*From rakehell prince
and heir to an empire
to England's
incomparable king—*

When Queen Victoria died in 1901, few expected that her son Albert Edward, Prince of Wales, would be able to take her place. As prince, he had defied Victorian morality and ushered in an era of unabashed opulence and sensuality. How could this flamboyant, untrained playboy possibly guide England's perilous destiny?

Yet Edward, the mortal man, became a beloved monarch and the First Gentleman of Europe—reigning with all the might and wisdom of his immortal heritage.

Be sure to read Volume 1 of *EDWARD THE KING*—*Edward the King: Prince of Hearts*—the enthralling story of his life and many loves during Victoria's reign.

Books by David Butler

Edward the Seventh: Volume I
Prince of Hearts
Edward the Seventh: Volume II
Monarch Among Men

Published by POCKET BOOKS

Edward the King

Volume II
Monarch among Men

by David Butler

PUBLISHED BY POCKET BOOKS NEW YORK

Chapter

1

The Queen was dying.

In her bedroom at Osborne, Victoria, by the Grace of God Queen of the United Kingdom of Great Britain and Ireland, Defender of the Faith, Empress of India, lay motionless, the right side of her face slightly flattened by the stroke which she had suffered five days before. Her thin grey hair was spread over the pillow on to her shoulders and all colour had drained from her features, leaving her skin pure and white, so that the watchers round her bed seemed to be gazing at a waxen death mask. Only the faintest occasional tremor of her high-arched nostrils showed that she still breathed.

For months her medical advisers had known that it was merely a question of time. In her eighties, almost blind, frail, crippled by rheumatism, only her indomitable will had kept her alive. While her armies struggled in South Africa, she would not surrender to her body's weakness. From somewhere inside herself, the aged queen had drawn the power to give determination to her government and courage to her soldiers. During the first disastrous year of the war while Britain's enemies triumphed, her energy and vitality had amazed and inspired her people. 'We are not interested in the possibilities of defeat,' she declared. 'They do not exist.' But once the tide of the war had turned and her troops, now better led and better equipped, began to drive back the Boer armies, the power which had sustained her gradually faded, exhausted by age and infirmity, by distress at the appalling lists of casualties, by sleeplessness and loss of weight.

It was a time, too, of private sorrow. The relief which the first victories brought her was swept away by the sudden death from cancer of her second son, Alfred, Duke of Saxe-Coburg, and by the secret news that her eldest daughter, Vicky, Dowager Empress of Germany, was dying also of the same disease. In September, she was told that her grandson, Prince Christian Victor, was dead in South Africa of enteric fever and, on Christmas Eve, old Lady Jane Churchill, the last of her close friends, died of heart failure at Osborne on a night of dreadful storm. It was the last link with the past and her beloved husband, Albert, the Prince Consort, whom she had outlived for so long. The opening year of the new century which had seemed so full of bright promise ended in despair. Victoria's strength failed rapidly and her mind became clouded.

In the early weeks of January 1901, her ministers complained at the delays in official business. When they braved the storms to reach the Isle of Wight, they found that her secretarial staff had been advised not to show her anything that might agitate her. The piles of routine work waiting staggered them. The amount which Victoria had regularly and uncomplainingly dealt with was far greater than they had realised, but now her ability to concentrate had gone. Yet she was still the Queen and would allow no one, not even her eldest son, the Prince of Wales, to deputise for her. Her doctors forbade any attempt to force her. The knowledge that she had been replaced could only hasten the end, while she had shown superhuman powers of recuperation before and might even recover. But the stroke on Thursday 17th slurred her speech and threw her mind into deeper confusion. Members of the Royal Family hurried from all over Europe to join her remaining children and grandchildren at her bedside and the first cautious bulletin was issued to the public, stating that the Queen's nervous system had been affected by the cares of the past year.

On her right, her pillow was supported by Sir James Reid, the Royal Physician, and on her left by Kaiser Wilhelm the Second, Emperor of Germany. For over two hours, since four o'clock that afternoon, they had crouched without moving, unable to change sides because the Kaiser's left arm was weak and only partially developed since birth. Hearing of the Queen's collapse while he celebrated the two hundredth anniversary of the establishment of the Prussian monarchy, he had cancelled the court festivities in Berlin at once and hastened to London. Germany had championed the Boer Republics openly in their fight to push the British out of South Africa and he was unsure of his welcome. Nevertheless, he came, this time, not with arrogance but in humility and sorrow as the eldest grandson. When his uncle, the Prince of Wales, met him at Charing Cross Station, Wilhelm said simply, 'I am here purely as my mother's son.' On the island he had behaved with unusual tact and dignity, staying in the background until the Prince came to the drawing-room to announce that the end was near. 'I would like to see Grandmama once more before she dies,' he said humbly. 'But if that is not possible, I shall quite understand.' No one could deny his sincerity. The strain in his right arm which supported the pillow had passed beyond pain to a numbness which he no longer even noticed. He was conscious only of the slow ebb of life in the one person he had revered and loved since boyhood, the one person with the right and authority to restrain him and whose admiration he had always tried to win.

Opposite him knelt Alexandra, Princess of Wales, holding the Queen's hand, the beautiful, gentle Alix whose coming to England from Denmark as the bride of her son nearly forty years ago had slowly given Victoria renewed interest in life after the tragic early death of the Prince Consort. The older woman's hand which had clutched hers so desperately a few hours before as she struggled to speak now lay inert while Alix stroked it, smoothing the wrinkled skin of the little, stubby fingers. Her touch had seemed to soothe and reassure the Queen as it had done so often in the past. At fifty-six, Alexandra still had the slim figure and clear complexion of a woman half her age, her hair swept up to a mass of small curls still a rich auburn, her brow unlined.

She was only three years younger than her husband, Albert Edward, Prince of Wales, who was kneeling beside her on one knee, yet Victoria's heir showed every one of his years. He was now stout, the black waistcoat under his frockcoat stretched across his girth by his kneeling position. His hair still held a trace of gold but had thinned to a few wisps in front; his full moustache and clipped, pointed beard were grizzled. The last word his mother had spoken had been to him. She had looked at the people assembled round her bed, searching for him. When he leant towards her, she whispered, 'Bertie,' his name in the family, and smiled, that rare, sweet smile of hers, just for him, before her eyes closed. He had sobbed and fallen to his knees, covering his face with his hands.

Now he gazed at her, seeing not the fragile, wasted shape

3

on the bed but a series of images of her as he remembered her, a severe young woman, her glossy brown hair parted in the centre and looped round her ears, a shawl pulled primly round her shoulders, staring at him as his father read aloud the disappointing reports of his tutors, the same young woman in a light day dress shrieking with laughter as she played skittles with him and Vicky and Affie in the Long Gallery at Windsor, or flushed and excited in a tartan gown and sash, dancing a reel with his handsome father at Balmoral. An awesome little figure in black bombazine and white widow's cap telling him for the hundredth time that, until she could rely on his discretion, she would give him no official position, the voice sharp and cutting, the face older, the cheeks pouchy and the drooping nose more pronounced. That face transformed, tender and compassionate, her arms holding him as he wept for the death of his infant son. The little, old lady, plump, nearsighted, stiff with rheumatism, in her black dress and embroidered cape and new bonnet, smiling through tears as her open landau moved in procession along six miles of London streets, while the largest crowds in history roared out their tribute of loyalty and affection on her Diamond Jubilee.

At the foot of the bed, stood Victoria's only other surviving son, Arthur, Duke of Connaught, and her daughters Helena, Louise and Beatrice. Behind them were the husbands of Helena and Louise, Prince Christian and the Duke of Argyll, Bertie's son, George, Duke of York, with his wife, May, and the other grandchildren. Again and again they had called out their names, urgent and pleading, hoping that the Queen might react to one of them and be drawn back from the dark threshold at which her spirit was hovering, but for some time now they had fallen silent. The only sound in the room was the quiet murmur of prayers spoken alternately by the Bishop of Winchester and the nervous Vicar of Whippingham, the local clergyman, included by the Queen's own invitation in case he felt slighted.

Elsewhere in the great house, the younger relations and great grandchildren were gathered in the main drawing-room with the lords and ladies-in-waiting. Staff and servants lined the corridors, fearful, waiting for news.

Outside, the darkness of the January evening had settled on Osborne, designed by the Prince Consort himself in the Italian style with a loggia and towers like campaniles to be a home for his young family on the Isle of Wight, nearer to

4

London than Balmoral yet away from court society and ceremony. A ring of policemen surrounded the house so that no premature news could be leaked to the throng of reporters who waited beyond the ornamental gates for the latest report on the Queen's condition. Muffled against the cold, shuffling their feet for warmth, they spoke in whispers or stood watching the lit upper windows, wondering behind which one the Royal Family kept its vigil.

The wind had dropped and the air held an unnatural stillness. After the storms had come dense fogs, but the fog had now lifted and one could even make out the distant glimmer of Portsmouth and Gosport across the Solent. On the mainland, many people stood on the quays and high places, straining to see the lights across the water. All over the kingdom, thoughts were on that tiny island in the south. From the crowds massed outside Buckingham Palace and the Mansion House to the clubs of Piccadilly, from suburban terraces to country farms, in city tenements and highland crofts, men and women waited for the announcement which they knew must come but could not believe. The same sense of disbelief, of sudden uncertainty about the future, was felt throughout the Empire, the huge collection of dominions, colonies and protectorates, all owing allegiance to the Queen. On every continent, her administrators and troops and subjects waited with the same feeling of grief and unease.

Generation after generation had been born and grew up knowing that the Queen was on her throne, a guarantee of order and stability. Most of her more distant subjects had never seen her. To them she was almost a mystical figure, to be worshipped and appeased, a ruler whose name had magical authority. To some she was a symbol of hatred and oppression, to others a promise of justice and liberty. Even in her own kingdom many of her people had never seen her. When her husband died she had withdrawn from the world, expecting in her despair to follow him within a few months. Her mourning had been respected but, as the months grew into years, respect had turned to resentment at her continued seclusion. Not the most determined efforts of her ministers could bring her to show herself in public. Gradually her place in society was taken by Bertie and Alix, the handsome, gregarious Prince of Wales and his beautiful, high-spirited Princess, while the Queen became more and more remote, shut away in her residences at

Windsor, Balmoral and Osborne between which she travelled by closed carriage and private train. In her isolation she acquired an insatiable appetite for work. No law was passed nor government appointment made, no contact abroad nor development at home was allowed unless she had been consulted. She found ways to let her opinions be known on everything from childbirth and education to music and morality and her insistence on respectability and decorum became the ideal of millions. In time her remoteness became accepted and created round her an aura of unapproachable majesty. To be invited to meet her became the rarest and highest honour and eminent men found themselves trembling at the thought of standing in her presence. In later years when she began to make infrequent public appearances, the merest sight of the small, dignified figure in black sent the crowds into a tumult of excitement and adoration. She had become a legend, imperishable and unaging in her remoteness. While she lived, the future was secure and certain, the known way of life, the world she approved would not change. But now it was to end.

As in Britain and the rest of the Empire, so in the nations beyond peoples who owed her no personal loyalty felt an imminent sense of loss, an indefinable bewilderment. From Rome to St. Petersburg there was anxiety and distress. State balls and receptions were cancelled. In Paris, the French Chamber agreed to suspend its sessions and, in Washington, a special prayer was said in the Senate for the Queen's recovery.

To the people in the bedroom at Osborne, time seemed to be standing still. Reid and the Kaiser crouched, unmoving, holding up the Queen's pillow. Beatrice, Victoria's youngest daughter and constant companion since her own young husband, Liko, had died on the Ashanti expedition, sobbed quietly between her two sisters. The Bishop of Winchester, Randall Davidson, had begun to murmur again the prayer for the dying. 'O Almighty God, with whom do live the spirits of just men made perfect, after they are delivered from their earthly prisons: We humbly commend the soul of this thy servant, Her Gracious Majesty the Queen, into thy hands, as into the hands of a faithful Creator and most merciful Saviour; most humbly beseeching thee that it may be precious in thy sight.'

Kneeling beside Alix, Bertie looked from his mother to his son, George, Duke of York, slim, handsome, with Alexandra's straight nose and clear blue eyes. Like Bertie he wore his beard short and pointed, in the naval style. He stood braced and erect as though on the quarter-deck of his ship, his hands clasped tightly in front of him to stop their trembling. Next to him, his wife, May, full-figured and already growing matronly after the recent birth of her fourth child, also saw the trembling and slipped her arm through his as if for support but really to comfort him. He swayed slightly towards her and steadied himself. Poor boy, Bertie thought, knowing that behind the discipline and manliness which his son cultivated, he was sensitive and vulnerable. For fifteen years he had enjoyed his career in the navy, until the death of his elder brother Eddy from pneumonia had suddenly made him second in succession to the throne. Conscious, overconscious of taking his brother's place, with Bertie's help he had conquered his feeling of inadequacy and carried out his own duties admirably. The first of these had been to marry and produce an heir himself. They had been lucky to find for him a girl as sensible and intelligent as May.

Bertie looked at his nephew, the Kaiser. The skin of Willy's face was stretched tight over his high cheekbones and a small muscle jumped in the corner of his right jaw. His curiously flat eyes were fixed, staring at his grandmother as if to will strength and life back into her. For years Bertie had loathed that sleek, handsome face with its moustache standing up at the ends in arrogant spikes. Willy had followed his gentle father as Kaiser at the age of twenty-nine and proceeded to show the world how an emperor should behave. His bombast and conceit amused the family. He was highly intelligent, even brilliant, but erratic, and his dreams of military glory made him dangerous. At one time he had admired his Uncle Bertie extravagantly, but he always had to be the best and when he found that his uncle's popularity was greater than his, that his uncle, not he, was the leader of European society, he set out deliberately to take his place. That he had not succeeded made it worse.

He challenged the Prince's position as the world's champion yachtsman. Using his vast, imperial resources, he employed the designer of Bertie's racing cutter, *Britannia,* to build him a bigger and faster vessel, but his determination to win at all costs turned sport into politics. His uncle shrugged and withdrew from the contest. Wilhelm's victory was hollow. The fact that Bertie had then concentrated on his stables and that his race horses had won the Grand National, the Two Thousand Guineas, the Eclipse Stakes, the St Leger, the Newmarket Stakes and, twice, the highest palm of all, the Derby, was insupportable. To score over his uncle became an obsession. He sneered at his morals, doubted his courage, belittled his experience and achievements. 'The old popinjay,' he called him. In one area he could always win. As an emperor, he took precedence over the Prince of Wales and he used it to snub him, to keep him standing and make him late for meals. It was petty and ridiculous and finally the Queen was forced to take notice. She let it be known that she thought his insistence on being treated as an emperor, even in private, vulgar. 'If he has such notions, he had better never come *here*.' Wilhelm had wept, protesting that he was misunderstood.

Although by birth and upbringing he was German, part of him was English through his balanced, intellectual mother, Victoria's daughter, whose influence he had rebelled against since his teens when he first became intoxicated by uniforms and the gleaming bayonets of the Prussian army on parade. Sometimes he longed to flout them all, to cut himself off, yet the need for his grandmother's approval, to be accepted as one of the family, never left him. He would not admit it but his happiest memories were of holidays spent as a boy at Windsor, of walking in the woods at Sandringham with Uncle Bertie and his cousins, of being more than half in love with his beautiful Aunt Alix, and of Victoria telling him never to forget that he was Albert's first and dearest grandson. At this moment, supporting the Queen's pillow to ease her breathing, he was wholly English and at peace because he had surrendered to his need and been accepted. Watching him, Bertie felt able to understand him at last, and to forgive. How unhappy he must be, he thought, how torn.

The quiet murmur of the Bishop's voice went on. Bertie closed his eyes. He tried again to pray but he could not find the words. Once he had wanted desperately to be king, to be his own master and not merely his mother's shadow. But no more. Through the Queen's mistrust, he had been denied a true position in the affairs of the country. To be of service, he had learnt to work in his own way, through social contacts and pressures, developing friendships in all political parties, with financiers and industrialists, in the arts and sciences, becoming the leader of fashion from his London home at Marlborough House, the First Gentleman of Europe. Successive Prime Ministers had valued his help, especially in foreign affairs, but it was mostly unofficial. He was not used to routine. He had been given no training for kingship, no experience in government. As the years passed, his ambitions faded. He told himself he had had to wait too long. He was nearly sixty. His mother had probably been right to exclude him from any real responsibility. He loved her without resentment, content to be her Master of Ceremonies. She was the Queen and the world without her was unthinkable. Like most of her subjects, the miracle he hoped for was that she would survive, that somehow life would continue as it was.

He heard Alix give a short intake of breath beside him and looked at her. She was staring down at the Queen's hand which had just moved in hers. The little fingers stirred as if life were returning to them. Alix's sigh was echoed by others in the room. Davidson's voice faltered and stopped. Victoria's eyes were opening.

She blinked slowly in the light of the oil lamps. Wilhelm leant closer and she looked up at him. She nodded, seeming to recognise him with pleasure, then her eyes moved to her daughter, Louise. Then to Beatrice and Helena and to each person in turn, recognising them, until she came to Bertie and Alix. For a long moment she gazed at them tenderly, then her glance moved beyond them as though to someone waiting in the shadows. She smiled, the shy smile of a young girl in love, and her eyes closed for the last time. All the prayers in all the tongues, to so many different gods, had not been enough.

When he had recovered, Bertie left the others kneeling round the bed and went with George to break the news to the younger members of the family. They and the Minister in attendance, Arthur Balfour, First Lord of the Treasury, the lords and ladies-in-waiting and the senior members of the Household had to be brought for a last glimpse of the dead queen. As they paced slowly down the corridors, the watching servants saw from their faces what had happened and knelt in silence, stunned, some of them crying. Victoria's little white Pomeranian, Turi, ran ahead of them, excited, barking, until one of the equerries caught him and quietened him.

The telegraph wires had been closed until Bertie gave his mother's Private Secretary the official message to be sent to the Prime Minister, the Archbishop of Canterbury and the Lord Mayor of London. 'My beloved mother, the Queen, has just passed away, surrounded by her children and grandchildren.'

The news was broken at last to the reporters waiting outside the gates. 'Her Majesty the Queen breathed her last at 6.30 p.m.' For seconds they stood, unable to believe it, then the panic began. Those with carriages or bicycles scrambled for them, while others began to run, all racing for the post office in Cowes. And as they ran, they shouted, announcing the end of an era. 'Queen's dead! The Queen's dead!'

In London and the other principal cities, huge crowds heard the news in silence, then dispersed quietly to their own homes. Each individual felt the loss personally, as though someone in his own family had died, someone whose existence had been relied on. There was no mass show of grief. It was too soon for that. Many were afraid, like children suddenly abandoned. The Widow of Windsor had seemed to be immortal, an essential part of the fabric of national life. How could it go on without her?

At Osborne, the members of the Royal family and the Household began to realise that Bertie, the Prince of Wales, was now King and should be addressed and treated as such. Yet to do so seemed oddly wrong. Bertie himself was embarrassed and did not insist on it, not with his mother still lying on her bed and her servants weeping for her. Alexandra was horrified when Wilhelm begged to be the first to kiss her hand. She would not let herself be acknowledged as Queen until Victoria was buried. 'There can only be one Queen until then,' she said.

It was a situation which Balfour and the others knew could not continue. He urged the Prince to call an immediate Accession Council but Bertie refused. Only when the Prime Minister, Lord Salisbury, sent a coded telegram to explain the urgency did he consent. Officials of State and Government, Members of Parliament, Judges, officers in the armed services and many others took their commissions directly from the Crown. They had to be confirmed in their appointments and positions. Orders and proclamations needed the sovereign's signature. Bertie agreed to travel to London the next day.

No one was quite certain what to do. It was sixty-four years since the last sovereign, William the Fourth, had died and no one could remember the correct procedure. The secretaries were sent to search the records. In the royal bedroom, Wilhelm had taken command. The late Queen was now dressed in white. She had a horror of undertakers and had forbidden them to touch her body. Wilhelm himself measured her for her coffin. When it was brought, he would have lifted her in if Bertie and Arthur had not insisted it was their right as her sons. In her coffin, her white widow's cap was placed on her head, flowers were scattered on her dress and the silver crucifix from above her bed laid in her folded hands. Last of all, her white lace wedding veil, yellowing with age, was drawn over her face.

The large dining room had been converted into a chapel. The walls were shrouded in draperies and palms spaced round them, separated by wreaths. To one side hung a Union Jack as the backing for an enormous cross of gardenias. The coffin, covered by the Queen's crimson and ermine robes of state, was placed on a raised platform covered by the Royal Standard. On the coffin, on a crimson velvet cushion, lay her diamond Imperial crown and her Order of the Garter. Round it were set eight tall candles in silver candlesticks and at each corner stood a Grenadier Guardsman in full uniform, scarlet tunic and busby, his head bowed, his hands crossed on the butt of his rifle, the muzzle resting on his foot. An officer of the Household kept watch with them and the guard was changed every hour, in slow time, for the ten days that Victoria's body lay in state.

Early in the morning after she died, Bertie crossed over to the mainland with George and Arthur and travelled to London by special train. He left Kaiser Wilhelm in charge on the island.

It was a raw, blustery morning and because he was tired, Bertie felt the cold more than usual. He had slept very little. There had been arrangements to make, so many arrangements, for the lying in state, the funeral procession and interment, for the reception of foreign mourners and the changeover of households. He had watched and prayed

11

by the body of his mother and comforted his sisters. He had scarcely had time to be with Alexandra, yet after so long there was little need for words. When the Queen was laid in her coffin and all was done, Alix had taken his hand. They had looked at each other and, in that moment of silence, everything that was needed between them had been spoken. Now he sat, hunched, in the day saloon of the Royal train, watching the glowing tip of his cigar and its reflection in the window without noticing the sombre landscape that rushed by outside. Despite the companionship of his brother and son, he felt isolated, more alone than he would ever have thought possible. The day he had once longed for and then dreaded had come.

In London, the Government, the great officers of State, the archbishops and dignitaries of the realm waited for him. He knew that, like him, they would still be shaken, grieving for the loss of a sovereign they had admired and loved. And he knew that among them were some of his fiercest critics. Not all of them realised how hard he had worked behind the scenes, how often his advice and help had been asked. His influence and prestige abroad had been invaluable, but his diplomatic triumphs had largely been planned and carried out in secret, the credit for them taken by a series of Foreign Secretaries. At home he was seen as a dignified but genial ceremonial figure, a pleasure-loving sportsman with a fine appreciation of good food and pretty women, his private life a target for scandal and gossip. That statesmen like Disraeli, Gladstone and Rosebery respected and honoured him was considered an aberration. For it was obvious that his mother did not trust him, and with reason.

All his life his main desire had been to please her. But his brilliant father in a misguided attempt to make sure that the heir to the throne would be a paragon of wisdom and morality had devised a gruelling system of education into which he had been forced at the age of seven, exhaustive hours of study with private tutors under the strictest discipline. He was to be made into the perfect man, morally, intellectually and physically. Any relaxation, any tendency to idleness or pleasure was ruthlessly stamped out for his own good and the future good of the country.

To Albert, Bertie was always a failure. Although he loved him, his chief fear was that Victoria might die young and their son become king before he had learnt a sense of responsibility. But it was Albert who died, leaving Victoria a widow at the age of forty-two. She blamed Bertie for his father's death. It was disappointment over his son's lack of academic success and worry over his misconduct, his first short-lived affair with a music hall singer, which killed him and not typhoid, as the doctors said. She never fully forgave Bertie. At first, she could not bear even to see him. Later, when she was forced to take up again the work of government, the burden had been crushing but she would not let him help her nor share it in any way. He was not worthy to have even a fraction of his father's place at her side.

That was why Bertie had learnt to work in secret. With his energy and talents, he could not be idle. The one thing his father had managed to instil in him was a desire to be of service to his country. Yet whenever his advice had been accepted, when he had given his support to a reform he believed in or used his diplomatic gifts to resolve a crisis, his mother had acted at once to forbid any further contact between him and the minister or government department concerned. Victoria used every hint of scandal against him, every human indiscretion as an excuse to exclude him.

It was only in the most recent years when the Queen's health had begun to fail and he had to be ready to deputise for her that he had been sent details of Cabinet discussions and Foreign Office despatches. Often he only heard of what had been decided or of important developments abroad when he read of them in the newspapers. It was humiliating. Even in these past weeks when it was evident that he would become King or Regent at any moment, the humiliation had continued. After his mother's first collapse, when he wanted to go to her, her advisers prevented him in case the sight of him alarmed her. He was kept from her deathbed until the last minute as, by her orders, he had once been kept from his father's. Restless, unable to settle he had left Alix at Sandringham and gone to London to wait at Marlborough House for news of the Queen. He heard at last that she had said, hesitantly, to her doctor, 'The Prince of Wales will be sorry to hear how ill I am. Do you think he ought to be told?' In the stilted words he had sensed her need for him and gone to her at once.

In spite of everything she had done to him, he had loved her with the same natural, unquestioning love since childhood. And she loved him. In spite of her jealousy and mistrust, she had never doubted his obedience or goodness

13

of heart. She could see how hurt he was by her refusal to let him work with her, yet she was only being true to Albert's judgement of him. Sometimes she yearned for someone to share her labour, but it could not be him. It was a pity, since he was always so attentive and loving.

There was one immediate problem which troubled Bertie above all others. It was purely personal. He had been christened Albert Edward, Albert after his father and Edward after his mother's father, the Duke of Kent, a younger brother of George the Fourth. Albert Edward. It was unknown for a King of England to have two names. When he had mentioned the difficulty once to his mother, she had stiffened.

'What difficulty?' she demanded. 'It was beloved Papa's wish, as well as mine, that you should be called by *both* when you became King, and it would be *impossible* for you to drop your Father's. It would be monstrous!'

He had soothed her. 'I agree, Mama. And if I took only one name, it could not be Papa's.'

'Indeed not,' Victoria agreed. 'Albert alone, as you truly and amiably say, would *not do*. There can only be one ALBERT!'

Bertie coughed on his cigar. His mother had been very insistent, and her wishes were well known. It was still difficult. He had to make a decision before the Council in London. His Private Secretary, Francis Knollys, who had helped him with many tricky questions over the years was at Marlborough House and could not be consulted. Well, he would have to leave it to his own inspiration. He would think of something when he came to it.

He coughed again and the ash dropped from the end of his Havana cigar on to the toe of his boot. He grunted and leant forward to brush the flakes from his grey spat. As he straightened, he caught sight of his reflection in the window. His lowered head emphasised how far his hair had receded. His shoulders were hunched, his neck sunken, an old man's image. In the glass, spattered with rain, the face he saw was drawn and pale, the heavylidded eyes tired, the cheeks sagging. Is that me? he wondered. Is that what I've become? The face disappeared but he could still see it in his mind. An old man's face. How could he take on the responsibility for a mighty Empire? It was madness for him to try. No one could blame him. There were many who would applaud his recognition of his own unfitness. His life

14

need not change. It could still be carefree and enjoyable. He could stand aside and leave the burden to younger, stronger shoulders.

He glanced round. Arthur, white-haired and full-moustached, wearing his Inverness cape, was asleep in his bucket chair. Near him, George, in naval uniform, sat shivering with cold. The thumbnail of his left hand plucked nervously at the nails of his right in turn. He looked up and saw his father watching him. He smiled, a shy, diffident smile, and clasped his hands together. He's afraid, Bertie thought, but he's more afraid of showing it. He's afraid that something might happen to me, that he'll be left to carry on alone. He heard an echo of his own father's voice, the soft German accent.

'One day you will be head of the family. Always try to do what is right. And remember, we cannot live as other people. We must always think of our country, and of the example we set.'

Bertie nodded. Even if he could only bear it for a short while, the burden was his. He could not abandon it to George, who was even less prepared than himself. He smiled to his son, reassuringly. 'Ring the bell for the steward,' he suggested. 'We'll all feel better for a glass of brandy.'

The Council Chamber of St James's Palace was crowded with Privy Councillors, Church dignitaries and Officers of State. The black mourning worn by most of them contrasted with the robes and uniforms of the others and gave the gathering an added solemnity. A proclamation of the new King's accession had been agreed to and signed and now they waited for him. Conversation was muted but excited. *The Times* leader that very morning had hinted openly that the new King was not fit to reign. Some were indignant, others sceptical, almost amused as they thought of the future. Although they talked quietly in private groups, all eyes turned constantly to the doors which were closed.

Charles, Lord Carrington, one of Bertie's oldest friends since his undergraduate days at Cambridge, stood with Reginald Brett, Lord Esher, who had become a member of the Prince's inner circle through helping to organise the Diamond Jubilee procession. Younger than the urbane Carrington, he was a handsome, feline man with intelligent, watchful eyes. They had moved slowly round the room, listening to the buzz of conversation. Through a gap ahead, they could see the crimson and gold Council Throne.

'Well, Reggie,' Carrington said softly, 'it's here at last. He's had to wait longer to become king than anyone in history.'

'Nearly sixty years.'

'Can you hear them? They're all wondering if he's up to it.'

Esher nodded. 'A great deal depends on what happens this afternoon.'

'Look at Salisbury. He doesn't seem too happy.'

'I expect he's wondering what change he'll get out of the new Sovereign,' Esher drawled.

The aged Prime Minister, the Marquess of Salisbury, had been talking to Frederick Temple, Archbishop of Canterbury. Salisbury was white-haired, heavily bearded, in his early seventies. For the last quarter of a century, his relations with the Prince of Wales had been perplexing to him, his opinion veering between admiration and outright disapproval. He was a troubled man. He bowed to the Archbishop and turned to find his nephew, Arthur Balfour, and Lord Lansdowne, the Foreign Secretary, at his elbow.

'Now is the time to insist on constitutional reform,' Balfour said urgently. 'He can't rule in the same way as his mother.'

'As Prince of Wales he was lightweight, Prime Minister,' Lansdowne insisted. 'Undependable.'

Balfour smiled. 'Let him wear his fancy dress uniforms and entertain visitors—he's good at that. But he must not interfere with the government.'

'We needn't worry. All he wants is the position, with none of the responsibility,' Lansdowne assured them. 'He must know all the betting's against him. He won't even try.'

Salisbury considered them. They were old in politics, but young in experience of the Prince. The King, he corrected himself. He had learnt not to be astonished at anything. The doors behind them were opening. 'Well,' he murmured. 'We'll soon see.'

George, Duke of York, Arthur, Duke of Connaught, George, Duke of Cambridge, Victoria's cousin and Prince Christian of Schleswig-Holstein, her son-in-law, had withdrawn from the chamber to inform the King, according to tradition, that the Privy Council was sitting. Footmen in livery opened the doors. The Lord Chamberlain, the

Lord Steward and the Master of the Horse led the procession of the Household, walking slowly backward, facing Bertie. He was followed by the four royal messengers. He wore the dress uniform of a Field Marshal with the blue sash of the Garter. Round his upper left arm was a black mourning band. He halted, sensing the tension in the chamber. At first he could make out no individuals in the crowd, then Carrington and Esher stepped forward and were the first to bow. He smiled to them faintly and to the Duke of Devonshire, the Lord President of the Council, before moving across towards the throne.

Reaching it, he acknowledged the bows of the assembly, then bowed himself to the Prime Minister and the Archbishop. There was a pause as he looked at the empty throne. The carriage taking him from Victoria Station to Marlborough House had passed through streets filled with people, standing silent and bareheaded. They had not come to cheer him, but to show him that they shared his mourning. As he turned, his head rose.

'Your Royal Highnesses, My Lords and Gentlemen—' For a few seconds, there was almost consternation in the assembly as they realised he intended to speak. It was followed by complete stillness. His voice was quiet and steady. 'This is the most painful occasion on which I shall ever be called upon to address you. My first and melancholy duty is to announce to you the death of my beloved mother the Queen, and I know how deeply you, the whole nation and, I think I may say, the whole world, sympathise with me in the irreparable loss we have all sustained.

'During her long and glorious reign, she set an example before the world of what a monarch should be. I need hardly say that my constant endeavour will be always to walk in her footsteps. In undertaking the heavy load which now devolves upon me, I am fully determined to be a constitutional Sovereign in the strictest sense of the word and, so long as there is breath in my body, to work for the good and well-being of my people. In this I do not merely mean the people of these islands, forged from so many different elements to create the nation of which we are so proud, but the development and well-being of my subjects beyond the seas.'

As he spoke, the age and tiredness seemed to drop from him. Balfour and Lansdowne glanced at Salisbury, who was standing very erect. Was this the man they had just written off?

He told them of his faith in the Empire, a force for stability and right in a changing world. He saw his duty as not only to hold but to build on the achievements of the past. He hesitated briefly. 'I was christened Albert Edward, in the expectation that, as Albert Edward, I would come to the throne. However, I am resolved to be known only by the name of Edward, which has been borne by six of my ancestors.' He paused at the almost incredulous murmur which swelled for a moment. 'In doing so I do not undervalue the name of Albert, which I inherit from my great and wise father. But by universal consent, he is known—I believe deservedly—as Albert the Good, and I desire that his name should stand alone.

'In conclusion, I trust to Parliament and the nation to support me in the arduous duties which now transfer to me by inheritance—and to which I am determined to devote my whole strength throughout what remains of my life.'

When he finished, there was a profound silence. Many of those present, like Salisbury, stood straighter in the presence of their King. Carrington wanted to cheer. Beside him, he heard Esher clear his throat. Looking across the room, he saw Earl Roberts, the Commander-in-Chief, a dapper, indomitable little man with a bristling moustache, blink tears from his eyes. Like Carrington, he realised the courage that speech had taken.

There were those who would complain that the King's first act had been to set aside the wishes of his mother. But he had also used it to serve notice on his critics that he did not intend to be merely a figurehead. He would resist any attempt to restrict the full power and privilege of the Crown. Already the Prime Minister and the Earl Marshal, the Duke of Norfolk, were congratulating him ceremoniously on his speech. When they discovered that he had spoken without notes or preparation they were shaken. They asked permission to publish as much of it as could be remembered.

In front of the Privy Council, the King took the oath to govern according to the laws and customs of the realm, then the Councillors, in order of precedence, knelt before the throne and gave the oath of allegiance. The first was George, as heir apparent. When he knelt to kiss his father's

18

hand, Bertie held his left hand over his bowed head in blessing.

How different, Salisbury thought, how very different from his own treatment as heir. It was touching in its natural affection. Then it was his turn to kneel stiffly before the throne. 'I, Robert Arthur Gascoyne Cecil, Marquess of Salisbury, do swear that I will be faithful and bear true allegiance to His Majesty King Edward the Seventh, his heirs and successors, according to law. So help me God.' He handed up his seal of office which was returned at once. He kissed hands and rose. One by one, the rest of the Ministers and Councillors followed, some grudgingly, some embarrassed, but most with a newfound respect, glad to do homage.

On the following morning, Lord Roberts and his staff in full dress uniform rode into Friary Court on the east side of St James's Palace at the head of a detachment of Grenadier Guards. A flag party carried the King's colours draped in black. From the palace came the marshalmen in scarlet coats and gold-corded shakoes.

The guards formed a square, facing the colours, below the balcony on which Victoria, nearly sixty-four years ago, had first shown herself to her people as Queen. On to the balcony came the Earl Marshal in his robes, followed by the Kings of Arms, Norroy, Deputy Garter and Clarenceux, in their glittering costumes, the heralds, York, Lancaster, Windsor, Chester, Somerset and Richmond, and the Pursuivants, Rouge Croix, Blue Mantle, Rouge Dragon and Portcullis, in their sleeveless tabards decorated and quartered with gold emblems. Behind them came four state trumpeters in gold ornamented tunics and caps and four of the King's sergeants-at-arms, carrying the King's maces, in their dark uniforms laced with silver. To the side were the Lord Steward and the Lord Chamberlain in their robes of office. In a moment, the old stone courtyard had been turned into a blaze of medieval pageantry.

At a triumphant flourish from the State trumpeters, two of the macers stepped forward with Norroy King of Arms who raised his scroll to deliver the proclamation.

'Whereas it has pleased Almighty God to call to his mercy our late Sovereign Lady Queen Victoria, of blessed and glorious memory, by whose decease the Imperial Crown of the United Kingdom of Great Britain and Ireland is

19

solely and rightfully come to the High and Mighty Prince Albert Edward: we, therefore, the Lords Spiritual and Temporal of this Realm, being here assisted with those of her late Majesty's Privy Council, with numbers of other Principal Gentlemen of Quality, with the Lord Mayor, Aldermen, and Citizens of London, do now hereby, with one voice and consent of tongue and heart, publish and proclaim, that the High and Mighty Prince Albert Edward is now, by the death of our late Sovereign of happy memory, become our only lawful and rightful liege Lord Edward the Seventh, by the Grace of God King of the United Kingdom of Great Britain and Ireland, Defender of the Faith, Emperor of India. To whom we do acknowledge all faith and constant obedience, with all hearty and humble affection; beseeching God, by Whom Kings and Queens do reign, to bless the Royal Prince Edward the Seventh, with long and happy years to reign over us.

'Given at the Court of St James's, this twenty-third day of January, in the year of our Lord one thousand nine hundred and one.

'God Save the King.'

Chapter

2

The Royal Yacht *Alberta*, escorted by eight black torpedo-destroyers, carried the Queen's body on the eight-mile journey from the Isle of Wight to Portsmouth. The coffin, draped in a white satin pall emblazoned with a cross of gold and the Royal Arms, stood on a dais in a crimson pavilion erected on the quarterdeck.

The sea was calm and the winter sun sparkled on the surface of the water as the small yacht steamed slowly towards the mainland, preceded by its escort in double file and followed by the Royal mourners in the *Victoria and Albert*, the *Osborne*, the *Trinity* and *Admiralty* yachts and the Kaiser's Imperial battleship, the *Hohenzollern*. Nearer the island were moored, in tribute, a German squadron of four ironclads, a French warship, a Japanese battleship sent by the Mikado, and others from the Kings of Spain and Portugal. The tribute was impressive, yet it was dwarfed by the awesome, majestic spectacle that lay ahead, an unbroken line of giant warships, battleships and cruisers of the British Fleet, stationed two and a half cables apart, stretching out of sight, all the way to Portsmouth Harbour. It was visual proof of the invincible might of the Empire. The canopy of the pavilion was looped back so that the sailors lining their tops, bridges and lower decks could salute the coffin as it passed. As soon as the *Alberta* had sailed into the roadstead and turned, the huge guns of the fleet began to crash out all along the line at intervals of a minute.

On the bridge of the *Victoria and Albert*, Bertie stood apart from the others, his hands gripping the rail. The guns roared again, sudden red tongues of flame leaping out ahead of columns of smoke that billowed up and shrouded the little yacht bearing his mother's body. A succession of red flashes pierced the haze, followed by the terrifying thunder of the explosions extending into the far distance.

21

Then the light wind that swept the Solent rolled back the grey clouds of smoke and he could see the *Alberta* clearly again, moving slowly on past the towering shapes of the ironclads.

Among the members of the Household on the forward deck of the *Osborne* was Sir Arthur Bigge, the late Queen's Private Secretary, a pompous, prickly man. Near him stood Frederick Ponsonby, Assistant Private Secretary and Equerry. In his early thirties, formerly an officer in the Guards, he was popular with the rest of the staff for his wit and sense of style. Normally humorous and relaxed, on this day he was tired and worried. It was he who had telephoned Marlborough House with the news of the Queen's serious condition. Perhaps because of this, the new King trusted him and had put him in charge of all the funeral arrangements at Windsor. It was a heavy responsibility, with no real precedent to go by and so many expectations to satisfy. Especially since he still had to carry out his duties on the island. He had travelled up to Windsor and to London, to find chaos at the Earl Marshal's office and the War Office. With the backing of the Commander-in-Chief, in two frantic days he had drawn up a programme with orders for the troops, guards of honour and police, lists of the English Royal Family, Foreign Sovereigns, Representatives and Suites and their place in the ceremonies. He had only arrived back on the island in the middle of the night and had to rise very early to put on his dress uniform and take his place in the cortege.

Beside him, Bigge snorted disgustedly, 'It's absolutely beyond belief! I knew he was vain but that is inexcusable.'

'What is?' Ponsonby asked.

Bigge pointed curtly ahead. Round the bulk of the *Victoria and Albert*, they could just make out the *Alberta*, with the Royal Standard at the masthead. On all the other vessels, flags were flying at half-mast. Ponsonby grunted without commenting. Like the others he had been surprised when the King had ordered the flag to be raised, but now he thought he understood. It was the Sovereign's personal Standard. Ever since the Queen had died, the newspapers had been full of fears for the future, of what would happen to the country now she was gone. Public speakers had described her death as a national calamity. How could the Empire survive without her guiding hand? It was the natural extravagance of sorrow but dangerous if allowed to

22

continue. This was King Edward's way of showing his people, while they mourned, that the throne was not empty. Just like the show of force today, to warn hostile countries not to try to take advantage of the nation's distress. Subtle but unmistakable. That was the kind of king Ponsonby wanted to serve, especially after years of coping with a capricious old lady. The trouble was, the King already had his own staff and would be reluctant to accept any of his mother's Household who might be prejudiced against him. And Ponsonby had no illusions. He knew that, if there were the slightest mishap in the ceremonies at Windsor, he would lose any chance of being taken on at all.

The tension in the crowds who waited at Portsmouth was growing. All that long afternoon they had gazed towards the island along the majestic line of battleships, their excitement stirred by the thunderous salute of the guns, but already daylight was fading and only glimpses of the naval procession could be made out through the smoke. Then the sun touched the horizon and the western skyline burst into glory, the sleek, black torpedo-destroyers emerged from the smoke of the last salute and the *Alberta* sailed out into the golden path of the sunset. In the heightened clarity of the light every detail of her deck could be seen, the crimson pavilion, the officer at each corner on watch and the shimmering whiteness of the pall that covered the small coffin on its bier. Many people cried out and all eyes followed the little yacht as it moved slowly behind its escort across the final, clear stretch of water and disappeared into Portsmouth Harbour.

For long minutes no one moved, then the light was gone. The moon shone palely above the silent line of warships and people shivered in the sudden cold of the wind.

That night, the *Alberta* lay next to Nelson's flagship, *Victory*. In the raw morning, after a service on deck, the coffin was carried to a special train. The King travelled on ahead to London with Alexandra and the other mourners and their suites. Only a few of the oldest ladies-in-waiting accompanied the Queen's body on this stage of its journey. At each station on the route crowds had assembled to see the train as it passed, its carriage blinds drawn, and in the fields at the side of the track groups of country people and farmworkers knelt bareheaded in the rain to pay their respects.

At Victoria Station, Bertie waited with the men of the Royal Family. The Kaiser was now not the only foreign member present. Cousins and relations had poured into London, the King of the Belgians, the Kings of Greece and Portugal, the Czarevitch, Grand Duke Michael, representing Victoria's grandson by marriage, Czar Nicholas and Archduke Franz Ferdinand, heir to the Austrian Empire, representing the aged Emperor Franz Joseph. With them were the Crown Princes of Germany, Rumania, Denmark, Norway and Sweden, with Princes, Grand Dukes and Dukes from Saxe-Coburg to Sparta, representing branches of the family and the other Royal Families of Europe.

As the daughter of a soldier and Queen of a nation at war, Victoria had commanded a military funeral. When the train arrived at the platform, the coffin was transferred by Coldstream Guards to a gun-carriage, the pall was stretched over it and the Royal Standard laid on top, then the crown, the two orbs and sceptre, a splendour of rich colours, gold and diamonds. Years ago she had decided that black plumes and trappings were wrong for a funeral. The colours should be bright, to symbolise the soul rejoicing to join its Maker. The streets were hung with purple and white and Highland pipers in regimental tartans marched ahead of her, playing their wild lament.

The route from Victoria Station to Paddington was lined by police and 30,000 troops leaning on their reversed rifles.

Marching at the side of the gun-carriage, Ponsonby was impressed by the size and reverence of the crowds. A dense mass of people, dressed in black, had gathered since dawn in Buckingham Palace Road, the Mall, St James's Street, Piccadilly and Hyde Park, waiting patiently in the intense cold. Their numbers were uncountable, yet there was none of the bustle and chatter of former occasions. Along the miles of the route there was profound silence, broken only by the occasional sound of weeping that mingled with the tramp of the horses and the creak of the gun-carriage. All eyes watched it devotedly as it passed, then moved to the King.

Bertie rode immediately behind the cortege on a dark bay cavalry horse. To his right was Kaiser Wilhelm on a white charger and, to his left, his brother Arthur on a roan. All three were cloaked, wearing the scarlet uniform of a Field Marshal in the British Army and white-plumed hats. Bertie's cloak was thrown back, showing his decorations and the sash of the Garter. He was pale and haggard, yet he rode proudly, immensely moved by the silent tribute of the crowds, aware of the strained, white faces and the muffled sobbing. Not all their concern was for the dead Queen. Many had wondered at the absence of the King's son, George, Duke of York. Now they had learnt that he lay seriously ill at Osborne, nursed by his wife, May. Struggling against what seemed to be a severe cold, he had collapsed and was found to have measles, with the fever threatening to turn into pneumonia. They remembered how the King's elder son had died from pneumonia, less than ten years ago, and their hearts went out to him. Grieving for his mother, was he also to lose his heir?

Then their eyes were taken by the pageant of Kings and Princes which followed, by the plumes and cloaks, the orders and sashes and the magnificence of the costumes. And behind the great parade of Royalty came the closed carriages with the ladies of the family. Alexandra sat in the leading carriage with her daughters, Louise, Victoria and Maud, dressed and veiled in black. Although she knew her thoughts should be on the dead Queen, she could not stop herself thinking of George, dear Georgie left behind at Osborne. She remembered the awful sweating, the raving and whistling gasp for breath when Eddy died. She longed to be with May. To be so far from her son's bedside was torture. Sitting beside her, Toria saw the anguish which her mother tried to hide. She slipped her hand between Alexandra's which lay on her lap and Alexandra held it tightly as the procession moved slowly on.

At Paddington, the coffin was carried on board the Royal train for the last stage of its journey to Windsor, through crowds whose emotion was all the more expressive for its silence. It went beyond mere tradition and loyalty. Many of the foreign princes who had come out of duty found themselves affected by the same sense of respect and awe.

At Windsor Station, the procession reassembled with the mourners now on foot. Ponsonby was relieved to see the detachments of the Army and Navy drawn up as he had directed, the military bands in position and the Artillery horses standing ready, harnessed to a gun-carriage. As soon as the coffin was secured and covered as before, he asked the King's permission to start. He stepped to the side, held

25

up his hand, the drums beat and the head of the procession moved off. But the horses had been kept motionless too long in the cold and the leaders were sluggish. The ones nearest the wheels, straining against the full load, began to plunge and rear. The traces of the harness snapped and the gun carriage started to roll back. For a second, it looked as if the King, who was standing immediately behind, might be injured, but the horses were held up. In the confusion, Ponsonby had enough presence of mind to send a sergeant at the double to halt the head of the procession which had already marched out of sight round the corner.

Ponsonby told the King embarrassedly what had happened, then ran back to find the officers of the Artillery trying to calm the horses and to work out how to draw the gun-carriage with the two traces still left intact. No one had foreseen such an accident and there were no spares. But it was obvious that two horses alone could not pull the heavy load up the steep hill to the Castle. In the near panic, Ponsonby realised that any longer delay would turn the Windsor procession into the fiasco he had dreaded, then Prince Louis of Battenberg, a Captain in the British Navy, reminded him quietly that sailors were used to manhandling guns. He returned to the King who watched him impassively, wrapped in his cloak.

He bowed. 'Do I have Your Majesty's permission to take out the horses and let the naval guard of honour drag the gun-carriage?'

The King contemplated him and Ponsonby held his breath. The King nodded. Ponsonby hurried to the Commander of the naval guard and told him. The sailors piled their arms and moved in on the gun-carriage, to the fury of the Artillery officers. In whispers, they protested violently at the insult. Bigge sided with them and told Ponsonby angrily that he was ruining the dignity of the entire ceremony. In any case, there was no rope, so the sailors were useless. But within minutes the naval guard had stripped the remaining traces off the horses, looped them together and attached them to the sides of the gun-carriage.

When the procession started off again, the crowds massed along the route had no idea that anything had gone wrong and were touched to see the ordinary seamen, in their blue uniforms and flat, white, widebrimmed hats, drawing their precious burden. Along the High Street and Park Street and through the gates at the end of the Long Walk, the cortege moved, ever closer to the tolling of the Sebastopol bell, only rung at the funeral of a sovereign, and the dull booming of the minute-guns. At St George's Chapel in the Castle precincts, the naval guard withdrew and a bearer party of the Coldstreams carried the heavy oak coffin up the steps, banked with wreaths, and along the nave to a purple bier placed above the tomb of George the Third in the Choir.

The Queen had come home to Windsor and here the darkness which she had so hated was finally dispelled. Inside the Chapel, all was brightness and splendour. Yeomen of the Guard in their scarlet and gold Tudor dress and black caps lined the passage of the nave. The seats and stalls were filled with the nobles and dignitaries of the whole kingdom, bishops and archbishops, in their embroidered copes, Privy Councillors in robes of state, the Knights of the Garter in their flamboyant feudal costumes, Gentlemen-at-arms in silver and white plumed helmets and scarlet coats. The dark cloaks and overcoats that had covered the uniforms of the royal mourners were removed and now they followed the bishops, the heralds and the King, a shifting mosaic of colours, blues, greens, magenta, grey, white and crimson, shining with jewelled orders, medals and stars, towards the Choir hung with the resplendent banners of the Knights. Alone in that gorgeous throng, one man wore the black dress of mourning, the American Ambassador, Mr. Choate. Among the glittering diplomatic uniforms, he was a figure of dignity and simplicity.

The service was short, read by the Archbishop of Canterbury and the Bishop of Winchester, then the Deputy King of Arms spoke again the proclamation of the new sovereign and, to the music of Beethoven's Funeral March, the coffin was taken to lie in the Albert Memorial Chapel.

Immediately after the service, Bertie and Alix hurried to the Private Secretary's Office, where Francis Knollys had put through a call to Osborne. Alix tried to speak to May but her deafness made it almost impossible to make out what her daughter-in-law was saying on the crackling line. As her agitation increased Bertie took the receiver from her. The news was better than he had nerved himself to expect. George's fever had lessened and he was out of danger as long as he was kept quiet. He left Alix resting in her own apartments and went to his private sitting-room in

27

Edward the Third's Tower. He sat in the armchair by the fire and laid his head back, closing his eyes. He had not let any of them see how concerned he had been. Now he felt exhausted with the emotion and strain of the processions and the worry over his son. He felt as if he could sleep for a week. Yet there was so much to do—the foreign visitors to be entertained, Ministers to be seen and a vast accumulation of business left by his mother to be cleared up. Above everything else, the war in South Africa still continued. Among his guests were some who had slandered the Queen and himself in their jealous hatred of Britain's foreign policies. He forgave and honoured them for coming here now, like Willy, but their countries were still hostile. The war must be won for Britain to keep her place in the first rank of world powers and it must be won speedily before other nations became involved.

In their last conversation together before his death, Bertie's father had told him how he dreamed that one day the rulers of Europe should be united by family ties and work together in friendship for the good of all. An impossible idea, perhaps; even his great father had failed to achieve it, yet it seemed the only way to create a lasting peace. His mother's aloofness over the years had made it more and more difficult, but in this gathering of princes, linked by reverence for her memory, he could see a faint beginning. Someone had to take the first steps. And he was now head of the family.

He had been faintly aware of a soft knock at the door and looked up to find Ponsonby beside him, bowing. He remembered he had sent for him. 'Yes, well done, Fritz,' he muttered. 'Well done.'

Ponsonby straightened in surprise. He had been trying to apologise to Arthur Bigge who had not hidden his malicious satisfaction when the summons came. He had expected a reprimand at the very least. Instead, the King had complimented him and called him by his nickname.

'Nasty moment, that,' the King was saying. 'But you coped very well. Now there's only the private family burial on the fourth. See to the arrangements, will you?'

'Me, Sir?'

The King nodded. 'Keep it simple. Just the bearer party and guard of honour. You know the sort of thing.'

Ponsonby stared at him. He had begun to relax, relieved that his responsibilities were over. Now he was being given

28

one day in which to organise the most important final stage of the funeral. 'That's Monday, sir,' he pointed out. 'The day after tomorrow.'

'Yes,' the King said.

Ponsonby spent a frantic evening working out the complete list of the family and foreign guests and their precedence, drawing up a suitable programme and arranging for it to be printed. He made his peace with Bigge. The King had been impressed by the spontaneity and unaffected dignity of the bluejackets, but Ponsonby had pointed out that the Artillery would feel insulted if the sailors replaced them again. He chose two bearer parties, one from the Life Guards and one from the Foot Guards and, on Lord Esher's advice, held a lantern-lit rehearsal of the final ceremony at the Mausoleum at eleven o'clock that night. It was an eerie scene with the men shuffling in the dark under the weight of a substitute coffin and stumbling on the steps of the Mausoleum. It was a difficult manoeuvre to turn the coffin at the door and Ponsonby was glad they had rehearsed it. He could not afford another mishap.

The King had agreed to all his suggestions, including the use of the horses, but his last words had been, 'Very well, but if anything goes wrong, I shall never speak to you again.'

Ponsonby was summoned to the King again the next morning after breakfast. He found the Royal party in the Long Gallery. The Kaiser, the plump, amiable King of Portugal, Dom Carlos and the raffish, bearded King of the Belgians, Leopold the Second, stood by the open fire. They all wore black frock coats and cravats. For a moment, Ponsonby could not think what was wrong, then he realised they were smoking cigars. That anyone should be smoking in public at Windsor was unthinkable, terrifying. Wisps of blue tobacco smoke were even drifting towards the Queen's study. Then he remembered. As they looked at him, slightly surprised, he bowed and moved on.

The King was standing further down the corridor with his son-in-law, the Duke of Fife, Princess Louise Victoria's pompous, self-important husband. Ponsonby bowed to the King. He allowed himself the trace of a smile, feeling rather pleased with himself. The King turned to look at him. He was holding a copy of the printed programme which had been rushed out and Ponsonby saw at once that something was very wrong.

'What do you mean by this, Ponsonby?' he rumbled.

'Your Majesty?'

'The Duke of Fife's name has been omitted!' the King thundered.

'I have never been so insulted,' Fife said stiffly.

Ponsonby quickly looked down the column of names when the King handed him the programme. In his haste, he had left the Duke's name out. It should have been at the bottom of the list. He wanted to say that he had done his best, that the King had checked the list himself before it went to the printers, but he thought better of it.

'It was purely inadvertent, sir,' he said. 'I'm very sorry.'

'That's not good enough!' the King told him angrily. 'How could you forget my own son-in-law, the husband of the Princess Royal?' Ponsonby was silent. He saw the Duke of Fife draw himself up. 'How can I have any confidence in you,' the King went on, 'when you make omissions like this? It is absolutely inconceivable to me how anyone like you, accustomed to arranging ceremonies, could have left out so important a person as my own son-in-law! Very well, that's all,' he finished curtly.

The Duke bowed to the King and stalked off down the corridor, satisfied at the reprimand. Ponsonby had not moved. He was tired and upset. He wanted to excuse himself, to make his peace with the King, but did not know how. It seemed very unjust. 'I—I am truly sorry, sir,' he said.

The King's eyes were heavy-lidded. The right lid closed slowly and opened again. Ponsonby nearly mistook it for a wink. Then he realised he had not been mistaken, when the King's mouth twitched. 'There, there, Fritz,' Bertie murmured. 'I know how difficult it's been for you—and I think you've done wonders.' He took Ponsonby's arm and walked with him to the window at the side, where they were screened from the others by a huge Dresden vase. 'No, you see it's all a question of balance, between pride and diplomacy. After all, Fife is Louise's husband. I had to say something strong. The poor fellow was so hurt he came to me and said he presumed he could go to London as he was apparently not wanted.' He chuckled and Ponsonby found himself smiling back, as if to a friend the same age and rank as himself.

On the day of the funeral, services were held throughout the country in every town and city of the Empire. All over

Europe, mourning was observed by Heads of Government and, in many places, public businesses were suspended. In the United States, the exchanges in all the chief cities were closed. In Washington, President McKinley and his Cabinet, with members of the Supreme Court, the two branches of the Legislature and the Army and Navy, attended a solemn memorial service.

Aa Windsor, all the public pomp and processions were over. Now, there was only the family, the late Queen's Household and the Royal mourners.

The stately mausoleum, built by Victoria nearly forty years before to house the remains of her adored husband, Albert, the Prince Consort, lay south-east of the Castle at Frogmore, near the house where her mother died. When she was at Windsor, she had paid a daily pilgrimage to his tomb and, every day, longed to join him, at first desperately and then with resignation, wondering how long her life must last before they could be together.

The day was bitingly cold and a thin snow fell as the slow cortege moved on foot across the Great Park towards Frogmore, led by the band and the Queen's Company of the Grenadier Guards. The dark horses drawing the gun-carriage with the coffin, draped in its pall and regal insignia for the last time, were quiet and subdued. Behind the coffin, Bertie with the Kaiser and Arthur led the Kings, heirs and Crown Princes. Following them came Alexandra with the ladies of the family and Household, then the other royal mourners. Seen fully for the first time, the dress of the ladies made a striking and solemn impression. In the same way that no one could remember the procedure for a Royal funeral, no one had known what to wear. The enormous bonnets and bombazine dresses of the past were too old fashioned. Princess Marie Louise, Helena's daughter, who had recently returned to England after the annulment of her marriage to the preposterous Prince Aribert of Anhalt, had experience of the mourning worn in the courts of Germany, In consultation with her, Alix devised a black dress of cashmere trimmed with crepe, the high neck swathed in white chiffon and with deep white chiffon cuffs. The headdress was a Mary Stuart cap, peaked over the forehead and covered to below the shoulders, with a filmy, flowing black veil that shrouded the head and face. The effect, with the Queen's daughters, granddaughters and

ladies all dressed alike, was strangely beautiful and un-
earthly.

Reaching the gates to the grounds at Frogmore, the
band and the Grenadiers moved to the sides, lining the
road, and the Queen's own Highland pipers, playing the
heartbreaking lament, 'The Flowers of the Forest,' led the
cortege in slow time to the Mausoleum. The Household
officers removed the insignia. The bearer parties in relays
carried the coffin up the steps aud over the threshold.

Inside the Mausoleum, shaped like a Greek cross and
richly decorated with mosaics, marble, frescoes and stained
glass, black hangings had been forbidden. In their place,
by the King's command, were palms, white lilies and clusters
of scarlet geraniums. The main, central chamber was
octagonal and there, under the lofty dome, lay the tomb of
the Prince Consort. The sarcophagus of dark-grey granite
stood on a black marble base, guarded at each corner by a
kneeling, bronze angel with outspread wings. On the sarcophagus, a recumbent, life-size effigy of the Prince in white
marble glimmered in the light of gas lamps. For nearly
forty years, Victoria had mourned her husband and prayed
to join him and here, to the singing of St. George's Chapel
choir, she was laid at last by his side.

After the service, the foreign guests and the Household
withdrew leaving Bertie and Alix and the Royal Family
kneeling by the tomb. Then they in turn retired. The doors
were closed and the lamps were left burning. Victoria and
Albert were together and alone.

Alix had never cared for Buckingham Palace. In contrast
to her own charming, comfortable home at Marlborough
House, it was gloomy and old fashioned and, as the late
Queen had hardly ever used it, much of it had a dusty,
uncared-for look. When Lord Esher took her on a tour of
inspection, as permanent secretary to the Office of Works,
he was surprised to find that she did not know her way
around. As Princess of Wales, she had only ever visited the
public and semi-public rooms used for receptions and state
banquets.

He was showing her the Royal study, surprisingly small,
decorated in a dark, early Victorian style and cluttered with
mementos. It was not long after the funeral and she still
wore the black mourning dress which was obligatory for
six months, with the veil tied back indoors. Esher admired

the way it suited her slim figure and fair complexion. She was biting her lower lip as she looked round.

'It's very dismal, isn't it?' she said.

'Perhaps a little, ma'am,' Esher smiled. 'It has been left exactly as it was, when it was used by the Prince Consort.'

Alix nodded and turned towards one of the two doors. 'And what's through there?'

'The Queen's private apartments,' he told her. She smiled slightly. It was an expression he had come to recognise, meaning that she had not heard. He spoke louder. 'The late Queen's private apartments. She always used these rooms on the few occasions in these last years that she stayed at the Palace.' He moved to the door and opened it. 'Would you care to inspect them, ma'am?'

Alix hesitated. All the time she had been in England, she had never once been in her mother-in-law's really private rooms in the Palace. She felt a touch of almost superstitious fear. She wanted to refuse, but Esher was waiting, smiling, and she crossed slowly towards him.

Bertie sat in the small red Audience Room, waiting for her. They were to receive the foreign ambassadors in order of importance and members of their suites. He had Charles Carrington and Francis Knollys, his Private Secretary, with him. They were smiling, remembering the Accession Council at St James's. 'I thought Balfour's face would crack,' he said.

'And Salisbury's knees,' Carrington added.

Bertie chuckled. 'Well, it didn't go too badly.'

Carrington paused. 'May I compliment you on your speech, sir? It was unexpected, but most appropriate. And moving.'

'I think everyone agrees, sir,' Knollys said. 'Nothing that could have been written for you would have sounded so sincere.'

Bertie was touched. 'Thank you, Francis—Charles. Thank you both. No, I felt something was called for. Had to break the ice.'

There was a knock at the door and Ponsonby came in. He was wearing his Equerry's uniform. The day after the funeral, the King had asked him to join his personal staff as Assistant Private Secretary. Bigge had been made secretary to the Duke of York and, although he had not yet been fully accepted by Francis Knollys, Ponsonby was the happiest young man in the Household. He bowed.

'What's going on out there, Fritz?' Bertie asked.

'The Ambassadors are arriving, sir. And the Prime Minister and Mr Balfour are waiting.'

Bertie grunted. 'Salisbury drags his nephew round with him like an old tugboat towing a battlecruiser.' They laughed. 'Well, we'd better have them in.'

Ponsonby bowed and left. Bertie looked round. 'Where the deuce is the Queen?'

'The Queen, sir?' Knollys asked, surprised. As Bertie glanced at him, he realised. 'I beg your pardon, sir.'

'Yes, it takes a little getting used to,' Bertie nodded. 'But now Alix is Queen, I hoped she'd be a sight more punctual. She can't keep the whole diplomatic world waiting!'

One end and one wall of the narrow dressing-room were taken up with wardrobes, full of clothes in a style not worn for thirty years. On the dressing table was a miniature of Prince Albert and his silver hairbrushes. The sofa and other pieces of furniture were heavy and covered with dark brocade. It smelt faintly of dust and camphor.

Alix coughed. 'I thought it would be bigger,' she whispered. She was still nervous, feeling guilty yet excited at being here.

'The Prince Consort's bedroom is through there, ma'am,' Esher told her. 'Of course, it has not been used for many years. The Queen's bedroom is here.' He hesitated. 'Would you care to see them?'

Alix had noticed the hesitation. 'Will it be all right?'

'Of course, ma'am. They are yours now,' Esher explained. 'I merely thought—His Majesty is waiting to receive deputations.'

'Yes, I know,' Alix said.

'It cannot begin until you are there,' Esher warned. 'He will become impatient.'

Alix laughed. 'Let him wait. It will do him good.' Consumed with curiosity, she moved past Esher and pushed open the door to the Queen's bedroom. 'Oh, dear,' she sighed when she saw it. Esher smiled and followed her.

In the Audience Room, Salisbury and Balfour had presented themselves to the King. They watched with the others as he paced, trying to control his irritation. He stopped and turned. 'Well, who should we see first?'

'If I might suggest, sir,' Balfour said; 'the German Ambassador. There is agitation in Germany that the Kaiser is still here.'

34

'My nephew is still distressed by the death of his grandmother. He is staying on as a member of the family, not as the German Emperor.'

'The gesture has made Kaiser Wilhelm very popular here,' Carrington pointed out.

Bertie nodded. Willy's behaviour had been a model of tact and sympathy. With none of his usual brashness, he had unobtrusively taken George's place temporarily at his uncle's right hand. His strength and comforting presence had been invaluable. 'It might give us a real chance at last of reaching an understanding with Germany.'

Balfour coughed. 'That will be for discussion between his ministers and yours, sir.'

Bertie glanced at him, annoyed. The most able member of Salisbury's Cabinet, Arthur Balfour was a handsome, patrician man, tall, with a full moustache. His amusements mainly intellectual and literary, he had little in common with the King, with whom his manner was often stiff and lecturing. Bertie respected him but had no intention of being treated as a powerless figurehead. However, that problem could be thrashed out later. 'Where the devil is Alix?' he muttered. He moved to the principal chair of state and sat drumming his fingers on the arm-rest. The others shifted uneasily. 'This is intolerable! Well, let's do something. We'll have Soveral in.'

Salisbury was surprised. 'The Portuguese Ambassador, sir?'

'He's a friend of mine,' Bertie snapped. 'And at least, the rest will know something's happening. I cannot bear being thought impolite.'

Knollys nodded to Ponsonby who was waiting by the door. He went out. 'Perhaps I could send a messenger to look for Her Majesty?' Knollys suggested.

Bertie glared at him and Knollys subsided. It was a new experience for Balfour. He had known the King as Prince of Wales, smiling and affable in public and, in private, charming, polished and diplomatic. Now he could see that his staff, even the Prime Minister, Lord Salisbury, were in awe of him. As he looked at the powerful, seated figure, the face set, the beard jutting, he had a fleeting touch of that awe himself and wondered at what lay ahead. In rage, the King would be terrifying.

The door opened as Ponsonby entered again. 'The Marquis de Soveral,' he announced.

Luis de Soveral, the Portuguese Minister in London, was a strongly built, good-looking man in his late thirties. His hair was black like his moustache. During the five years he had been in England, he had made love to many ladies and become the friend and confidant of many influential men. Behind his light, frivolous manner, he concealed an acute intelligence. Although his jaw was clean-shaven, his skin always showed a dark shadow. That and his infectious, mischievous smile had earned him the nickname, The Blue Monkey. He advanced and bowed.

'Your Gracious Majesty,' he said, 'may I tender the sincere thanks of my sovereign, King Carlos, for your recent hospitality at this trying time and repeat his deepest condolences in your irreparable loss. Also, his heartfelt felicitations on your accession. To which I have the honour to add my own.'

'I thank you, Luis,' Bertie said and gave him his hand. Like Carrington, Soveral's wit and discretion had made him one of his closest friends.

As Soveral bowed low again, Alexandra came in from the study followed by Esher. She nodded, smiling, as the gentlemen bowed, and headed for the red and gold chairs of state. When she reached them, Bertie muttered thunderously, 'Alix, where have you been?'

'Oh, dear,' she asked, unruffled. 'Have I kept you all waiting?'

Bertie pulled his fobwatch from his waistcoat pocket. He held it up and said heavily, 'Only for fifty minutes.'

Alix smiled. 'Well then, it's not too bad, is it?' Bertie gave up gracefully. She looked round at the others who were trying not to smile. 'Now, what do I have to do?'

'If you would take the Consort's throne, Your Majesty——' Knollys proposed. Alexandra glanced at him as if for a moment she were about to object, then raised her hands in a small gesture of assent. She took the chair next to Bertie. When he had put his watch away, she nodded to him and sat up erect, the very pattern of grace and dignity.

The King and Queen were ready to take their first audience.

Chapter

3

George had recovered. He was still pale and had lost weight but he would no longer let anyone treat him like an invalid. There was too much to do. At Osborne, he had chafed at being away from everything. He bitterly regretted having missed the funeral and was almost as excited as the children to see the cinematograph film of the procession through the streets of London.

They were in the main white and gold drawing-room of Marlborough House. The projectionist had set up his equipment on a table and the images were thrown on to a collapsible screen, supported by two posts. Ponsonby was assisting him. George leant on the back of a small sofa on which his second son, Prince Albert, known as Little Bertie, knelt between Alix and her spinster daughter, Princess Victoria. Bertie sat in front of them with George's elder son, Prince Edward, known as David, aged six, perched on his knees. To the side, May sat with Alix's friend, Lady de Grey, and other ladies-in-waiting, who were very aware of Kaiser Wilhelm standing behind them with Esher and Francis Knollys.

As the pictures flickered and the gun-carriage drawn by its pale cream horses jerked past, they were all hushed. Then Bertie jogged David. 'Watch now,' he said. 'There's Grandpa. And Cousin Willy of Germany. And King Carlos!'

The children laughed. 'He looks very important,' David said.

'Doesn't he?' Bertie chuckled. 'And Uncle Willy of Greece. The Archduke of Austria and the Russian Grand Duke. And there—you see the tiny man in the cloak and the white helmet? That's the Crown Prince of Siam.'

'Look at the soldiers!' Little Bertie shouted.

'Yes, lots of soldiers,' Alix agreed, smiling.

The picture blurred, slowed into indistinct single frames and cut off and the film whirred inside its spool as the reel ended. A footman standing by the doors turned on the electric lights. Little Bertie cried out in disappointment.

'Again!' David pleaded. 'Let's see it again, Gran'pa!'

'No, no, David,' May said primly. 'Don't clamour. That's the third showing.'

As David's face fell, Bertie ruffled his hair. 'We'll look at it again tomorrow,' he promised. He kissed the top of David's head. 'Time you were in bed.'

David rose reluctantly as his mother stood. He knew it was useless to protest. Alix rose, too. 'I'll help you with them, May.'

'There's no need, Motherdear,' May said quickly. 'Nanny can manage.'

'No doubt,' Alix nodded. 'But so can I. Come on.' She took Little Bertie's hand as he jumped up and led him towards the door. May flashed a quick look at her husband and followed her. She adored her mother-in-law, but like George, felt that she spoilt the children abominably. They were always much more difficult to manage after they had been to stay with their grandparents.

David was gazing at Bertie, hopefully. 'Will you come up and see us, Gran'pa?'

'In a little while,' Bertie assured him. 'Off you pop.'

David smiled happily and went out with his Aunt Toria. Lady de Grey and the ladies-in-waiting had risen. They curtsied to the King and followed them out. Bertie laughed quietly. He could hear David shouting, 'Don't forget, Gran'pa!' from outside in the corridor and being hushed.

He pushed himself to his feet as the Kaiser came to him. 'They admire you so much,' Willy said quietly. 'I know how they feel. When I was a little boy, I wanted nothing so much as to be just like my Uncle Bertie.'

Bertie was touched. 'Thank you, Willy,' he muttered. There was a box of cigars on the table beside him. He took one and offered the box to Wilhelm, who shook his head. George had been helping Ponsonby to roll up the screen. He moved in and struck a match to light his father's cigar. 'Yes,' Bertie puffed. 'David's a chip off the old block. D'you know what he said when we told him his great grandmama had died and gone to heaven?'

Wilhelm looked at George. George smiled. 'He said— "Oh, she won't like that".'

Wilhelm frowned, surprised. 'Why did he say that?'

Bertie paused. 'That's what we asked him. And he said, "Well, you see—she'll have to walk *behind* the angels".'

As he understood, Wilhelm laughed. 'How very perceptive.'

'Wasn't it?' Bertie agreed. 'Still, she was a great Queen.'

'And the greatest assembly of crowned heads ever seen honoured her passing,' Wilhelm added, serious again. 'I was proud to be part of it.'

The others had come closer. Bertie included them. 'Ponsonby here helped to arrange things,' he said. 'I'm thinking of adding a new section to the archives, a Cinematograph Section. I may ask him to take charge of it.'

'What a splendid idea!' George exclaimed. 'I was most impressed. The quality's improved so much in a short time.'

Bertie blew softly on the tip of his cigar. 'It could be an important development in the future.'

'Yes,' the Kaiser conceded. 'Yes, but it would have to be carefully controled. Properly used, it could be very effective. Still, one would only wish people to see what it is fit for them to see.'

Bertie shrugged noncommittally. He had meant a simple record of state occasions and family gatherings. 'If it were censored, Willy, it would not be a true record.'

'What is truth?' Wilhelm smiled. 'Everyone has heard the camera cannot lie. But we could so arrange things that these moving pictures would only show what we wanted them to, like in the theatre.' His quick mind had already grasped the possibilities for propaganda and self-glory. He could visualise a whole pageant with himself as the central figure on the screen, in his white uniform, reviewing his crack troops. It could be shown to schools and colleges, at public meetings to inspire loyalty.

'Well, of course,' Bertie said, 'we could always dress up and do theatricals for the camera. They could charge admission to show it at Drury Lane.' They laughed. Ponsonby passed them, carrying the screen. 'Yes, you wanted to ask me something, Fritz. What was it?' Ponsonby stopped, glancing at the others. 'Yes?'

Ponsonby was embarrassed. 'It was only—I am still a serving officer, sir, in the Grenadiers. Many of my friends have fallen in South Africa.' He hesitated. 'I would like your permission to join my regiment there before it is too late.'

The group was very quiet. The Kaiser came to attention. 'You are an honour to your country,' he told him.

Bertie nodded. He had come to appreciate Ponsonby's efficiency, but he could not refuse. 'Very well. As soon as Francis can spare you.'

Ponsonby bowed and moved to help the projectionist dismantle his equipment. He was still embarrassed. He had not meant to make a parade of his request like that. George followed him. 'Lucky devil,' he said enviously. 'I wish I could go with you.'

Bertie sat again. He respected Ponsonby still more. Yet it saddened him. So many young men he had known and admired, gallant, patriotic, had gone out full of courage to die on those stony hills, that arid veldt. In the first six months of the war, the British forces had been near defeat. The Boer armies, numerically superior, more efficiently commanded and equipped with better and heavier guns by Holland, Germany and France, had smashed into them without warning. Their object, backed by the same Powers, was to expel the British settlers and turn the whole of southern Africa into a Dutch Republic. They had nearly succeeded, except for a few small garrisons which managed to hold out amid frightful privations until reinforcements arrived from England under Lord Roberts, with Kitchener as his chief of staff. Their combined tactics and determination had defeated the invading armies and the President of the Transvaal, Kruger, fled with an immense fortune to Europe where he was hailed as a hero. But the rest of the Boers fought on, refusing to surrender. They were skilled and brave guerrilla fighters and many lives were still lost.

'You see no end to the war?' Wilhelm asked.

'They are determined to wear us down,' Esher said.

Wilhelm grunted. He had no more illusions about the prospects of a Boer victory. It had been a forlorn hope. God favours the big battalions. His last belief in their chances had died with the flight of Kruger. Unlike the French President and the Queen of Holland and despite popular demands in Germany, he had refused to receive him. 'Ja, es ist klar,' he muttered. 'You are bound to win.'

'Of course,' Bertie sighed. 'Yet the needless slaughter goes on.'

'At least it has proved one thing,' Wilhelm declared. Bertie looked up at him. 'That the British Empire will fight to the finish for what it believes is right. Some of us had

forgotten that.' He paused. 'Perhaps it is not the time, but
. . . I have wanted to talk to you.' Bertie waited. 'You and I
are heads of the strongest nations in the word. We should
work to forge a lasting alliance between our two countries.'

Bertie was silent. In the days they had been together, he
had forced himself not to raise the subject. For it to have
a possibility of success, the proposal had to come from
Wilhelm, himself. He had to want it and believe it was his.
Tomorrow he was returning to Berlin. It had almost been
too late. 'It has been my dream for many years,' he said
quietly.

Wilhelm smiled. 'I had not realised until these last
weeks how similar in so many ways we are. Not only the
natural ties of affection. We both have a sincere desire
for peace and order.' He turned a chair that was beside him
and sat near Bertie, leaning forward. Esher and Knollys
moved closer, listening, caught by his enthusiasm. 'With our
empires united in friendship,' Wilhelm went on, 'together
we could police the world! The practical advantages for
both our countries would be enormous.'

In the study at Downing Street, Lord Salisbury sat behind
his desk. The study was panelled, a functional but comfortable room with wide windows looking on to the garden.
Balfour stood by one of the windows. Lord Lansdowne, the
Foreign Secretary, sat near the fire. They were listening to
Esher who, at the King's request, was reporting the gist of
the conversation.

'What particular advantages?' Salisbury enquired.

'The Kaiser believes that the chief danger to all of us is
the growing ambition of Russia.'

'They are ambitious for territory,' Balfour agreed. 'But
Czar Nicholas is incompetent and his country virtually
bankrupt.'

'He has been negotiating with financiers in the United
States,' Esher warned. 'They will lend him money to develop his empire in Asia.'

Salisbury tensed. 'How will that affect us?'

'The Kaiser promises to protect our interests in India
and the Middle East,' Esher told him, 'if we protect his in
Africa and South America.'

Behind him, Lansdowne laughed. 'Does the King really
believe any of this?'

'He believes the German Emperor is sincere in his desire for an alliance with this country.'

Balfour moved from the window to the end of the desk. He was frowning. 'Then why was the German Ambassador not instructed to discuss it with the British Government?'

Esher shrugged. 'Kaiser Wilhelm wanted the King's views first.'

Lansdowne was angry. A detached, aristocratic man with a faintly supercilious manner, he had had a long career as a politician. He had recently taken over the Foreign Office from the ailing Salisbury and, as a professional, deeply resented interference by someone he considered an amateur. 'Does he think the King of England is like him and can tell his government what to do?' he snapped.

Esher looked at him. 'Surely such an offer is to be considered, Lord Lansdowne, whichever channel it comes through?'

Salisbury shook his head. 'We have never found an acceptable basis for an Anglo-German alliance before.'

'The King is convinced of its sincerity,' Esher stressed. 'He feels it essential that we join in closer ties with Europe. If we do not, we shall be squeezed out between the United States and Russia before the middle of the century.'

There was a pause. Lansdowne laughed again. Balfour smiled. 'He's giving us the benefit of his political thoughts, is he?'

Salisbury cleared his throat. 'No, don't underestimate him, Arthur. He has always been interested in foreign affairs.'

Lansdowne smiled. 'Affairs, yes. Foreign, on occasion.'

Salisbury's fingers tapped slowly on the desk. 'That is no way to speak of your Sovereign, sir,' he said gently.

Lansdowne stopped smiling, rebuked. Balfour glanced at him. He agreed with Lansdowne completely, although he liked the King well enough as a man. However, the issue of who was to rule the country, the King or the Government, was too vital to be left undecided, certainly more important than this delusion of impossible alliances. 'I am prepared to take him seriously,' he said, 'when he tells me what are the right clothes to wear or who sits next to whom at dinner. At that he is an expert.'

Esher was incredulous. Having assured himself of the Kaiser's good faith and ability to influence political opinion in Germany, the King had stepped aside, as was his duty

42

as a constitutional monarch, passing the handling of the negotiations on to his government. Yet through pride and misjudgement of his experience and intentions, the leading members of the Government were rejecting the opening he had given them. He turned to Salisbury. 'Am I to tell him that you will not consider any of his recommendations?'

'I trust you will not tell him any of this, Lord Esher,' the Prime Minister said pointedly.

Esher enjoyed a privileged position. He had frequently been asked to enter Parliament, offered posts of power and responsibility. He preferred, however, to work behind the scenes where his influence and power were all the greater for being unseen and not attached to any one party. He had direct access to many government departments and his advice was often asked by the Cabinet. If he told them his real opinions in this case, that influence could be ended. He nodded shortly. He picked up his hat, gloves and cane and rose. Making for the door, he stopped and considered them in turn.

'He is learning fast,' he murmured. 'And may surprise you.'

Few people knew the owner of the smart, one-horse brougham, a little, four-wheeled closed carriage with no arms or monogram on its sides, which sat so many afternoons outside the house in Portman Square. The house belonged to the Hon George Keppel, a tall, good-natured man with impeccable manners, a younger son of the Earl of Albemarle, and those few who might recognise the brougham would change their minds if they had been thinking of calling, for its presence meant that Mrs. Keppel was entertaining a most distinguished guest to tea.

Alice Keppel, in her early thirties, was a strikingly beautiful woman, her rich chestnut hair piled high above the perfect oval of her face, her eyes a vivid turquoise under delicately arched brows. Her voice was low, slightly husky. For nearly three years, she had been Bertie's mistress and confidante and was still his favourite because, like Alix, she understood him and did not expect him to be entirely faithful. Wise and witty as well as beautiful, her love for him was genuine and she never took advantage of her position. The situation was accepted by her charming, older husband and by almost the whole of society, whose members admired her poise and discretion.

Bertie was sitting on the sofa in the drawing-room. Alice's children, two little girls whom he adored, had been brought to meet him and their Nanny had taken them back upstairs. 'They didn't tire you?' Alice asked.

'No, no.' He shook his head. She took the empty cup and saucer from him and moved to lay them on the side table. Out of deference to him, her afternoon dress was of black with a border of boldly patterned, dark purple lace. The sleeves were soft and flowing to the elbows, then tapering in the same lace to the wrists. The close fit of the skirt emphasised the fullness of her hips, the curving hour glass figure with its slender waist, which had needed tighter and tighter corseting since the birth of her second child.

She was conscious of him watching her as she turned and came back to sit beside him on the Chesterfield, stretching out her arm along its back. He took her hand and turned it, moving it to his lips. As he kissed her palm, he murmured, 'You are very lovely, my dear, as always.'

His deep, almost guttural voice still had the same effect on her as on the first time they had met, wholly feminine and uncontrollable. She wanted to reach out and touch him, draw him to her, cradle him against her. Instead she smiled and he lowered her hand, still holding it, to rest between them. His thumb moved gently as if to feel the texture of her skin, but she could see he was not really thinking of her. Normally they laughed together, trading news and pieces of gossip. Today he had been unusually silent. As he was now.

'Is something troubling you?' she asked.

'There's so much to be done,' he said after a pause. 'Hard to know where to begin. I'd hand some of it over to George, but he and May are leaving for Australia next month.'

'I read the announcement in your speech.'

He nodded. 'The trip's been arranged for some time, to mark the establishment of the Australian Commonwealth. He's to open the first Commonwealth Parliament. I thought of going myself, but it's too soon after the funeral—and the experience will be good for George. I want him to be brought forward, to learn a bit about government, and work with me. I don't want him to be shuffled aside like I was.'

'It will be good for them both,' Alice said.

'Yes,' he agreed. 'May's a fine girl. But too serious. It'll help to draw her out.' He smiled briefly. 'When I told her they were going to New Zealand and Canada as well and they'd be gone for seven or eight months, she nearly had kittens.'

'Why?'

'We've to look after the children while they're away. She's terrified we'll spoil them for some reason. I don't think she really understands children.'

Alice laughed quietly but he did not join in. His eyes were preoccupied again. 'Is there something else?' she asked.

For a moment, she wondered if she had said something wrong, then he shook his head. 'Nothing you can help with, my dear. My sister, Vicky.'

'The Empress Frederick? I thought it was strange she didn't come from Germany for the funeral.'

"She couldn't,' he said flatly. 'She's dying, herself.'

Alice was upset. She had been hideously tactless. 'I'm sorry,' she apologised. "I had no idea.'

'Neither had I. Just one more thing that was kept from me.' He breathed out heavily. 'She has cancer. The same thing that killed her husband—and my brother, Affie.' He looked at her and his eyes were wet. 'I'm leaving for Friedrichshof as soon as I can. I don't think she knows it—but I may be seeing her for the last time.'

The following Sunday, when the *Victoria and Albert* drew in to the jetty at Flushing, Bertie heard the sound of a large Dutch crowd further away on the quay singing hymns. The singing was loud and passionate, but he could not understand why they repeated the same hymn over and over again. The British Minister at the Hague explained when he came on board. They were singing 'De Volksved', the Boer national anthem. Some of the crowd had been violent and the police held them back behind barriers.

Bertie was travelling with only his personal physician, Sir Francis Laking, and Ponsonby as Secretary. Despite protests from the Government that he should be properly attended, he had become used to travelling light, as Prince of Wales, and saw no need to change that now he was King. It was not official, he insisted, purely a private visit. Last time he had travelled on the Continent. taking Alix to visit her family in Denmark, a youth had leapt on to the running-board of their compartment, while the train was standing in Brussels Station, and shot at them, the bullet ripping into the cushioned headrest between them. He remembered the smashing glass, the smell of cordite and the white, staring face as the boy jerked again at the trigger. They were only saved because the gun misfired but, when the Minister suggested that Embassy Staff accompany him for his protection, he refused. He would not let a shouting mob think they had made him afraid.

Throughout the night, he heard that hymn at every station the train stopped at on its way to Germany.

At Homburg, Kaiser Wilhelm was waiting on the platform. Affectionate and friendly, he had respected his uncle's wish to do without ceremony and they set off at once, in a sleigh drawn by two greys, for Freidrichshof, the home built by Bertie's sister in memory of her husband, the gentle Kaiser Frederick, who had only reigned for three months before dying of cancer of the throat.

The Empress Frederick had never ceased to be homesick for England and Friedrichshof, situated in pleasant, wooded countryside, under the Taunus Mountains, was in the style of an English country house, standing in its own spacious grounds. The thick wooden beams chequering its stone walls gave it an Elizabethan effect, strengthened by groups of high, Gothic turrets. A guard of honour was drawn up outside the main entrance, Prussian soliders in spiked helmets and greatcoats reaching to their ankles. In the massive hall, the Empress's Household stood in line to be presentèd. Also waiting were the Empress Frederick's three daughters. When they told them that she had insisted on being up to greet her brother, the King and the Kaiser hurried upstairs at once to her sitting-room.

Victoria, eldest child of the Queen and the Prince Consort, was a pretty, round-faced girl when she married Fritz, Frederick Wilhelm, Crown Prince of Prussia. Quietly imperious, artistic, with a lively mind, she had converted her husband to her own pacifist, liberal opinions. For a time they had been carried away by pride in Prussia's sweeping achievements, the defeat in turn of Denmark, Austria and France and the creation of the German Empire, but when they saw that their country was becoming a military dictatorship, they dedicated themselves to the idea of reducing the power of the army and introducing a liberal democracy when Fritz succeeded his autocratic father as Kaiser. All their hopes were destroyed by Fritz's untimely death.

Their son Wilhelm had no sympathy with his mother's pacifist beliefs and her last years had been bitter.

Her private sitting-room, like most of the other rooms in the house, was very English in its furniture and decoration, except for an enormous, tiled stove in one corner. In the fashion of Osborne, and Windsor, there were photographs, statuettes and mementos on every available surface. The heavy curtains were tied back but a screen of frost on the outside of the windows obscured the view of the park and the hills beyond, which the Empress Frederick loved because they reminded her of the hills of Scotland, of Balmoral where she had been so happy as a girl, and where dear Fritz had proposed to her just before her fifteenth birthday.

Dressed in full mourning, she was lying, partly on her side, propped up by cushions on a chaise longue. Her eyes were fixed on the door. Only sixty, she looked much older, haggard, wasted by suffering and disease. The cancer which had attacked her spine made each day she lived an agony and the Court doctors could give her no relief. She plucked anxiously at a quilt which covered the lower part of her body, listening eagerly for any sound outside. When she heard voices in the corridor, she nodded quickly to the nurse in attendance to help her to sit up more.

Wilhelm opened the door and held it for Bertie to enter. Bertie stopped. Seeing her, he needed a moment to compose himself. Wilhelm passed him and crossed to the chaise longue. 'So, you're dressed, Mama,' he said, surprised. He kissed his mother's cheek perfunctorily and turned, smiling. 'Well—here he is!'

Bertie moved forward. He had been remembering his elder sister as a young wife and, although he had schooled himself, her appearance shocked him. Now he had recovered. 'Splendid, Vicky!' he laughed. 'We thought to find you in bed.'

She held out her hand and he came to her, taking it. '. . . Bertie,' she whispered. Her voice was weak and hoarse. 'I have been longing—longing to see you.' Her hand held his tightly, not letting it go.

'Now, don't keep him too long, Mama,' Wilhelm said. 'I have promised him a sleigh ride this afternoon.' He went to the door which the nurse hurried to hold for him. He bowed. 'Till later.' When he left, the nurse curtsied and closed the door, then moved to sit unobtrusively by the far wall.

Vicky was still holding Bertie's hand. She drew him down to sit beside her. 'Bertie . . .' she whispered again, gazing at him. He had always been her favourite brother. They had had their differences but, for many years, had been as close again as they were when they were children.

'How are you, my dear?' he asked after a pause.

She waved the question away. 'Let's not talk about me,' she smiled. 'The children, are they well?'

'All thriving.'

'And Alix?'

'Never better.' He chuckled. 'I think she enjoys being Queen.'

He grimaced as he realised what he had said. Vicky patted his hand and lay back. Sitting up was too exhausting. 'I was heartbroken I could not be with you,' she faltered.

'We missed you. But Willy behaved admirably. He won all hearts,' he assured her. 'I hadn't realised how devoted he was to Mama. He supported us all in her last hours.'

Vicky nodded. She tried to smile. 'And you are King at last.'

'In name.'

'When will you be crowned?'

He shrugged. 'Not until the war is over. It would not be right to hold a Coronation, to ask my people to rejoice when the country is not at peace.'

The tears which Vicky had been fighting came at last. But they were silent tears. 'I had so hoped to be there,' she whispered.

'But you will,' he told her. 'You will be!' She shook her head. From her chair by the wall, he saw the nurse sign to him. He had promised to stay only a few minutes. 'I must leave you now, let you rest.'

She looked around at the nurse and back to him. 'No, no,' she pleaded. 'No, please . . . Stay with me! Tell me how she died. Did—did she speak of me?'

That afternoon, Kaiser Wilhelm took Bertie and his suite for a drive in sleighs across the snow-covered countryside to an old castle which he owned nearby. It was welcomed by Laking and Ponsonby who found the stiffness and formality of the Prussian Household very difficult. It was especially difficult for Laking, a distinguished London physician, whose presence was resented by the Empress's doctors.

48

He had been warned not to discuss her case unless he was asked. An unnecessary precaution as they would scarcely talk to him. Ponsonby, as a mere Captain, was treated with insolent politeness by the Kaiser's staff of Generals and Colonels. Sir Frank Lascelles, the British Ambassador in Berlin, had arrived and sat next to Ponsonby in his sleigh. He seemed nervous. Ponsonby understood why when they reached the castle. Count Metternich, the German Ambassador in London, was there. The Government had obviously sent Lascelles to make sure that the King was not having secret meetings on the question of the alliance. The Kaiser and the King went off to talk alone. Lascelles was left with the silent Metternich.

As the days of the short visit passed, Laking and Ponsonby grew more uncomfortable, aware of a growing tension that lay just beneath the surface. At dinner in the evenings, Laking was largely ignored. Ponsonby was placed between General von Scholl, the Kaiser's Aide de Camp, and the gruff, English-hating General von Kessel. He was conscious all the time of Count Eulenberg, the Kaiser's closest friend and Marshal of his Household, a plump, suave man, watching him with malicious amusement. And grateful to the Empress Frederick's daughters, Wilhelm's sisters, who were excited at being with their famous uncle and whose gay chatter at least gave him an excuse to listen rather than make forced conversation.

Wilhelm was as affable and friendly as he had been in London, but there was something hidden behind his banter and laughter. Here he was on his own ground and he knew that the members of his staff were watching to see how he treated his uncle whom he had so often sneered at in the past. Though not yet crowned, his uncle was now also a King and Emperor. With an empire far larger than Germany's. If Bertie was aware of any strain, he gave no sign. He joked with his nephew, took Laking to visit the chest sanatorium at Falkenstein and worried Ponsonby by protesting that there had been thirteen every night to dinner. Later, when Ponsonby explained that he could see no way to avoid the unlucky number without offending their host, he laughed and said it was all right. He had found out that his niece, Princess Frederick Charles of Hesse, was going to have a baby. He was determined to create the impression of a happy family party and his reward was that Vicky seemed to improve. One day she was well enough to be wheeled in her bathchair in the park for an hour beside him and, later, to sit with him and the other guests in the main drawing-room after dinner.

He was so delighted that he insisted on wheeling her back to her private rooms himself. He wanted to speak to her alone. Her cheeks were slightly flushed and she laughed when he threatened to spin her round as he turned her chair. 'You're looking so much better,' he assured her.

'It's having so many of my children with me,' she said. 'That has not happened for a long time. And it is thanks to you.'

'Not only that,' he smiled. 'I am sure you are getting better. Your doctors are more confident.' She shook her head. 'Now listen, Vicky. I didn't want to trouble you before, but you know I've brought Laking with me. I want you to permit him to examine you.'

Her smile faded. 'They won't let me see him,' she said quietly.

Bertie was puzzled. 'Not see him?'

Her eyes moved quickly to the door and back to him. They were still alone. 'Will you close the door?' she whispered. He shut it carefully and turned, waiting for her to speak. 'You don't know what it's really like here, Bertie,' she said at last. 'The soldiers you see are really guards. No one is allowed to talk to me without a permit from Eulenberg. I cannot invite my friends or even send them letters.'

"That's not possible,' Bertie breathed

'It has been going on ever since Fritz died. At first, I could find ways to get round it. I had my old servants .But since I have been ill . . .' She coughed. 'My visitors are turned away. My letters are read.'

'You are the Emperor's mother,' he said, horrified.

'I am English,' she reminded him. 'I have never been accepted. My son's advisers know that I have always worked for peace and been against the power of the Army.'

Bertie was unwilling to believe it. He came closer to her. 'Those days are gone in Germany,' he protested. 'Willy, himself—he sincerely offered me his friendship. And he meant it.'

'Yes,' Vicky agreed. 'He does today—and perhaps tomorrow. Maybe even next week. But one day he will change.' Bertie stared at her. Her voice had been bleak, unemotional. Now it began to break. 'He cannot help it. Oh, he was

50

moved by the funeral and being accepted as one of the family. Part of him has always longed for that.'

'Yes.' He sat near her, on the chaise longue.

'But you are head of the family now.' She looked at him. 'He has always admired, and envied you—but he cannot accept anyone as greater than himself. He is the Kaiser. One day he will have to open a door for you or not be able to sit until you sit and all his hatred and envy of England will come back—worse than ever.'

Bertie knew she was right. She was speaking of her own son. Although they had been estranged for many years, she was one of the few people who understood his strange mind. 'I hoped, this time it would last,' he said. He was saddened. He wished he could find an excuse to take her away with him, but realised it was not possible.

'I had to warn you,' she said.

He nodded. 'Thank you, my dear. I'll be careful.' He sighed. 'Nothing is what it seems any more.'

He gazed at her, seeing the lines furrowed by suffering. He felt an angry impotence, knowing there was nothing he could do to ease her pain. It need not have been such torture. At least, Laking would have given her larger doses of morphia than the German doctors permitted, although they agreed that she would never recover. Two of his brothers were gone, Alfred and Leopold, one sister, Alice. And soon Vicky. Time and disease, he thought, but time is the chief enemy. Time takes everything. And he had wasted so much of it.

Chapter

4

Ponsonby could not work. He had excused himself early after dinner, having so much to do. Every day a messenger brought despatch boxes to Friedrichshof for the King's attention. Many of the contents were orders needing only his signature, but others had to be thought over and answered carefully. Ponsonby had to compose and write out all the replies, often twice when the King made corrections. He still had several to finish to complete the latest batch, but he could not concentrate.

In the morning, he had walked in the park with the King and his nieces, and the Empress Frederick was brought out again to join them for a short while. When it was time for her to leave, he had been near her. She said to him, 'My nurse takes tea at three-thirty. Will you come and see me then?' He had, of course, accepted the invitation with pleasure. As the nurse came to wheel her inside, she added very quietly, 'Don't tell anyone I asked you.' For the rest of the morning and all through lunch he had wondered what it could mean.

At half past three, he had gone upstairs to her sitting-room. He found her lying back on the chaise longue, supported by cushions. She was drawn and pale. The mask which she wore in public had dropped and she was obviously in extreme pain. The middle-aged German nurse sat in a chair near her, reading.

'How kind of you to call,' the Empress said, as though surprised to see him. Ponsonby was more intrigued than ever.

The nurse had risen. The Empress looked at her. 'It's all right, Anna,' she nodded. 'Captain Ponsonby will sit with me for a minute or two.' The nurse hesitated uncertainly, then curtsied and left the room. Ponsonby waited, aware of the Empress watching him.

'I remember you as an Equerry of my mother's,' she said at last.

He bowed. 'I had that honour, ma'am.'

'Of course, I knew your father well.' His father had been adviser and Private Secretary to Queen Victoria for many years. He bowed again. 'And you are married?'

'I have that honour, too, ma'am,' he smiled. 'Although it took nearly three years to convince her late Majesty that it would not lessen my duty to *her*.'

Vicky smiled briefly. 'Do, please, sit down,' she said.

He removed the nurse's book from the chair and brought it nearer to the chaise longue. As he sat, waiting for her to speak, he secretly examined the room. It was like a museum, crowded with fifty years of family history. Most prominent was a heroic bust of the Emperor Frederick. Round its neck hung the laurel wreath given to him by his wife after the Franco-Prussian war, brittle and faded. Flanking it were portraits of Queen Victoria and the Prince Consort, both draped in black crepe. Mounted on velvet under a glass dome was a small sprig of white heather. In many of the portraits and statuettes, the faces were unknown to him but one photograph he recognised from a copy at Windsor, of Queen Victoria holding her little grandson, now Kaiser Wilhelm, on her knee. Just in front of it was a matching pair of marble busts. The beautiful young woman was Queen Alexandra as a girl. The other was of a remarkably handsome young man. With a slight start of surprise, he realised it was the King as Prince of Wales, on his wedding day.

He was bursting to ask the Empress why she had invited him to visit her, but could not. With Royalty one did not ask questions. One could not start a topic, but had to wait to be spoken to.

She eased her position on the cushions. 'My brother tells me you are to go to South Africa.'

'When we return from here, ma'am,' he told her. 'As soon as a replacement is needed in my regiment.'

'I shall pray for you,' she said softly.

He was grateful for her concern, especially as she, herself, endured so much suffering. Yet he could not think why she was so interested in him. He thought he understood when she began to question him, insisting that he must be perfectly frank in his answers. She seemed to want reassurance about conditions and attitudes in England. She

53

asked him about the war with the Boers, how it was really going, about the King's health and popularity, the state of the Government, his own reactions to criticism of his country from abroad, about the unrest in Ireland. Behind it all, he felt that something was troubling her, something serious. Questions poured from her. She gave him no chance to be diplomatic, but he tried to keep his replies concise, for he could see that conversation was very tiring for her.

When the nurse came back half an hour later, she was disturbed to find him still there. 'Your Imperial Majesty,' she protested, 'I really must insist that you rest.'

The Empress sat up suddenly, very erect. 'Captain Ponsonby is telling me intimate details of the funeral at Windsor,' she said sharply. 'You may return in five minutes.' The nurse seemed about to object but, under her mistress's steady gaze, she gave way. She bobbed and retreated into the corridor, closing the door.

Ponsonby had risen. He was thrown. The Empress's voice, clear and commanding for a moment, had been so like her mother's. And also, the funeral had never been mentioned.

Vicky's head was lowered. The effort of dismissing the nurse had nearly been too much for her strength. She straightened slowly. 'You have been wondering why I wished to see you,' she panted. 'I want—I want you to do me a service.'

'Willingly, ma'am,' he assured her.

'It is not without danger,' she warned. He was silent, more puzzled. Her eyes searched his face. 'You do not ask questions. That is good. But I must tell you, so that you may know its importance.'

'Yes, ma'am.' He was impressed by her intensity.

'Over the last forty years I have had many letters from England,' she told him. 'Most of them from my mother, the late Queen. They were family letters, not diplomatic. I have kept them all.' He nodded. 'I want you to take charge of them.'

Ponsonby's mind was racing and he realised that in their earlier conversation she had been testing him, satisfying herself that he could be trusted.

'They are too important to destroy,' she went on, 'but they must be got away from here before I die. They contain many things which would not now be . . . accepted—which could be used politically against your country.'

54

'I see,' he muttered.

In her weakness, Vicky almost wept with relief. She had despaired of finding the man she needed, yet she still had to be certain. 'No one must know they have been taken away,' she stressed. 'In particular, my son must not have them, nor even learn they are in your custody.'

'As you wish, ma'am,' he said.

She paused, wincing with pain. 'There are secret police everywhere,' she whispered. 'I am watched, that is why I could not smuggle them out before this. Can you do it?'

'I shall do my best, ma'am,' Ponsonby promised. 'Where are they?'

'I shall send them to you at one o'clock tonight,' the Empress said. She broke off as the nurse came in again. Ponsonby bowed. There was much more he wanted to ask, but this time, it would seem suspicious if he did not leave.

It was now late at night and he was waiting in his room. As he paced, he heard the clock in one of the distant turrets chime and strike one. The sound died away and he stood still, listening. Outside, there was utter silence. He moved to the door.

The long corridor was dark and shadowed, lit only by a small shaded oil lamp at each end. He went quietly down the corridor, past the rooms where the Kaiser's ADCs slept, to the landing which overlooked the main staircase. Keeping out of the glow of the lamp, he eased forward to the balustrade. Beyond the curve of the stairs, the great hall seemed deserted. Here, the silence was more profound, the shadows impenetrable. The logs in the massive fireplace had burnt out. Moonlight from the narrow windows was reflected dully on the shoulders and casques of a row of suits of medieval armour along one wall. Then he heard a muffled cough and the scrape of a rifle butt on the flagstones by the end doors. Prussian sentries were on guard. He stepped back noiselessly and returned to his room.

He made himself sit on the chair by his writing table. His heart was thudding. He told himself he was a fool. If he had been seen, it could have spoiled everything. He had been aware of the fear in the Empress's eyes, which she had tried to conceal. She had reason for it. He remembered his father describing the Emperor Frederick's death in the ornate Neues Palais in Potsdam.

For days, the voiceless Emperor had been growing weaker and weaker, able to breathe only through a cannula inserted in his throat. The Empress had lain at night on a sofa outside his bedroom door, awake, listening to the hideous wheezing and bubbling of the air through the artificial tube, terrified that another fit of choking would bring on a haemorrhage. Their friends had begun to desert them, giving secret allegiance to their son, Prince Wilhelm. The night before the Emperor died, when it became certain that he could not live more than a few hours, units of the army, commanded by the Prince's supporters, moved stealthily into position in the palace grounds. In the morning, Prince Wilhelm in his scarlet hussar's uniform waited impatiently by his father's bed. As soon as he died, he gave his signal and immediately the palace was ringed by bayonets. All exits were barred and armed soldiers moved into the passages. No one, not even members of the Imperial family, was permitted to leave without a pass signed by the new Kaiser. All unauthorised messages, letters, telegrams were forbidden, all packages checked. While aides went through the contents of his father's desk and rooms, Kaiser Wilhelm searched his mother's apartments, pulling out the contents of drawers and cupboards, tearing open cases and boxes. He was looking for his father's private papers and diaries, for secret correspondence between his mother and liberal sympathisers, letters from abroad with critical comments on himself or affairs in Germany, anything he could use to incriminate her. To his fury, he found nothing. Everything had been carefully removed weeks before. Only public reverence for the late Emperor and stern objections by Queen Victoria put an end to the open persecution of his mother.

Ponsonby knew the same would happen here. To justify his treatment of her, those personal papers were one of the things Wilhelm most wanted. The soldiers were already standing by. The moment the Empress Frederick died, the Kaiser and his staff would ransack Friedrichshof.

It was ten past one. Ponsonby lit a small cigar, forcing his fingers to be steady. He sat motionless, smoking. The huge house was completely hushed, so quiet he could even hear the tick of his pocket watch which he had placed on the mantelpiece. The minutes passed slowly. The cigar was nearly finished. He rose and looked at the watch. It was twenty-five past. Obviously, the Empress had not found a way to send the letters to him or it had been too dangerous.

The worst possibility was that, somehow, he had misunderstood her last whispered instructions.

There came a swift, barely audible knock at the door. He tensed and flicked the cigar into the fireplace. 'Herein,' he said.

The door opened and four men came in. They wore blue serge breeches and riding boots under cloth jackets and carried two boxes between them. They were stablemen, chosen because they would not question orders. They set the boxes down in the corner where Ponsonby indicated and left as silently as they came. When they had gone, he moved quickly to the door and locked it, then stood very still, listening intently. There was no sound.

When he was satisfied that no one had been disturbed, he turned and looked at the boxes. They were much larger than he had imagined, about the size of trunks. He crossed to them. They were wrapped in black oilcloth, bound tightly with cord. On the side of each was a blank white label. He tried to lift one. It was heavy, very heavy. He had only expected a package of letters, perhaps several parcels which he could easily hide in his own luggage, but the size of the boxes made the problem much more difficult. It would be impossible to get them out without being seen. He did not even have a servant to help him. As he looked at them, he began to realise the immensity of the responsibility he had been given. These were no ordinary letters but the whole intimate, correspondence of Queen Victoria and her daughter over many years. The Queen wrote as she thought, freely and forcefully, leaping from private matters to national and international politics, personalities, often controversial, sometimes indiscreet. To her daughter, she would have been even more unguarded. These boxes contained priceless historical documents. That the Kaiser would destroy them Ponsonby had no doubt. But first he would mine them for secrets and political statements which he would use at will to affect England's relations with every country in the world. If they came into his hands, it would be disastrous.

He thought briefly of asking the King's advice, but changed his mind. If anything went wrong, the King must not be even remotely involved or there could be a serious international incident. Also for some reason, the Empress had not entrusted the letters to her brother. There were bound to be critical references to him, too, revealing the Queen's innermost feelings about past scandals and quarrels.

The Empress Frederick had meant Ponsonby to take responsibility not only for keeping them safe, but also for judging the right time to reveal their existence. It could not be now. Such material could not be made public for decades, some of it never.

It was hours before Ponsonby decided what he must do. The letters must be got away, but there was no chance if he tried anything elaborate. His only hope lay in simplicity, in not attracting suspicion. At least, that would give him time to think. On the label of the upper box, he printed his name and, underneath it, 'BOOKS WITH CARE'. On top of the boxes he laid out his dress uniform and his sword, and went to bed.

For the next two days, whatever he was doing, working with the King, riding, eating, walking in the park, he thought of the boxes. When he looked up at dinner to find the eyes of the sinister, effeminate Eulenberg fixed on him, or the Kaiser suddenly barked one of his abrupt, joking remarks at him, he could see them standing in the corner. He imagined the maid who dusted his room being curious about them, mentioning them casually, the contents being examined and Von Kessel waiting for him with the guards when he returned. It was only too possible. The Prussian secret police were notoriously efficient. What would happen to him personally he could not foresee, but the Dowager Empress and those servants who were still loyal to her would be treated without mercy.

He had no further opportunity to speak to the Empress Frederick alone. On the evening before their departure, Laking and he said their goodbyes. He bowed over the Empress's hand and kissed it. Her smile to him was grateful and trusting. Afterwards, the Kaiser shook a finger at him. 'I believe my Mama has a soft spot for you, Ponsonby,' he laughed.

The next morning they were leaving Friedrichshof. Ponsonby had considered and rejected several plans as too risky. His safest bet was still to rely on simplicity, helped by the fact that the Kaiser's staff scarcely thought him worth noticing. On the second label, under his name, he printed 'CHINA WITH CARE,' then dragged both boxes out into the corridor to await collection with the rest of his luggage.

He and Laking were standing in the hall with King Edward and Kaiser Wilhelm. The Kaiser's aides formed a stiff group near the main doors, barely hiding their relief that they and their visitors were leaving. Relays of soldiers and lackeys were bringing bags and cases down the stairs and outside to open wagons which would take them to the station at Homburg. Over the King's shoulder, he could see the boxes being carried down the stairs. There was a delay in loading the wagons and luggage was piling up inside the hall. The orderlies taking out the boxes set them down between the Royal party and the door, then went back upstairs to fetch the rest of the cases. Wrapped in their black oilcloth, the two boxes contrasted sharply with the ordinary trunks and portmanteaux beyond. To Ponsonby, the newness of the cord round them was startlingly obvious. The white labels caught the eye automatically. He saw the tall adjutant, Von Scholl, glance down at them. The palms of his hands grew damp. He brushed them unobtrusively against the sides of his coat.

The Kaiser was hesitating. He had thanked the King again for coming to Germany so soon after his accession and explained why he had not decorated Laking and Ponsonby. Because, he regretted, it was not an official visit. 'However,' he went on, 'the memory of your presence on this historic occasion is enshrined in my heart.' Laking and Ponsonby bowed. Wilhelm was perfectly sincere in his thanks. The visit had touched the sentimental side of his nature. Also, to avoid criticism, he had needed to spend time with his mother. His uncle being here had made agreeable a stay which otherwise would have been provoking and irksome. Politically, it had confirmed the family ties between Great Britain and Germany. That could have far-reaching results.

Everything he needed to say before the formal farewells at the station had been said, yet he still hesitated. He had not resolved a problem which had occupied him since his valet woke him that morning. The matter of seniority between himself and his uncle had not been settled. A regiment of his favourite Prussian Guards was drawn up outside. A military band waited to play the national anthems. If he allowed his uncle to go through the door first, it would establish a precedent and the Imperial Staff would resent it. On the other hand, if he were to go first, it might give offence to his uncle and damage the goodwill that had been built up. At last, he found the solution. He must appear first, but he would step back on the threshold and lead his uncle out as though presenting him as a guest to his troops. It would be natural and effective. He strode towards the door.

He stopped. The pile of luggage was directly in his path. 'What are these doing here?' he rapped. 'Who left them here?' They had spoilt the spontaneity of his exit. He moved forward, glaring at the boxes wrapped in oilcloth. 'What are these boxes?'

Ponsonby had followed with the King. His throat was dry.

The Kaiser turned slowly and looked at him. 'Are these yours, Ponsonby?' he asked. Ponsonby could not speak. For a second, he did not realise that the Kaiser was smiling. 'You English——' Wilhelm shook his head. 'You cannot go anywhere without your clothes and your comforts.' He chuckled. His staff echoed him. 'Come, Uncle Bertie,' he said, his humour restored. He linked arms with the King and they walked through the door side by side.

The Imperial staff clicked their heels and came to attention, then went out after them. As they left, the fat General Von Kessel muttered, 'He'd better not take so much to South Africa. If he runs away, the Boers will catch him.' The others laughed. It was offensive, spoken loudly enough for Ponsonby to hear. He flushed, but made himself smile as he and Laking followed them.

After the playing of the anthems and the inspection of the guard of honour, he stood by his carriage, watching until he saw the boxes hoisted on to the last wagon on the start of their journey to England.

Lord Esher was extremely busy. The King had returned from Friedrichshof like a man obsessed by the passage of time, determined to cram years of work into a few months. With Esher, Knollys and his old equerry, Sir Dighton Probyn, now Keeper of the Privy Purse, he had already discussed the Royal Household. It was antiquated and wastefully run between the rival departments of the Lord Chamberlain and the Lord Steward. The King was the first heir ever to come to the throne solvent, but his financial resources were restricted. Most of his own money had been spent on keeping up the appearances of his position as Prince of Wales, on entertaining, foreign travel and charities. His mother had lived comparatively simply but she had left her vast accumulated fortune to her younger children. Economies had to be made. Directed by the King, Esher and Probyn had reformed the staff, rooting out unnecessary officials and duplicated posts, cutting disused traditional odds and ends like the Royal Buckhounds and organising the entire Household on a business basis.

The current Poet Laureate, the successor to Tennyson, was the ludicrously inept Alfred Austin, celebrated for his deathless lines in an ode written many years before when the King, then Prince of Wales, lay seriously ill.

> Flash'd from his bed, the electric tidings came,
> He is not better; he is much the same.

The King disliked hurting anyone's feelings. He told the Prime Minister that Austin could remain as Laureate, provided he received no pay.

The most urgent matter concerning Esher was the condition of the Royal residences. The King owned the splendid, fashionable Marlborough House in London and the comfortable Sandringham House in Norfolk. He had now, in addition, inherited Buckingham Palace, Windsor Castle, Balmoral Castle and Osborne. They were all in a half-neglected condition, inconvenient, unhygienic and completely in need of modernisation.

Buckingham Palace had to be the principal residence of the monarch in London. With Esher and Lionel Cust, Curator of the Royal Art Collections, the King prowled from room to room and along its labyrinthine passages, assessing the state of repair. The Queen had disliked the Palace and only spent a reluctant two or three days a year in it. Here, as elsewhere, she had tried to freeze time at the moment of her husband's death. The decoration was heavy, mid-Victorian, illuminated by crude gaslight. There were signs of dilapidation everywhere, dust, damp, mildew in the lower corridors. In the ballroom and drawing-rooms, the crystal chandeliers were dark with soot from the gasjets below, the gilded mouldings and plaster reliefs grimy. In one salon stains could still be seen from a State visit of the Shah of Persia. He had commanded a sheep to be sacrificed on the carpet.

Bertie's face grew more set, more expressionless as the tour continued. There were no amenities for the staff. The servants' quarters were cramped and inadequate, the plumbing everywhere disgraceful. Traces of the superb mansion

61

built by Nash for George the Fourth remained, tarnished by the neglect of half a century. They reached the Queen's private apartments and, beyond them, the rooms kept sacred to his father.

Bertie felt the full weight of the past press down on him. He had not been here since he was a boy. Everything was just as he remembered it but as he looked, he saw that the curtains and carpets were faded and moth-eaten. In the study, on the desk, unanswered letters lay curling at the edges, brown with age. The ink in the silver inkwells had turned to black dust. In the music room, the upright organ at which his father had composed his chorales still stood in the corner. Bertie pressed one key. It gave without resistance, making no sound. The organ had perished. Esher and Cust were watching him, silently. The air in the rooms was close and smelt of decay.

'We'll start here,' he muttered. 'Everything—everything must go.'

The amount needing to be done in Buckingham Palace alone was staggering. And it would all cost money. A lot would depend on how much Parliament voted in the new Civil List for the Crown's upkeep and expenses, for that determined the scale on which the modernisation and decoration could be carried out.

Esher was reasonably pleased with himself. He had come to Westminster to sound out a few sympathetic Members of Parliament and explain the King's need of an income to match his dignity and position. They had promised their support in the debate. He had strolled for a while on the terrace of the House of Commons, overlooking the Thames. He did not regret his days as a Member, but smiled to think how narrow his life had been then. He was returning to the main entrance when, further along the passage, Balfour and Lansdowne came out of a committee room. He slowed down, but Balfour had seen him and waved the papers he was holding in greeting. Lansdowne, slim, immaculate in his grey frock coat, was more distant.

'Well, well, Reggie,' Balfour smiled. 'Come to tread the corridors of power?'

'Just chatting,' Esher told him.

'That's what we've been doing,' Lansdowne said waspishly. 'About this German business. We are being hounded by the Kaiser. Apparently the King has encouraged him to believe that the question of an alliance can be settled in weeks.'

'Couldn't it be?' Esher asked innocently. 'At least, an agreement in principle.'

'That is impossible—as surely even the King can realise,' Lansdowne said. 'In many areas, our interests conflict with Germany's. We cannot even begin to talk until our positions are defined.'

'Best fly-fishing in the world,' Balfour observed loudly. Lansdowne was startled, then realised that Edward Grey, Opposition Spokesman on Foreign Affairs, was coming down the passage with Winston Churchill, the new young Member for Oldham.

'I'm sure it can't compare with Lansdowne's in Ireland,' Esher said, smiling. He bowed to Grey and Churchill. When they had gone past, he went on quietly, 'All the King asks is that the door isn't shut in the Kaiser's face. At any rate, make a show of talking. If he becomes impatient, Wilhelm will do something foolish.'

Lansdowne sighed. 'Does our foreign policy have to depend on the Kaiser's moods?'

'In this case, it does,' Esher told him seriously. 'But the King undertakes to manage him.'

As Lansdowne stiffened, Balfour intervened, changing the subject. 'I believe His Majesty has other concerns at the moment,' he said drily. 'The last I heard, he was looking into the possibility of restoring Hampton Court as his palace.' Lansdowne laughed.

'He thought of it,' Esher agreed. 'But only because of Queen Alexandra's reluctance to move into any apartments formerly lived in by Victoria.'

'I can understand that,' Balfour said.

'She will have to eventually, of course,' Esher shrugged.

Lansdowne smiled sardonically. 'Then let him study tact and diplomacy by finding a way to convince her,' he suggested.

Alexandra was excited. It was really like all the Christmases of one's life rolled into a few days, she told herself. The knowledgeable Lionel Cust had shown her the art treasures of Buckingham Palace, sculptures, magnificent paintings by Van Dyck, Rubens, Titian and many others, collected by Kings of England since the time of Charles the

First. She could hardly believe that they all belonged to Bertie and her.

Now they were at Windsor. Her guilt at going into hiterto forbidden rooms and opening locked cupboards was overcome by the excitement. In spite of the mourning dress, with her flushed cheeks and quick, eager smile, Cust thought she looked like a girl, younger than her daughter, Princess Victoria, who was with them. Toria, Alexandra's middle daughter, was a long-faced, thin, intelligent young woman with little trace of her mother's beauty or charm. Although both her sisters were married, Louise to the Duke of Fife and Maud to Prince Charles of Denmark, she had never found a suitable husband. In her early thirties, she was slightly embittered and inclined to be critical, but her mother's delight had infected even her. They were like children as they scurried from the Library to the State Apartments, up to the attics and back to the galleries.

Windsor was a treasure house. It was not only the splendours of the art collection which was greater than the one in Buckingham Palace, but all the other unexpected discoveries. There was so much they had never noticed before, in hidden corners or in disused rooms. Superb tapestries, cabinets full of exquisite snuff-boxes collected by George the Fourth, bronzes, suites of delicate French furniture, banished in favour of mahogany, overblown upholstery and brocade. Stuffed into huge cupboards, almost at random, were all the trophies and gifts of Victoria's long and prosperous reign. Rolls of silk, golden keys, matchless jades sent by the Emperor of China, silver trowels with mother of pearl handles, jewelled armour and weapons from India. In one attic, they found a pile of rotting giant ivory tusks. The old Queen had never thrown anything away. An unending range of trunks held baby clothes, the camisoles and pantalettes she had worn as a girl, slippers, shawls, Court Dresses, riding skirts. Boxes and boxes of prints and photographs, gilt caskets set with gems in which loyal addresses had been submitted. And everywhere, the tributes from her two Jubilees, gold ewers, vases and baskets, and vast golden centerpieces in fantastic, allegorical designs.

The chief treasure to Alix was the porcelain; fragile, single pieces, immense, Oriental bowls and cupboard after cupboard filled with services of Dresden and Meissen china. It hurt her to see how carelessly some had been stacked so that plates and tureens were chipped and cracked. George the Fourth's priceless sets of Sèvres were still, fortunately, intact. For such a wicked man, Alix thought, he really did have superlative taste. She stood, gazing at them. 'Aren't they beautiful, Toria,' she marvelled.

'Yes, Motherdear,' Toria agreed. 'We must go now.'

'But they're all unused,' Alexandra said. 'Just for looking at.'

'Yes, Motherdear.'

Alix turned to Cust. 'Aren't they the most beautiful things you have ever seen?'

'As pieces of china, ma'am,' Cust smiled.

Toria took her mother's arm. 'We really must go,' she said loudly. 'Papa will be waiting and you know how impatient he gets.'

For once, Bertie did not mind waiting. He had been to London to receive deputations from the principal universities and had driven back in his motor car. He had had his first ride in one two years before and, from that moment, was converted. He liked the comfort and the sense of speed. Horseless carriages, motor cars, automobiles, whatever you choose to call them, they are the thing of the future, he maintained against those critics who complained they were noisy and impractical. He already owned a Daimler, a Mercedes and a Landaulette. In the Daimler, he had returned to Windsor that afternoon in just under an hour.

'Not bad going,' he complimented his chauffeur, delighted.

He was back earlier than he expected. Ponsonby was in attendance but he excused him. There was something he had to do, which he had been putting off, and which he had to do alone. The visit to his parents' most private rooms in the Palace had been an ordeal, but he had Esher and Cust with him and the memories were of long ago. Here at Windsor, the associations were much more recent. The Queen's presence could still be felt as though she were next door and might come in at any minute. He had to walk through those rooms, open the doors that had always been closed to him and take possession.

Slowly, he paced through his mother's apartments, some of which he had never been in before. Albert had planned the decoration. It had not been changed. Paintings by great masters were hung in awkward corners or high on the

65

walls to give pride of place to family groups and portraits. There were busts everywhere from close family to distant relatives, friends and favoured servants. Painted plates with views of Albert's boyhood home and innumerable framed photographs and engravings were ranked on the shelves, mantelpieces and tables. Above her bed hung an enlarged head and shoulders photograph of Albert lying dead.

In his father's suite, nothing had been touched. His suits and uniforms filled the dressing-room. Chairs were left at the angle in which he last sat in them. A book lay open beside an unfinished memorandum. A spoon and glass and medicine bottle stood on the table beside the bed in which he died. The illusion that he, too, had only just stepped round the corner was carefully kept up. Every evening his clothes were laid out in his bedroom, the jug filled with hot water on its stand and a clean towel placed beside it. Standing in the Blue Room where he had seen his father die, Bertie tried to recapture the grief he had known then, but the reality of it had gone. He shivered involuntarily. It was not only the chill of the room. He felt a revulsion at this perpetuation of the moment of death.

Alexandra and Toria found him in the family sitting-room. He had ordered the fire lit and was smoking a cigarette as he looked at the photographs. 'You should have come with us, Bertie,' Alix scolded. 'I'll never remember everything.'

He smiled. 'We'll have it catalogued.'

She noticed one of the mounted snapshots on the piano. It was of Bertie at the wheel of his racing yacht, *Britannia*. 'Oh, look! I took that of you myself, at Cowes,' she said. 'And that one of Mama at Balmoral.'

Toria shook her head, glancing round the room. 'Strange. It all seems like something out of another age already.'

'Don't be silly, Toria,' Alix laughed. 'Of course, it is. We're in the twentieth century now.'

'Yes, Motherdear,' Toria said. She smiled to her father. 'Tastes have changed, you know.'

'Yes, Motherdear.'

Alix sat in an armchair by the fire. I'm dropping!' she confessed. 'Why didn't you tell me there'd be so much?'

'What did you make of it all?' Bertie asked.

'Staggering,' Toria said. 'Rubens, Rembrandt, Canaletto——'

'The Titians, Leonardos—a whole art gallery,' Alix broke

in, not realising Toria was speaking. 'Not to mention the furniture. And the china! Some of it's beyond price. I've never really examined it before.'

'Well, it's all ours now, my dear,' Bertie told her.

'I suppose it is,' Alix said dubiously. 'What on earth can we do with it?'

Bertie did not answer at once. He had been using a sweetmeat bowl as an ashtray. He stubbed out his cigarette. 'Let's—let's take a look at the study,' he proposed. He moved to the connecting door and opened it, waiting for Alix to rise. As she passed him, he signalled to Toria to stay where she was.

In the Royal study, Victoria's desk was still in its position near the windows. Behind it, a lifesize white marble bust of Albert stood on a plinth. The blinds were drawn most of the way down and the sepia light that filtered through them added to the brooding, sombre feel of the room.

Coming in, Alix stopped and glanced nervously at the door to the small Audience Room and the far door that led to the private apartments. 'I don't like it, Bertie,' she whispered. 'It doesn't seem right to be in here.'

'I know,' Bertie nodded. He moved to the desk. On it were a silver inkstand and penholder, a green blotting pad, a smaller gold bust of his father and one of his mother as a young woman, a magnifying glass.

'It's as if we're being watched,' Alix said. She followed him to the desk. Among the other family mementos that lay on it were little bronze models of children's hands. He was running his fingertips over one. 'What's that?' she asked.

'It's a cast of my hand. When I was a baby,' he said quietly.

Alix was touched to think it had lain on his mother's desk all that time. She watched as he went round the desk to the nearest window and wrenched the blind up to let in more light.

'She should have had electricity put in, with her eyesight,' he muttered. He glanced at the bust of his father, then moved past it, assessing the room. He stopped. On a wall stand near Albert's bust, only slightly smaller, was a gilded plaster bust of a handsome, strong-featured man with a curling, fringed beard. He lifted it down.

Alix could not see the face. 'Who's that?' she asked.

'The Queen's Highland Servant,' Bertie said tonelessly.
'John Brown?'

'Yes. The Great John.' He returned the bust to its stand but as he raised his hand, his fingers opened and the bust fell to the floor, shattering, its head rolling beneath the desk.

'Bertie!' Alix gasped.

'How clumsy of me,' he murmured dispassionately. He turned to look at the study properly. Like the other rooms, it was dingy, old fashioned and cluttered. 'Still,' he said, 'we'll have a better idea of what redecoration's needed when we get all this stuff cleared out.'

'Redecoration?' Alix echoed, puzzled. She assumed that everything was to be left untouched, as a memorial.

Bertie had deliberately moved away. 'Yes,' he said. It had to be settled between them. He was already working out plans for more bathrooms, central heating. His father's suite was the best situated and most convenient in the Castle. He would have its contents reverently packed away, then the rooms would be painted and papered and brought up to date for himself. He turned to Alix.

She was staring at him as she began to understand what he meant. 'We're not going to live here?' she queried. 'I thought, in the State Apartments occasionally—but not here!' She was horrified.

He took a step towards her. 'Alix . . .'

'No! No, Bertie,' she protested. 'For years as Princess of Wales I was never allowed to do as I pleased. Now everyone keeps reminding me I am Queen and I shall make my own decisions.'

'Some decisions are forced on us,' he explained gently.

'I will not sit at her table and live in her rooms!' Alix told him vehemently.

Francis Knollys had finished his work for the day. As he came out of his office in Marlborough House, he heard the sound of voices, raised voices from the main staircase. He recognised the King's, loud, insistent.

'We must live there,' he was saying. 'There and at Buckingham Palace.'

Then a woman's voice answered angrily, 'Must! All my life it has been "must"! When am I to be allowed to choose for myself?' It was a second before he realised it was Queen Alexandra. He could not think when he had last heard her so angry. He hurried along the corridor, just in time to see her sweep into her own drawing-room with the King behind her. Princess Victoria followed them, looking troubled and upset.

In the drawing-room, Alix would not face Bertie. 'No! No, no, no,' she reiterated. 'Out of the question!' She was adamant.

'Alix . . .' Bertie pleaded. He was trying to be patient, not to lose his temper. He knew very well what had hurt and provoked her. 'I've told you about Osborne. We needn't go there. But Buckingham Palace and Windsor are another matter.'

'*This* is my home!' Alix declared. 'Most of our children were born here. All my memories are here.'

Knollys came in. He bowed, hoping his arrival would distract them, but they ignored him. A footman in scarlet livery and powdered wig was standing by the door, embarrassed, trying not to hear. Knollys signed to him and he went out quickly, shutting the door behind him.

The King was saying, 'That is true. But Marlborough House will be needed for Georgie and May.'

Alix spun round. 'Why should they have it?'

'They will shortly become Prince and Princess of Wales,' Bertie explained. 'It is their right.'

Alix looked at her daughter. 'Toria—what do you say?'

Princess Victoria was torn. It was the first time she had heard her parents quarrel loudly in public. Staying at home, she had become her mother's constant companion and usually took her side, protecting her. In this she could not. 'I'm afraid I agree with Papa,' she faltered.

Alix stared at her haughtily, then turned and strode to the window. Bertie glanced at Toria gratefully. Alix stood gazing out at the trees in the spacious garden. They had not lost their winter bareness but soon the daffodils beneath them would open and the green shoots of the spring flowers burst into colour. She loved this house, the first home of her marriage. She told herself she was not being unreasonable. For so long, a large part of her life had been controlled by Bertie's mother, whose rulings had often seemed biased and unfair. Yet she had accepted them as her duty, while longing, like Bertie, for the time when she would be free to do what she liked, to manage her own affairs. She had thought that happy time had arrived, earned by her patience, and now they were asking her to give up her dearest home in the name of that same pitiless duty.

They watched her until she spoke at last, dully, her back still turned to them. 'Very well . . . I concede Windsor. And Georgie shall live here.'

'Thank you, my dear,' Bertie breathed, greatly relieved.

She turned. Her face was bleak. 'But you will not force me to accept Buckingham Palace,' she told him firmly. 'It is unacceptable and ugly.'

'Then where are we to live in London?' he demanded.

'Anywhere but there,' she said. 'We can discuss it tonight at dinner, with the family.'

Bertie had had enough. They had been arguing for hours and he was exasperated by the complete veto on the Palace. He caught Knollys's eye and nodded imperceptibly.

Knollys coughed. 'I'm terribly sorry, Your Majesty— have you forgotten that you are dining tonight with members of the Cabinet?'

Bertie appeared to be surprised. 'Tonight?'

'At your club, sir.'

'Why didn't you remind me of this before, Francis?' Bertie objected wrathfully. He turned to Alix. 'I can only apologise, my dear.'

Alix was looking at Knollys, who stared straight ahead, expressionless.

'I wouldn't have had this happen for the world,' Bertie declared.

Alix smiled fleetingly and moved back to the window. 'It's quite all right,' she said. 'I fully understand.'

The King's Smoking Room in Covent Garden Opera House was an elegant salon behind the royal box. It had seen many fashionable gatherings and many discreet supper parties after the performance, while he was Prince of Wales. Tonight, the group was even more carefully discreet than usual, for reasons of convention. It was not possible for the King to enjoy himself too conspicuously in public only a few months after the funeral.

Bertie sat in the Smoking Room with some of the leading members of his *Cabinet,* an exclusive group of his most intimate friends. Chief among them were Lord Esher, Luis de Soveral, the Portuguese Ambassador, and Ernest Cassel, the millionaire financier who had become Bertie's adviser on all money matters. He was Jewish and self-made, a naturalised immigrant from Germany, which could have prevented him from reaching any notable position in society. But his incredible business ability, his honesty and unsparing gifts to charity, together with a fanatical devotion to the interests of his adopted country, had opened many doors. Although ten years younger than Bertie, they were very similar in appearance and Cassel was often flattered by being mistaken for the King. Their tastes, too, were similar and the friendship they had formed was immediate and lasting. With their lady guests, they were laughing quietly at a slightly risqué story which Soveral was telling very expressively. Through the partly open door of the box, they could hear the music of 'Les Sylphides'.

Bertie was sitting nearer the door of the box with Alice Keppel. The men were in evening dress and, as a special concession, the ladies had been permitted to wear half mourning, deep purple, lilac, white and silver. Alice wore a pale violet evening gown, trimmed round the hem of the skirt and under the full swell of her bust with elaborate, silver passementerie. Her hair was looped up in a coronet of soft waves, with one tapering curl on the centre of her forehead. She was ravishing, amused as she watched Soveral. Bertie was leaning back, abstracted.

'So there they were at the house party for the weekend,' Soveral was saying. 'Unfortunately, the hostess was not in on the secret and had put Beresford and the lady in opposite wings. What was he to do? . . .' The others laughed as he rolled his eyes. 'Well, he waited until he was sure everyone was asleep, then crept in his nightshirt from the east wing across to the west wing. No one saw him. He reached her floor and counted along the doors until he found her room. He let himself in very quietly. A tiny lamp burned low on the bedside table. His heart was pounding. At last, they were together. He threw off his nightshirt and leapt on to the bed, flapping his elbows. "Cock a doodle doo!" he cried. The occupant of the room turned up the lamp.' He paused. 'Unfortunately, Beresford had miscounted the doors. He was in bed between the Bishop of Chester and his wife!'

The group laughed more loudly, the ladies pretending to be shocked. Alice smiled to Bertie. He nodded but he had clearly not heard. 'Tired?' she asked.

'H'm?' He shook his head. 'No, my dear. Just thinking. An unusual occupation for me, I admit.' He was smoking a thick, dark cigar which he drew on. She waited for him to

71

continue, if he wanted to. He shrugged. 'I've been shut out for so long. And here I am when everything should be different, still behind a door—listening to the music of a ballet I'm not allowed to see.' He had been thinking how similar his problem was to Alix's, although their needs were different.

'That's only till the end of official mourning,' Alice said.

'You're too matter-of-fact for me,' he grunted. 'I was looking inward—what's the word? . . . Introspective.' He stopped and glanced at her. 'But of course, you knew that.'

Alice smiled. Sometimes he was not an easy man to be with. His tremendous vitality could be exhausting. In a passing mood of despair at his lack of achievement he could withdraw desolately into himself, or his restlessness could make him irritable. But because she loved him, she understood him.

He smiled ruefully. 'You're right. I mustn't let it show. Must be a bore for you, sitting out here instead of in the box.'

'Not at all,' she assured him quietly.

'Only I can't show myself, not even dine out, till the end of half mourning. And that's another three months.' He broke off, apologising. 'You've just said that.'

They sat in silence for a moment. Alice leant towards him. 'Would it help you to tell me?' she asked gently. 'I don't want to pry.'

'You never do,' he said. 'There are so many things, Alice. The war—I want to do something positive, but the Government takes little notice of my opinions. All I can do is make sure that more doctors are sent out and the medical supplies are stepped up.'

'That is a great deal,' she told him.

'But not enough,' he insisted. He hesitated, drew on his cigar. 'And then . . . there's the Queen. I cannot convince her that the Palace must be our home in London.'

Alice was surprised. 'What is her objection?'

'She finds it depressing,' he growled. 'Oh, I can appreciate why. The damned palace is a sepulchre. But where else is there?' He picked up a glass of champagne from the low table beside him and finished it.

Esher came to them and bowed. He smiled, seeing his glass empty. 'Some more champagne, sir?'

'No thanks, Reggie.'

'Mrs Keppel?'

Alice shook her head. Esher sensed that it was better to leave them alone for a little longer. La Keppel would bring the King out of his depression in her own fashion. He bowed again and returned to the group. Soveral had started on another story, his arms gesticulating. One of the ladies giggled.

Bertie sighed. 'Off again? He's in his anecdotage.'

Alice gurgled, then bit her lower lip to stop herself laughing too loudly. Bertie glanced at her. When she laughed, she raised her chin, bending her head back. It made the line of her shoulders and throat sweeping down to the rich surge of her breasts perfect. It was that maturity combined with good sense and the vivacity of a girl that fascinated Bertie. As she lowered her head, he smiled. 'I envy Luis,' he said. 'He'd still be telling a story in front of the firing squad.'

Her eyes laughed into his. His spirits were buoyed up and he chuckled, holding out his hand. She laid hers in his. Her eyes never left him. Her lips were parted and he could feel the throb of the pulse at her wrist.

'I don't see the point of staying here much longer. It's getting late,' he murmured.

'Very,' she agreed softly.

Chapter
5

      Alix was heartbroken when George and May left for their tour to Australia. With Bertie away so often and so many new adjustments to be made in her life she had wanted and needed their support. She had her old friend, Charlotte Knollys, her woman of the bedchamber, and Toria, of course, but she could not really confide in them. Her comfort was that she had her grandchildren to take care of, the two boys and their little sister, Mary, aged four, and the baby, all with her at Sandringham. She was happiest when she was with children. She could enter into their world and they responded eagerly to her. It brought her closer to Bertie, also. When he was not too busy and could join them, it was like when they were younger again.

    To the children, the months when their parents were gone were paradise. They had been terrified of their great grandmother and were rather in awe of their own father and mother but Granny Alix and their grandpapa, Kingy, were wonderful, never cross, always interested and thinking up exciting things to do. Even going to bed was fun, with games and fairy stories and pillow-fights. At mealtimes, they could talk and ask questions. Granny Alix had left their governess behind in London so there were no lessons. Instead, they went for walks in the park with all the dogs running and barking round them and Kingy took them for long drives in one of his motor cars and up to the Military Tournament where they saw real elephants dragging cannons and Mary could hold her grandmother's hand and feel very safe, even when the big guns fired.

    Bertie loved children as much as Alix did. He had been deprived of so much of his own childhood, he could not bear to see a child neglected or intimidated. He thought George disciplined them too harshly as if he was their commanding officer in the Navy and, although he was devoted to his daughter-in-law, he found May too serious and intellectual. Neither of them could relax with their children. David was an extrovert and could cope but Albert was a shy boy with a tendency to blush and stammer, just as he had been. He needed to be given confidence and encouragement, to be shown he was just as special as his elder brother.

They were in their favourite room in Sandringham, the hall to the left entrance, really a large living-room with high, oak crossbeams and oak-panelled walls, covered with pictures, prints, photographs, mounted heads of deer with branching antlers and ornamental groups of swords and battleaxes. At one end were round-topped arches which gave the effect of a minstrels' gallery. There were colourful flowerstands, comfortable armchairs and screens to deflect stray draughts, desks, a gleaming grand piano and occasional tables strewn with magazines and periodicals. From the centre of the ceiling hung a huge, electric chandelier, its curling, gilded arms ending in opalescent globes but, during the day, tall windows filled the room with light. This was the family salon, opulent but informal, where they did most of their entertaining.

Alix laughed as she saw Bertie trot round the fluted columns of the arches with little Bertie perched on his shoulders. They were playing Bears and growling as they chased David who shouted as he dodged them. Toria was at the piano with Mary on her knee, teaching her to use one finger instead of all ten at once. Bertie lumbered across the hall and dumped Little Bertie on to his back on a sofa, then collapsed beside him, winded.

'More, Kingy!' Little Bertie pleaded.

'No, no,' Bertie panted. 'The bear has to rest for a minute.'

'You're smoking too much,' Alix said.

David had crept round behind the sofa. He jumped up and clapped his hands over Bertie's eyes. 'Oho, who's this?' Bertie rumbled. He caught David's arms and hauled him over the back of the sofa, struggling. He straightened him up and held him. 'Why, it's a little rabbit,' he growled. 'And it's going to get its nose bitten off!' As he pulled David towards him, pretending to snap at his nose, David froze. Little Bertie squealed and Mary banged the piano keys in fright.

'All right, come on.' Alix laughed. 'That's enough. Let Grandpa get his breath back.'

Bertie hugged David and drew him down beside him, chuckling. He sat with one arm round him and the other round Little Bertie. They snuggled in.

'Can we go fishing tomorrow, Grandpa?' David asked.

'Not tomorrow, I'm afraid,' Bertie said. 'I shan't be here.'

'Don't go yet,' David objected, disappointed.

Alix was surprised. 'Where will you be?' she asked.

'I've decided to run down to the Isle of Wight for a few days,' he told her. 'There are things at Osborne I must see to.' Alix nodded. They had still not settled between them where they were to live, but on one point they were in complete agreement. Neither of them would consider Osborne, the house where the old Queen had died. To Alix it had always seemed cold and cheerless and it held too many unhappy memories for Bertie, the years of unrelenting lessons in its classroom when he was a boy, the terror of the visits to his father's study. He would never live there again.

'And I've promised to have a look at Tommy Lipton's new yacht,' he added. 'He's entered it for the America Cup.'

It was a clear, crisp day when Bertie arrived at Southampton. Alice Keppel was with him and, to avoid crowds, they hurried to the quay and went straight on board Lipton's yacht, *Shamrock II*.

The last two days had been difficult. The trip to Osborne was depressing and the news from South Africa brought no relief. The remaining Boer generals, Botha, Delarey and Christian de Wet, had split their forces up into over seventy commandos, highly mobile, collecting provisions from outlying farms and townships and supplied with French and Dutch guns and ammunition smuggled in through German East Africa. The most daring of them, De Wet, had overreached himself in an attempt to invade the Cape Colony. His forces had been routed and driven back over the Orange River, but constant attacks by Botha, Delarey and others over an area of thousands of square miles prevented the British troops from uniting and following up their success. The Boers wiped out isolated posts, ambushed supply trains and cut lines of communication, still hoping that one of the Powers would enter the war openly on their side. Their agent in Europe, Dr. Leyds, joined the fugitive Kruger in whipping up mass hatred of Britain, presenting the Boer ambition to conquer South Africa as a glorious stand against

Imperialism. They were strongly supported in many countries. In Ireland, the Nationalists used it as a weapon in their agitation. Even in England, the Liberal party was split into groups which approved or violently condemned the war. The situation was critical and dangerous.

Another disturbing factor was a rumour that had spread throughout the country, of an old prophecy that the King would not live to be crowned. It had even been reported in the newspapers. Bertie laughed about it with his friends but it touched a secret fear of his that he told no one. He was relieved to be able to relax for a few hours, to feel a deck beneath his feet and the clean rush of the air as the yacht moved away from the quay.

Sir Thomas Lipton had welcomed him and Alice Keppel aboard. He was a millionaire tea merchant whose quick wit and frank manner appealed to Bertie. A wiry, active man with a passion for yacht racing, his ambition was to win back the America Cup which had been held for so long by the New York Yacht Club. His *Shamrock I* had beaten Bertie's racing cutter *Britannia* but had failed against the Americans with their more streamlined hulls. The modified *Shamrock II* was a beautiful craft and Bertie admired her as his host showed them round.

'She's perfert, Tommy,' he told him. 'You'll show a clean pair of heels to anything from here to the Med.'

'What about the Yanks, sir?' Lipton asked.

'Well now,' Bertie chuckled, 'you never know what surprises they'll cook up.' He sighted along the yacht's lines and examined the towering steel mast that carried a vast expanse of canvas, set flat in the new style. 'Bit tricky to handle with all that weight up top?' he queried.

'Not a bit, sir,' Lipton assured him. 'Responds to a touch. And that mast's indestructible.'

Bertie nodded. He was very impressed and tempted to suggest he captain her himself. But this speed trial was too important. To show her capabilities, she was being matched in a race against *Shamrock I*. He moved to join Alice by the rail. Her lips were slightly parted and her eyes sparkling with excitement as the yacht leapt forward under its full press of canvas.

The sea was choppy in the stiff breeze and he suggested that she sit to avoid the spray. He remained standing, himself, balancing easily, liking the faint shiver in the planking and sensing the smooth shift of the yacht to the controls.

77

In the right conditions, her speed would be remarkable. It was difficult to estimate but she was already doing a fair number of knots. His sailor's instinct told him that a stronger wind was on its way. He smiled to Alice, responding to her excitement as she watched the prow slice through the grey billows and the spume foaming back.

Shamrock I was already moving into position between the coloured buoys. *Shamrock II* began to tack to cross the starting line, a simple manoeuvre of changing direction to make use of the side wind. As *Shamrock II* turned, Bertie staggered and glanced round at the helmsman, who had misjudged his turn. The yacht lurched as it drove across the wind. At the same moment, the wind Bertie had been expecting hit her even more strongly than he had anticipated. He heard Lipton shouting orders to the crew as the full force of the blast struck the sails and wrenched them round, but they were too late. With a crack like a sixteen-inch gun, the great steel mast snapped, tearing free of its stayropes. Bertie grabbed Alice and pulled her to her feet, turning as the mast under its huge weight of spars and canvas crashed on to the rail inches from them and toppled over into the water. Broken steel ropes lashed the air and pieces of rigging smashed on the deck around them.

People watching from other ships and on the shore screamed, certain the King had been killed. Lipton and his mate came running, horrified. Alice was ashen, and trembling, clinging to Bertie but they were only shaken. They had escaped by a miracle. Lipton tried to take hold of Alice to help her away. Bertie shook him off and told him curtly to see to his yacht before she drifted into the marker buoys or capsized.

The other boats came crowding in and they transferred to the nearest of them at once, while Lipton and his crew struggled to save the crippled *Shamrock II.*

The worst of the accident was the added impetus it gave to the rumour. Hardly anyone had believed it before. Now they whispered that fate had decreed the King would never sit on the throne. Many prayed for him.

Bertie was touched by an emotional letter from Kaiser Wilhelm congratulating him on his escape but, soon afterwards, heard he had joked about it in private. Willy could not resist sneering to his friends in Berlin. 'What a pity,' he was reported as saying. 'what a pity if my uncle had been killed—while nonchalantly boating with his grocer.' Which am I to believe? Bertie wondered. What are his real feelings?

The letter from his other nephew, Czar Nicholas, also seemed sincere, but carried a sting at the end. He suggested Bertie might have been spared to put a stop to the struggle in South Africa, 'which looks like a war of extermination against a small people desperately defending their country'. It was little comfort. It took all Alice's tact and charm to console him.

They had dined alone at her house in Portman Square and she noticed that he was drinking more than usual, although it seemed to have no effect. 'Nothing seems to stimulate me,' he explained. 'Everything is crowding in, getting me down.'

After dinner he had stayed on. He was waiting for her in her boudoir and she thought of him as her maid helped her out of her heavy purple evening dress and untied the tapes of her layered petticoat which rustled to the floor. Alice slipped her silk drawers down and the maid crouched, holding them as she stepped out of them and over the crumpled ring of her petticoat. She moved to the dressing table. She undid the emerald choker from round her neck and smoothed the faint mark it left on her skin. The maid followed her and began to loosen the laces at the back of her stiffly boned pink satin corset. Unlike many women, she did not need pads to emphasise the curves of her hips and bust. In recent years, it had been her waist that needed the tightest lacing, with an extra double row of metal tags. She twisted open the fastenings of the busk that supported her full breasts, then, raising each leg in turn, undid the clips of her long, ruffled suspenders. Her pale lemon stockings were still kept up by silk garters, beaded with pearls.

She felt the easing of the compression at her waist and sighed as the laces slackened in the last of the tags. She held her corset in front while the laces were withdrawn, then passed it round under her arm. She was left in her high-heeled shoes and stockings and a filmy chiffon chemise, creased and moulded to her body by the corset. She plucked it away from her skin and stretched. It hung from the tips of her breasts and clung to the rounded swell of her hips. The maid stood the rigid corset in the wardrobe and returned with a negligée of silk, faintly tinged with violet and covered by white lace.

Alice slid her arms into the short sleeves that ended in a

79

cascade of lace at the elbows and tied the sash loosely at her waist before sitting at the dressing table. The maid took the jewel-headed pins and the hidden grips carefully from her hair, then lifted off the woven ball of false curls round which her upswept coiffure had been built. Alice shook her head and the thick waves of her own dark auburn hair unwound and slithered to her shoulders and down her back. She reached for her hairbrush and smiled to the maid, dismissing her. The girl could be trusted but she did not want her to see how impatient she was.

She had been thinking all the time of Bertie. They had been so near death. She could still hear the grinding crash and feel the shock as the mast struck the rail beside them, smashing it to pieces. The thought that he had been in danger, or of the scandal if they had been injured together had not even occurred to him. He had only been concerned about her. 'What would I do if I lost you?' he had said. She could not tell him, but she knew it would have been far worse if she had lost him. He would always have someone else, his friends, his duty. But she had no one. He had become her life. Her husband, even her children were only a tiny part of it. The rest was him.

He was sitting in an armchair by the fire in her boudoir. It was their private place. Normally, in this warm, richly-furnished little room he could relax, but he was tense, smoking his cigar in quick, restless puffs, It felt wrong to be sitting idle. In spite of the immense amount of work he did, catching up with the mound of unfinished business left by his mother and the details of her estate, as well as the day to day letters and despatches, the continuous receptions and meetings and public appearances, his energy was not used up. The need to be active drove him on relentlessly. He could not be alone.

He was relieved when Alice came to join him. 'I've been thinking. I shouldn't have snapped at Tommy like that,' he said. 'I was just anxious.'

'I'm sure he understood,' she told him. She came to him and kissed his cheek. She lingered bending over him. Her hair touched his face and he could smell the delicate perfume of her skin, the slight natural aroma of fresh blossom that was peculiarly hers. The tension lessened in him but he did not reach up to hold her.

She moved to a table on which there was a lamp, a cigarette box and match stand. She lit a cigarette. As she drew the smoke in deeply, she wondered if she had left him alone too long. He might have decided to go back to his study, to the piles of unanswered letters. She understood the reason for his restlessness. He had so many years for which to make up. Once he could absorb himself in pleasure and forget: now while he rested or enjoyed himself, he felt guilty. Yet he had to unwind, forget his obligations for a time, or he would exhaust himself.

The lighting of the cigarette deepened the atmosphere of intimacy between them. Bertie fought against it. He had made up his mind to finish his cigar, then return to Marlborough House and finish reading the colonial despatches. Standing at the table in the silk and lace negligée, her hair loose like that on her shoulders, Alice looked enchanting. When she turned, the light of the lamp was behind her and he could see the dark outline of her body through the thin material.

He made himself sound matter-of-fact. 'Do you think I should drop him a line?'

'Why not?' she smiled. 'All you need to say is that you hope the yacht wasn't too badly damaged. That will convey everything.'

He nodded. She moved to a low settee facing the fire and lay back on it. 'I've been thinking, too,' she murmured. 'Has it been agreed yet where you and Her Majesty are to live?'

'Not yet.' He flicked his cigar in irritation. He had ordered the cleaning and clearing out to begin at Windsor, but nothing had been settled between them about Buckingham Palace. 'Everyone agrees the Palace must be the centre of the new Court. Everyone except Alix, that is.' It was a problem that nagged at him.

'Is she determined?'

'Adamant.' He shrugged. 'Of course, the private rooms are not very convenient. And the whole place would have to be done up—modernised, if it's to be a real home.'

'That's what I've been wondering,' Alice said casually. 'If you asked her advice on the decorations—perhaps even to choose everything herself . . .' He looked at her. She smiled. 'What woman could resist redesigning an entire palace?'

Bertie sat up straighter, taking her point at once. Knowing Alix, he was certain she could not resist the challenge. 'Now why didn't I think of that?' he breathed.

'You've had far too much on your mind, and been trying

to do everything yourself as usual,' Alice told him. He grunted. 'She has perfect taste. You couldn't find anyone better.'

'And as usual, you are completely right, my dear,' Bertie said. He smiled to her. He had not wanted to force Alix. With so many things still undecided, much more important things, the argument over where they were to live had been especially disturbing. The more he reasoned with Alix, the more stubborn she became. This could be the ideal solution. He rose and moved to the table. He stubbed his cigar out on the base of the match stand, feeling an elation, a disproportionate sense of relief at the prospect of doing something positive.

Alice was lying back on the settee, watching him. She held the cigarette poised near her lips. Her legs were crossed at the knees and the negligée had parted revealing the full shape of her thighs and the strong curving line of her legs with their surprisingly narrow ankles and small feet in their glacé shoes with jewelled heels. With the light colour of her stockings shading into the ivory of her flesh under the fine stuff of the chemise, it was an unconsciously provocative pose. She was pleased that he had taken her suggestion so readily and was now no afraid that he was leaving.

He had not made love to her since his visit to Friedrichshof. He had come back from there with his vitality restored, yet it was as if he had none to spare for her. So often when she had wanted him, as she did now, he had left her abruptly, driven by his awareness of time passing and the need to work. But when he turned and smiled to her, she realised that tonight he did not mean to leave.

She rose slowly and tossed her unsmoked cigarette into the fire. As she stepped towards him, the sash at her waist came undone. His arms slipped round her under the negligée and he drew the soft warmth of her body close to him.

The responsibility for the redecoration of Buckingham Palace and Windsor was exciting and absorbing. It was what Alix needed. She had refused to be called Queen Consort. After so long, she was the Queen. But there was no challenge in her life. She had resented Bertie making most of the decisions and telling her what to do. For many years, in return for the freedom which she allowed him outside, he had let her be complete mistress in her own home. There, everything was arranged and organised by her. With his preoccupation and inability to let her share his new duties in any way, she had felt shut out, excluded, and had withdrawn to Sandringham where she tried to pretend that anything outside her immediate circle did not exist. Now she was alive again, of use, part of his world.

While she had paid a short visit to Vicky in Germany, he had all his mother's treasures and mementos moved out of her apartments and stored away with his father's belongings in one room at Windsor. She would not have dared touch them herself, but the last shred of her reluctance vanished with them and she threw herself enthusiastically into the plans for redecoration. She chose the colours and the curtains and carpeting. She selected the furniture and worked out how it was to be redistributed, which pieces were to be scrapped and which to be polished and restored. She chose the rooms for herself and Toria and her ladies-in-waiting, keeping one to hang her own watercolours in, which she did not want anyone else to see. Esher helped her and saw that her ideas were carried out as she wished. With Lionel Cust, she picked out the best of the paintings and sculptures for the most important rooms. Bertie was delighted by her enthusiasm and approved of everything she did. Only one thing he insisted on, that he was consulted on where the pictures were to be hung.

'I may not know much about Art,' he said. 'But I know a lot about arrangement.' With all the plans and preparations and her grand-children to look after, her days were full. Yet it was not enough.

She had taken Toria and a party of their friends to inspect progress in the State Apartments of the Palace, then they had dined quietly with Bertie at Marlborough House. Lord Carrington had been charming and complimentary. Even Toria who was so hard to please had been quite animated. She was grateful for their praise, but felt unsettled. It was past two o'clock and she was in bed, unable to sleep. One of the worst drawbacks of her deafness was that she could not hear what was happening in the house. She did not know if Bertie had gone to his rooms or not.

She rose and put on her dressing gown. The corridors were brightly lit but deserted. The door to Bertie's dressing-room was partly open. She looked in and saw his Austrian valet, Meidinger, sitting with his arms folded, asleep. She smiled and hurried down the stairs.

The light was on in Bertie's study. She knocked and went in. He was alone, seated at his desk, reading. He had been writing a short comment in the margin of a report, so engrossed he was not aware of her. She watched him for a moment, concerned, seeing how drawn and tired he looked. 'Aren't you in bed yet?' she said.

'H'm?' He glanced up, surprised to see her.

She moved nearer. 'You'll do no good by wearing yourself out.'

'There's so much I have to catch up on,' he muttered. She had not heard and he spoke louder, tapping the sheaf of notes and memoranda in the nearest tray. 'So many Ministries, so many departments, all with their own interests and problems. I should know about them.'

'Not everything is of the same importance,' she told him. 'You should be more selective.'

He shrugged. 'I suppose so.'

Alix paused. 'And you take too much on yourself,' she said. 'You should let me share more with you.'

Bertie laid down his pen. He moved it parallel to the top edge of the report he had been reading, not looking at her. 'I'm sorry, my dear.' He shook his head.

'Why not?'

From her voice, he could hear she was hurt. 'For the same reason that I must learn,' he explained. 'I have made a beginning, but too many people expect little of me. I have the position, but I must also earn it.'

'And what about me?' she asked. 'Have I waited so long, too, for nothing?' As he made to speak, she went on quickly. 'I know what you're going to say. There are the children, and the renovations. But think, Bertie. In a few months, George and May will be back and the children will go to them. And the work at Windsor and the Palace will be finished. What will my concerns be then—only to look pretty and arrange flowers and preside at Charity Meetings? What is the point of it all if I cannot do something worthwhile?"

He saw that she was taut, desperately sincere. The difficulties of his own position had been so pressing, he had not stopped to consider hers. He had been unfair, undervaluing her ability just as others had done to him. Her duties were mainly social, yet she, too, was not content to be merely a figurehead. People saw her as beautiful and charming, though not very clever. He had been able to make his own opportunities, but she had seldom had the chance. If they

84

could find even one thing—— Her head lowered and she began to turn away, thinking his silence meant he had rejected her. It was the last time she would appeal to him.

'I—I should have realised,' he said, stopping her. He rose and came round the desk to her, taking her hand. He kissed it, then held it between both his. 'You're cold. Come and sit down.' He led her to the small sofa by the fire. He had not noticed the fire was nearly burnt out and jabbed it with the poker to stir the grey coals back to life. Alix shivered and leant forward, holding herself.

Bertie was thinking aloud. 'There's the London Hospital —the Royal College of Music . . .' He turned to her. 'No. I have it! Something that would be really useful. Those military nurses you sent to the Cape——'

'Yes?'

'That's a service you could extend.'

Alix bit her lower lip, dubious. 'I have often wished to,' she said. 'Even tried. But the War Office makes so many difficulties.'

Bertie sat beside her. 'Go straight to the top. You said it yourself. You're the Queen now. Have a word with Lord Roberts.' He smiled. 'I doubt if he'll be able to resist you. Any more than I can.'

Alix smiled at him shyly and nodded. 'Thank you, Bertie,' she said.

How lovely she is, he thought, like a young girl. I could never hurt her. He put his arm round her shoulders and they sat quietly, watching the fire where a tiny, forked flame flickered up unsteadily in the embers. It was the first time they had been alone together in weeks.

The Commander-in-Chief, Lord Roberts, was grateful to the Queen. He was only too aware that the medical facilities in South Africa were inadequate, almost criminally inadequate. Of the appalling number of deaths, more than half were not caused by wounds but by enteric fever and other diseases. The Army's Medical Service had been despised and undermanned for far too long, owing to snobbery and prejudice at the War Office. Recently the King had campaigned with some success for a better standard of doctors and increased efficiency and the Queen, when Princess of Wales, had sent out a body of nurses at her own expense and organised and equipped a hospital ship to be based at

Cape Town. It had saved many lives and been an invaluable incentive to others to give voluntary aid.

At nearly seventy, Lord Roberts was still spry and vigorous. It was hard to believe that his Victoria Cross had been won nearly fifty years before, during the Indian Mutiny. After a lifetime spent in the army, his slight figure was erect and soldierly. His hair was white, his moustache full and bristling, covering his mouth, but the impression of fierceness was softened by light-coloured, humorous eyes. Devoted to the welfare of his men and revered by them for his fairness and care, he was known to officers and privates alike as 'Bobs'. He had served in Abyssinia and pacified Afghanistan, capturing Kabul and, in 1880, leading the heroic march to the relief of Kandahar. For eighty years, he was Commander-in-Chief in India for which he received his title. He returned to England as a Field-Marshal and seemed to be gradually working towards retirement when the Boer War broke out. After the first disasters, he was sent to South Africa with Lord Kitchener as his second-in-command. Within months they had wiped out the memory of the initial Boer successes, capturing Johannesburg, Bloemfontein and Pretoria and occupying the Transvaal and the Orange Free State. He was recalled to England to take charge of all British forces and in the last official act of Victoria's reign, was created Earl.

He sat in an armchair in Alexandra's private sitting-room in Marlborough House, very conscious that she sat opposite him and that her daughter, Princess Victoria, was pouring tea for them. The Queen had already invited him and his wife to dinner the following week. He was overwhelmed, but suspected that he was being softened up for something, although he could not imagine what it was.

'It is heartening to see how many ladies have volunteered to help in the hospitals in South Africa,' she said. 'And how many societies have been formed to send medical supplies.'

'It is indeed, ma'am,' he agreed. 'May I say, following your example.'

She smiled briefly. 'Yet I have been discussing it with Mr Holland, Chairman of the London Hospital, in which I take an interest, and we are agreed that it is disgraceful that men fighting for their country should have to depend on charities for proper care.'

'I cannot dispute that, ma'am,' Roberts acknowledged.

'It is a disgrace.' He had an odd feeling that the Queen was, for some reason, relieved.

'The war has shown once again that the present army medical arrangements are insufficient and unsatisfactory.'

'On that we also agree, ma'am,' he said. 'In fact, strictly between us, it is one area that I intend to reform as soon as possible.'

'I would very much like to help,' Alix told him.

Princess Victoria had brought his tea. 'Thank you, Your Royal Highness.' He sat back, more at ease. He had not known what to expect. His conduct of the war had recently come in for some pretty strong criticism from unexpected quarters and he had been on his guard. But this was safe ground. The Queen was waiting for him to comment. 'I'd be delighted, ma'am,' he assured her. 'What do you propose? Some more nursing sisters—a new hospital ship?'

'Something a little more permanent,' she said levelly. 'A total reorganisation of the Army Nursing Service.'

Roberts blinked. He set his cup and saucer down carefully on the table beside him. 'That is quite a proposal,' he observed.

'It is long overdue, Lord Roberts,' Alix said firmly. 'I do not blame the army doctors. They cope nobly in impossible conditions. But their field hospitals are poorly equipped and understaffed. Far too many patients die, not from enemy action, but needlessly, from fever and dysentery.'

'That is true,' Roberts conceded. 'It has always been the case.'

'But it must not continue. Plans must be drawn up for a corps of trained, professional nurses, actually serving with the army.'

Roberts nodded. That would be the perfect answer, but it could not be done at a stroke. 'It would have to be submitted to the War Office and go through the proper channels.'

'If we do that,' Alix said, 'they will still be discussing it in committee ten years from now.'

Roberts smiled shortly. Ten years was not an excessive estimate. At least the Queen understood one of the major problems, but there were many others. What she was suggesting was a very sweeping change. He tried to explain. 'You see, ma'am—these plans you mention would have to be fully worked out, clause by clause, the nature of this

87

corps agreed and its relationship to existing services. It would have to be very thoroughly organised and have someone at its head whom the Chiefs of Staff would accept.'

'Would they accept me?' Alix asked. He looked at her, surprised. 'To save time and avoid wasteful discussion,' she went on, 'I have already drawn up plans, with my daughter's assistance, for the recruitment and training of nurses and the formation of an efficient unit. I think it covers most of the points.'

Toria had moved to her mother's desk. She brought back a sheaf of pages in Alexandra's scrawled handwriting which she gave to Roberts. He ruffled through them quickly, seeing notes on establishment and organisations, figures and statistics, what seemed to be the complete breakdown of a training programme, command structure. 'The Chairman of the London Hospital helped with many of the practical details,' Toria said.

'Yes. Ah, yes,' Roberts muttered. He felt more than a little rushed. He turned back to the top page. 'The Imperial Military Nursing Service,' he read out. 'I take it, it would go under your name, ma'am?'

'Of course,' Alix said. 'Fortunately, my husband approves.'

Queen Alexandra's Imperial Military Nursing Service. Of which the King approved. He could hardly see anyone opposing it. 'And what would my role be in all this?' he asked.

'Firstly to give advice on the details of military organisation,' Alix told him. He nodded. 'And secondly, to cut through those endless miles of red tape.'

Roberts smiled. He had walked with open eyes right into an ambush from which, he realised, he had no great wish to escape. The ponderous dinosaurs of the War Office could do with a Royal rocket up their backsides.

The Queen was puzzled by his silence. 'Don't you think we can do it?' she asked.

'On the contrary, ma'am,' he assured her. 'I believe if anyone can, it is you. As you say, it is long overdue. And I should be proud to help you.'

'I'm so glad,' Alix smiled. 'As I know how busy you are. Perhaps you would like to take these proposals of mine and make some comments on them, from the army's point of view? There's no hurry. You can bring them with you when you come to dinner next week.'

Roberts felt that, somehow, until the Queen's Nursing Service was in operation, he was going to be much busier.

Bertie's hopes for an understanding between Britain and Germany were growing fainter. In his mind, the situation was simple. As the two most powerful nations, if they agreed to work together for the common good, a pact between them would ensure peace in Europe for the next fifty years. As a stabilising force, its effect would be felt throughout the world. He accepted his government's reluctance to commit itself until agreement had been reached on various aspects of world policy, a difficult matter since the attitudes of the two nations were different, and, in some cases, their interests clashed. On the other hand, the German Government insisted not on an understanding but on an outright alliance, binding each party to complete support of the other's actions. It was a tricky problem, but not insoluble, except for the fact that Germany's actions were to a large extent dictated by the Kaiser. He sounded genuine in his desire for an alliance, at least an understanding, but he was a creature of capricious moods and his vanity and rashness made him undependable.

Bertie had suggested that, if there were any special areas of disagreement in the negotiations, Wilhelm should write to him direct. It unleashed a torrent of freakish letters, one of which was so unrestrained in its criticisms of Salisbury and Lansdowne and the British Foreign Office, 'a set of unmitigated noodles', Willy called them, that Bertie had to summon Baron von Eckhardstein, Chargé d'Affaires in the German Embassy in London, to warn him. If it got out, such a letter could cause the immediate collapse of the talks.

Eckhardstein was embarrassed. 'Perhaps Your Majesty should treat it as a joke,' he suggested.

Bertie laughed. 'Probably the only thing to do,' he agreed, then grew serious. 'Unfortunately, I have already had to put up with many of these jokes of the Kaiser's—even worse than this one. And I suppose I shall have to put up with many more.'

This was possibly the best opportunity there had ever been to make his father's dream a reality. If there was to be any hope of success, Bertie could not fall out with Wilhelm and he arranged to meet him again in Germany. Three weeks before they were due to meet, Vicky died. As soon as could be arranged, Bertie left with Alix for the funeral.

Chapter

6

Although it had been expected, Vicky's death affected Bertie deeply. The news was given to him when he landed wth Alix at Cowes after wishing Godspeed to Commander Robert Falcon Scott and inspecting his ship *Discovery*, which was leaving the next day for a voyage of exploration to the Antarctic. He had himself driven, alone, to Osborne and walked through the grounds to the little Swiss Cottage. If Vicky's spirit lingered anywhere, it would be here.

There had been only a year's difference in age between him and his elder sister. As young children they had been very close, sharing a nursery, governesses, toys. Vicky was intelligent and precocious, their father's favourite. Even sensing that had not made Bertie love her less. Separated from him for a time by her early engagement and marriage, she had used her influence to persuade their parents to treat him with more understanding. She had found Alix for him and she and Fritz had been their first friends. No quarrel between them had continued for long and, in these last years, he had felt closer to her than ever.

When he thought of the bright, hopeful girl who had left for Germany, the vicious antagonism she had endured in her father-in-law's Court, the bitter end of all her hopes and ambitions with the death of her husband and the agonising martyrdom of her widowhood, he nearly broke down. He sat in the living-room of the cottage, at the table at which Vicky had so often been hostess at their children's tea parties. He tried to remember her as a round-cheeked, laughing girl, but all he could see was the lined, careworn face of the Dowager Empress and the pain hidden behind her eyes. He seemed to hear the ghostly echo of children's laughter and he shivered, although the air in the room still held the heat of a long August day. He looked round at the plain, wooden furniture, the tiles and the homely mottoes in German on the walls, knowing it was for the last time. He would not come here again.

Alix and he travelled to Homburg with his brother, Arthur, Duke of Connaught, and the old Duke of Cambridge, their mother's cousin who had been like an uncle to him and Vicky. As it was an official visit, they brought a suitable number of servants and staff with them, including Frederick Ponsonby as Assistant Private Secretary. The Kaiser and his sons met them at Frankfurt and accompanied them to Homburg where a guard of honour and a horde of dignitaries waited to receive them before they drove to the Hotel Adler.

Greeting the officials and inspecting the guard of honour, the smiling and strutting of the Imperial staff, had been distressing to Bertie. It made a mockery of private grief. And Wilhelm had been distant at first.

'It is six days since my mother died,' he said. 'I felt sure you would have come at once.' A strange sentiment, Bertie thought, when a great part of his sister's unhappiness had been caused by her son's rejection. Wilhelm was brusque and unfeeling throughout the reception but in the hotel, when he described his mother's death, he wept. In the final weeks, even her indomitable courage had not been proof against the pain and she had sobbed and cried out in agony. On the last morning, she asked for a window in her bedroom to be opened so that she could see the tree-covered hills. A butterfly fluttered in from the sunlit garden and hovered over her. She smiled, gazing at it, and died.

Later, alone with Bertie, Wilhelm tried to justify himself. 'She was always suspicious of me,' he said. 'She saw everything in shadows, everything I did was wrong. If only she had lived just a little longer, until our countries were allied, she would have understood that our ambitions have always been the same.' If only matters had been settled, he went on, but the British Foreign Office was too cautious, too prejudiced.

Bertie could see that Wilhelm was full of questions and complaints, impatient to begin discussion of the issues that were still unsettled. He was still distressed and had no wish to argue or reason with him, certainly not until after the funeral. Before leaving London, he had asked Lansdowne for a list of the subjects which divided the two governments, with a brief statement of the British position on each to guide him in his talks with the Kaiser. He decided on a gamble.

Wilhelm was becoming agitated, pacing, the hand of his undeveloped left arm clutching the ceremonial dagger at his belt, the other stabbing the air.

'Why don't they trust me?' he demanded 'You say you are forced to leave the discussions to your Foreign Office. Well, why don't they tell me what they really think?' Bertie felt in the inside pocket of his coat and took out Lansdowne's memorandum. He rose from his chair and gave the typed pages to Wilhelm. Wilhelm was puzzled but, as he unfolded them, his expression changed.

'These—these were meant for your eyes only,' he stumbled.

'That proves that on my side there is nothing to hide,' Bertie said. 'And that I trust you.'

For a moment, Wilhelm could not speak, then he reached out impulsively and gripped Bertie's shoulder. 'I am in your debt forever,' he muttered.

The funeral ceremonies began with a simple service in the Church of St. John in Cronberg, the village near Friedrichshof where the Empress Frederick had worshipped. Bertie and Alix placed a cross at the head of the catafalque in her memory. The burial took place two days later in Potsdam. A superbly decorated hearse drawn by eight black horses carried Vicky's body along the route, lined by soldiers ranked four deep, from the Neues Palais to the mausoleum chapel in the Friedenskirche. Massed bands playing the Dead March preceded the hearse and it was followed by the Kaiser and his uncle, King Edward, and the rest of the Royal Family, on foot.

There was so much squabbling over precedence among the delegations and representatives of other countries that the English suite decided to let them all go first and took up the rear of the procession. Walking last of all as a junior member of the staff, Ponsonby sincerely mourned the dead Empress whose courage he had admired, and was disturbed by the German officers ahead of them who laughed and called out joking remarks to their friends in the crowd.

Some of what they said, he could now understand. He had hoped by this time to have rejoined his regiment but he had still not been posted. He carried on working uneasily under Francis Knollys who was suspicious of a

93

young man whom the King obviously liked and trusted. Ponsonby realised that the best way to be accepted was to make himself useful. Surprisingly, in the whole staff, including Knollys, there was no one who spoke German. He bought a dictionary and set himself to learn ten words a day. In the past months, he had mastered several thousand words and, although he could not string sentences together properly himself, he could make out the gist of what was said.

'Saying goodbye to the widow?' someone in the crowd shouted.

'She's gone at last, die Engländerin,' a Prussian colonel in front of him laughed back.

The stout Major beside him snorted. 'Why didn't they wrap her in a Union Jack and send her back to Windsor?'

Stanley Clarke, the senior Equerry, walking ahead of Ponsonby, looked round and whispered, 'What are they saying?'

Ponsonby shook his head, his lips compressed. If he told Clarke, an official protest would have to be made and it could have a disastrous effect on the relations between the King and his nephew. After the business of the Empress's letters, when the King had chosen him to accompany him, he had been apprehensive about meeting the Kaiser again. But Wilhelm had smiled and shaken hands graciously. Obviously the search for his mother's papers had uncovered nothing. He must think they had been destroyed long ago.

He was jolted out of his thoughts as Von Scholl, the tall ADC he had met at Friedrichshof, marched back down the procession towards them and fell into place beside him.

'His Imperial Majesty has sent me,' he said gruffly. 'The English suite are to move up the line and take position immediately behind the Royal Family.' The Kaiser had given his mother's countrymen pride of place.

After the funeral, Alix went to visit her father in Denmark. Bertie dismissed most of the suite and returned to Homburg with only Ponsonby, Clarke and a Groom-in-Waiting.

Homburg was an elegant expensive town, famous for the curative value of its mineral waters. As Prince of Wales, he had visited it at this time every year to take the

94

waters and enjoy himself, incognito. The fashionable crowd which was also there for the cure had always respected his anonymity. This year, however, his photographs were everywhere, in illustrated magazines, newspapers, shop windows, and people followed him whenever he appeared, staring and pointing. After several days their curiosity was satisfied, but his pleasure in the town was gone. He drove out most afternoons into the countryside to escape. He would have left altogether except for the meeting with his nephew that had been arranged for months.

On the day, he travelled by train with the three remaining members of his staff to Wilhelmshoehe. He wore the dark trousers, long tunic with the double row of buttons and the flat, black-brimmed hat of the First Prussian Dragoon Guards, of whose regiment he was Honorary Colonel. He had hoped to lose weight at Homburg but the interrupted cure prevented that and the uniform was tight and uncomfortable.

He had intended the meeting to be private because of mourning, a quiet lunch and talk. Wilhelm met him with ostentatious, military ceremony, bands and flags and ranks of officers. He was an imposing figure in helmet and thigh-length jackboots and a resplendent white uniform, the gold epaulettes covered by black crepe. At the castle, they reviewed an hour-long march past of fifteen thousand troops. The whole display was tasteless and unnecessary. Bertie kept telling himself it was only his nephew trying to impress him. Wilhelm wanted to show his delight at the visit. It was the only way he knew how.

The lunch was in the banqueting hall of the castle. The King and the Kaiser sat on one side of the long table with Sir Frank Lascelles, the British Ambassador. Opposite them, Ponsonby and Stanley Clarke were next to the plump, fair-haired Eulenberg, head of the Imperial Household. The other places were taken by senior staff officers. Throughout the meal, Wilhelm was ebullient and lighthearted. When he chose he could be very amusing. As a centrepiece on the table was a solid gold vase with a gold rail round its lip to hold in the flowers. It was a gift he had devised for his uncle and he made an effusive speech, presenting it and explaining that the rail was a new conception. Bertie spoke courteously in reply, thanking him for his welcome and the magnificent gift.

Eulenberg clicked his teeth disapprovingly. 'He should

have mentioned that it was designed personally by the All-Highest.'

'By whom?' Clarke asked, ingenuously.

Eulenberg frowned. 'His Imperial Majesty.'

'Very clever idea, that rail,' Ponsonby said quickly. He had already warned Clarke to be careful what he said to Eulenberg, who was the Kaiser's most intimate friend. Everything would be sure to go straight back.

Wilhelm had not heard what was said across the table but his attention was drawn to Ponsonby. He was slightly irritated that his uncle had not sufficiently praised his invention and, as always when he was irritated, had to find someone to take it out on.

'Well, then,' he observed sarcastically, 'I see the brave Ponsonby has changed his mind about going to South Africa.'

'Not at all,' Bertie said. 'He's been trying to get out there for months. In point of fact, he's leaving in a few days' time.' Wilhelm was staring at him. Bertie smiled. 'Yes, Fritz has got a replacement posting at last. I've given my permission.'

Wilhelm flushed. He realised he had been unjust and it heightened his annoyance. He rapped on the table with his spoon for silence. 'Your Majesty—gentlemen, a toast!' he called. 'To Captain Ponsonby who is leaving shortly to fight for his country. Fritz!' He raised his glass and drank. The others round the table called out 'Fritz!' also and drank.

Embarrassed, Ponsonby rose to his feet. He knew the ritual here was to drink to his host in reply. The glass in front of him was empty. He saw the Kaiser smile maliciously across to Eulenberg and, a second later, understood why. The wine decanter in front of him was also empty except for the dregs at the bottom. He had no choice. He poured an inch of the brown-tinged sediment into his glass.

'Your Imperial Majesty,' he toasted and drank.

'You'll ruin your digestion, you know,' Wilhelm laughed, shaking his finger, 'drinking the dregs of bottles.' The laugh was taken up round the table and Wilhelm settled back, chuckling, his humour restored.

After lunch, Wilhelm and Bertie walked in the castle gardens with the British Ambassador. This was the moment Bertie and Lascelles had been waiting for, but Wilhelm would not talk seriously. He was still excited by the feeling of power the march past had inspired in him. Bertie smiled and quipped back, humouring him. Lascelles was bewildered. He had expected a frank discussion, but the Kaiser kept skirting round it, enjoying himself. Finally Wilhelm mentioned the visit his cousin, Bertie's nephew, Czar Nicholas the Second, had just paid to Paris.

'A great success, I believe,' he said. 'They could have parcelled up the Eiffel Tower in all the red carpet they put out for him.'

'I believe so,' Bertie smiled. 'I thought he might have offered to visit me afterwards. I'd like to have seen Nicky.'

'Many people were surprised he didn't;' Wilhelm agreed. 'It almost looked like a demonstration against England.' He waited but his uncle did not rise to the bait. 'Of course, he was obviously there to make sure of France's support in his troubles with Japan.'

'Obviously,' Bertie said. Something in Wilhelm's manner made him wary. They walked on for a minute in silence.

Wilhelm stopped, looking at a border of white chrysanthemums. 'They need cutting back. Dead heading, as Mama used to say,' he observed. His mouth was twitching. He could not keep it to himself any longer. 'Extraordinary communication, that,' he chuckled. 'The one you gave me. So full of little inaccuracies.'

Bertie was aware of Lascelles's puzzlement. 'It was not meant to be a communication, Willy,' he said warningly. 'Only some notes, written in haste.'

'In great haste, apparently,' Wilhelm smirked. 'As I pointed out to your Lord Lansdowne.'

Bertie froze. 'You pointed out?'

'Yes. I prepared a memorandum covering the same topics, which I sent to him. He should find it instructive,' Wilhelm laughed. 'Do you know, he actually said Kuwait was to be the terminus of the Transcaspian Railway? A strange ignorance of geography for a Foreign Secretary! Of course, he meant the Anatolian Railway.'

Bertie was furious and barely able to restrain it. 'Those notes were given to you in confidence, Willy,' he growled. 'Not to be used as ammunition.'

'Blank cartridges, I assure you,' Wilhelm said airily.

'I gave them to you in proof of friendship!' Bertie fumed. Already he could imagine his Government's reaction and

Lansdowne's scandalised disapproval. He would have to bluff it out, somehow.

'Exactly,' Wilhelm said, unrepentant. 'Having learned how close we are, they might have more belief in my assurances.'

Lascelles was looking from one to the other. Something was very wrong but, without knowing what, he could not even attempt to smooth it over. He moved with them as they turned towards the ornamental fountains, the Kaiser smiling, the King clearly having difficulty in stifling his anger.

'It is not merely the inaccuracies,' Wilhelm went on. 'There are the little omissions. Like the Anglo-Japanese Agreement.'

Bertie stopped and stared at him. Lascelles felt that now he could intervene. He bowed to the Kaiser. 'I regret having to contradict you, sir. There is no such Agreement.'

The Kaiser smiled crookedly. 'Indeed? I am told that talks have been going on at the highest level and that Britain and Japan are almost ready to sign a treaty of alliance.'

Lascelles was shaken. 'I have heard nothing of this,' he muttered. He turned to the King.

Bertie was motionless. With the expansion of Russia into the Pacific and its threat to the independence of Korea and China, he saw an alliance with Japan as an important stabilising force in Asia, as one with Germany would be in Europe. The talks with Japan had been delicate and completely secret, ending centuries of Japanese isolation and suspicion of foreigners.

'How did you know about them?' he asked quietly.

'One learns things.' Wilhelm smiled. The agreement would protect Germany's interests as much as anyone's, but he felt aggrieved. It was a diplomatic triumph and his agents had brought him the information too late for him to become involved.

'No treaty has been finalised yet,' Bertie said to Lascelles.

'But it will be,' Wilhelm told them. 'At any moment. Yet there was no mention of it in this innocent memorandum. It is just another instance of the deceitfulness of your Foreign Office.'

'Deceitfulness?' Bertie growled.

'Perfidious Albion,' Wilhelm declared. 'The phrase is

well-coined. Throughout history, the deviousness of the British Government has been notorious.'

'You will not call my Government deceitful!' Bertie snapped.

'I must protest also, sir,' Lascelles said.

Wilhelm drew himself up. 'It is not something to quarrel over. Only something one must accept!' He had not meant to fall out with his uncle. 'I do not connect you with this in any way, Uncle Bertie,' he swore. 'After all, because of your strange system, many decisions are taken before you are even consulted. I am upset on your behalf as much as my own.'

Bertie controlled himself. 'As you say, our system is different.'

'And clumsy,' Wilhelm insisted, 'when your left hand does not know what your right hand is doing. You have often complained that your Cabinet keeps you in the dark.'

'Does your Government tell you every transaction it's involved in?' Bertie countered.

'I *am* my Government!' Wilhelm asserted imperiously. 'There is no will but mine!' His arrogance exalted him. He stood erect, his head lifted as though to catch the sound of distant music. 'I am sole master and arbiter of German foreign policy and the Government and country *must* follow me. Their destiny has been given into my hands.'

Bertie was silent, watching him. He remembered Vicky's hoarse, urgent voice. 'Bear with him, Bertie. For my sake. If you abandon him, our world will end in ruin.'

Bertie returned to Homburg. The dangerous corner in his talks with Wilhelm had been turned. They parted with more ceremony and professions of friendship, but the meeting had been abortive. Bertie had wanted to reassure his nephew, to strengthen the family tie. Instead, he found that all his uneasiness with him had returned. Wilhelm clearly desired an alliance, yet it had to be on his own capricious terms, and behind all his jokes and banter there was a hint of malice. He kept referring to the difference between them, to his own authority and his uncle's dependence on his Ministers, 'jumped-up lackeys' he called them. He could not resist showing how well-informed he was. Casually, he mentioned the unrest in Malta and said, 'I hear your Colonial Office is considering giving them self-government.' Bertie could not confirm or deny it. As the Kaiser had suspected, he had not been told. It weakened his position immeasurably. Wilhelm seemed to be saying, 'Why should I be serious with you? Do you have the power to negotiate?'

The last week of Bertie's stay in Homburg did nothing to lessen his depression. Before Ponsonby left for the Cape, he wrote a letter of protest to the Colonial Office, to be told curtly in reply that the Secretary of State for the Colonies was responsible only to Parliament and, unlike the Foreign Secretary, did not even have to consult the King. A further letter brought a grudging promise of fuller information. At the same time, attacks on Bertie in the German newspapers, cartoons and criticism of the war, became more frequent and more vicious, stimulated by politicians who were against the possible alliance. The Kaiser regretted them but could not interfere with 'the freedom of the press'. And rumours circulated about the dead Empress Frederick, how she had asked in her will to be given an Anglican funeral, how she had wished to be wrapped naked in a Union Jack and sent for burial at Windsor, but her son had patriotically refused. There was no official denial.

On the day before he left, a flash came informing them that President McKinley had been shot by an anarchist at the Pan-American Exhibition in Buffalo and lay critically wounded. The news shocked and saddened him. He had won the President's respect by his restraint and calmness during the crisis of the Spanish-American war and they had remained friends. They had hoped that the bond between them would draw their countries closer together. In Bertie's life all the certainties seemed to be shifting. He wrote personally to Mrs McKinley before leaving to join Alix in Copenhagen.

King Christian of Denmark was over eighty, still vigorous and mentally alert, a charming, old fashioned gentleman with mutton-chop whiskers and a curling moustache. The loss of his beloved wife, Louise, three years before, had prostrated him, but he was consoled by the love of his people and his children.

Alix came to Denmark every spring when the whole family gathered to celebrate his birthday, then she returned in the late summer to join her favourite sister, Minny, now the Dowager Empress Marie Feodorovna of Russia, widow of Alexander the Third. This year their brother Willy, King George of Greece, and their younger sister, Thyra, Duchess of Cumberland, were visiting too. With Minny was her son, Czar Nicholas, and his wife, Alexandra, named after Alix. As a family they were very devoted. Most of their pleasure was in talking and simply being together. In private there was little or no formality and they kept public engagements to a minimum.

Bertie's arrival caused an uncomfortable chill at first. As a boy, Nicholas had idolised him. His uncle had comforted him at the funeral of his father in St. Petersburg and stood by him at his wedding that followed a few days later. He had wanted to rule as Bertie advised, with justice and understanding for his people, but both his young wife and his mother had convinced him that to grant reforms was to show weakness. He was the Czar, the Autocrat of all the Russias, and must be unyielding, as his father had been. Gradually, he had become what they desired and grown away from his uncle. The age-old suspicion between their two countries now divided them.

Bertie had not met Nicky for some years. He was amazed to see how like George he still was, although his hair had begun to recede. The same clear eyes and straight nose above a short neatly-trimmed beard. It hurt him that their initial meeting was so strained, but he would not force intimacy on him. He realised that much of his nephew's criticism of him had been dictated by politics. Now Nicky felt guilty and embarrassed. He would only come round, if at all, in his own time. He treated him with cordial politeness. And his niece, the Czarina, known as Alicky to distinguish her from her aunt, was a beautiful, reserved young woman, with golden hair and cornflower blue eyes. Bertie had hoped that marriage would warm her, but she was still detached and aloof in company. Only with her children, the little girls and the new baby, Anastasia, did she show any real animation. 'Princess Sunshine', she had been nicknamed. She was now a Snow Queen. Between her and her mother-in-law, the Empress Marie, there was an ill-concealed hostility. Minny still tried to dominate her son, to control his thoughts and actions, while Alicky fought to make her husband independent, Czar in his own right.

With Alix's sister, Minny, Bertie was more relaxed. He had known her since she was a girl and her occasional grand manners amused him. He remembered how pleased she was when he came to her wedding. Most of her own relatives were too poor. Minny had once been a gay, attractive girl. In middle age, her face had become sharp, her voice imperious. He almost preferred Alicky's reserve which he knew did not come from disdain but from a crippling shyness. Minny laughed at her interest in mysticism and tongue-tied silence at meals. Bertie scrupulously avoided taking sides.

They were staying at the Amalienborg Palace in Copenhagen, four great rococo mansions round an octagonal piazza. Bertie found the routine of its life, set by the old King, extremely dull but he endured it each year for Alix's sake, the heavy meals, the old world card games, the endless family conversation. He schooled himself to visit the art galleries, museums and historic churches of the town for perhaps the twentieth time, with an occasional evening at the theatre.

It was Alix's younger brother, Willy, the King of Greece, who saved him from complete boredom. He was an amusing, raffish man, tall, with a long, drooping moustache. Elected King of the Hellenes while still a naval cadet in his teens, he was friendly with some of the less solemn members of Copenhagen Society, including two dashing and amiable countesses on whom they were able occasionally to call. Another interest he shared with Bertie was a passion for motor cars and he organised excursions and picnics for the family at Royal residences out in the country, at Fredensborg Palace and Bernstorff, the unpretentious white château where Alix had spent her childhood summers. It was through these drives that the breach between Bertie and Nicky was healed.

Three open limousines took the family, with another three for servants and the Russian detectives who acted as the Czar's bodyguard. Willy laughed at them but Minny explained that in Russia they would have been completely surrounded, as the only means of ensuring their safety. Bodyguards went in the first car, then came Alix with Minny and Thyra, followed by Alicky with the children and their governess. Bertie, Nicky and Willy were behind them and more bodyguards and servants brought up the rear.

Sitting in their Mercedes, Bertie and Willy kept up a flow of conversation and Nicky began to join in. He was almost lightheaded at the sense of freedom, driving in the Danish countryside with so few guards. It reminded him of his visits to Sandringham when he was a boy, running free in the estate with his cousins, picnicking with his uncle Bertie and aunt Alix. He had never wanted to leave. He had dreaded the return to St Petersburg, to the sentries and machine guns that ringed its palaces and the high walls round the stone court in which he was allowed to walk, like a prison yard. He laughed embarrassedly when he remembered his first visit to Balmoral as Czar, when his mother had insisted on him taking fifty policemen. They had even surrounded him when he went deerstalking on the moors.

'Uncle Bertie was so annoyed,' he told Willy. 'It ruined the sport.'

'They sounded like a herd of elephants,' Bertie laughed. 'Frightened all the game away.'

'And you really still have no bodyguard?' Nicky asked. It seemed incredible.

'There's never been a need for one,' Bertie assured him. 'The British people and I trust each other.'

It brought back what Bertie had said to him over and over again in the long days of vigil when they travelled together in the black-draped train carrying his father's body the thousand miles from Livadia to St Petersburg to lie in state in the little baroque church in the Peter and Paul fortress beside the Neva.

'Trust your people,' Bertie had counselled him. 'Let them see you trust them. Give them at least part of the liberty they have begged for. It cannot harm you and means a whole world to them.'

He had often wondered how different things would be if he had taken his uncle's advice. Both his mother and Alicky had objected that English methods would not work in Russia. Perhaps he had been wrong. But it was too late to change.

The cavalcade swept along the avenue of elms to the Château of Bernstorff. It was quite plain, with semi-circular steps before a rounded entrance hall, only two floors and a series of attic rooms under a steeply-pointed, tiled roof, but the pinewoods round it and the miles of deer forest beyond were superb. Picnic tables were already laid out on the lawn. Willy had ordered a supply of bicycles and, after

103

lunch, he raced Alix round the outside of the house. In spite of her lame leg, she won.

Her gaiety was infectious and she soon had Minny and Thyra also wobbling about the drive on ladies' bicycles. Even Alicky was persuaded to leave the children with their governess and join in. They set off down the avenue, shouting with laughter, to see Alix's favourite view of the Sound.

Bertie and Nicholas sent for horses from the stables, to the consternation of the detectives, only one of whom could ride. The horses had to be sent back. Nicholas flushed. He felt humiliated, repelled suddenly by the thought that even here it was not safe for him to move without protection. He suggested a short walk in the woods to his uncle and, as they set off, commanded his bodyguard sharply to stay out of sight. Bertie could see that he was disturbed and kept silent. The day was perfect, the sky blue and serene, the air among the pine trees lightly fragrant. The only sound was the call of songbirds. They reached a glade in the wood, a clear space of springy turf flecked with tiny, white, starshaped flowers.

Nicholas walked into the centre of it and turned slowly, gazing round. 'I had forgotten how beautiful—how simple . . .' he began. He blinked as though to stop tears and sank to his knees.

Bertie moved closer, sensing the need to remain silent. Nicky plucked one of the tiny flowers and knelt, holding it, and the words began to tumble out, his uncertainties and fears, his fragile hopes. For too long, he had had no one he could confide in, no one to whom he could open his heart. Between his mother and his strong-willed young wife he was in torment. He loved them both, but they were tearing him apart.

He bitterly regretted the estrangement from Bertie. It had been gradual, caused by Russia's necessity to extend her sphere of influence. But everywhere they were checked by the ramparts of the British Empire. They faced aggression from Japan in the Pacific and the threat of the new Empire founded by the United States with the occupation of the Philippines and Guam. His sole ally was France but she was untried, a Republic, many of whose people were critical of him.

At the same time, there was widespread unrest at home, civil disturbance that only harsher and harsher methods could contain. He did not know which of his advisers to trust and all final decisions had to come from him. He was only an ordinary man, not very clever, yet the fate of millions rested on his shoulders. He longed for rest, for peace. That was why he had organised the International Conference on Disarmament which his uncle had mocked. He could not understand why. Nicholas was trembling. His fingers shredded the little flower unconsciously.

Bertie began to speak, quietly and reasonably. To him the idea of disarmament, unless all countries agreed, was sentimental and impractical. He believed in nations solving their disputes by discussion and arbitration, not war, but until that became the rule the only chance for peace lay in the strength of the alliances between Powers. It was the best protection, too, for the smaller nations.

'So how do you justify your war against the Boers?' Nicky muttered.

'I don't have to. You have been listening to their propaganda,' Bertie said. 'You are thinking emotionally, not remembering the facts. We protested to them against their mistreatment of British settlers and workers in their mines. Their reply was to attack without warning, hoping to drive our colonists into the sea. They looked for glory and our rivals rejoiced. Now they are defeated and, suddenly, we are the villains. Their brutality is forgotten. But when peace is restored, they will be given good government and equal rights with every other citizen of the Empire. That is our promise. Can you tell me when England has ever failed to keep it?'

Nicholas was motionless for a time, then shook his head.

'You have no call to be suspicious of us,' Bertie went on. 'We are not seeking any more territory. Neither should you be, Nicky.' Nicholas looked at him. 'Your greatest danger is from the agitation inside your own country. It can only grow worse. If your ministers turned their thought and energy to that, instead of on hatred of Britain and preparations against Japan, you could cure it in a few years.'

'I can't discuss it,' Nicholas said curtly and rose.

'Listen to me, Nicky' Bertie urged. 'You would only be carrying on what your grandfather began by freeing the serfs and allowing district assemblies.'

'He was murdered for it. That was his thanks, to be blown up by anarchists!'

'And for the crime of a few, your father punished his whole people. Instead of forgiveness, he brought back oppression.' Nicky had moved away, but stood still, listening. 'All our countries are changing, with new ideas, new freedom,' Bertie said. 'Even in Russia you cannot hold back the clock. There must be change. Whether it comes violently or is controlled and gradual depends on you.'

He waited, tense, realising he might have said too much. Nicholas sighed. When he spoke, he could hardly hear him. 'It is impossible to choose where to begin.'

'Your people only ask for justice,' Bertie said. 'They must be given hope. All you have to do is grant a few simple reforms and you would be the most loved Czar in history.' Nicky's head lifted. 'They call out to you in the streets, "Little Father, protect us!" Do you rule your own family by fear? Do you want your children to fear you?'

Nicky swung round. Bertie expected anger, instead Nicky raised his arms helplessly. 'You don't understand,' he faltered. 'I have no choice . . . no choice.' Again, the barrier was down. His voice shook as he tried to explain himself. He was not a cruel man. It hurt him to see his children growing up, separated from their fellow countrymen by barbed wire. He had wanted to be a more liberal ruler, but any attempt to alter his father's policy had been shouted down by his mother and his father's brothers. He could not stand against them. Now it was too late. Bertie tried to reassure him, but he went on more excitably. The only time he felt at peace was when he was alone with Alicky. She supported him against the others. Yet even she charged him to stand firm, to be strong, when all he wanted was to escape with her, to somewhere in the country, with the children, a small estate, a farm where they could live without cares and responsibility. That could never happen. If only they could get away, perhaps she would be able to have the boy, the male heir they longed for. That was why she studied the occult and went to faith healers, driven by her desperate desire to give him a son.

Bertie smiled gently. 'Sons do not come from faith healers,' he said.

Nicholas nodded. 'I knew, Uncle Bertie. But I would not oppose anything she believes, if it might help. I love her. She is my world. Without her, I could not carry on for a day.'

In the struggle to control her husband, Alicky had already won. Sooner or later, the Grand Dukes and the Dowager Empress would find they had no more influence.

What use the Czarina would make of her power, Bertie could imagine, but he felt compassion for Nicholas. In his own search to learn how to rule, he was helped by a wise and honoured Constitution, by conscientious ministers and a people schooled by centuries of justice and liberty. How much more formidable, perilous, it must be to have total authority, answerable and responsible to no one. Wilhelm boasted of having such power, but it was a delusion. He would have gloried in it. Nicky possessed the reality, but it terrified him.

When Alix and her brother Willy came to look for them, they found Bertie walking back with Nicholas, arm in arm. Bertie was smiling but she did not think she had ever seen his eyes so sad.

Chapter

7

As soon as he returned to London, Bertie received Mr Choate, the United States Ambassador, in special audience. Choate, a dignified, serious man, had come to convey the thanks of Mrs McKinley and the American people for his continued sympathy 'through the darkest hours of their distress and bereavement'. McKinley was dead and had been succeeded by the Vice-President, Theodore Roosevelt.

When the Ambassador bowed and left, Bertie sat motionless for a while, brooding. While greeting the crowd at the Exhibition in Buffalo, McKinley had been shot twice at point blank range by his assassin, with whom he was shaking hands. He had lingered for some days and died, saying, 'It is God's way. His will be done.' Behind the words, Bertie could feel the anguish and bewilderment of his wife and family. He had recently begun his second term of office. He had been against the war with Spain over Cuba but, once Congress voted in its favour, he had led his country to victory and the United States had taken her place among the Imperialist Powers. Bertie had welcomed it. Alliances within Europe were essential, yet he saw a larger concept of world peace ensured by the friendship of the English-speaking peoples. He knew it would not be easy for America to learn how to use her new wealth and strength. Opposed by militants and isolationists, an understanding would not come automatically but, with a man as far-seeing as William McKinley as President, it had not been impossible.

He wondered what his murderer had thought to accomplish. He was a Polish immigrant, a member of Free Society, an anarchist group in Chicago. There were numbers of those small societies springing up everywhere, in every country, calling for revolution and an end to all established government, private property and business. They were advocates of chaos and their only recognisable argument was violence. This man was chosen by lot to kill. Probably he had not thought at all, only seen the President as a symbol of authority. It took no intelligence to pull a trigger, but it had ended a life of dedication and high purpose.

Francis Knollys was with Bertie in the Audience Room, watching him. He was concerned. Usually the King returned from Homburg relaxed and fitter for losing weight. This year, he had put on more. He looked far from well and seemed under constant tension.

Bertie twisted uncomfortably in his chair and took his cigar case from an inside pocket of his frock coat. 'What do you know about Roosevelt?' he asked.

Knollys had learnt to keep a supply of matches handy. He struck one and held it as the King puffed one of his thick black cigars alight. 'Bit of a firebrand, sir,' he said. 'He's from a fairly rich family. Made his name as President of the Board of Police Commissioners in New York, fighting against corruption. Became a national hero when he formed the Rough Riders during the Spanish-American War. He's also done a bit of daredevil exploring and written books about it.'

Bertie nodded and sat back. It confirmed what he knew. His American friends had been full of Roosevelt at one time. He remembered Jennie Churchill reading out a description of the Battle of Kettle Hill. Exploits like that had swept Roosevelt into the governorship of New York and then the vice-presidency. He was a tough fighter, a fiery orator and a politician. But he was an unknown quantity as a statesman.

Well, McKinley was dead. And the world was poorer for the loss of a man of goodwill. He sighed. 'Send the new President my congratulations, Francis,' he said. 'No. No, I'll write to him myself.'

Bertie had forgiven Jennie Churchill. Now in her mid-forties, he had known her since she was nineteen, the debutante daughter of a New York financier, Leonard Jerome, a vivid girl with dark, passionate eyes and raven hair which she was said to have inherited from some Cherokee ancestor. She was intelligent and amusing and he had found her irresistible. He had introduced her himself to Randolph Churchill, the younger son of the Duke of Marlborough, and Francis Knollys had stood as best man at their wedding. After the collapse of her brilliant husband's political career and the horror of his creeping death from syphilis, she had turned to Bertie for support and comfort. She had been his intimate favourite for some time, until she was replaced by the bewitching, uninhibited Daisy, Countess of Warwick.

Even after that, they had remained close friends. As with many of his former favourites, he had a lasting interest in her wellbeing and happiness. He advised her and teased her when she fell impetuously in and out of love. But he had not laughed when she returned from a short spell as organiser of a hospital ship in South Africa and announced that she was going to marry his godson, George Cornwallis-West, twenty years younger than herself, the same age as her son, Winston. What made it worse was that, just as he had introduced her to Randy, it was he who had brought her and George together.

He had asked Daisy to invite his godson to one of her lavish weekend parties at Warwick Castle. The boy had danced with Jennie, rowed her on the lake, and it amused Bertie to see him so obviously smitten. An affaire had started which he thought harmless, if unsuitable, another of Jennie's escapades, but marriage was another matter. It was not merely that society was shocked. Jennie had shocked it before. He was worried about her. He had pointed out the difficulties to her and to George but against his advice they had married. He had been disappointed and angry until it occurred to him one day that, if their ages had been the other way round, he would have had no objection. Jennie had loved young George enough to marry him. And certainly she had a right to find happiness if she could, and for as long as she could. To show his forgiveness, he invited her and her new husband to spend a weekend at Sandringham. Alix was delighted. Sometimes her tolerance surprised him. She had always liked Jennie.

They had joined a select party of guests, Lord Carrington, Soveral, Lord Roberts, the elegant Lady de Grey, Balfour and Lord Salisbury, the Bishop of London and the Arthur Sassoons.

'A pretty mixed bag,' George Cornwallis-West whispered to Jennie. 'A Liberal peer, a diplomat, a field-marshal, a society beauty, two Conservatives, a Bishop and a Jew.' Jennie laughed and told him not to be stuffy. If the King had no prejudices, neither should he.

At lunch they had congratulated George and May who had just returned from their tour of the Empire. As a token of their success and his love, the King had created them Prince and Princess of Wales, Queen Alexandra made everyone laugh. 'Whenever anyone says, 'The Princess of Wales, I always jump up,' she complained. Afterwards they had driven to Walsingham to see the ruins of the famous old Abbey and returned in time for tea, when the little princes, David and Albert, and Princess Mary had joined them. That was when Jennie had noticed signs of strain.

The children had been playing Bears, their favourite game, with most of the gentlemen crawling on all fours to let them ride on their backs. The Bishop of London, who was extremely tall, had bowed to David and asked, 'Would you care to ride on my back, Your Royal Highness?' David had eyed him carefully for a moment, then said, 'I don't like giraffes.' The King had roared with laughter, and so had the other gentlemen, but she could tell that Prince George was annoyed. Princess May sat straight as Nelson's Column, unsmiling. Jennie was sorry for her. She had known her as an intellectual but animated girl before she married the King's heir. She had taken on all George's stiffness and correctness of manner. They were both scandalised at the freedom their parents had allowed the little princes in their absence. Jennie stepped in and suggested that the children might like to show her the maze. It was a game they had played before. May was about to object but Alix jumped up, delighted. She insisted on joining them. David and Little Bertie took their hands and led them out into the gardens with the others trooping behind.

Near the Rosery, behind a screen of bamboos, was a maze made of yew and box hedges. Once inside, many visitors to Sandringham had spent an anxious hour trying to find the way out. Both Alix and Jennie had discovered the secret of it but it made an exciting adventure for the children to think that they were completely lost. The others waited outside, amused, listening to the shrieks and shouts for help from behind the hedges. When Alix finally led them all out, David and Little Bertie were two of the happiest boys in England.

May had had enough. She told them firmly it was time for their governess to take them back to York Cottage, their own home on the other side of the garden. She would not listen to any protests and marched them off, in spite of Alix's plea to let them stay on a little longer. The King had obviously been irritated, but he would not argue with his son or daughter-in-law. He led the party back into the main house in silence.

Now the ladies had gone up to rest and change for dinner and the men were having a drink in the salon before doing the same. George Cornwallis-West felt distinctly ill-at-ease. For two reasons. One was that he was so much younger than anyone else. It was all right while Jennie was with them, but without her he was out of his depth. The other was something that he realised was unworthy. Looking round a group like this, he could not help wondering which of them at some time in the past had been his wife's lover. He absolved Prince George, the Marquess of Salisbury and the Bishop of London. Apart from that, he could not be certain. He listened to Sassoon talking to the Prince about India, from which he had originally come as a merchant banker. He moved on unobtrusively to the far corner under the arches where the King stood with Lord Roberts and the politicians. It was strange that Carrington could attack Salisbury vehemently in the House, yet here they were hobnobbing quite happily. They were listening to Lord Roberts.

'Kitchener has beaten them, sir,' he maintained.

'Yes, but they won't surrender,' the King growled. He still seemed irritated.

'It's only a question of time, sir,' Roberts explained. 'His system of blockhouses and concentration camps has made it impossible for the Boer commandos to operate.'

'They're saying abroad that it's inhuman,' Carrington said. 'A disgrace to a civilised nation.'

Roberts stiffened. He did not take kindly to criticism by civilians. 'It's the only means of bringing the war to a successful conclusion,' Balfour replied for him.

Cornwallis-West knew there was bitter censure of the Army's policy in South Africa. Kitchener had experience of this kind of fighting before, against the Mahdi's dervishes in the Sudan, and had realised that conventional warfare would not work. He was facing an enemy whose forces were scattered over a vast terrain, skilled horsemen with an intimate knowledge of the territory, able to pick up supplies from hundreds of upcountry homesteads and villages. They ambushed slow-moving infantry columns, blew up railway tracks and attacked remote garrisons. By day, many of them posed as simple farmers and, at night, raided as guerrillas, butchering sentries and pickets and cutting telegraph wires. Kitchener moved his garrisons back closer to his lines of communication. Every mile along the railway tracks he built small blockhouses, connected by telephone to larger camps at all stations and bridges. The blockhouses were carried on across the whole territory, until there were over five thousand of them dividing it into eight irregular squares. Inside the squares, all food and livestock was slowly gathered in and the civilian population moved into large camps of concentration to prevent aid, supplies or information reaching the enemy. The camps were well-planned, with medical services and teachers for the children.

Kitchener reinforced his infantry with thirty thousand mounted rifles from Britain and the colonies, Canadians, New Zealanders and Australian Bushmen, lightly armed and highly mobile, as skilled in rough country as the Boers themselves. As they cleared each square, it was occupied by the South African Constabulary, a special mounted force under Colonel Baden-Powell, the hero of Mafeking. The enemy commandos were gradually pushed back against the line of blockhouses where they had either to fight or surrender. The system of strangulation was uniquely effective. Unfortunately, in many of the camps, insanitary conditions spread disease and a great number of women and children died. In the nations opposed to the war, Britain was furiously condemned. In the country, itself, opinions were sharply divided. In the political parties, most, but not all Conservatives were determined that the war must be brought to an end by whatever means were necessary. Among the Liberals and their allies, the Socialists, most, but not all condemned Kitchener's methods as barbarous and clamoured for the resignation of the government that permitted them.

'What's the point of winning the war if we lose our prestige?' Carrington asked.

'Kitchener can't stop now, when he's so near victory,' Roberts told him. 'I repeat, it's only a question of time.'

'But in that time more lives will be lost,' the King said. 'Can't they see it's futile to go on?' His godson realised that what he had taken for irritation was really an urgent anxiety. The others were silent as the King went on. 'I've had letters from young Ponsonby. Winston Churchill confirms what he tells me. I think I know those Boers. They hang on with a kind of desperate gallantry. Surely they understand we'd give them honourable terms?'

113

'Negotiations are ready to begin, sir,' Roberts answered. 'As soon as they wish.'

'How long will it take?'

Roberts hesitated. 'Six or seven months, sir.'

'Six months?' The King echoed. He sighed. 'Can I depend on that?'

'It must be over by May of next year, sir,' Roberts assured him.

'Then the Coronation could be in early June,' Salisbury said. We could celebrate it and the end of the war at the same time.'

The King nodded. 'As soon as possible. Thank you, Lord Roberts.'

Roberts bowed, 'Your Majesty.'

The King walked past and headed for the door to the stairs. George Cornwallis-West watched him leave. He would never make him out. Was he worried about the carnage of the war—or only about when he would be crowned?

Alice Keppel admired the Queen. Alexandra was always unfailingly kind to her and never for a moment showed that she knew her friendship with her husband was closer than any of a number of others. Alice was invited to Marlborough House, even to Sandringham, although Alexandra had utterly refused to accept Daisy Warwick as a guest there. But then, Daisy had exulted openly in being Bertie's mistress and could not resist demonstrating her hold over him. Seeing her so gracious to Alice, people wondered if the Queen had conquered all jealousy, perhaps she no longer had any real feelings for her husband. It was not that Alexandra was unaware of the relationship. She simply chose to ignore it.

Footmen were setting up tables for cards in the drawing-room at Marlborough House after dinner. Alice sat with the Queen, Princess Victoria and Charlotte Knollys, listening to Luis de Soveral who was describing a boar hunt he had been on in Albania. Bertie stood with Francis Knollys, Esher and Charles Carrington. They were all in evening dress, the ladies still in black or dark purple. This damned mourning, Bertie had muttered to his valet, it makes everything so depressing. It had been correct and fitting at first, but now it had become irksome. He was grateful that Alix and he had real friends they liked spending the evenings

114

with and that the long year was nearly done. Never again, he vowed. It's far too long to be cooped up. If he were to make his mark at all on the country, it had to be out where he could be seen.

'I'm sure Albania is very beautiful, Luis,' Alix said. 'But you must come with us to Denmark this year.'

'I'd be honoured, ma'am.' Soveral bowed and moved to join the gentlemen. He smiled to Bertie. 'It appears you have a travelling companion, sir. You have often told me of the round of simple pleasures there. Once you have visited the museums, heard the opera and sampled the cheeses, what do you do?'

'Start at the beginning again,' Carrington drawled.

They laughed. 'Exactly,' Bertie agreed. 'Most days our most strenuous occupation is trying not to fall asleep.'

'The Amalienborg must be the dullest place in Europe,' Knollys chuckled.

Bertie's eyes fixed on him, narrowing. 'How dare you say that?' he growled. The others stopped smiling at once. Knollys was frozen, afraid of one of his sudden blistering rages. 'Oh, I forgot, Francis,' Bertie added casually. 'You've never been to *Bernstorff.*'

He rumbled into laughter and the others joined in, relieved.

Alix had been watching them, trying to hear. 'I wish you'd speak up, Bertie,' she said. 'I can hear what Luis says perfectly, but you always mumble.'

'Sorry, my dear,' he apologised, then repeated louder. 'Sorry!'

Alix winced. 'There's no need to shout.' She rose. 'Now everyone who wants to play Bridge, come along.' She took Soveral's hand. 'Luis shall be my partner, then I can hear what he calls.' She led him towards the two card tables. Carrington and Esher escorted Toria and Charlotte Knollys.

As she sat at one of the tables, Alix turned and saw that Alice Keppel had stopped beside Bertie. He murmured to her and smiled.

'Come along, Bertie!' she called.

'You'll have to excuse me,' Bertie said. 'Francis and I have work to do.'

'Nonsense!' Alix protested. 'You started before breakfast. Now come and behave like a human being.'

He hesitated, then gave in, smiling. 'Oh, very well.' They came to the table where Soveral stood facing her. Knollys

115

handed Alice to one of the spare seats and Bertie sat opposite her. Then Soveral sat and the others at their table.

'You'd better keep score, Francis,' Bertie said. 'I'm no good at counting.'

'Why do you want to work so hard, anyway?' Alix asked.

'There's a lot to catch up on,' Bertie grunted. 'And when mourning ends, we'll have to go out in society, show ourselves. There won't be so much time.'

Alix had not really heard him. She shook her head and turned to Esher at the next table. 'Could I possibly have one of your cigarettes, Reggie?'

'Motherdear!' Toria exclaimed.

'Certainly, ma'am,' Esher said. He rose, offering his case.

As a footman lit the Queen's cigarette, Alice caught herself staring and looked away. Somehow, she had never imagined Alexandra with a cigarette. She saw Bertie twinkling and smiled back briefly. Esher held his cigarette case towards her and she took one.

'I'm so glad we have a little vice in common, Mrs. Keppel,' Alix said. About to light her cigarette, Alice glanced up. The Queen smiled. 'Only an occasional one with me. I picked up the habit from my sister. Of course, she smokes those horrid Russian things, cardboard tubes with half an inch of old rope at the end.' Soveral chuckled as he dealt. Alice Keppel smiled. She wondered, as many had done before her, just how artless the Queen's apparently innocent remarks were. 'What are we playing for?' Alix asked.

'Whatever you like,' Bertie said, sorting his cards.

Alix shrugged. 'Well, nothing too much. Remember Parliament didn't vote me nearly as much money as you.' The people at both tables laughed. She looked over at Soveral. 'What do you suggest, partner?'

Soveral screwed up his face as though in intense concentration. 'Would penny points be too much?'

'As long as the cards don't run against us,' Alix sighed. She started to assemble her hand.

'How are the redecorations going, ma'am?' Alice asked her.

'Perfectly. Perfectly. We're only staying on here until they are complete.' Alix paused. For a second, her face was pensive. 'Funny to think that in a few weeks this house will be Georgie's.'

'You give one up—you get two bigger ones in its place,' Bertie muttered. He winked across to Alice.

116

Soveral had sorted his hand very quickly. He closed it and fanned it open again. 'I see the first official Ball at the Palace is the day before full mourning ends,' he observed.

'Yes, it's awkward,' Bertie agreed. 'Still, it can't be helped.'

Alice looked at the Queen. 'I wanted to ask you what to wear, ma'am,' she smiled.

Alix was still arranging her cards into suits, her cigarette in the corner of her mouth. 'Whatever you like,' she said, not glancing up.

'The ladies were hoping for a directive from you,' Alice went on. 'Are we to come out of black?'

'I am trying to concentrate, Mrs Keppel,' Alix told her. 'You must wear what you think most suitable.' She took her cigarette from her mouth, flicked it and sat back considering her hand.

Alice queried Bertie silently. He shrugged his arms, unable to interfere. Alice took stock of her cards. 'No bid,' she said.

They waited for Alix. 'Three no trumps,' she announced.

Bertie chuckled and turned. Soveral's face was an actor's mask of despair. As he gazed across at Alexandra, she looked up and smiled at him.

Redecorated and restored, the ballroom at Buckingham Palace was stunning in its magnificence. By far the largest of the State Apartments, this was where Bertie planned to hold not only balls but presentations and investitures.

At one end was the Royal dais. Under a high, carved arch hung a huge, bell-shaped crimson canopy, richly embroidered, with the Royal arms in gold on its central panel. The front of the canopy was looped up and back to reveal the golden chairs of state for the King and his Consort. On either side of the thrones were scarlet sofas for the members of the Royal Family. The dais was flanked by tall Corinthian columns in marble, with gilded capitals. Against the wall at the opposite end of the ballroom was an organ, in front of which sat the orchestra.

The walls of the great salon were panelled in crimson silk. The floor was of polished inlaid oak and the ceiling, above superb plaster mouldings, was coved and gilded. Built into the walls were pairs of stucco Corinthian columns, painted to resemble porphyry. Between them hung full-length portraits of Queen Victoria and the Prince Consort, and Van Dyck's Charles the First and Henrietta Maria.

Along either side of the hall were three tiers of seats. The old gasoliers with their encrustment of soot had been replaced. The lighting came from gilt-bronze candelabra on the walls and a range of crystal electric chandeliers hanging from gold bosses in the ceiling.

The guests gathered in the ballroom had been impressed by the splendours of the rooms of the renovated palace, glimpsed on their journey from the entrance courtyard. The ballroom astounded them. The King had kept his promise and the Queen had fully justified his trust in her taste. The new court was proving to be the most colourful and sumptuous the palace had ever seen. The lights glittered on the gold lace, stars and decorations of the many diplomatic and military uniforms. Yet the overall appearance of the guests was sombre, so many of the gentlemen in black evening dress, and all the ladies in black or dark purple gowns, relieved only here and there by lighter violet or silver. Most eyes kept turning to the massive sculptured doors at the end near the dais. One led to the supper room, the other to the anteroom. The orchestra played softly, quiet background music, and everyone waited for the entrance of the King and Queen.

Bertie was waiting with George and May in a small chamber off the anteroom. He was furious. It was their first Royal Ball and Alix was late. His son and daughter-in-law and equerries watched as he paced, almost at the limit of his patience. He was just about to send an aide to demand the Queen's immediate presence when he was told she was arriving. He strode out into the anteroom and stopped, staring. Alix was coming towards him, followed by Toria and Charlotte Knollys.

In the ballroom, the buzz of conversation rose to an audible gasp and then ceased totally as the King and Queen entered. The men bowed and the ladies curtsied, gazing incredulously at Alexandra. She was dressed from head to foot in pure white, a dazzling snow-white ballgown, and white, elbow-length gloves. Her upper arms were bare and the neck of the gown was cut low and round, ending in slight puffs just below her shoulders, revealing the entire slope of her shoulders and the creamy swell of her high bosom. Round her slender throat was a choker of diamonds and pearls. Her burnished copper hair was swept up into a multitude of small curls. and set on it was a tiara made of a diamond circlet and three diamond fleurs-de-lis. Even her fan was of ivory. In contrast, the sky-blue of her eyes and the red gold of her hair seemed more vivid. She was radiantly, astonishingly beautiful and she smiled, delighted by the effect she had produced.

Alice Keppel was standing with her tall husband and Soveral. She became aware that her mouth was open and closed it as Soveral smiled at her. After a moment, she smiled back. She glanced round the salon as their Majesties advanced and the guests bowed and curtsied individually. Among the King's charming favourites here, she could see Mrs Willy James, Mrs Ronald Greville, Mrs Arthur Paget and Daisy Warwick, herself, still lovely but putting on far too much weight. They all looked shaken. She smiled and curtsied deeply as the Queen passed on the King's arm, acknowledging her victory.

The Chamberlain signed to the orchestra and they began to play a waltz as the Queen had requested. She and Bertie opened the Ball. After they had made one complete circuit alone, the other dancers joined them. Bertie was smiling to Alix, proud of her. As the dancers swirled and turned, she seemed to glow with her own light, singled out among the dark dresses of the court.

Alix had transformed the private apartments. Her own rooms, once Victoria's, she had made bright and attractive. They were not less cluttered with photographs and mementos than they had been, but the furniture was comfortably modern and the colour schemes were much lighter. Bertie was with her in her bedroom, looking round.

'Toria and Charlotte are happy with their accommodation at last, so that's a blessing,' she said.

'It's charming, my dear,' Bertie told her. 'Charming. I honestly never thought these rooms could be made so pleasant.'

She smiled and kissed his cheek, before leading the way out into the dressing-room. Bertie paused before following her. His weight had noticeably increased. He was slower and not feeling well, but hiding it.

'I was worried about our rooms facing north,' Alix said as he joined her. 'But it doesn't seem to matter.' The small dressing-room was in a restful, pale green, picked out in gold. She clicked her tongue. 'It's ridiculous that in this enormous barracks we should have so little space for ourselves. Still, I have some ideas.'

'I'm sure you have,' he smiled. He sat gratefully on one of the painted white chairs.

'You said I could have a completely free hand.'

'It's your home,' Bertie assured her. 'Here, we do as you say.'

Alix had realised how pale he was. 'Are you all right, Bertie?'

'A little tired, that's all,' he conceded. He rose as she moved to the door, heading for the private sitting-room.

He was pleased also by the sitting-room. It was bright and sunny and the accent was on elegant but solid comfort. The portraits of past Royalty by Lely, Kneller, Gainsborough and Lawrence had been hung again in their places once the walls had been repapered. There was a piano for Alix, a desk and masses of flowers in Dresden vases. In addition to the sofas and armchairs, there was a wide seat under the deep bay window. Alix was waiting for his verdict.

He nodded. 'I feel at home—already.'

She was delighted. 'I thought we'd be troubled by traffic, but you can't hear anything.'

'Very true,' Bertie agreed. He could tell by her expression that she had not heard what he said. He chuckled. 'Everything you have done is perfect.'

Alix smiled. 'Why don't you sit down? I'll ring for tea.'

'I can't, unfortunately,' he told her regretfully. 'Knollys is waiting.'

'You're not going to work any more today,' Alix protested, disappointed.

'It has to be done.'

'What?'

'Well, for example,' Bertie said, 'in her last illness, Mama left thousands of Army commissions unsigned. I'm not going to send young men out to die with a rubber stamp. I'm trying to see to as many as possible myself.'

The King's study, too, had been modernised. As in the rest of the palace, electric light had been installed. 'I'll be spending more time here than in the Throne Room,' Bertie had said, so it was comfortable as well as businesslike. There were welcoming, leather armchairs, cabinets of reference books, a telephone on the walnut dask and some of his favourite sporting prints, photographs of his yacht, *Britannia,* under sail and his racehorses, Persimmon and

Diamond Jubilee, on the walls, with watercolours of Balmoral and Windsor.

Bertie was seated, reading by the light of a desk lamp. Knollys and Arthur Davidson, who had taken over from Ponsonby as Assistant Private Secretary, were standing, waiting for him to finish the day's correspondence. Davidson was almost asleep on his feet. He could not imagine how the King kept going. Bertie glanced round at them. 'Why don't you sit down?' Knollys and Davidson hesitated. Bertie waved his hand at them. 'Come on, none of that nonsense.'

Knollys sat at the side of the desk near Bertie and Davidson eased into a chair by the door. 'Thank you, sir.' Knollys said.

Bertie grunted. He initialled the report from the Home Office he had been reading and laid it aside. He picked up several pages in meticulous, italic writing. 'What's this, Francis?'

'It's a protest, I'm afraid, sir. From Cardinal Vaughan on behalf of the Roman Catholic community.'

'What about?'

'They took great exception to the Protestant bias of the declaration, in your first speech from the throne on the opening of Parliament,' Knollys reported.

Bertie swung round to face him. 'I *told* Salisbury,' he said, annoyed. 'The whole thing is centuries out of date. All that stuff about the sacrifice of the Mass and the invocation of the Virgin Mary being idolatrous and superstitious.'

'It would need an Act of Parliament to change it, sir,' Davidson pointed out, diffidently.

'As head of the Church of England, you were required by law to make the declaration,' Knollys added.

'Otherwise I should not have,' Bertie stated. 'But there's no reason why my son should have to when it's his turn.' The other two were silent. 'Surely in this day and age, some new declaration could be worked out that would not give offence to a third of the country? Arthur, write to whoever's responsible—the Chancellor—and tell him I want it done.'

'I shall inform him of Your Majesty's opinions and wishes,' Davidson said carefully.

Bertie missed Ponsonby's directness. 'Be as diplomatic as you please,' he snorted. 'Only make sure they do something about it.' He scribbled a few lines at the foot of the Cardinal's letter to indicate the shape of the reply to be sent. 'Get this off at once, will you?'

As Davidson rose to take the letter, there was a knock at the door. He opened it and an Equerry came in, carrying a telegram on a silver salver. He bowed to the King. 'It was sent *en clair*, sir. From His Imperial Majesty, the German Emperor.'

Bertie unfolded the telegram and read it. He read it again more carefully and looked up at Knollys. 'My nephew,' he said slowly, 'my nephew congratulates me on the generosity of the surrender terms we've offered the Boers.'

Salisbury watched in silence as Lord Lansdowne read the telegram. They had been received in the small Audience Room. Contrary to his usual custom, the King had not asked them to sit.

Lansdowne had told the Prime Minister that he intended to protest most strongly at being summoned like a schoolboy to the headmaster. In the King's presence, seeing the clear blue eyes fixed on him, his self-assurance had dwindled. Out of the corner of his eye he could make out the heavy figure, seated, his beard jutting forward and the fingers of his right hand drumming on his thigh. Lansdowne shook his head and handed back the telegram. 'I am at a loss to understand it, sir,' he confessed.

Bertie's fingers stopped their impatient tattoo. 'Is it true?' he rapped.

Lansdowne glanced at Salisbury. 'It is true,' the Prime Minister began, 'undoubtedly true that Kitchener has given the Boer commanders an opportunity to meet, to hold a conference to discuss their situation without fear of attack, south of Johannesburg.' Bertie nodded. 'Also we may assume that the High Commissioner in South Africa, Lord Milner, as Your Majesty agreed, has conveyed to them the conditions on which we would accept their surrender.'

'What the final terms were or whether they have been acceded to, we have not heard,' Lansdowne added.

'Then perhaps you should ask the Kaiser?' Bertie suggested drily.

Lansdowne's mouth opened to object but Salisbury spoke first. 'It might be as well, sir,' he agreed. 'As you have frequently mentioned, the German Intelligence service is remarkably swift and accurate. Would you care to communicate with him?'

'I would not,' Bertie said flatly. 'I will not be forced again into revealing to the Kaiser my lack of knowledge of important developments inside the British Empire.'

'In this case, your Government does not have the information either,' Lansdowne protested.

'Can you imagine what sport the German Foreign Office would make of that?' Bertie observed. Lansdowne stiffened. The very idea was humiliating. Bertie smiled briefly.

'Perhaps it may give you and your colleagues some inkling of how I have so often been made to feel in the past.'

'Quite so, sir,' Salisbury conceded. 'However, it would be very unfortunate if the terms of the peace were to be generally known in the Wilhelmstrasse before they were announced in London.'

Bertie looked from the Prime Minister to the Foreign Secretary. It was a matter that needed an oblique kind of diplomacy at which neither of them was adept. 'Very well,' he sighed. 'Get in touch with Lascelles in Berlin. He can call on the Kaiser on my behalf. No doubt, my Imperial nephew will be only too pleased to enlighten him with the details over lunch.'

When Salisbury and Lansdowne had bowed and left, Bertie sat for some minutes until the pain which had gnawed at his belly throughout the interview, and which he had concealed, receded. It left him pale and drained. If Wilhelm's information was correct, as it usually was, then the war would soon be over and peace confirmed by the date Roberts had predicted. The long-delayed Coronation could go ahead. He pushed himself to his feet and winced, holding his side, as the pain stabbed him again. He walked slowly through into the study, where his new friend, Caesar, was waiting for him. Caesar was a white, long-haired fox-terrier, an intelligent, alert little dog of great character. Between them there had sprung up an instant rapport and he responded to Bertie's moods in a way that was almost uncanny. He stood up, wagging his tail questioningly.

'No, no, Caesar,' Bertie told him. 'I have to work.' Caesar trotted over to Bertie's chair and stretched out beside it as Bertie sat heavily at the desk, which was covered with papers, lists of appointments, letters and reports. He grunted and reached for his pen, refusing to admit to himself that he was tired, more tired than he could ever remember. He told himself it was only this weight he kept putting on. His waistline seemed to increase daily although he was trying

123

to eat sensibly as his friend Agnes Keyser, Sister Agnes, had recommended and to cut down his smoking as Alix insisted. The pen slipped in his fingers and he made himself concentrate. He had decided against inviting crowned heads to the Coronation, only heirs and representatives. Even so, the numbers to be accommodated and entertained would be enormous and the difficulties of precedence immeasurably complex. It was too complicated to trust to others. He found the preliminary list of foreign guests he had made and began to write quickly, annotating it for his staff.

The door behind him opened and Alix swept in. She was wearing a lavender afternoon dress with a high-standing, lace collar and carried some sheets of sketching paper. 'I cannot get any sense out of them!' she declared. Bertie looked round, startled. 'No one has the faintest idea what is the correct dress for a Queen Consort to wear at a Coronation.'

Bertie realised what was troubling her and nodded. He turned back and went on writing.

Alix came to stand beside him. 'The Grand Duchess Augusta is the only one old enough to remember what Adelaide wore at William the Fourth's,' she said. 'That was over seventy years ago and it sounds frightful!' She dropped the sketching paper on top of the list Bertie was working at. 'Look at these.'

'My dear——' he protested.

'I've designed them myself,' Alix went on, paying no attention. 'I know better than all the milliners and antiquaries. I shall wear exactly what I like.'

'Of course, of course,' Bertie muttered. He glanced at the sketches. They were line drawings of various styles of gowns and robes. 'Yes, very nice.' He pushed them aside.

'Come and see,' Alix said.

'Alix,' he explained patiently. 'I have invitations and arrangements to make.'

'What arrangements?'

'Well . . . what honours do I give? Who has to be met personally?'

'Leave all that to your secretaries,' she told him.

'I cannot,' Bertie insisted. 'Where do we put people up? More than half the princes in Europe will be coming.'

'There's lots of room here. And Georgie can have some at Marlborough House,' Alix decided. She took the pen from his hand and laid it back in the stand. 'Now, come on —I want to show you some material I've chosen.'

'Alix——!' Bertie warned.

'Don't you care what I'm going to wear?' she asked, surprised. 'You insist on knowing everything else.' She stood her ground, gazing at him until he gave in and rose to follow her. She did not notice his choked-off grunt of pain as he pushed himself to his feet. 'Come on, Caesar,' he sighed. 'Let's go and look at the frocks.'

Peace in South Africa was agreed on the last day of May, 1902. It was greeted with great rejoicing throughout the British Isles and the Empire. Yet the celebrations were oddly muted. The victory was disproportionate to the effort, the fearful loss in materials and men. Because the victory had also been inevitable, the length of time it took before it was achieved robbed it of much of its triumph. Britain's popularity abroad had been damaged immeasurably and her prestige had suffered from a war that was forced on her and brought little immediate gain in return.

Bertie attended a thanksgiving service at St Paul's with Alix and George and May. As he knelt in prayer, he thought of the friends and sons of friends who had died, the crippled and maimed, the children in the camps. In my lifetime, it will not happen again, he swore. As he had promised Nicholas, and as Wilhelm had reported, the terms given to the defeated Boers were more than generous. Milner became Governor of the two new possessions, the Transvaal and the Orange Free State. There was to be no death penalty for those who had been British subjects and had rebelled. In return for the others laying down their arms and swearing allegiance to the Crown, all prisoners were released and returned to their homes. Dutch was to be taught alongside English in the schools. Civil government was established and arrangements made for Boer participation, and the British Cabinet granted millions of pounds to restock the Boer farms. Magnanimity in victory did something to restore British prestige, but Bertie had no illusions. Even that had its dangers.

Yet, after so long, the people felt the need to rejoice full-heartedly and the Coronation, fixed for June 'he twenty-sixth, gave them the cause. There could be no reservations about that. The King's obvious care for his roops, his personal sorrow, his self-denial in waiting until peace

125

was declared to be crowned, the persistent rumour that his life was in danger, all had built his popularity to a staggering height. The end of the war had scarcely been announced when the excitement and the frenzied preparations began. Designs for commemorative medals had been approved, for mugs, tin trays, tea-sets, chocolate boxes and coloured prints. An army of workmen began to erect the great wooden stands for visitors and sightseers along the route of the procession and the decorations, the flags and bunting and banners, were hung. Every house in the United Kingdom had its window display, every street its flags and streamers, every town prepared its bonfires and fireworks and every city its festivals, concerts and civic parades.

In perfect weather, the foreign guests and their suites began to arrive in London, the Crown Princes, Archdukes, Nabobs and Maharajahs. Members of the Royal Family met them at the principal stations and crowds gathered to cheer as squadrons of mounted Life Guards escorted them through the streets. For reasons of state, none of them were staying at Buckingham Palace. Some were at Marlborough House. Others were guests at many of the fashionable houses, whose owners had been asked to offer accommodation. London society burst into a flurry of entertainments, brilliant receptions, balls and dinners. From all over Europe and the Empire, nobles and dignitaries flocked to the capital, from the Middle East, the New World and Asia. The Savoy, Claridges and the new Ritz and all the other leading hotels had been booked out for months. Unheard-of prices were asked and paid for seats with a view of the Coronation parade. Visitors arriving from the provinces with nowhere to stay slept on boarding house floors or camped in the public parks. And still more crowded in. And contingents of troops brought back from the Cape and from the Dominions to line the route and march in the procession spilled out of the barracks into tented cities in Hyde Park and St James's Park, and a bewildering variety of colours and styles of uniform mingled with the gay summer dresses and the parasols and straw hats and bowlers in the streets.

The King was indefatigable, receiving guests, replying to deputations, supervising arrangements and preparations, driving on his staff to ensure that every detail was impeccably organised. A genial, smiling figure at dinners, at the theatre, opening the military tournament, he refused to rest or delegate the smallest duty. He became unusually short-tempered and critical. At times he would lapse into an exhausted, almost despairing silence, suddenly losing all interest in what he was doing or the people around him. He gave up all attempt to diet and his weight increased alarmingly until none of his clothes fitted him. He was drinking more than his friends had ever seen before and chain smoking cigars and cigarettes. He seemed to be urging himself to the limit of physical endurance. Even his closest friends could not discover what was goading him.

George was worried and tackled his mother one day when she came back from a rehearsal of the ceremony at Westminister Abbey, but Alix refused to interfere. She knew that Bertie's doctor, Sir Francis Laking, had advised him to cancel his engagements for a few days to rest and had been angrily shouted down. Bertie would not accept any alteration in the arrangements for the Coronation and became almost violent at the slightest suggestion that he was not well. She could understand why. As the years of waiting dwindled into days, his secret fear was that, somehow, at the last moment, the crown would be denied him.

To honour his army and to celebrate the peace, Bertie travelled down to the huge military establishment at Aldershot in Hampshire where a Coronation Review of forty thousand troops and a presentation of colours to the heroic Highland Light Infantry were to take place. Alix and Toria, George and May were with him, and his brother, Arthur, and his wife and the old Duke of Cambridge. With only a week to go to the Coronation, many of the most important Royal guests were invited.

They stayed in the bleak, comfortless Royal Pavilion. The weather, which had been so perfect and had been looked on as an omen that nothing could go wrong, had begun to change. The Saturday on which they travelled down was cold and damp and, by the time they reached Aldershot, heavy rain was falling, washing the colour from the bunting with which the camp was decorated. The Royal standard hung sodden on its mast and the ground round the pavilion turned into a quagmire. But that night, in spite of the cold and the rain, detachments of the Foot Guards of England, Ireland, Scotland and Wales, the home counties, turned the recreation ground into a scene of weird splendour. The soldiers carrying blazing torches, the sections accompanied by their own bands playing their own folk tunes marched and countermarched. The King and the Royal party watched from a stand in front of the pavilion. Bertie was slumped in his chair, pallid and sweating. The Grand Duke Michael of Russia tried to joke with him about his first visit to St Petersburg when they had driven in sledges by torchlight to a ball at the Winter Palace, but got no response. He asked Toria what was wrong.

Toria complained to Alix, 'Papa is being too boring. Do tell him to take more interest.'

Absorbed, Alix did not hear her. The English Guards had halted facing the stand. The others marched into position, forming a hollow square, and the bands joined together to play 'Rule Britannia', the National Anthem and a final hymn. As the notes of the hymn died away and the fading torches sputtered in the rain, a lone bugle played 'Lights Out' and the tattoo was ended.

Bertie excused himself and went straight to his room. Alix stayed for dinner with the guests in the main salon, gossiping and laughing. She was an incomparable hostess and soon the chill of the surroundings and the King's absence were forgotten.

Some time later, on her way to bed, Toria saw the light on in her father's room and looked in to say goodnight. She found him on his feet, fully dressed still in his uniform. He was bent over a table, supporting himself with both hands. His eyes were staring and his face congested as he fought for air. 'Quick . . . quickly . . .' he gasped. 'Undo my belt—I can't—can't breathe. . . .'

Shaking with fear, she hurried to him to unfasten the buckle of his belt, but the belt was strained so tightly round the bulk of his body that she could not move it. She only hurt her fingers. She left him and ran to his valet's room. The valet had been drinking with the soldiers and was fuddled. He could not even understand what she wanted. Hurrying back to the corridor, Toria saw her mother saying goodnight to May and the Duchess to Connaught. She signalled to her to come urgently, without alarming the others. Alix could not make out what Toria whispered to her but saw her agitation and followed her quickly into Bertie's bedroom.

He was still leaning on the table, weaker, gulping in shallow breaths which scarcely reached his lungs. Alix saw at once what was wrong. Without panic, she told Toria to help support him and looked round the room. On a stand by his bed was a tray of lobster salad and fruit that had been left for hm. She grabbed the knife from it and sawed at the belt, cutting it in two. He collapsed on to the couch at the foot of his bed, tearing open the buttons down the front of his tight tunic.

As he sprawled back against the couch, sucking in air, trembling, his eyes glazed with pain, Alix realised why he had been so unlike himself these last months, so abrupt and bad-tempered, seeing for the first time how ill he really was.

Chapter

8

Sir Francis Laking was an extremely able doctor, but he also knew his patient. Summoned to Aldershot in the middle of the night, his examination confirmed what he had already suspected. The King's condition was critical and he ought to be operated on without delay. That would mean an indefinite postponement of the Coronation which, in the King's present state of weakness and restless excitability, could cause a violent reaction that might well be fatal. The only other hope he had of survival was if he rested completely and kept to a strict diet. If so, there was just a chance that he could stand the strain of the ceremony and the dangerous operation might even be avoided. Laking decided against alarming the King unless it became absolutely essential.

To calm Alix's anxiety, Bertie had told her that he was only suffering from a chill and a touch of bronchitis and he accepted Laking's diagnosis eagerly, that the chill had brought on a severe attack of lumbago. He objected to the treatment of rest and diet but bouts of giddiness, high temperature and the recurrent pain in his lower abdomen made him submit. He could not attend the church parade on the Sunday and, next day, he returned to Windsor, twenty miles at walking speed in a closed, horse-drawn carriage, with every jolt and lurch an agony. Alexandra took his place at the Coronation Review, seated in an open barouche at the saluting-point with Toria opposite her and George, Prince of Wales, stationed on horseback behind their carriage. During the hours of the march past and the presentation of the colours, none of the men seeing her poise and smiling interest could have told that it hid a deep and growing distress.

The general public was not unduly concerned until the following day when the King was expected to attend Ascot Races to inaugurate the new stands. The return of better weather tempted many thousands to the course for what was to be a joyous social occasion. The arrival of Alix, alone in her carriage with George and May, made all the rumours that had been circulating about the King's health suddenly more disturbing. Surely nothing except serious illness would have made him miss the first visit of his reign to Ascot? Yet the public was reassured by the official medical bulletins saying the King only had a severe chill and needed to rest.

At Windsor, Bertie chafed and protested at having to stay in bed on a milk diet, when there was so much still to do, so many final details to be checked. He insisted on getting up in the late mornings and working through the afternoons with Knollys and Davidson. He received the officer bringing the peace despatches from Lord Kitchener and went for short drives round the estate, with Caesar perched up beside him like an extra Equerry. He felt exhausted now by the slightest activity, yet he would not show it, and he forced himself to ignore the constant pains, passing off the moments of faintness and breathlessness with a chuckle, as the result of too much smoking. Those who did not know how ill he really was were impressed by his vigour and remarked at the obvious good his rest was doing him. Only Laking knew how much effort it cost and he became increasingly concerned as he realised the King's condition was deteriorating.

Members of the Cabinet and a few of Bertie's closest friends joined him in a house party at Windsor the weekend before the Coronation. He refused to worry them by cancelling it or by staying in bed. He had missed a great part of the festivities and entertainments to which he had been looking forward so eagerly and he would not give up this final moment when he had asked his friends to celebrate with him.

The weekend began badly when Lansdowne told him the Government had invited the Shah of Persia to pay a State Visit later in the year. It was a purely political invitation, an attempt to counteract the influence of Russia on Persia. Since the Treasury had refused to back an enormous loan which the Shah needed to prop up his corrupt regime, he had turned down the invitation until it was suggested to him that, if he came, he would be sure to be given the Order of the Garter, the most noble and coveted order of chivalry in the world. Bertie was furious. He could not make the infamous, dissolute Shah a Knight of the Garter nor let it be used as a pawn in a political game. Lansdowne retreated, confused. The Duke of Devonshire, the former Lord Hartington, now President of the Privy Council, advised him to drop the whole matter. Apart from anything else, the Garter was an exclusively Christian Order and the King was right to protect it from becoming debased.

Bertie's other friends brought more cheering news and he was relieved to hear from Esher that the arrangements for his Coronation Dinner were progressing well. This was the project that meant most to him personally of all the year's festivities, a gigantic dinner to be given to all the poorer people of London, over half a million of them spread throughout the metropolitan districts to be fed and entertained at the King's expense. He had organised it, himself, with the Lord Mayor and the Mayors of the various boroughs and his yachting friend, Sir Thomas Lipton. The meal was to be served by voluntary helpers at the same time on the same day in public buildings, halls and parks all over the city. He had provided thirty thousand pounds to pay for it. Touched by the King's generosity, many people offered to contribute but he would not let the committee accept money, only gifts in kind. An anonymous donor presented five hundred thousand specially engraved invitation cards. Fifteen hundred musicians and music hall artists volunteered their services. Among the presents from many leading manufacturers were china beakers, a King's Cup for every guest from the Royal Doulton Company, twenty-eight thousand gallons of ale from the Bass Breweries and a box of chocolates with the King and Queen's portraits for every guest and helper from Rowntrees of York. The assured succes of his dinner delighted Bertie.

At his house party that weekend, Esher, Luis de Soveral and Alice Keppel were concerned about him. Although he seemed tireless and joked and laughed with them, they could tell that he was in pain and that only his strength of will kept him going. Alice was very afraid for him. Soveral had seen less of him recently than the others and was appalled by the change in him, his haunted, darkly shadowed eyes, his swollen body, his breathlessness. Sensing their anxiety, he tried to reassure them by showing how active he was. Animated, hearty, he ate, drank and exerted himself to amuse them. After lunch on the Sunday, he took them on a guided tour of the magnificently redecorated castle, himself, with Caesar running ahead of them, wagging his tail. He marched them from the library with its oriental miniatures and illuminated manuscripts to the Waterloo Chamber, the picture gallery and the armoury, the Rubens room, St George's Hall and the restyled red, green and white drawing-rooms. His father's former apartments overlooking the East Terrace had been completely renovated for his own use and now included a smoking and billiard room. The colours here were mainly crimson and gold, except for his bedroom which was a soft, dark green.

He would not let them pause in any one place. They purposely walked slowly so that he could rest but he urged them on to see everything. By the time he led them out on to the terrace, they were limping and exhausted. It pleased him to see them more out of breath than he was.

Soveral tried to delay him by telling him stories of the flamboyant Prince Danilo, Crown Prince of little Montenegro, who had waltzed into London for the Coronation with a pretty woman he had met on the journey.

Bertie chuckled. 'Where's he keeping her?'

'At his side, day and night,' Soveral told him. 'He takes her to all the best dinners and receptions and introduces her as his wife's lady-in-waiting.'

'He's not married,' Bertie said.

'Precisely, sir,' Soveral agreed. 'But short of causing a diplomatic scandal, what are the hostesses to do?'

Bertie laughed and marched on, determined to finish the circuit. When they reached the Great Drawing-room again, his guests were ready to collapse. 'There now! How was that?' he asked triumphantly.

'It was the most enjoyable forced march I have ever endured,' Soveral gasped. The others laughed.

'No stamina, that's your trouble, Luis,' Bertie smiled. He snapped his fingers. 'I know—after tea we'll get the old skittles set up.'

'Please—Your Gracious Majesty,' Soveral protested, 'spare us the skittles. I doubt if I have strength even to deal a pack of cards.'

Chuckling, Bertie handed Alice to the sofa and sat beside her. He hoped she had not noticed his unsteadiness as they walked along the last corridor. He did not want her upset. Alice was grateful to sit down, but more grateful that he was off his feet. He looked greyer and was perspiring heavily. She wished he would tell her what was wrong. She was very worried.

Leaving them alone, Soveral moved to examine the paintings on the wall. He stopped by a portrait of the children of Charles the First, pretending to study it. 'Reggie,' he called, 'You know about pictures—who's this by?'

Esher joined him. 'Van Dyck, I fancy.'

Soveral glanced at the King who was talking quietly to Alice. He lowered his voice. 'Why is he behaving like this?'

'He's trying to prove there is nothing wrong with him,' Esher murmured.

'That's obvious,' Soveral said. 'But what *is* wrong? Is he ill?'

'He won't admit it,' Esher sighed. 'And he won't pay any attention to his doctors, not with the Coronation only three days away.'

'Is there nothing we can do?'

'Tell him to postpone it? When the whole country's geared to it?' Esher shook his head. 'He's waited too long already.'

Bertie had recovered his breath. His head was singing but the pain in his abdomen had stopped when he sat. 'Well, what do you think of Windsor?' he asked Alice.

She smiled. 'Most impressive.'

He nodded. 'It's good to get away from Town for a few days, isn't it? I couldn't stand all that fuss. There'll be enough to do after . . . afterwards.'

'I thought you had come here to rest,' she chided him gently. 'But you seem to be doing more than ever.'

'Can't stop,' he muttered. 'It's all too important.' He turned. 'Reggie—how are the preparations going?'

'The workmen have nearly finished in the Abbey,' Esher told him. 'You won't recognise the place. And most of the stands are up along the route.'

'Good—good,' Bertie panted.

'The town's filled up already,' Soveral said. 'I don't think I've ever seen London so crowded. You can't get a table at the Ritz. Cesar says the Coronation will make his fortune.'

'Really?' Bertie chuckled, pleased. That reminded him. 'And the dinner—everything's ready?'

'I believe so, sir,' Esher answered. 'Tommy Lipton's got the cooking and delivery all organised. And the gifts are piling up. Oh—the latest is, we've been promised seventy-two thousand gallons of lemonade.'

'It's enough to refloat *Shamrock II,*' Alice said. They laughed.

'The King's Coronation Dinner to the Poor,' Esher murmured. 'It will be the biggest feast in history.'

Bertie was smiling. 'And they've all had their own invitation,' he said, proudly. 'I made up the wording myself. "King Edward heartily bids you welcome to his Coronation Dinner".' He paused. 'It's a day on which I don't want anyone to go without.' He leant back on the sofa, breathless, spent.

'I think perhaps we should leave you,' Alice suggested quietly.

'No, no,' Bertie objected. 'No, I'm perfectly all right,' He pushed himself forward to sit upright, smiling.

Alice nearly wept for him. She made herself smile back. 'Well, if you'll excuse me, I think I should have a little rest before tea.' She glanced at Esher and Soveral and rose.

'I believe that's a good idea, Mrs Keppel,' Esher said, realising what she meant.

'Yes,' Soveral agreed quickly. 'I could do with forty winks. Or fifty.'

Bertie wanted to protest, to keep them with him, but suddenly the idea of being alone, of not having to hide the pain that made him nearly cry out was irresistible. An hour or two of rest and he could get through the evening. He struggled to his feet. 'Hope I haven't walked you all off your feet,' he chuckled.

Esher and Soveral bowed and Esher moved to open the door for Alice. As she reached it, Alix came in and stopped, seeing them. The men bowed again and Alice curtsied. 'You're not all leaving?' Alix asked, surprised.

'We thought we might rest before tea, ma'am,' Alice explained.

She gave her words just the right emphasis and Alix understood at once. 'Ah . . . good. I'll make sure you're called.'

They smiled and went out, closing the door. Bertie sat again abruptly and Alix moved past him, searching among the framed photographs on the sideboards for one of Friedrichshof which she had promised to show Lottie, Duchess of Devonshire. 'Bertie, you really must try to take things a little easier,' she said, not looking at him. She could not find the photograph and turned, annoyed. She gasped. Bertie was lying back in a corner of the sofa, clutching his side, his mouth open in agony. 'Bertie——!' She hurried to him. 'Oh, my darling . . . I'll send for Laking.'

'. . . No.'

'Your own doctor—he'll help you,' Alix said.

Bertie forced his mouth closed and leant over, grunting as a sharper spasm of pain lanced through his intestines. 'No! It will pass,' he told her. And added to himself, Dear God, how long can I bear it?

Alix sat beside him. She could no longer pretend to herself that it was nothing serious, that he would conquer it as he had always done before. 'What is it?' she pleaded. 'Why won't you tell me?'

'Nothing—nothing to be done,' he muttered. 'Laking told me. It can wait.'

But this time it could not wait.

The next day, he had to return to London for a great reception and dinner in the evening at Buckingham Palace for all the Royal guests. Alexandra begged him to stay at Windsor, but he said he would get to the Palace if he had to walk. All night he had been in torment, sweating and feverish. The train journey to Paddington was torture for him and, at the station, dense crowds were waiting. To thunderous cheers, he walked slowly and steadily to the open carriage at the end of the red carpet.

The relief of the crowds at seeing him was intense. Stories had been circulating about his illness and all the old rumours had revived, only slightly lessened by an announcement from Francis Knollys that there was no word of truth in them. Now seeing him in his carriage with Alix beside him, waving and smiling, all their fears were forgotten. Bertie drove through streets filled with shouting, cheering people, flourishing hats and flags, and prayed that he would not faint before he had reached the privacy of the Palace courtyard. At his side, Alix was calm and gracious, smiling at the people's enthusiasm and compelling herself to show neither to them nor Bertie the anguish that filled her.

George had entertained his cousin, the Crown Prince of Germany, to lunch at Marlborough House. As soon as he could excuse himself, he drove to the Palace to hear the latest news of his father. He found his mother and Toria in the private sitting-room. They both looked so distressed that he was almost afraid to ask.

'Papa is ill,' Toria told him. 'Very ill.'

Alix sat on the window seat, gazing out towards the park. She turned as George came to her and kissed her cheek. She took his hand and held it tightly. 'He would not let me cancel the reception tonight,' she faltered. 'But I have forbidden him to go to it.'

'Of course, he mustn't,' George said.

'You will support me?' she begged. 'He is very angry. I sent for Sir Francis Laking but now he will not let himself be examined.'

George hesitated for a moment, as she gazed at him. In these recent months, his father's anger had been unpredictable and frightening but, for his own good, he had to be faced. There was no one else to do it.

Laking had brought another specialist, Sir Thomas Barlow, with him, a dry, taciturn man. They had been with the King for an hour, attempting to reason with him, and had not insist, but was determined not to leave. He glanced failed to get his agreement to an examination. Laking could round as Prince George came in.

Bertie was sitting near the door to his bedroom. He had suffered the doctors' arguments as patiently as he could but his temper was now frayed. 'Not you as well, George . . .' he growled.

'I came to see what Sir Francis said,' George replied, easily.

'I have not yet examined His Majesty,' Laking informed him.

'Things are bad enough without half the doctors in London poking and prodding,' Bertie said. 'I've stood it so far. I can last another two days.'

'What do you think it is?' George asked Laking, ignoring his father.

'I would rather not say until I am certain, sir,' Laking answered. 'Not until it is confirmed by Sir Thomas.'

George paused. He could see his father scowling at him. For all their mutual affection, he was secretly terrified of him. 'Then to set all our minds at ease,' he proposed calmly, 'particularly my mother's, perhaps you should begin?'

Laking held his breath. In the silence, the sound of hammering could be heard from outside where the carpenters were erecting the last of the public stands. Bertie rose slowly to his feet. Without looking at George, he went into his

137

bedroom, leaving the door open. Laking and Barlow bowed to George and followed him in.

Left alone, George blinked and suddenly felt in need of a drink. His own firmness had surprised him.

Laking's examination was short, then he stood back to make room for Barlow. The King's bedroom was not large. Indeed, it was fairly cramped, containing only a three-quarter-sized bed with a chair beside it, a washstand and chest-of-drawers and a draught screen. The walls were covered with a floral paper and, above the bed, was a portrait of Albert Victor, Duke of Clarence, the King's elder son who had died of pneumonia ten years before.

When Barlow finished, he stepped back, folding his stethoscope and replacing it in his leather bag which was on the washstand. Bertie sat on the edge of the bed. He was in his shirtsleeves, doing up his waistcoat. 'Well?' he asked tensely.

Barlow was very grave. 'I am afraid I concur with Sir Francis, sir,' he said. 'It is what we suspected. You are suffering from severe perityphlitis.'

Bertie glanced from him to Laking. 'What's that?'

'It is a suppurating abscess, caused by inflammation of the appendix, a small tube in the intestines,' Laking explained. 'A condition sometimes known as appendicitis.'

In the shock of relief, Bertie felt lightheaded for a second. He swayed and closed his eyes. 'I'm sorry. Sorry, Laking,' he muttered. For months he had been remembering the slow, agonising deaths of his brother and his sister. It had seemed inevitable that he had become a victim of the same hideous disease. He breathed out deeply. 'I thought . . . it might be cancer.'

'Unfortunately—at the stage it has reached,' Laking said, 'it is just as serious.'

Bertie's head rose. He stared at the two doctors.

'You must have an immediate operation, sir,' Barlow confirmed.

'Out of the question!' Bertie snapped.

'Sir——' Laking began.

'No!' Bertie controlled himself. 'Do you know what happens the day after tomorrow?!'

'It is my duty——' Laking continued steadily.

'After the Coronation you can cut me in two if you like,' Bertie roared. 'But not till then!'

'Sir, I beg you to listen,' Barlow pleaded.

'How can you suggest it? Do you know what—what I have been going through? I'll stand no more of this!' He pushed himself to his feet and turned his back on them, dismissing them.

The doctors were shaken by his anger. Laking wondered if he should have prepared the King more gradually. In any case, it was too late. He realised the seriousness of cancelling the most solemn and important national ceremony, that had needed immense planning and expense, that involved the Government, the Churches and Armed Forces, thousands of distinguished visitors from abroad, and had roused great excitement not only in Britain but in countless millions throughout the Empire. Cancellation or even postponement of it would result not merely in disappointment but in considerable financial loss to many people. Many of the arrangements for the Coronation were unrepeatable and the unique atmosphere in which it was to be held could never be recaptured. All this was what troubled the King.

Laking had weighed the consequences but the gamble that the operation could be delayed had not come off. He signed to Barlow, discreetly. Barlow hesitated, then took his bag from the washstand and went out, closing the door.

Bertie had busied himself with the buttons of his waistcoat. He turned with a sigh, hearing the door shut, to find that Laking had not moved. 'Leave the room,' he commanded, dangerously quiet.

'Sir, I cannot,' Laking answered. Bertie drew himself up, furious. Laking did not yield. 'I would fail in my duty if I obeyed you.'

His sincerity checked Bertie's anger. 'Laking—I will be crowned,' he said determinedly. 'I shall go to my Coronation, if I die in the Abbey!'

'That is exactly what will happen, sir,' Laking informed him, keeping his voice level and unemotional. 'If you are not operated on by tomorrow morning, it will be too late!'

Bertie was shocked. He had always trusted Laking, yet he could not accept it. 'It's not possible,' he blurted.

'Believe me, sir—nothing is more certain.'

Bertie's legs would not support him any longer. He sank back on to the bed. 'I've borne it for months,' he muttered. 'I can last a few days longer.'

'You have only survived because of the strength of your constitution and your stamina,' Laking said bluntly. 'But

139

now, peritonitis has set in. At the moment, it appears to be localised. If it spreads any more, it will be inoperable and fatal.' The King sat completely motionless, listening. Laking went on, more gently. 'I would have given anything to prevent this becoming inevitable, sir. I have considered all the possibilities—and I do know what a postponement of the Coronation will mean—both to you and to the country.' The King's silence encouraged him. 'In my opinion, it would be too dangerous to move you. I have contacted Sir Frederick Treves, the surgeon, and asked him to attend you tomorrow morning. Tonight we shall fit up your dressing-room as an operating theatre. I have many preparations to make. Do I have Your Majesty's permission?'

Bertie's face was expressionless. He sat so still that Laking wondered, at first, if he had heard. Then his head nodded once, almost imperceptibly. Laking realised his throat was dry. He swallowed, easing the tension in himself, and bowed. He retreated to the door and went out.

Bertie sat, gazing at the wall straight ahead of him, alone and desolate. All his hopes, his ceaseless work, his struggle against unbearable pain had been useless. The secret threat, which he had never been able to forget, had become a reality. 'Will my people ever forgive me?' he whispered.

At the magnificent dinner and reception that night, Alix welcomed the Royal guests, smiling and serene. Not even her children, George and the girls, realised what an ordeal it was for her. Laking had told her that her husband's condition was critical and that he had agreed to undergo treatment. What the treatment was to be, he had not said, and she suspected the King's doctor was being considerate to her, holding something back so as not to make her duty as hostess more difficult. Being aware that she had not been told everything almost made it worse.

There were over two hundred guests, from the Archduke Franz Ferdinand to the dashing Prince Danilo, all of them animated and excited. No announcement had been made that the King would not be able to appear and they were all impatient to see him and congratulate him on his recovery from his illness. They all brought messages from other friends and relations. They had to be greeted and reassured that the King was merely resting before the great day. Toria nearly spoilt everything by telling a few of the nearest relatives the true facts, but the reception was a

140

striking success. It was long past midnight before Alix could get away.

As she headed for her private apartments, with George, she saw Laking waiting for her and her heart turned over. He reassured her at once. The King was asleep under sedation and professional nurses were taking care of him.

Alix accepted the news of the operation much more calmly than Laking had expected. After months of worry and uncertainty, it was a relief to hear that something positive was to be done. Although the word had never been spoken between them, she too had been afraid of cancer. She was perfectly controlled and composed until she entered the dressing-room between her bedroom and Bertie's. A folding metal operating table had been smuggled in, portable lamps, trolleys for surgical instruments and enamelled bowls to hold swabs. The floor was covered by a rubber carpet. She swayed slightly at the finality of it and George held her arm.

'This operation,' she breathed, 'is it dangerous?' Laking hesitated. 'I want the truth.'

'The disease of the appendix has only recently been discovered, ma'am, and the technique is fairly new,' Laking told her, reluctantly. 'The operation has only been performed in acute cases. Not always with complete success.'

George felt his mother tremble. 'And if it is not attempted?' he asked.

'Then His Majesty has no chance whatever.'

In the morning, Laking and Barlow were joined at the Palace by the surgeon, Sir Frederick Treves, and another two specialists, Sir Thomas Smith and the aged Lord Lister. The brilliant Lister had been retired for ten years but still knew more about antiseptic surgery than any living man. Bertie had helped him to found his famous Institute and it was said that his discoveries had saved more lives than were lost in all the wars of the nineteenth century. After examining the King he was very worried at the extent of the internal abscess, yet he had confidence in Treves. He finally agreed that the operation could not be delayed and signed the bulletin to be issued to the public.

The streets of London were thronged with over a million visitors. Others were still pouring into town from every corner of the world. In a holiday mood, they marvelled at the fabulous red and gold decorations and some were already staking out places along the route of the procession. Hawkers sold semi-official programmes, flags, rosettes and painted periscopes. Everywhere there were portraits of Edward and Alexandra, on picture postcards, banners, boxes of sweets, glassware, matchboxes, trinkets and medallions. Foreign envoys were arriving from more distant countries and hurrying to the Palace to present themselves. In Westminister Abbey, the Dean was holding a full choral rehearsal of the ceremony.

The sightseers near the noticeboard on the railings of Buckingham Palace expected only a routine announcement when the bulletin was pinned up. It read: 'The King is suffering from perityphlitis. The condition on Saturday was so satisfactory that it was hoped that with care His Majesty would be able to go through the Coronation ceremony. On Monday evening a recrudescence became manifest, rendering a surgical operation necessary today.' The news struck the crowds like a bombshell. Disbelieving, they struggled to read it for themselves, then stood stunned, to be pushed out of the way by others. The same shock and disbelief was felt throughout the capital as the news spread. Women and men wept in the streets and the music and gaiety and laughter stopped. In Westminster Abbey, the organist called for silence and the Bishop of London stepped forward and announced the indefinite postponement of the Coronation that was being rehearsed.

'We cannot do better,' he said, 'than kneel down and pray.' As all present knelt, the litany was intoned, then the officials and the choir and orchestra were dismissed. The great abbey, prepared for the ritual and containing the precious emblems and relics, was locked and placed in the charge of the Earl Marshal.

In the King's bedroom, Alix and one of the two nurses helped Bertie to rise. He was wearing an old fashioned nightshirt for the operation and the nurse hung a dressing gown on his shoulders. The pain was now intense and he had spent a wretched night.

'Lean on me,' Alix told him as he limped towards the door.

'I apologise to everyone,' he muttered.

'There's no need,' she assured him.

'All those people . . .' he said. 'The Coronation Dinner—whatever happens—it must not be stopped. They mustn't be disappointed.'

'Of course not, my dearest,' Alix promised. She would not show him how near she was to weeping for him.

Laking, Barlow and the second nurse waited in the dressing-room with Sir Frederick Treves. He was a gentlemanly, unpretentious man, his reserve a contrast to Laking's urbane worldliness. He bowed as the King entered, supported by Alexandra.

'Are you still decided, Sir Frederick?' Bertie asked.

'Emphatically, sir,' Treves replied. His voice retained just a trace of a Dorset accent.

Bertie nodded and the nurse took his dressing gown as Alix and Laking helped him on to the operating table. The second nurse brought a mask of wire mesh, covered with cotton wool, and a bottle to Laking. 'Chloroform, sir,' he explained. 'Would you please relax and breath deeply.' The mask was laid over Bertie's mouth and nose and a few drops sprinkled on it.

Alix had stayed at Bertie's side. She saw his fingers clench and then stretch out as he tried to relax. More of the anaesthetic was dripped on to the mask and its cloying, honey-sweet smell spread through the room. Bertie's complexion darkened and his chest began to labour as his lungs fought for pure air. He was panting loudly and his shoulders heaved but Laking and the nurse held him down. His arms were threshing and Alix caught them, pressing him down too as he struggled. She had been perfectly controlled till now but had never seen anyone going under chloroform before and was frightened.

Treves was anxious to start his preparations. With the King's chest condition caused by heavy smoking, he did not wish him to be under anaesthetic too long.

Alix looked round, frantic. 'Why don't you begin?' she implored.

Treves hesitated, appalled by the realisation that the Queen meant to stay in the room. Laking saved him. 'If we might ask you to withdraw, ma'am? . . .' he suggested.

Alix was surprised. She was not squeamish and had thought that she might help in some way. She saw the doctors and nurses, the professionals, looking at her. 'Oh . . . if I could——' she stammered. By their embarrassment, she understood that her presence inhibited them. 'Of course,' she said meekly and moved to the door of her bedroom. One of the nurses opened it for her. The doctors bowed and she smiled briefly, to show her confidence in them, before she went out.

When the door closed, Treves signed briefly to the nurses. With the Queen gone, he could think of the King at last merely as a patient. He stripped off his frock coat and folded back his shirt-sleeves. One of the nurses hung up his coat and poured a carbolic solution into a bowl for him to wash his hands and arms. The other brought him his rubber apron, passed the tapes over his head and tied it at the back. The King was breathing more easily, his body inert, as Laking established just the right amount to keep him unconscious.

In the Queen's bedroom George had been waiting with his sisters, Toria and Maud. When Alix came in, she stood gazing at them, unable to speak. Toria took her and sat her in the chair by her dressing table. They had heard their father's hoarse panting and the muffled words from next door. Now there was complete impenetrable stillness.

From all over London, people converged slowly on the Mall and Buckingham Palace. Outside the railings, ringing the whole courtyard, a vast, silent crowd waited, watching the windows and the Royal standard as it floated at the top of its pole against a cloudless sky. Many of them wondered if by the evening they would see it lowered and many remembered the prophecy which the King, himself, had laughed at. The foreign princes and envoys were awed by the depth of real feeling in the streets. The secret was that, throughout his life, Bertie had always seemed human. Even his faults and indiscretions were human and easier to forgive. As Prince of Wales, he had become a stimulating and colourful part of national life. People had joined vicariously in his pleasures, pitied his sorrows and cheered his triumphs. Even in scandal, when the level of his popularity fell, he had never hidden behind a Royal mask but had faced the country. He was human and approachable, yet no one had more natural dignity nor a more regal presence on the great occasions of pomp and circumstance. The thought that they might lose him, that he might die just at the moment when they could show him at last, openly, unashamedly, how much they loved him was unendurable.

In the dressing-room, Treves had made the first incision, cutting surely and cleanly. He knew the operation would be made more difficult by the King's excess weight but he did not hesitate as he cut deeper into lower layers, the nurse opposite him swabbing away the blood that clogged his fingers.

In the bedroom, Alix sat tensely with her children, counting the minutes. Churches all over the city and the whole country had opened and filled with people in a mute, spontaneous vigil. The Moslem officers of the Indian Army in London for the Coronation were at a reception of the Bishop of London's in Fulham Palace. Hearing the news, they bowed and left. In the grounds outside, they laid down their mats and knelt in prayer for two hours, supplicating for the life of their King-Emperor.

In the dressing-room, Treves had reached the abscess and examined the extensive damage it had caused in the tissues surrounding it. The decision now was how much to risk cutting out without leaving or spreading the deadly infection. He glanced at Laking who nodded back encouragingly. The King's colour was good and his pulse fairly regular. Treves was perspiring. The nurse who managed his instruments used a swab to dab his forehead and temples as he rinsed his fingers. He took a clean scalpel and bent again over the incision.

In the bedroom, Alix felt her nerves grow more taut with each passing second. Forty minutes had gone by since she left Bertie stretched unconscious on the table, forty minutes in which she had lived again their whole life together from the first moment she had met him, golden-haired and smiling, in the cathedral at Speyer. a reticent, young man, so shy and handsome, who had chosen her at his mother's bidding to be his wife. She still remembered the wonder and tremulous excitement when her parents finally told her that the meeting was not accidental, that one day she would be his Queen.

'He knew it would happen,' she whispered. 'He always knew he would never be crowned.'

George was standing at the window. He turned.

'Don't say that, Mother,' Toria sobbed, her voice breaking. Beside her, Maud was trembling.

There was a soft knock at the door. They looked at one another, tensing. As George moved towards it, Treves came in. He had washed and fastened his shirt cuffs, but still wore the apron. He bowed. 'It is all over, ma'am,' he announced. 'And I believe, successful.'

Alix rose, biting her lip.

'I thank God,' George muttered.

Treves led them back into the dressing-room. One of the nurses was cleaning up. The other steadied Bertie as Laking took his pulse. He was just coming round from the anaesthetic. As his eyes opened, he seemed troubled. 'Where ... where's George?' he faltered.

George stepped to the foot of the table. 'I'm here, father.'

Bertie nodded, contented. His head turned, his eyes searching. The nurse moved aside and Alix came nearer. She was trying not to cry. 'Alix . . .' Bertie breathed. He smiled faintly and his eyes closed.

The next bulletin said that the King had borne the operation well but that it would be several days before it could be certain that he was out of danger.

After a service of intercession at St Paul's the following day, at the time the Coronation should have taken place, most of the foreign guests left for home. But the crowds outside the Palace railings remained, for three days and nights waiting for each bulletin as it was passed up. And the churches throughout the country and the Empire stayed open, houses of worship of all creeds and denominations, until the Saturday when it was announced that the immediate danger was over.

Weak, suffering intense pain from the continual dressing of his deep wound, Bertie was troubled most by the disappointment his illness had caused to so many, especially the poorer children who had been looking forward to their treats. Thousands of boys and girls from the East End were gathered in Victoria Park and given bags of sweets and cakes. Twelve hundred children from the city's orphanages had been invited to see the Coronation procession from stands outside Marlborough House. George and May gave a party for them in the gardens to which they brought David and Little Bertie. For the guests from the colonies and India, planned entertainments, investitures and reviews went ahead with George, Prince of Wales, standing in for the King. The Coronation Honours List was published, including baronetcies for Laking and Treves, and the first members of the King's new Order of Merit were appointed, for distinction in their chosen careers, among them Roberts, Kitchener and Lord Lister. And most spectacular of all, the King's Coronation Dinner was carried out with triumphant success at eighty-six different locations from Olympia and Paddington to Greenwich and Lewisham, the numbers of poor

146

guests ranging from fourteen thousand in Bishops Park, Fulham, seated at two and a half miles of tables, to one thousand in Hampstead Town Hall. The princes, princesses and dukes of the Royal Family represented the host at each centre and read out the bulletin from the doctors, issued that very day, reporting that his life had been saved.

The nurses, who had stayed on at the Palace, had never had a more extraordinary patient. The day after his life was despaired of, they found him lying in bed smoking a cigar and reading a newspaper. To them, the speed of his recovery was a miracle. The only time he grew angry was when they chased Caesar out when he sneaked in to visit him. Alix helped devotedly in his nursing but, because of the strain of trying to make her hear, he often pretended to be asleep when she was with him. Two weeks after the operation, he was able to receive Salisbury in audience, propped up on pillows.

Salisbury was more grave than usual. And looking older, Bertie thought. The Prime Minister's beard was more shaggy than ever, his shoulders stooped, his hands shaky. After a discussion of Cabinet business and the news that all Boer arms had been surrendered and the work of reconstruction already begun in South Africa, he paused. 'I regret that I shall not be able to keep Your Majesty informed personally for much longer,' he said slowly. The words came reluctantly. 'Increasing ill health forces me to consider resigning in the near future. I made myself stay on till the end of the war and hoped that I would be Prime Minister at your Coronation—but I must make way for someone younger.'

Salisbury's work and loyalty to his country were his life. A Member of Parliament for fifty years, Leader of the Conservative Party after the death of Disraeli, a notable Foreign Secretary and three times Prime Minister, if he was now resigning, the decision must be irrevocable. 'We have known each other for many years,' Bertie said gently. 'I shall be very sorry to lose you.'

Salisbury had not expected to be emotional at this moment. He had often disapproved of Bertie as Prince of Wales and it had taken him a long time to discover why Disraeli so admired him. He always regretted that he had not made more use of the King's diplomatic gifts but of course the old Queen had been an insurmountable obstacle. Rather to his surprise, he was touched by the King's sincerity and realised that he would miss their meetings and

147

discussions. It would never do to be tearful. An old man's weakness.

'Thank you, sir,' he replied, curtly.

The delay before he had spoken told Bertie a great deal. There was regret, acceptance, even affection in it. How different much of the past would have been, if he and Salisbury had been able to work together. 'Have you chosen a successor?' he asked.

'I would ask your Majesty to send for Mr Balfour,' Salisbury said without hesitation.

Bertie pursed his mouth. 'Downright nepotism,' he murmured. Salisbury straightened and Bertie chuckled. 'No offence, Lord Salisbury. Your nephew is the ablest member of the Cabinet. He will do very well.'

The Prime Minister smiled stiffly. He had not appreciated at first that the King was joking with him to make the act of resignation less painful. Lightness of touch and consideration for others' feelings, valuable qualities. How often had he been mistaken, perhaps, in accusing the King of frivolity? How often, when it was too late, one began to see the qualities in people one had missed. He knelt with difficulty by the bed and kissed Bertie's hand.

After Salisbury had withdrawn, Bertie shifted his position, drawing up his right leg slightly to ease the ache in his side. Enforced leisure had given him time to think many things through, things that had to be done. Now that he knew he was to live, he had a chance to achieve something positive. He had counted on Salisbury backing him. With Balfour and the prickly Lansdowne it would be more difficult and he would have to proceed more cautiously. In politics there was always change when one needed continuity. Salisbury's resignation was only part of the changing of the old order, the old certainties. Although he knew it must come and he must adapt to it, it saddened him. He thought again of the old Prime Minister, honouring him. For thirteen out of the last sixteen years he had been head of the Government, shrewd, untiring, but the years of struggle in South Africa had finally worn him out. In a war, there were more casualties than those on the battlefield.

148

Chapter
9

Four days after Salisbury's resignation, Bertie was well enough to travel by train to Portsmouth, where he was carried on board the Royal Yacht *Victoria and Albert* on a stretcher to start a convalescent cruise. Treves travelled with him to make sure there was no relapse.

In the group accompanying the King and Queen was Frederick Ponsonby. He had been invalided home from South Africa at the end of the war, in which he had served with distinction, being promoted Lieutenant Colonel. Back in London his prospects had not seemed too promising. Francis Knollys had made it clear that he was not needed in the secretarial staff and he had been given only a very minor job as one of the escort of the younger brother of Kaiser Wilhelm at the Coronation. With the cancellation, his employment finished and he had just decided he would have to look for something else when the surprise invitation to join the cruise arrived.

After lunch on the first day, he was sent for. He reported to the King in the deck cabin which had been fitted up as a sickroom with a bed in the centre, surrounded by tables for dressings and medicines. He had expected to find him in bed, wan and ailing. He was certainly pale, but lying on top of the bed in a blue flannel suit, smoking a cigar. Ponsonby was bemused. A mere three weeks ago, the King had been at the point of death. He had been one of the millions who had prayed for him, convinced that even if he lived he would be infirm and sickly for months to come.

Bertie was pleased to see Ponsonby and suspected that things had been difficult for him. He had only heard by chance that he had returned. It was typical of Ponsonby that he had accepted an insignificant post without complaint, but he deserved better and Francis should have made more use of him.

'Hello, Fritz. Back from the wars?' he said. Ponsonby

bowed and was startled to discover that the King had followed his progress in South Africa with interest. He stammered his thanks. 'Well, I won't praise you,' Bertie smiled. 'You did no more than I looked for from you.' He winced. 'I little thought when I last saw you I'd be like this now.'

'You have made a remarkable recovery, sir,' Ponsonby said. 'I understand you were in considerable pain.'

'At first,' Bertie nodded. 'The worst of it's over.'

'I can't tell you the dismay, the anxiety your illness caused,' Ponsonby told him. 'I was in Regent Street when the papers came out with the news that Your Majesty had survived the operation. The relief on people's faces was indescribable.'

Bertie blinked. He was still weak and easily moved by sympathy. 'Most kind,' he muttered. Then, seeing Ponsonby's embarrassment, he steadied himself. 'When I nearly died twenty years ago, exactly the same thing happened,' he recalled. 'All at once my sins were forgiven and I discovered that everybody loved me. It's not a bad idea for Kings to be ill from time to time.' After the briefest pause, Ponsonby grinned. Bertie chuckled back. That was one of the things he had missed. Ponsonby always knew when he was joking.

There was a spatter of paws on the deck and Caesar scampered in through the partly open door. He barked twice in greeting and leapt up on the bed, frisking over Bertie's legs and swarming up to lick his face, his whole body wagging with his tail. 'Now, then! Now, now. Caesar,' Bertie protested. 'Be a little more decorous.' He pushed him further down the bed and Caesar licked at his hand. Laughing, Bertie ruffled his ears. 'You'll have to forgive us,' he explained to Ponsonby. 'We haven't seen each other properly for weeks. Fritz, this is Caesar.—Fritz.'

'How d'you do?' Ponsonby said, smiling.

He stepped back and bowed as Alix came in. She saw the little dog with Bertie. 'So there he is,' she sighed. 'I might have known it. He shouldn't be on the bed.'

'He's fine,' Bertie assured her. Caesar had settled down beside him and watched Alix warily, his head cocked.

'You realise what the doctor will say?'

'If he touches Caesar, I'll have him keelhauled,' Bertie growled.

Alix began to laugh, but stopped. 'Oh, Bertie, look at

you!' she exclaimed. 'You came down here for sea air and you're filling your lungs with cigar smoke.'

'Tastes better with sea air,' Bertie answered.

Ponsonby decided it was time for him to leave. He bowed. 'If you'll excuse me, sir?'

'H'm? Oh, yes, fine,' Bertie said. As Ponsonby retreated to the door, he added, 'We'll go through the letters tomorrow, Fritz. I expect Francis will only send the essentials, so we'd better see to them.'

It was said so casually it was not until he was outside that Ponsonby grasped that he had just been taken on again as Assistant Private Secretary.

On the *Victoria and Albert*, Bertie's health improved rapidly and he grew stronger every day. The yacht was anchored in calm waters off Cowes and steam launches patrolled round it to keep other craft at a distance. With the dressing on the wound still needing to be changed frequently, he had to stay in bed but, after a week and a half, he had had enough of immobility and ordered the anchor weighed. The yacht sailed slowly round the Isle of Wight and he took his first tentative steps, leaning on a sailor's arm. The following day he summoned Prince George, Lord James of Hereford and the Duke of Devonshire and held a Privy Council in the saloon, seated in a wheelchair. To their amazement, he announced that the postponed Coronation would take place in two weeks' time.

Arthur Balfour still felt strange to be sitting at the Prime Minister's desk in the study of 10 Downing Street, with his uncle in the armchair by the fire. But Lord Salisbury only attended meetings now as an adviser. Out of office, he had suddenly become an old man, his health and powers crumbling. Lansdowne was with them.

Lord Esher had just brought them the news. 'The ninth of August,' he repeated.

'Surely that's too soon?' Balfour queried.

'He has made an astonishing recovery,' Esher said. 'And does not wish to wait any longer.'

'I don't think it is possible,' Balfour objected. 'There are far too many arrangements to make.'

'The same arrangements would serve,' Esher pointed out.

'No, no,' Lansdowne said dismissively. 'There would not

be time to co-ordinate all the foreign princes and envoys. They'll need several months' notice.'

Esher looked at him. 'The King does not care about that. He insists that the Coronation only really concerns himself and his people.'

Lansdowne flushed. 'It also concerns his Government,' he maintained. 'Already he has refused some of my suggestions for appointments and decorations.'

'That is his privilege,' Esher reminded him. 'In the past he was unsure and reluctant to claim his right to be consulted—but then he was unwell. Now he is fit again, you will find him a different man to deal with.'

Salisbury nodded in agreement. 'If he was popular before, his illness has made him much more than that,' he said quietly. 'If he chose to form a political party, he would win every seat in the country.'

'Then it's perhaps as well the constitution prevents him from dabbling in politics,' Balfour remarked drily.

'I have warned you before,' Salisbury stressed. He glanced from Balfour to Lansdowne. 'Do not underestimate this new Edward. I have watched him develop. Despite all his critics, he will prove . . . every inch a king.'

Inches were a matter of pleasure to Bertie. He had lost eight of them from round his waist. He was several stones lighter and, although his face was drawn, he was tanned and looking years younger. After three weeks' cruise, he was not only fit, he had regained the vigour and appetite for life of a man half his age.

It was as well that he was also better able to control his temper. He needed patience in dealing with his sisters, Louise, Lenchen and Beatrice. On his trips round the Isle of Wight, he had come to a final decision about Osborne House. He had offered it to George and May but they politely refused it as too expensive to run. It occurred to him that one wing would make an ideal convalescent home for officers of the Army and Navy. The other wing and stables could be turned into a Naval College for cadets, and the central pavilion which included his mother's rooms remain as a shrine and family museum. In her will, Victoria had left a share in Osborne to all her children. Arthur did not care, but his sisters were more attached to it. He had given them houses in the grounds but they still complained and protested bitterly. 'Can you afford to keep it up?' he

asked them. 'Well, neither can I. Nor have I the inclination.'
He wrote to Balfour, presenting Osborne as a gift to the
nation.

When the word spread that Alix and he were on their
way back to London, people left their shops and offices and
the streets were thronged. Seeing him bronzed and smiling,
like the Prince they remembered, their reaction was a loving
storm of greeting. Yet it was only a foretaste of what was to
come.

The foreign princes and archdukes who had returned to
their own countries were not invited again, only those who
were directly related to Edward or Alexandra. In the six
weeks since the operation, the whole concept of the Coronation had changed in Bertie's mind. It was no longer to be
an ostentatious pageant of the heirs of all the ruling houses
in the world, a festival of monarchy, but a solemn act of
consecration and homage, essentially personal, national and
imperial.

It was imperial in that, instead of foreign heirs, pride of
place was given to the Dominion and Colonial premiers,
the princes of India and the viceroys and governors of other
territories owing allegiance to the Crown. The recent war
had knitted the Empire together as nothing else could have
done and this was the first coronation of a British Emperor.
The thousands from the free colonies who had answered
the call to arms had been under no compulsion to fight.
That they had come voluntarily to the assistance of the
Mother Country, which only one in a hundred of them had
ever seen, was visible proof that they were one people,
united by a common inheritance, prepared to stand or fall
together. It was not purely emotional. Men of different
creeds and races, they were ready to die in defence of something they knew to be unique, a system which guaranteed
stability, freedom and prosperity, a league of countries
linked together by destiny, yet each independent, under
democratic governments based on the ancient laws and
hard-won liberties of England.

It was national in that the Coronation confirmed the
covenant between the King and his people, his oath to rule
according to law and their recognition of his right to the
throne. Although responsibility for running the country had
now passed to Parliament, the throne was not a mere symbol, but a promise of continuity, the cornerstone of the

constitution, a check on any group of politicians or single party assuming total power. That promise and recognition was now extended to the whole Empire, which received its consecration in the anointing of the King.

To Bertie, it was the most solemn act of his life, the moment for which he had been born. He had, in fact, succeeded to the throne immediately on the death of his mother. Following the Privy Council's proclamation at St James's Palace, his reign had formally begun. There was a time when the King's peace was suspended and he had no right to the allegiance of his subjects until the crown had been placed on his head. This was no longer the case, yet both to Bertie and his people the act of crowning was more than a colourful tradition. It had a spiritual significance, difficult for them to put into words, an almost mystical exaltation, combined with pride and security and an inspiring affirmation of national existence and progress.

Because the Coronation was to be more personal it allowed him to show more honour to his family, his younger brother, Arthur of Connaught, an old fashioned soldier with whom he had little in common, and his sisters, the artistic, unhappily married Louise, Duchess of Argyll, Helena from whom he had been largely estranged since her marriage to the dull Prince Christian of Schleswig-Holstein, and the youngest, Beatrice, who had been an infant when he married Alix, now a slightly embittered, withdrawn widow herself. And he was faithful to his friends, making sure they all had a place in the Abbey. Among the noble lords assisting in the procession, Carrington carried St Edward's Staff and Lord Roberts one of the Swords of Justice. Cassel was there by virtue of his recent appointment as a Privy Councillor. Soveral was with the diplomatic corps, representing Portugal. Harty Tarty, the Duke of Devonshire, was in attendance as the Lord President and his wife, Louisa, formerly Duchess of Manchester, sat in the front rank of peeresses.

Bertie checked the list of invitations carefully with the Duke of Norfolk. A tricky problem lay in finding places for his intimate favourites, among whom were several whose rank did not entitle them to a seat in the Abbey. He solved it by having a special box built for them. On the day, the other guests gazed in astonishment at the beauty and exquisite dresses of its occupants, among them Jennie Churchill and her sister Leonie, Mrs Arthur Paget, Lady

Kilmorey, Mrs Hartmann, Princess Daisy of Pless, Sarah Bernhardt and Alice Keppel. When Carrington finally informed him that some of the racing fraternity were calling it the King's Loose Box, Bertie frowned, trying to look severe, but his eyes gave him away.

'Well . . . why not?' he chuckled.

Another problem lay in providing seats for his godchildren whom he wished to be present. For some it was easy, they were officially the sons of peers or had married peers. For others, more elaborate arrangements had to be made. His favourite, Olga Alberta, his daughter by the provocative, mysterious Duchess of Caracciolo, brought up discreetly in Dieppe, had just married. Bertie persuaded his friend, the King of Saxony, to make her husband a baron and Chamberlain to his court, so that they could be given official invitations.

The day before the Coronation was unseasonably cold and heavy rain threatened but, by nightfall, people without tickets for the stands were already claiming vantage points along the route of the procession. Among them were many from Australia, New Zealand and South Africa. Over five thousand visitors had come from Canada alone. By dawn, the numbers had swelled beyond the possibility of counting.

They still had many hours to wait but they were patient and good-tempered and, as the detachments of troops moved out to help the police to line the streets, there was always something new to catch their interest, famous British regiments, Highland pipers and drums and a bewildering variety of unfamiliar uniforms. Shoulder to shoulder, three or four deep, from Buckingham Palace, along the Mall, through the Horse Guards Arch and down Whitehall and Parliament Street to the west door of Westminster Abbey, were contingents of troops from every corner of the Empire. Spaced out by military bands were Lancers from New South Wales, Rifles from South Australia, Bushmen from Victoria, Mounted Infantry from Swan River, Brisbane and Hobart, Maori soldiers from New Zealand, men from Ceylon in white, gigantic Fijians in blue, white and crimson, Swahillis from the King's African rifles, Haussas in short, scarlet jackets and loose trousers, Hong Kong Police, Mohammedan Police from Cyprus wearing red fezes, the bodyguard of the Sultan of Perak in Malaya, West Indians, Dyaks from North Borneo and, straight from South Africa, Remington's Tigers, the Imperial Light Horse and Kitchener's Fighting Scouts. Most resplendent of all were the detachments of the Indian Army, Lancers and Guides, Grenadiers, Infantry and Artillery, made up of every caste and race from Cape Comorin to the Himalayas, Sikhs, Gurkhas, Mahrattas, Rajputs and Pathans. Then the interest quickened when the doors of the Abbey were unlocked at seven o'clock and the first carriages of the guests began to appear, with liveried coachmen and footmen in powdered wigs. Soon the parade of the famous and distinguished was continuous. Among them, the crowd applauded one Royal carriage in which were two nursing sisters in grey uniforms, the King's nurses.

Inside the Abbey, the wooden throne made more than six centuries before for Edward the First stood at the entrance to the sanctuary. It was built to hold, under its plain seat, the Stone of Destiny on which the ancient Kings of Scotland had always been crowned and which the conquering Edward brought south from the Abbey of Scone. Next to it stood the throne made for Mary the Second. In front of them were two Chairs of State to be used by the King and Queen before the crowning. The nave and the central dais were carpeted in deep-blue, the galleries hung with draperies of blue and old gold. The high altar was covered in scarlet and dazzled with gold plate. By nine o'clock, the towering galleries in the nave were filled with knights in the dress of their medieval Orders, officers and courtiers in scarlet and gold, Judges, Civil and Church dignitaries in ceremonial costumes, their ladies wearing, as the King had requested, ballgowns and their finest jewellery. In the choir were the ambassadors and foreign princes, the Privy Councillors and Indian rajahs in a blaze of diamonds, rubies and emeralds, orders and decorations. Among a row of sombrely dressed representatives of the Church of Scotland sat the Aga Khan. In front of him in a pure white robe was Ras Makunen from Abyssinia, direct descendant of the Queen of Sheba. With the statesmen were the Prime Ministers of Canada, Australia, New Zealand and Newfoundland, the Minister of Natal and the governors of the Crown Colonies. On the screen above the choir were the musicians and singers in white, gold and scarlet. In steeply banked tiers in the north and south transepts sat the peers and peeresses, wearing crimson robes with ermine capes,. Spaces for the princes of the Royal Family were to the right of the King's throne, while the Archbishops, Bishops, the Earl Marshal and nobles with parts to play in the ritual gathered in the Sanctuary, the clergy in jewelled and embroidered copes and cloth of gold, the officers of state in court dress covered by peers' robes or the blue mantle of the Garter. Through the grey pillars and soaring arches of the venerable Abbey, the diffused light of the stained glass windows softened the vividness of the scene and turned the eight thousand people assembled within into a living tapestry of rich but subdued colours, highlit by the flash of a myriad gems from bracelets, necklaces and diadems.

In his robing room at Buckingham Palace, Bertie was already dressed in a shirt and satin breeches, with silk stockings and buckled shoes. Watched by the Master and Groom of the Robes, Chandler, the Superintendent of his Wardrobe, helped him into a red tunic reaching to his knees. All he had to do now was put on his cap and outer robes. As he smoothed the tunic down from his chest to his waist, he touched the dressing over the scar left by the operation, which had nearly healed. There was no pain.

In half an hour, the procession was due to leave the Palace. All the years of waiting had shrunk to a few minutes. He could sense the tension in those around him, yet he felt perfectly calm. When he examined him that morning, Laking had been surprised to find his pulse and blood pressure normal and had asked if he did not feel nervous at the thought of going through the strain of a long, unfamiliar ritual under the eyes of the whole world. Nervous was the wrong word. Expectant would be better, buoyant, hopeful, reverent, all of these. He remembered the day he discovered he was destined to be crowned. He was twelve or thirteen and his tutor, the harsh, pedantic Mr Gibbs, had given him the Tables of the Kings of England to learn. He had been puzzled that Henry the Eighth's son, Edward the Sixth, had succeeded his father instead of one of his elder sisters, Mary or Elizabeth. Up till then, he had always assumed that Vicky, being older, would be Queen after their mother. When Victoria had confirmed that, as the eldest son, he was the heir, he had been shaken and afraid. 'I don't want to be!' he had wept. 'Why can't Affie be King? Or Arthur. He could do it!' She had kissed him and told him to be brave. 'It is not what we want to do,' she had said. 'But what we must, what is our duty.' How could he be nervous when, long ago, he had accepted the inevitable?

He became aware than another ten minutes had passed.

The lord-in-waiting who had gone to check on Alix's readiness had returned to tell him she had not started to dress. He sent pages to ask her ladies to stir themselves. He put on his Cap of Maintenance of crimson velvet edged with ermine, then his heavy purple cloak with a deep cape of ermine and the collar of the Garter.

'No sign of the Queen?' he asked.

'Not yet, sir,' the Equerry stationed at the door reported.

To the lords watching him, Bertie had become another figure, imposing, majestic, yet for the first time that day he began to feel anxious. Although he had promised himself he would be patient, he could not stop pacing. It was nearly time to leave, too late even to have a cigar. 'Where is she?' he exclaimed, exasperated. 'This is too much. Today of all days!' Flinging off his cloak, he strode out into the corridor, and marched into the Queen's apartments to throw open the door of her robing room.

Alix was with Toria, Louise and Maud, the Duchess of Buccleuch, Mistress of the Robes, and her ladies-in-waiting. They had just finished dressing her and she turned slowly to smile at him. Her gown was of white muslin, sumptuously embroidered in India with pure gold, over a lining of cloth-of-gold. Her arms were bare but veiled to the elbow in gauze. The neck was cut low, her bust and shoulders framed in a high-standing collar, richly encrusted with diamonds and gold embroidery. The waist was tight and narrow, the skirt extravagantly full, ending in a long train. Round her slender throat was a choker of diamonds above a superb diamond necklace. At her breast and waist hung the jewelled insignia of many orders and covering all were loops of pearls, matching her pearl earrings. She was slim, radiant, incredibly young and lovely.

For a moment, Bertie gazed at her, astonished by her unchanged youth and delicate beauty. Then he pushed the door more fully open. 'My dear Alix,' he growled, 'if you don't come immediately, you won't be crowned Queen!'

In the Audience Room, their grandchildren waited with some small friends and their parents. Bertie had wanted to give them a chance to see Alix and him close to before they set off. When they entered, posing in their Royal robes, they looked so regal that the children were overawed. Seeing their parents bow and curtsey to their grandparents who seemed so different, some of them were dismayed, even frightened.

Noticing, Bertie smiled to them. 'Good morning, children,' he chuckled and, raising the skirts of his robes, he danced a few steps to amuse them. 'Am I not a funny-looking old man?' he asked. They laughed in relief, realising that under the strange clothes he was still their adored grandpa.

The sky was overcast but, mercifully, although the clouds stayed sluggish and threatening, it did not rain. In fact, the clouds were welcome, for they lessened the heat of the August sun that would have been unbearable to the multitudes now concentrated along the route. Estimates of the numbers varied from three to six millions jammed into the sides of the streets, packing the stands, windows and rooftops, clinging to railings and lamp posts. Yet from all that vast throng there was curiously little sound.

As ten o'clock, the time for the start of the procession, came and went and there was no signal from the Palace, the feeling of uneasiness that kept the crowds subdued deepened. To the superstitious, the dark sky was an omen. The prophecy had still not been forgotten. Even when the band of the First Life Guards appeared at last, followed by a troop of the Royal Horse Guards in their magnificent State uniforms, forming the head of the cavalcade, a stir of excitement swept rapidly down the Mall, but there was no burst of cheering.

The Coronation procession was made up of three sections, each with its own escorts. First came a parade of carriages with the foreign princes and the princes and princesses of the Royal Family, including the King's sisters, and daughters. Then another squadron of Horse Guards preceded the Prince of Wales's procession with carriages for members of the Household and George and May in ermine robes. Their reception was warm and friendly and there were cheers for George and May but the crowds were still strangely hushed and uncertain. Then the roar of sixty-two cannons announced that the King's procession was leaving the Palace and a gasp of relief echoed all along the route.

All morning the suppressed excitement in the crowds had grown in intensity. As the advance guard of the Sovereign's escort rode out, Royal Horse Guards in shining helmets and cuirasses, those nearest the Palace surged forward, craning their necks to see over the motionless ranks of soldiers in front. The Guards were followed on foot by the King's Bargemaster and twelve Watermen in black velvet caps, scarlet, broad-skirted tunics embroidered with the Royal arms and tight, scarlet breeches and stockings. After them came the carriages of the maids of honour and the chief officers of the Household. They preceded a mounted troop of the King's aides-de-camp, a hundred distinguished officers of the Navy and Army and Volunteer Forces in a dazzling mosaic of dress uniforms, among whom the most colourful were the Maharajahs of Gwalior, Idar and Cooch-Behar. Riding side by side were Admiral Sir Edward Seymour who had recently captured Tientsin and opened the road to Pekin, Sir Alfred Gaselee who had relieved the legations besieged in Pekin, and Lord Kitchener, the avenger of Gordon of Khartoum and victor in South Africa. For the first time, seeing Kitchener, self-contained and handsome, with his piercing, light-coloured eyes and full moustache, the reserve of the crowds broke and the cheers and applause were loud and exultant.

All down the route, applause continued for the Headquarters staff and Lord Roberts, the Commander-in-Chief, who rode alone. When they had passed, the sound faded again and the ranks of Marshalmen, Yeomen of the Guard and the mounted cohort of Equerries went by almost unnoticed. The crowds were surging forward, their excitement stirred by the final escorts of Colonial cavalry in plain, fighting khaki with their rifles balanced upright on their right knees and the incomparable Indian cavalry in their turbans, many-coloured tunics and sashes. The murmur of excitement they caused died. Riding with the Equerries, Ponsonby was reminded of the feeling before a battle, the same electric expectance, the same stillness. The moment's silence was uncanny.

Behind the plumes and the turbans, the crowds had seen, drawn by the creams, the great, gilded State Coach with its golden crowns and tridents and garlands. Their reticence had begun as a mark of respect, a token of thanksgiving that the King's life had been spared. Yet as the morning wore on, the fear of a relapse and the need for reassurance, to see him with their own eyes, had become imperative and not until they were satisfied could their excitement find its release.

The silence lasted as the gilded coach moved slowly past the first press of the crowd. They saw Alexandra, eternally youthful and lovely, smiling, in her glimmering gown, her hair uncovered and, beside her, the King wearing his Cap of Maintenance and ermine robe. Although he was still tanned, the signs of suffering were unmistakable, the thinner face, the short beard which in a few weeks had become pure white, and they remembered the days of harrowing suspense when the nation had prepared to mourn him.

Bertie had been disturbed by the silence of the crowds. Even if they did not welcome his Coronation, this was partly their own Victory Parade. Listening from the courtyard while the princes and captains and all the rich panoply of the procession had advanced along the streets ahead of him with only a scattered, muted reaction, he had wondered if the people had lost the power to rejoice, or perhaps they had no desire to. Under the cover of their robes, Alix's hand touched his and squeezed it gently. He smiled at her and, as he turned to look again out of the clear windows of the coach, the keyed-up emotions of the crowd burst and a storm of cheering broke out around them. It had no trace of politeness or duty, sheer, naked emotion found its voice in a deafening thunder of cheering. The same silence followed by unrestrained jubilation was kept up the whole way, the pressure of excitement building in them until they, too, added to the frenzy. Many of them, men and women, in a delirium of affection and loyalty, thrust through the lines of saluting soldiers and marched beside the coach, shouting and sobbing, completely carried away.

The music of the regimental bands could not be heard. Even the pipes of the Highlanders were drowned in the cheering. All down Whitehall to Parliament Square the roar continued, always growing, a constant, heart-stirring thunder as the coach drew nearer to the Abbey where the Kings of England had been crowned for nine hundred years.

Inside Westminster Abbey, the excitement had mounted too as the assembled guests heard the tumult outside and the boom of cannon signalling the King's arrival. The members of the parade who had already entered moved to their places, the foreign princes and their suites and the princes and princesses of the Blood Royal. As he took his seat in front of the peers, George was unseeing, stunned by the reception given to his father. May crossed to the south side of the altar where David and Little Bertie were already in the roval box, irrepressible and animated until she came to keep them in order. She closed her eyes for a second or two in prayer, then composed herself and smiled to Toria, Louise and Maud, her sisters-in-law, who sat with their aunts.

The bishops and priests had blessed the regalia, brought from safekeeping in the Jerusalem Chamber and now forming part of the procession of the Sovereign and his Consort. To the sound of triumphal music, the Royal chaplains and the pursuivants in their silk tabards entered from the west door, ahead of the champions bearing the Standards of England, Ireland and Scotland, and the Union Standard. After them came four Knights of the Garter in their blue cloaks, chosen to hold the canopy over the King's head during his anointing, among them his friend, the former Prime Minister, Lord Rosebery. After the Duke of Devonshire and Arthur Balfour, as Lord Privy Seal, came the Archbishops of Canterbury and York, the Queen's Heralds and the officers of State carrying her regalia, all in court dress or uniform, the peers of the realm with their coronets carried behind them by gentlemen pages.

Then, as Alix appeared, a high shout rang out over the music from the boys of Westminister School in the gallery above the arches of the nave. 'Vivat Regina Alexandra!' And the hearts of all those watching rose as Alexandra progressed down the long nave, radiant and touchingly beautiful in her shimmering, golden gown. Escorted by two bishops in jewelled vestments and by gentlemen-at-arms, she wore her purple Coronation mantle suspended from her shoulders and stretching back from its ermine cape in a sumptuous velvet train. The train was edged with miniver and superbly embroidered in gold with a symbolic design of the rose, the thistle and shamrock, the historic crowns and the Star of India, set in a triple border. It was borne by eight pages in scarlet and its end held up by the Mistress of the Robes. Leading her ladies were the Duchesses of Marlborough, Montrose, Portland and Sutherland, all tall and beautiful, who were to support her gold canopy in the ceremony. Dignified and gracious, she advanced to her seat in the sanctuary.

At the entrance to the sanctuary, the Archbishop of Canterbury, the Lord Chancellor, the Lord High Constable, the Lord Great Chamberlain and the Earl Marshal were now waiting for the King. The music swelled and a flourish of trumpets greeted the entrance of the Heralds in their gorgeous costumes, leading the procession of the Royal regalia, a moving, resplendent pageant. First came the Duke of Argyll with the Sceptre of the Cross, then Earl Carrington with St Edward's Staff and the Dukes and Lords carrying the Golden Spurs, the sheathed Sword of Mercy and the Swords of Justice, one blunted, the other pointed. Following the Kings of Arms, the Lord Mayor of London and an array of the great Officers of State, came the Earl of Lucan with the Sceptre of the Dove, the Duke of Somerset with the Orb and the Duke of Marlborough bearing the Imperial Crown. And the voices of the boys again rang out. 'Vivat Rex Edwardus! Vivat Rex Edwardus! Vivat, vivat, vivat!'

A rustle and murmur of expectation had rippled through the Abbey, but now it hushed, Flanked by bishops, his purple train carried by pages, escorted by officers and Gentlemen-at-arms and followed by Dukes, Admirals and Generals, the gentlemen of the Household and Yeomen of the Guard, the King paced slowly up the choir, smiling and nodding very slightly to the guests, who were standing. Reaching the sanctuary, he bowed to Alix, then knelt in prayer at the stool, by his chair of state. Many in the assembly were asking themselves if he had recovered sufficiently to bear the strain of the ceremony, but the acclamation of his people and the colour and tension in the Abbey had raised Bertie above all thought of tiredness or pain.

As he rose, the eighty-year-old Archbishop of Canterbury, Frederick Temple, who refused to die until he had crowned his King, moved to his side for the Recognition. Facing the assembly, he called out the traditional formula, 'Sirs, I here present unto you King Edward, the undoubted King of this Realm; wherefore all you who are come this day to do your homage, are you willing to do the same?' There was a brief second of pause, then a universal, full-throated shout of 'God Save the King!' and the trumpets sounded. Then came the Communion Service, the recital of the Creed and taking of the oath, where the King swore to rule according to law, in justice and mercy. After the questions and replies of the oath, he knelt at the altar with his right hand on the Bible. 'Those things which I have here promised, I will perform and keep. So help me God.'

To the music of Handel's Anthem of Zadok the Priest,

the Lord Great Chamberlain helped him to take off his purple and crimson outer robes and the Cap of Maintenance. Dressed only in the red tunic, he sat in St Edward's Chair above the Stone of Destiny. This was the central part of the long ritual, beginning with the Anointing. Rosebery and the other three knights of the Garter held above him a canopy of golden silk. At the altar, holy oil was poured from the ancient Ampulla, shaped like an eagle, into the gold anointing spoon and it was brought to the Archbishop. With the oil, using his right thumb, the Archbishop marked the King with the sign of the cross on the forehead, on the breast through a slit in the tunic and on the palms of the hands, saying the ceremonial words and ending with a blessing. The most sacred element was over and the Knights carrying the canopy stepped back.

Now the King was clothed in the vestments of Kingship, the Colobium Sindonis, a white, sleeveless surplice, and the Supertunica, a short, cloth of gold coat, and a swordbelt. The Golden Spurs were touched to his heels and his scabbarded sword placed in his hand to be returned and rededicated at the altar. Then the King was dressed in the Imperial Mantle, a golden robe, gorgeously embroidered and decorated with silver eagles, and seated again in St Edward's Chair. He received from the Archbishop and handed back, also to be replaced on the altar, the Orb with the Cross, signifying that the whole world was subject to the power of Christ, a golden ball with a circle of rubies, pearls and emeralds and a cross of diamonds on top, set on a base of amethyst. Edward the Confessor's plain gold ring with a single ruby was put on the fourth finger of his right hand, then the Sceptre of the Cross as the sign of Royal power and justice was placed in the same hand and the Sceptre of the Dove, the rod of equity and mercy, placed in his left. After all the prayers and ritual, the supreme moment had arrived.

In the whole great assembly there was no sound. Throughout the ceremony, wrought up by their emotions, many people had sobbed uncontrollably but now there was no sound. Everyone watched the venerable Archbishop in breathless silence as he moved slowly to the altar and lifted up the Imperial Crown. Exhausted by the long prayers and rites, he was visibly weakening. The crown was heavy, a purple velvet cap enclosed by a circlet and hoops of silver, encrusted with jewels. On the circlet were crosses and fleurs-de-lis of diamonds and, at its crest, was a diamond orb and cross on an arch of pearls. They saw his hands tremble and could not hear him as he muttered the Coronation prayer, although his voice before had been strong and firm. Laying the crown on a cushion held by the Dean, he would have stumbled down the altar steps if his bishops had not caught him. In front of St Edward's chair again, he paused, gathering the last of his strength, before taking the Imperial Crown from the cushion and raising it above the King's head.

Glancing up, Bertie saw the flash of the ruby-like stone set in the Maltese cross in front, a jewel that had been given to Edward the Black Prince and worn by Henry the Fifth at Agincourt. Then the crown was turned and the Archbishop lowered it gently to rest on his brow. At the same instant, the standing peers all put on their coronets and a huge, exultant shout of 'God Save the King' filled the Abbey. The trumpets rang out, the bells began to peal and were answered in the distance by the massed guns of the Tower of London and the jubilation of the millions waiting in the streets.

St Edward's Chair faced east, away from most of the congregation. Rising, Bertie turned and displayed himself in the dress of majesty before moving to the throne, to be assisted ritually into it by the principal Officers of State and bishops. The old Archbishop, himself, was the first to kneel in homage on the steps of the throne, with the other bishops and priests kneeling behind him. After swearing his oath of loyalty to the King, he was finally worn out and could not rise. Bertie stood and, taking his hands, helped him to his feet. Supported by the Bishop of Winchester, he completed his oath by kissing the King's left cheek. Then came the homage of the Prince of Wales, kneeling at his father's feet. 'I, George, Prince of Wales, do become your liegeman of life and limb, and of earthly worship, and faith and truth I will bear unto you, to live and die, against all manner of folks. So help me God.' When he rose he touched the crown and kissed his father. As he stepped back, Bertie caught his robe and drew him back to hold him and kiss him in return. All in the assembly were deeply moved and Alix's eyes filled with tears as she saw the tenderness between her husband and son and remembered the other son who should have knelt with him.

Then the five senior peers representing their Orders knelt

on the five steps of the throne and, one by one, took the oath of fealty, the Duke of Norfolk, the Marquess of Winchester, the Earl of Shrewsbury, Viscount Falkland and the Baron de Ros. To save tiring the King with all the peers paying homage individually as was the custom, these five stood for all. When the last had kissed his cheek and retreated down the steps, drums rolled out and the trumpets sounded again in a fanfare. As Bertie looked from the Royal box to the transepts, the choir and the soaring galleries in the nave, the whole Abbey resounded to the triumphant shout, 'God Save King Edward! Long Live King Edward! May the King live for ever!'

His Coronation was over, and now it was Alexandra's turn to be anointed and blessed, presented with her regalia and crowned by the Archbishop of York. Then the peeresses, with a graceful, sweeping movement of hundreds of white-gloved arms rising from their robes, put on their crimson coronets and the Queen was conducted to her throne. After Holy Communion and the offerings to the altar, the King and Queen retired and changed into their robes of purple velvet. The processions reformed and the Sovereigns were escorted to their coach, announced by the joyous peal of bells and the crash of saluting cannons.

It was past two o'clock in the afternoon but the crowds had waited patiently, held by their excitement. Now, seeing the King in his crown, holding the Sceptre with the Cross in his right hand and the Orb in his left, they shouted and wept and sang. When the procession reached Buckingham Palace and the King and Queen came out on to the balcony to show themselves to the teeming multitudes packed into the Mall, the thunder of cheering and the delirium of the crowds surpassed anything that had gone before.

Gazing down at his people, his eyes wet with gratitude, Bertie knew at last that never in her long reign, not even at her mighty Jubilees, had his mother been given such loyalty and affection as this.

Chapter

10

It was a clear night and Bertie sat alone on the quarterdeck of the Royal Yacht, watching the dark coast of Wales slip past to starboard. Wrapped in an Inverness cape, he was smoking a last cigar and thinking over the events of the past few days.

On the advice of his doctors, he had resumed his convalescent cruise as soon as the celebrations and official functions were over. With the emotional stress of the Coronation coming so soon after his operation, they insisted on him taking time off to rest. The cruise had not begun as a rest. For nearly a week, events kept him in the waters between Cowes and Portsmouth Harbour. First, there had been an impressive Naval Review, when he had steamed along four lines of warships, each line more than three miles long, taking the salute from the bridge of the Victoria and Albert. Afterwards he had entertained all the captains and, at nightfall, the fleet had been illuminated, his touch on a button turning the heavy, menacing shapes of the men-of-war into delicate outlines, traced by curves and arches of little electric lights.

The next day, he had received the Boer leaders, Delarey, Louis Botha and Christian de Wet, who had arrived for talks at the Colonial Office. It had been a bizarre experience, seeing the launch approach, with Kitchener and Lord Roberts in dress uniform and the three Boer generals in black frock coats and trousers, black gloves and top hats. Alix had whispered that it was like receiving a deputation of undertakers. While he smiled and chatted, putting them at their ease, he had wondered what the impassive Kitchener was thinking. It must have been difficult for him to recognise these stiffly correct committee men as the savage fighters who had nearly turned the southern tip of Africa into a Dutch republic. He had said they were not to be

167

despised as enemies. Bertie hoped he welcomed them now as friends, as he did.

The real victory was that they had accepted colonial status in the Empire so readily, with the promise of full rights and privileges. Bertie had insisted on that. At a stroke, it wiped out any logical basis for attacks on Britain's policy by her European rivals. The war had been a disaster for both sides. On both sides there had been sacrifices and chivalry and heroism. If they recognised those qualities in each other and worked together, some lasting good might come of it in the end.

Two days after them had come another visitor, much less welcome, the Shah of Persia, Muzaffar-ed-Din, escorted by Lord Lansdowne. The Shah, a long-faced, autocratic man with suspicious eys, had come to England specifically to be invested with the Order of the Garter which Lansdowne had promised him. It was an extremely awkward situation for the Foreign Secretary as the King had flatly refused to confer it. To Bertie, the whole idea of diplomacy by the giving of decorations was ridiculous. He liked giving presents and decorations. They were a token of friendship, thanks and esteem . . . But he would not be dictated to. If the Government was concerned about Russian influence in Persia, the real way to solve it was by establishing better relations with Russia, not by pandering to a bankrupt and despotic Shah. In the course of the meeting, Lansdowne suggested that the officials of the Order ought to consider revising the statutes so that in future an altered version could be bestowed on non-Christians. He had brought a memorandum on the subject. Bertie nodded and promised to read it later.

The goodwill visit was a total failure. After lunch, the King presented the Shah with a miniature of himself, set in a gold frame covered with diamonds. The Shah refused it and ordered the members of his suite to refuse the decorations they were offered. He swept back to London, claiming he had been insulted. Bertie was angry, too, especially with Lansdowne, who did not have the courage to admit he had made a mistake and, by his weakness, had made a bad situation worse. He had put Bertie in an impossible position, where whatever he did was wrong.

The whole affair was embarrassing, even comical, if there had not been so many principles involved. Bertie was glad it was over.

For some while, he had been gazing at the light of a signal beacon on the coast. Its flash came roughly every twelve seconds and he had found himself counting out the pauses, oddly comforted by its regularity and the certainty of the moment of light. At first it had been away ahead. Then he had seen the cone of the beacon quite clearly on its pinnacle of rock against the sky. He realised that now it was far behind and the light only a tiny, uncertain flicker. The night air had grown colder. He rose and moved to the rail, pulling the cape closer about himself. One development in international affairs pleased him. He had managed to strengthen some of the ties between Britain and the New World. His courteously worded letter to President Roosevelt had brought an equally courteous reply and a cautious correspondence had begun, increasingly friendly. Also, to his surprise, he had been asked to arbitrate in a dispute over borders between the Argentine and Chile in the Southern Andes. It was a sign of trust, a hint that others had heard his plea for fair dealing between nations. If so, he had made a beginning.

It was time to go to bed. As he turned, he thought suddenly of Alice Keppel. This was the longest he had gone without seeing her for three years. She had written to him and he had sensed how worried she had been, behind the restraint of her carefully discreet letters. Not like Daisy Warwick's, extravagant, and tear-spotted, though nowadays they seldom met. He would have been more touched if Daisy had resisted mentioning her damned, radical politics. Even in bed, she had lectured him on Poor Relief and the wages of workers in the pen-making industry. Not Alice. He missed her and wished there had been some way to bring her on the cruise. He sighed and dropped his cigar over the rail. The night was so still, he could hear the faint hiss when it struck the water.

In the morning, the Royal Yacht tied up in Pembroke Dock and Ponsonby collected the mail and official boxes from the Government messenger. There were so many, his heart sank. Francis Knollys resented being left behind in London and had refused to let him bring a clerk. It meant starting at eight in the mornings on the routine mail, then going through anything more important with the King and, most days, carrying on till past midnight. In spite of that, Ponsonby enjoyed the work and was grateful that King Edward liked and trusted him enough to have chosen him as his travelling secretary. He did not know the other reasons, that Bertie thought him quicker witted than Davidson and more adaptable than Francis Knollys, who had become rather staid and old fashioned. Francis had also grown a little self-important, after so long acting as if his opinions were the King's. Bertie wanted to show him, gently, that he would not let himself be controlled by any single adviser. He would always make up his own mind.

After breakfast, Ponsonby took the day's delivery to the King's cabin. The messenger had said that one of the boxes from the Foreign Office was fairly urgent. Bertie had the key of the red despatch boxes, his proudest possession, owned long ago by his father. He unlocked the box while Ponsonby laid out the others, the letters and decoded telegrams on the desk. He expected some comment from the King, but there was silence. He looked round.

Bertie was sitting at the end of the desk, staring at what seemed to be a coloured drawing. His face was flushed and his hands shook with anger. 'It's unthinkable . . .' he muttered. 'Damned impertinence!' He glanced again at the letter he held in his other hand. 'Outrageous!' He flung the drawing away from him and it skimmed across the cabin, dipping out through the open porthole. Ponsonby took a step after it. 'Leave it!' Bertie roared.

Ponsonby turned. He had never seen the King so angry. His lips were drawn back in a snarl, his teeth clenched. His eyes, glaring up at Ponsonby, were sharp and dangerous. Ponsonby had heard of his rages, but never seen one. It was unnerving. 'He shall not have it!' Bertie growled, his voice thick with fury. 'I did not promise it. He is not fit to wear it! Write and say so!'

Ponsonby did not even know what had angered him. 'I— I am afraid, sir,' he stammered. 'I don't . . .'

'Read that!' Bertie snarled and thrust the letter at him. Ponsonby recognised Lansdowne's precise handwriting at once. The Foreign Secretary had written to say that the Shah had demanded the Order of the Garter and must have it before he left England in three days' time. Therefore, since the King had consented, Lansdowne had told the Court jewellers to make up a version of the Garter badge and star, leaving off the Cross of St George. He enclosed a coloured illustration of the new design. Ponsonby read the letter once more quickly. 'As you said, sir,' he agreed. 'It's unthinkable.' Silently, he cursed Knollys for not having warned him that this storm was in the air.

The King had risen and was pacing. 'And this is the man who was removed from the War Office for incompetence . . . The man who told our troops in South Africa they would not need horses! And how he's running our foreign policy!' he thundered. 'Great God in Heaven!' He stopped, breathing in slow, panted breaths to calm himself. 'Write to our distinguished Foreign Secretary, Fritz,' he commanded. 'And tell him his assertion that I agreed to present the Garter to his friend, the Shah, is a deliberate damned lie! To debase the most noble Order of Christendom and to try to use me in his shabby, political game is unspeakable. As for the Shah—it is outrageous for one Sovereign to dictate to another what he should be given. If he leaves the country in the sulks, like a spoilt child, then good riddance! If the Garter's to go to anybody, it should be the Emperor of Japan. At least he's an ally and is probably a damn sight more pleasant. The Government wants us to strengthen our hold on Persia. Very desirable, but you might point out that we would not have lost it if the Foreign Office had had any idea of the real nature of diplomacy!'

Ponsonby hesitated. 'Perhaps Sir Francis Knollys should communicate with Lord Lansdowne, sir, knowing the background,' he suggested.

Bertie shook his head. 'It would take too long,' he declared. 'That's to go off at once. And tell Lansdowne the subject is now closed! I'll have no more talk of it.'

Ponsonby bowed, took the despatch box and the letter and left the cabin. He was dazed. The King was absolutely in the right, but he could imagine the Foreign Secretary's reaction, not to mention the Shah's. As he moved along the passage towards his own cabin, a young naval lieutenant came down the companionway. He was carrving the coloured drawing of the remodelled insignia. 'This anything to do with you?' he asked.

'Ah—yes. Very grateful,' Ponsonby thanked him. He was relieved to have it back. He would have been hard put to it to explain how it came to be missing.

'Most extraordinary,' the lieutenant said. 'One of our stokers caught it. He was in the steam pinnace, heading for the quay, when it came shooting out of a porthole.'

'It just blew out of my hand,' Ponsonby explained lamely. 'Clumsy of me.'

'Blew?' the lieutenant repeated, puzzled. The morning air was completely still and windless. 'I see. Most extraordinary.'

In his own cabin, Ponsonby reread Lansdowne's letter. On a piece of paper beside it, he jotted down the King's reply and considered it. The problem was that if he sent it word for word, the Foreign Office would explode. On the other hand, if he changed it, the King could justifiably sack him. Oh, well, he told himself, time you earned your salary.

The cruise up the west coast continued, from Wales to the Isle of Man and by slow stages to the Hebrides. By the time they reached Skye, Bertie was completely recovered, so fit he went deerstalking. He was bursting with energy and impatient to get back to some real work. Alix was glad he had invited Soveral to join them. She could tell there was something serious in Bertie's mind. At least, Luis kept him amused. He was a fund of anecdotes about the Coronation.

He told them of the alarm after the ceremony, when they had left for the Palace, and the Duke of Norfolk heard what sounded like muffled gunshots coming from the crypt of the Abbey. Convinced that anarchists had got in, he crept down with a party of beefeaters to find Esher and his family having a picnic lunch. The gunshots had been the popping of the champagne corks. Their favourite story was of the Duchess of Devonshire. After the Royal procession passed on the way to the exit, she had hurried out to join on the end. To the consternation of many, who thought she was suffering from sudden folie de grandeur. The truth was that Lottie, now over seventy and having had to wait since eight in the morning, was determined to reach the conveniences before any of the other peeresses. Unfortunately, she was in such haste she tripped over her train and tumbled down the steps of the stand, to land at the feet of the Chancellor of the Exchequer in a flurry of ermine robes, her wig knocked awry and her coronet rolling away down the blue carpet. Soveral, himself, had helped her up, unhurt but more desperate than ever, clutching her red wig, while Margot Asquith, the unconventional wife of the deputy leader of the Liberal Party, had gone scrambling after the coronet.

Bertie capped it. When the aged Archbishop of Canter-

172

bury had tottered at the altar and the other bishops had rushed to support him, the whole audience had been deeply moved. Sitting upright on the throne, Bertie had been fighting to keep his face straight. One of the bishops had asked in a whisper if he ought to take over.. 'It's not my head!' the Archbishop snapped. 'It's my legs.'

Bertie always chuckled remembering that. He needed something to distract him. The Shah had left for Persia, indignant and insulted, but he had not had any positive reaction from the Government yet over his letter to Lansdowne. To some extent, he regretted its vehemence now, but it could not be helped. He needed to know where he stood with the Government, to find out if Balfour were prepared to let him take an active part in running the country or if he was to be considered as a figurehead. He hoped that Balfour would realise how much good could be achieved if they worked together, instead of letting the Government chip constantly away at the rights of the Crown. The Prime Minister had always kept his own attitude to Bertie carefully hidden. How he behaved in this business with Lansdowne would bring it out in the open and show Bertie how much to trust him in the future.

The cruise over, the Royal party went by train to Balmoral in Aberdeenshire, the baronial castle created by Albert as a Scottish retreat for himself and Victoria. It had been their favourite home. The house was set in magnificent, wooded country, surrounded by mountains, in the valley of the River Dee. Whenever he saw the pointed turrets of its tower appear over the treetops on the long driveway, Bertie felt his spirits lift. Here, more than anywhere else, he could feel completely natural and at home. Alix and he had left much of the decoration as it was, apart from toning down the riot of tartans in the principal drawing-room. His father's normally impeccable taste had been given a holiday when he discovered tartans, but guests could now enter the drawing-room without experiencing a momentary sense of shock.

Bertie went trout fishing and Alix and he attended the Braemar Gathering. In Scotland, he usually wore a kilt. As he drove about the estate, calling on the tenants and discussing their crops and harvests, he looked just like a country laird. With hunting, a Ghillies' Ball and a visit from George and May and the children, the time passed quickly. Shortly before they were due to return south, they had two other visitors, Lord Kitchener and Arthur Balfour. Kitchener had come to pay his respects before taking up his new appointment as Commander-in-Chief in India. Balfour was on holiday.

With consummate tact, Bertie did not raise anything controversial the first day and the Prime Minister, with equally perfect manners, simply enjoyed the King's hospitality. The following evening, after a morning and afternoon spent deerstalking, they met in the study before dinner. Balfour was pleasant and relaxed, reviewing Colonial and Home Affairs. He introduced the subject of Persia almost as an afterthought. He agreed that, of course, for the insignia of the Garter to be changed for political purposes was out of the question and that Lansdowne had no right to offer it to the Shah without the King's permission. 'In the circumstances,' he said, 'Your Majesty's reply was a model of restraint, making its points forcefully but without giving offence.' Bertie made a mental note to thank Ponsonby. Obviously he had used great skill. 'I believe,' the Prime Minister went on, 'that Your Majesty is here solely concerned with the not unfamiliar problem of having to deal with a public servant who, by mistake, has exceeded his instructions.'

Bertie smiled. 'As you say—not unfamiliar.' He was prepared to be generous to Lansdowne. It was not in his nature to be vindictive and he wanted to be more closely connected with the Foreign Office, not cut off from it by hostility. He was relieved. Best of all, the whole sorry business was leading to a better working relationship with Balfour.

'In fairness to the Foreign Secretary,' Balfour said, 'he was pressed for time and Your Majesty had, at last, given your consent.'

'I had not,' Bertie observed quietly.

'Ah, but when he mentioned the matter in the presence of the Shah at Portsmouth, you were seen to nod twice distinctly, in agreement,' the Prime Minister reminded him, his voice bland.

Bertie was puzzled, then he remembered promising to read the memorandum on the possibility of devising a non-Christian version of the order. So Lansdowne had used that, leapt on it as a sign of his consent to everything. To save his face, Lansdowne was prepared to make a travesty of his honour.

'The fact is,' Balfour continued, smoothly, 'mistaken or

not, he has repeatedly and explicitly pledged Your Majesty to bestow the Garter on the Shah. And now the question arises, is he to be thrown over or is he not? If he is prevented from carrying out his pledge, what will be his position? And if he resigned, could the matter stop there, in these days of Government solidarity?' He paused, not looking at the King.

Bertie had grown cold. The Prime Minister, who had seemed so friendly, was in fact threatening that the whole Government would resign if he did not give in. Incredibly, Balfour was prepared to ignore the beliefs and lower the prestige of the King, merely to satisfy the pride of the Foreign Secretary. Disbelief was replaced by anger. Yet he fought to keep control of himself. The resignation of the Government, on a charge of Royal interference, would bring about a national crisis.

Balfour waited, gazing with apparent interest at a hunting print on the wall. He knew he was bound to win. He would push this to the limit to prove, once and for all, that the elected government ran the country, not the King.

Watching his sleek, handsome face, Bertie had become aware of the arrogance behind it, the same haughty, intellectual pride as Lansdowne, only covered by a mask of indifference. He had already assessed his chances of winning a fight with the Government. He could count on a massive amount of popular support. But some of the peers and nearly all members of the House of Commons would oppose him automatically. It would split the country. At his accession he had promised to be a constitutional monarch, and he could not break that promise. He was a prisoner of the Constitution and would have to submit. For his oath and the welfare of his people, he had to accept humiliation. Balfour depended on his own sense of duty defeating him. 'What's to be done?' he asked, managing to keep his voice steady.

Balfour breathed out slowly. He had not realised how tense he was. 'Oh, I think it's best for the Garter to be sent straight to Teheran, sir,' he said. 'In its traditional form, of course. Our Minister there can hand it over at a suitable ceremony.' He did not let his satisfaction show. The King had accepted defeat with dignity and that was good. Balfour did not wish the dispute to become public knowledge, especially since it would be certain to affect his own standing and popularity.

Bertie had learnt how much he could trust and depend on the Prime Minister. For the first time in his life, he had not a single friend in the Government. Just when he needed support most, if he was to achieve any of the ambitions of his life.

Coveys of startled pheasants rose with a sudden whir of wings, their brilliant plumage flashing in the bright, late afternoon sun that slanted through the trees. The leaders wheeled and soared away from the line of beaters moving through the thick bushes below.

Out in the open, Bertie waited, attended by a group of loaders and keepers. He was wearing a Homburg hat, a belted jacket and knee-breeches, and carrying a shotgun. Beyond him, Carrington, Soveral, Joseph Chamberlain, the Colonial Secretary, and Francis Knollys were spaced out, all with their loaders. Beside him stood Kaiser Wilhelm in a tight, green tunic and breeches, with members of his staff kneeling behind him. Willy had come for a short stay at Sandringham and they were in the estate. The day's sport had been excellent. The King and the Kaiser were tying for the best bag and the shooting had become a contest between them.

Bertie was enjoying it. Normally, Willy was the better shot but, as the day wore on, he had grown over-anxious. Bertie's eye was in and he had recovered from a few early misses, after which Willy had considerately offered to lend him one of his own guns. He kept reminding himself that his nephew could not help being offensive. He had only invited him out of necessity. Their two governments had failed to reach any agreement on an alliance, through unwillingness on either side to make concessions. If the suspicion between them were not to develop into something worse, it was essential that Bertie kept up some form of friendly contact with his nephew, although it had become increasingly difficult. He could not give up the idea, cherished by his parents and Vicky and himself for so long, of the two nations united in the name of peace.

They were waiting for the last drive of the afternoon. A keeper nearer the trees raised his hand. 'Here they come, Willy,' Bertie warned.

A flight of birds swept out of the cover and skimmed across in front of them. The Kaiser's kneeling attendant passed up his loaded shotgun. He turned quickly, aimed and

176

fired. The shot missed. He had been too hasty and snatched the trigger. He fired again and one of the pheasants dropped. Nearly at the ground, it fluttered, recovering, and flew on.

'Oh, bad luck,' Bertie said. Another flight of pheasants came across, high and fast. He snapped up his gun, firing both barrels. Two birds plummeted to the earth. He changed his empty shotgun for a loaded one, as the other guns opened up all along the line. More birds fell. Beside him, Wilhelm was shooting with an intense, scowling concentration.

When it was over, Bertie was ahead by three birds. 'Good shooting, sir!' Carrington called.

'Yes, Uncle Bertie,' Wilhelm agreed. 'How clever to have the beaters trained to drive the birds directly in front of you.' His jealousy was ill-concealed.

There was silence in the people round them as Bertie turned to look at him. 'Well, I'm glad there's something we do better than Germany,' he said mildly. 'We'd better be getting back or we'll be late for dinner. Come, Willy. Thank you, all.' He nodded to the keepers and loaders who bowed or touched their caps. Wilhelm handed his gun brusquely to his loader and moved to join him as he headed for the cars.

Bertie's maroon Daimler with the Royal crest on the side stood on a rough track a short distance behind them. The chauffeur jumped down to open the passenger door. As the guest, Wilhelm climbed in first. He still felt riled at coming second and had to assert himself. 'I've been meaning to ask you, Uncle Bertie—what fuel do your automobiles run on?'

Bertie paused with one foot on the step. 'I haven't the foggiest idea.' He climbed into the back seat and sat beside Willy. 'Petrol, I suppose.'

'I thought so,' Willy laughed. 'Completely unsuitable.' The chauffeur closed the door and bowed, before getting up into the driver's seat. The others had come up and were sorting themselves out into the cars behind. Wilhelm raised his voice in order to catch their attention. 'I have been experimenting, myself, with a spirit distilled from potatoes.'

'Sounds like Dutch gin,' Bertie said.

'It will prove the only suitable propellant for motor cars,' Wilhelm told him stiffly. 'I shall send you some.'

'Good,' Bertie nodded. 'Then if the car won't start, we can sit at home and drink it.'

Willy bridled. As the Daimler moved off, the officers of

his staff were scandalised to hear Carrington and Soveral laughing.

A small orchestra was playing the last movement of a waltz by Franz Lehar in the hall. It was light and gay and the musicians were relaxed as they played.

They sat up more correctly as the door of the salon was thrust open and the King stalked out, followed quickly by the Queen. They were both in evening dress. The King glowered at the orchestra and strode towards the stairs.

Alix had paused to close the door. She hurried to catch him up. 'Bertie—you must go back.'

Bertie stopped with one foot on the stairs, fuming. 'No!'

'What shall I tell our guests?'

'Tell them I'm bored.'

'I can't,' Alix objected. 'Willy would be insulted.'

Bertie glanced at the closed door of the salon. 'Neither the fact that he's my guest, nor my nephew, nor the Kaiser, gives him the right to be a bore!'

Alix could not hear him properly for the music. 'Don't be difficult,' she said soothingly. 'You mustn't break up the party.'

'It's not a party!' Bertie roared. 'It's a damned one-man monologue from an arrogant booby who thinks because he wears a crown no one has the right to contradict him!'

'You're going to evict him?' Alix asked surprised.

Bertie paused. 'That's a damned good idea,' he nodded.

The orchestra came to the end of the waltz and there was quiet. 'Ah, that's better,' Alix smiled. 'Now, what were you saying?'

Conscious of the musicians, Bertie could not shout. 'I said, how long is he staying here?'

'Yes. I think you should,' Alix answered, patting his arm. He grunted in exasperation, glancing at the silent orchestra and back to her. 'I'm so glad you've changed your mind,' she went on. 'After all, you're the only one who can argue with him.'

As he looked at her, all at once, his mouth twitched. 'Evict him . . .' he chuckled. He gave a short rumble of laughter. 'Very well, I'll go back. But only to keep the peace. And only for you, my dear.' Smiling, he took her arm and tucked it under his.

In the salon, Kaiser Wilhelm sat alone in the centre of one of the sofas. Around him, seated or standing listening to

178

him, were his aides and the fellow guests who had been on the shoot. They had been joined by Toria, Charlotte Knollys and Lady de Grey. Seated near him were the amiable, bearded Sir Dighton Probyn, Keeper of the Privy Purse, and Admiral Sir John Fisher, Commander-in-Chief at Portsmouth. Fisher was a round-faced, forthright man in his early sixties, with white hair and very dark, fierce eyebrows. By many he was considered a genius, the greatest English sailor since Nelson. Unconventional and thrusting, he caused great concern at the Admiralty with his unceasing demands for modernisation and reform of the Navy. He was staring at the Kaiser with a rapt fascination which Wilhelm took as a compliment.

Wilhelm was holding forth, using the rest of the guests as an impromptu personal court. 'The British Empire may be the largest the world has ever known,' he declared. 'But it is also the most inefficient. You allow your Dominions far too much individual freedom.'

The Colonial Secretary, Joseph Chamberlain, a tall, monocled man, coughed warningly. Fisher had leant forward angrily, about to speak. He checked himself and sat back. Chamberlain answered the Kaiser, himself. 'That is because they are Dominions, and not colonies, sir.'

'Exactly!' Wilhelm announced, triumphantly. 'A situation which I would not tolerate. But then, my uncle is in the hands of his government, rather than them receiving their orders directly from him.'

'It is the democratic system, sir,' Knollys said.

'It is madness, Sir Francis,' Willy smiled. 'Democracy is only one step from anarchy. We can give a token recognition to it but only to keep the more radical elements quiet.'

The door opened and Bertie and Alix came in. As those seated made to rise, Alix waved to them to sit again. This informality was one of the features of his uncle's court which Wilhelm most admired. Informality, yet everyone knowing his place. Alix sat beside Charlotte Knollys. Bertie moved to take a cigar from the box on one of the tables. As he snipped off the end with his cigar cutter, he watched Wilhelm stonily.

'I do hope we haven't missed anything interesting.' Alix smiled.

'His Imperial Majesty was explaining to us the reasons

179

for our lack of preparedness at the start of the South African war, ma'am,' Chamberlain said.

Bertie grunted. He busied himself with his cigar as a footman struck a match for him. Alix laughed. 'It's perfectly simple. We didn't expect to have to fight.'

'Very true, Aunt Alix,' Wilhelm conceded. 'The British never expect to have to fight.' He smiled as if he had won a point. 'The British Army is chronically unprepared for wars. It should not engage in them.'

'Yet it contrives to win them, sir,' Carrington said innocently.

Fisher snorted with laughter and Wilhelm glanced at him sharply. 'Only through inability to accept the logicality of defeat!' he snapped.

'The logicality of defeat . . . ?' Fisher echoed, mystified.

Wilhelm sat up straighter. He was disappointed in Fisher, whom he now recognised as a trouble-maker.

Bertie stepped in. 'Sir John's a naval man, Willy,' he explained. 'The only logic he understands is a torpedo.' The guests laughed, easing the moment's tension. 'Still,' he went on, 'I didn't quite understand myself what you meant.'

Wilhelm shrugged, smiling. 'Well—take your war in the Cape. The Boers had beaten you in the first six months.'

'Ah, but you see, we didn't accept that,' Bertie murmured.

'Precisely!' Wilhelm said. 'And fortunately for you, I devised my strategic plan.' As Bertie raised his eyebrows, he added indignantly, 'The plan of campaign your armies followed in South Africa! I sent copies to you and Field-Marshal Roberts.'

There was consternation among the guests. Carrington and Chamberlain looked questioningly at Knollys. Knollys shook his head. Fisher was silently raging. Alix smiled to Soveral who had stayed well in the background. The Kaiser did not care for him.

'Well, now,' Bertie remarked. He blew softly on the tip of his cigar. 'I seem to remember Roberts considered your advice impractical.'

'He must have followed it!' Wilhelm exclaimed. 'How else could he have won?'

'How indeed . . . ?' Bertie wondered. 'I must say I am touched by your concern for our welfare. But I find it puzzling, in that case, why you advised us in your notes to admit defeat. And to reconcile it with your offer to the Boers to send them German marines as reinforcements.'

He had cut the ground completely from under the Kaiser. These were indiscretions of Willy's which he regretted, but he was too wily to be caught. He laughed indulgently. 'You of all people should not be puzzled by that, Uncle Bertie. I understand you had to be stopped from sending condolences to Kruger on the death of his wife.'

'That's not the same thing at all, Willy,' Bertie assured him. 'Not the same at all.'

Wilhelm shrugged and glanced away from him. 'Well, I must accept that you do not really understand the military mind,' he drawled. 'After all you have never served personally in a campaign.'

The others held their breath. The King's head rose tensely and he stared at the Kaiser. It was the cheap gibe the French and German newspapers always used against him. For many years, his constant fight with his mother had been over her refusal to let him serve in the Army. Wilhelm had scored a point at last, but had forfeited the last of his uncle's affection.

'War, war,' Alix sighed. 'The war's been over for six months but you men still talk about it.'

The guests shifted their position, trying not to look at the King or the Kaiser. Outside, the orchestra was playing a polka. It seemed inappropriately gay and lively. Soveral smiled to Alix. 'What would you have us talk about, ma'am?'

Alix's smile answered his. 'I don't want to talk at all. There's a perfectly good orchestra playing perfectly delightful music out there. I have been longing to dance for the last hour.'

'In the hall, ma'am?' Charlotte asked, surprised.

'Why not?' Alix laughed.

Soveral took a step towards her and bowed. 'Then if I may have the inestimable honour——?'

'No, no, Luis,' Alix said, rising. 'I want to dance with my handsome nephew.'

Wilhelm had seemed to have retreated into an imperious aloofness. He knew he was in the wrong but couldn't back down because his aides were watching him. He glanced at Alix who stood, smiling, radiant in her silver evening dress. His aloof pose melted. He rose and bowed, suddenly all charm. 'You have only to beckon, Aunt Alix,' he assured her, smiling. 'And besides—it is not every day one can dance the polka with an Empress.' Alix laughed. He bowed to Bertie and moved to her, crooking his arm. She laid her hand on it and he led her towards the door as the footmen opened it.

Carrington and Francis Knollys moved nearer to Bertie and stood with him, watching as Soveral, taking Alix's cue, led out Gladys de Grey. Chuckling, Fisher bowed to Charlotte Knollys and, over her protests, linked arms with her and marched her out into the hall where Wilhelm and Alix were already dancing. In a few seconds, the whole atmosphere had changed. She is amazing, Bertie thought. She seems to be aware of nothing, yet her touch is perfect.

Alix was laughing up to Wilhelm as they spun and hopped in the polka. Holding her, Wilhelm had become another person, younger, his face alight with enjoyment. Infected by her gaiety, he felt released.

Carrington glanced at the King, seeing him shake his head slightly. 'Know something, Charlie?' Bertie murmured. 'For years, I've been pinning all my hopes on him, trying to ensure the future through him. I've just realised—he's off his head.'

Chapter

11

To line the walls of his magnificent house in Park Lane, Sir Ernest Cassel had imported eight hundred tons of Carrara marble. In the hall, between pilasters of lapis lazuli, hung four superb paintings by Van Dyck. Everywhere was the gleam of gilt and crystal, an opulence that rivalled the Rothschilds.

Like his taste, his hospitality was lavish. His oak-panelled dining-room could seat over a hundred guests in comfort. The dinners he gave for the King were the ultimate in luxury, yet he was happiest when he was asked to keep the numbers to twelve or sixteen, just a few friends who could talk freely and, afterwards, divide easily into foursomes for Bridge, the third of the Royal passions which Cassel shared. The first two were the company of attractive women and the exercise of power. Their tastes bound them together. Like the King, he believed the strong had a duty to the weak, the rich to the less fortunate, and gave immense amounts to charity. Wherever possible, he used his business empire to further the interests and prestige of his adopted country, as in Egypt, which had recently come under British control, where he financed a vast irrigation scheme that transformed the lives of the peasant workers.

A reserved man, he preferred the smaller dinner parties, himself. He was human enough to enjoy his intimacy with the King and shrewd enough to realise its value. To their friendship, he owed his social position and his title. There were many people who were envious of him as the King's most trusted adviser, a jumped-up Jewish immigrant. Many were scandalised when, after receiving the heads of the Christian Churches at his accession, Edward had also received the Chief Rabbi and leaders of the Jewish community. They were shaken when Cassel was sworn as a Privy Councillor and refused the hat which the Clerk of the Council tactfully offered him. Obeying the last wish of his wife before she died, he had been converted to Roman Catholicism. It was typical of him that only his intimate friends knew.

Most of them were seated round his table. The King, Esher, Soveral, Francis Knollys, Admiral Fisher and Charles Carrington. Next to the King, he most admired Esher whom he had just induced to give up his post at the Office of Works and join him in the City. He doubted if it would last, as Esher was more suited to politics than to business. He respected Soveral for the astute mind he concealed behind the charm and high spirits and Knollys for his wide knowledge and loyalty to his master. Fisher fascinated him, on the surface a blunt, jovial sailor but, underneath, a brilliant strategist with a showman's feeling for publicity, combined with clarity of vision and the zeal of a crusader. The most likable was Charles Carrington, the King's oldest friend. A balanced, charming man, he seemed all relaxation and ease of manner, yet he was a reforming, liberal politician, had been an able Governor of New South Wales and was strongly tipped as a future Viceroy of India. One thing was common to them all, Cassel realised. Civilised, friendly, intelligent, they were all much more than they seemed.

Opposite Cassel, the King sat between Alice Keppel and the delicious, tawny-haired Mrs Willy James. Slim, vivacious, the daughter of a Scottish baronet, she refreshed Bertie with her lightheartedness. Next to Alice, she was his most constant companion. Somehow they shared his favours without jealousy and were even good friends. To one side, Cassel could see her dapper husband sitting beside another of the Royal favourites, Agnes Keyser. Mature, attractive, backed by Bertie she had turned her house in Grosvenor Crescent into a Nursing Home for Officers during the war. For her care and devotion to the wounded, she was known as Sister Agnes. They were laughing as Carrington protested, 'No, no. It's absolutely true.'

'What was the bet?' Mrs James asked.

'Five hundred pounds. And for that Beresford wagered that he'd walk naked at twelve o'clock midday, from Hyde Park Corner to Piccadilly Circus.'

'In broad daylight?' Agnes Keyser doubted.

'Of course, we took him up on it,' Bertie said. 'We didn't think even Charlie B had the nerve for that.'

'But he won his five hundred,' Carrington told them. As

the others waited, intrigued, he explained. 'He hired a hansom cab. He cut the bottom out of it, got in and took his clothes off and had it drive at walking pace down Piccadilly. All you could see was a pair of bare legs and feet plodding along underneath.'

Everyone round the table laughed, except Fisher. Alice clapped her hands. 'He deserved to win.'

'It was typical Beresford,' Fisher muttered. 'Cheating his friends.'

There was an uncomfortable pause. Admiral Lord Charles Beresford had been a close friend of Bertie's until they quarrelled over Daisy Warwick. Officially, they had made their peace but, now, Beresford had antagonised Fisher. When he was Admiral of the Mediterranean Fleet, Beresford had been his second-in-command and had taken over when he returned to Portsmouth. No sooner had Fisher left, than Beresford set himself up as the champion of the old school, opposing and ridiculing his former chief's attempt to reform the obsolete and unwieldy apparatus of the Navy. It was an explosive topic, but Alice Keppel did not let it develop. She looked across at Cassel. 'Are you a gambler, Sir Ernest?'

He smiled at her. 'All financiers are, to some extent, gamblers.'

'That's a very cautious answer,' Mrs James challenged.

'Shall we say, then—I have to be so very sure of the odds, that it holds little excitement for me.'

'Now you see why I asked him to handle my financial affairs,' Bertie said. Alice smiled to him, yet she was troubled. She could tell that he was brooding, forcing himself to appear relaxed. Carrington had sensed that, too, and had been joking to keep the atmosphere light.

'It is an honour, sir,' Cassel said.

'It has certainly left Your Majesty free to attend to other things,' Esher agreed.

'Yes, that was the theory,' Bertie nodded. 'And Ernest has carried out his part splendidly. I am free to fulfil my duties.' He swilled the wine round in his glass. 'But what duties am I allowed to fulfil? Nothing but empty ceremony. I ride first in the parade.' He finished his wine in one quick swallow.

It was rare for him to show his depression in public, even among friends. They were all serious, aware now of

185.

the bitterness that had been clear to Alice and Carrington. 'The Monarch is much more than that, sir,' Esher said quietly.

'So I used to believe.' Bertie set his empty glass down. 'And for a time, I thought I could be of use, that the Government would listen to me.'

'Surely they do?' Alice objected.

Bertie shook his head. 'You cannot advise when you are not given the information. Important questions are already decided before I hear of them.'

Fisher had not understood any of this. 'How can that be, sir? You are the King.'

Bertie grunted. 'And what's that? Only a signature these days. I am merely expected to give my consent.'

Cassel glanced from Esher to Carrington, hoping that one of them would step in to soothe the King. 'Well, of course,' Carrington said carefully, 'the Government has total responsibility under the constitution for all domestic affairs.'

'I accept that,' Bertie conceded. 'But all too often, decisions are not dictated by what is right for the country but by party politics.' There was a murmur of assent. 'And the Monarch has a right to be consulted. So that there is one continuous, unbiased adviser—whichever government is in office.'

'Hear, hear,' Francis Knollys declared. 'It is essential.'

'I tell you I detest being forced to accept decisions of which I do not approve!' Bertie growled. 'My advice should be listened to!' He was becoming belligerent, heartened by their support.

'I agree with you entirely—in principle, sir,' Carrington said. Bertie looked at him sharply, conscious of a reservation, but he went on. 'However, a head-on clash with your ministers would leave them with no alternative but to resign.'

'The Foreign Secretary's always threatening to do that anyway,' Esher remarked drily. Cassel was surprised at him. Instead of helping the King to stay detached, sometimes he almost seemed to egg him on. He could see the King scowl as if he had been touched on a raw spot.

'A case in point!' Bertie snapped. 'This present Government agreed with me that we must forge links with Europe. Yet they botched the German alliance which I had set up

186

and are taking no measures to lessen the hostility shown to us by France and Russia.'

'Perhaps they are being too cautious,' Carrington acknowledged. 'Yet there is no other way. They have to overcome centuries of distrust.'

'We are not merely unpopular,' Cassel added. 'We are detested abroad.'

Bertie nodded, accepting the truth of what they said. 'Still, they could surely find some new avenue of approach,' he muttered.

'Couldn't you suggest one, sir?' Agnes Keyser asked. 'After all, you have a unique knowledge of opinions and conditions in Europe.'

'Speaking as a foreigner,' Soveral smiled, 'I know that on the Continent people consider Your Majesty, and not your Government, as representing the views of this country.'

'Tell that to the Cabinet,' Bertie glowered. He signed to the footman behind his chair to fill his glass. 'Of course, I'd like to do something positive! But even there my hands are tied. Well, I had to watch impotently all the time I was Prince of Wales—and I refuse to sit idle while there is important work to be done!' He attacked the roast grouse on his plate, not appearing to notice that it had gone cold. All his irritation had returned. The others looked at one another, concerned, wondering if perhaps they should have left well alone.

The evening was spoilt and, although Bertie tried to respond to his friends, he could not shake off his depression. He would have preferred to be on his own with Alice or Mrs Willy or Agnes Keyser. They would have known how to distract him but he could not leave without hurting Cassel. Years before, the custom had been for the ladies to retire after dinner and the gentlemen to join them later, after an hour or two of brandy, cigars and exclusively masculine conversation. Bertie had stopped that, shortening the period to no more than half an hour. It cut down on hard drinking and made for a more enjoyable evening. Tonight, he chafed even at the half hour.

When they met again in the ornate upper drawing-room, Esher managed to seize a few moments with Alice Keppel. They watched the footmen strip the covers from new packs of cards and place them on the Bridge tables. 'Cassel is afraid he wants to go home,' he murmured.

'No,' Alice said. 'At times like this he dreads being alone.'

'I assumed you might be with him,' Esher smiled. 'I would welcome that. He is greatly influenced by you.'

'What do you wish me to do?' she asked.

Her directness threw Esher for a moment. He shrugged. 'Merely to encourage him.'

'I could not encourage him to defy the Government.'

'Of course not,' Esher agreed. 'But his instincts are completely right. He could be of great service to the country.'

He broke off as Bertie strode in with Cassel. He was smoking one of his thick, black cigars and was still strained and irritable.

'All set up, is it?' he coughed. 'Good. Come along, partner.' He nodded to Alice and they moved to sit at the nearest table. The others arranged themselves quickly into foursomes.

The atmosphere was still subdued and for a time nothing was heard but the slip and tap of the packs as they were shuffled. Esher and Cassel were playing against Bertie and Alice. Bertie had been watching them stonily and, as Esher began to deal, growled, 'We're here to play Bridge. Right? So no lectures.'

'We wouldn't presume,' Alice murmured.

'Ha!' Bertie snorted. 'I've already had one from Ernest. "Keep the peace at all costs." '

'It's not such a bad idea,' Alice said, sorting her hand as it was dealt.

Bertie frowned, his resentment ready to turn to anger. 'So I'm just supposed to knuckle under to Balfour and Lansdowne and all the others! Do nothing?'

'You're so good at handling people, I'd have thought you could find a way to do what you want without antagonising anyone.' She was offhand, concerned only with her cards, but her words struck home.

Bertie watched her, his mind turning, then became aware that Cassel and Esher were looking at him expectantly. 'All right, Alice,' he said gruffly, 'just concentrate on the game. Remember we're up against two of the foxiest players in England.'

'Oh . . .' Alice exclaimed. Her hand was made up of low numbers, scattered through the suits. She looked at it in mock dismay. 'Then God save the King . . . And preserve Alice Keppel.'

Bertie stared at her for a second, then began to chuckle. As Cassel smiled, the chuckle became a huge, infectious roar and soon all the other tables were laughing. The evening was saved.

Bertie was still chuckling when he came into his study at Buckingham Palace some hours later. For once, the cards had been with him and he and Alice had won two rubbers out of three. Esher had accompanied him home and was astonished to find that he intended to work. 'It's so late, sir,' he had protested. 'There's a lot to get through,' Bertie had said. 'And one or two things I want to get clear in my mind.'

He turned on the light of his desk lamp and sat. As he took out the key of the despatch boxes from his waistcoat pocket, the door behind him clicked softly open. He looked round surprised, wondering who would walk in without knocking. His visitor was Caesar. 'Hello, there,' Bertie chuckled. Caesar trotted across to him and jumped up on to his lap. 'Been waiting up for me? That's kind.' Bertie ruffled his ears. Caesar licked his hand and settled down happily, his chin on Bertie's knee.

It would have disturbed him to reach for the Foreign Office box and Bertie hesitated. He already had a fair idea what it contained. Since their chilly disagreement over the memorandum he had handed to the Kaiser and their warmer argument over the Garter, Lansdowne sent him the barest minimum of information, the briefest summaries of discussions and reports. Bertie got around it as he had in the past, by inducing his ambassadors in European countries to write to him direct. Many of them were personal friends and their letters were correspondingly frank. He checked what they told him discreetly with their opposite numbers in London, chargés d'affaires and ambassadors who were only too willing to accept his hospitality. More information came in letters from relatives in foreign courts and from observers stationed abroad, like Mackenzie Wallace of *The Times* who wrote from St Petersburg. In general, Bertie now had a more widespread and, in many instances, a more detailed knowledge of events and attitudes abroad than his own Foreign Office.

As he stroked the back of Caesar's neck, he thought of Wallace's description of the feeling in Russia. Still, deep discontent and unrest, more and more agitation from political extremists and harsher methods used to silence them, yet the bulk of the people seemed to be united behind the

189

Czar through growing fear of Japan. War fever was becoming more intense and now Britain was seen as an outright enemy because of the treaty with Japan. The main provision of the treaty was that if either party was forced into a war in the Far East, the other would remain strictly neutral, unless a third Power joined in, when it would come to the aid of its ally. The Russians could not see that the agreement was designed to discourage war or, if it began, to stop other nations becoming involved. 'What are we to do?' Bertie asked aloud and Caesar pricked up his ears.

Britain was isolated, had been deliberately isolated by policy. In itself that was not dangerous, as long as her fleet ruled the seas. Yet times were changing. America had taken a new importance in the world. How she would use it remained to be seen. Would she stay aloof or join in the scramble to increase her empire? The other major powers were all in Europe, split into the Triple Alliance, made up of Germany, Austria and Italy, and the Dual Alliance of France and Russia. The smaller countries were uncommitted and swayed in the wind. The whole of the Continent was in a state of armed peace, with the two blocs in a constantly shifting balance. The only thing they had in common was envy of the British Empire, whose very existence limited the size of their colonial expansion.

For more than fifty years the chief rival had been Russia. For most of that time, France had been mainly friendly but had been humiliated in recent years when troops under Kitchener ordered a force of French soldiers under Colonel Marchand to leave the area of Fashoda in the Sudan, which they had colonised. The threat of war was ended by France renouncing her claim to any part of the Nile Valley. It had never been forgotten and, at the outbreak of hostilities in South Africa, the French people clamoured for their country to take up arms on the side of the Boers. Up till that same war, the British had looked on Germans as their natural allies But the sudden revelation of unconcealed hatred in the German press, the vicious attacks on the British troops and the massive aid given openly to the Boers ended that completely. The libels and attacks still continued. Bertie had hoped that Wilhelm would have the wisdom and courage to put a stop to them, but he had proved undependable. Britain could no longer look to Germany.

As for the smaller countries, Bertie knew he could count

on the friendship of Denmark and Sweden. Spain stood apart after the loss of Puerto Rico, the Philippines, Guam and Cuba in her war with the United States. Holland was violently hostile, as was Belgium. Greece depended almost for her survival on Britain but the only actual ally was Portugal, an alliance going back many centuries. Yet even there Dutch and German agents had been at work. Much of the supplies smuggled in to the Boers had gone through Delagoa Bay in Portuguese East Africa. He knew from Soveral that the Government in Lisbon feared the bay would be annexed by British forces.

Bertie sighed. England was easily the most hated country in the world. The Government had at last realised the dangers of her position, but was too cautious and suspicious to do anything meaningful about it. And abroad, the caution was taken for unfriendliness and contempt. Somehow, a door had to be opened before it was too late.

The bombshell burst two days later when Arthur Balfour strode into the Foreign Secretary's office overlooking St James's Park. Lansdowne was jerked out of his normal urbanity. 'He can't be serious!' he gasped.

'I assure you, he is,' Balfour told him. 'Knollys informs me that the King has decided to undertake a "grand tour" of Southern Europe.'

'But none of his predecessors ever did anything like that!' Lansdowne protested. 'Queen Victoria only paid one State Visit throughout her entire reign.'

'Well, it's all arranged as far as His Majesty is concerned,' Balfour said.

Lansdowne was indignant. 'Without consulting the Foreign Office?'

'Apparently—since you hadn't heard of it.'

'It's out of the question!' Lansdowne snapped. 'Lord knows what he'd say or do. You remember that business with the memorandum? Just think what he might commit us to!'

'I agree,' Balfour said firmly. 'He must be talked out of it.'

The King received them in the red Audience Room. Now that he had decided, he had fully recovered his good humour. He was charming and listened to them attentively, but he was not to be swayed.

191

'Such a tour is without precedent, sir,' Lansdowne maintained.

'I am not a point of law,' Bertie replied. In spite of himself Balfour smiled. Bertie shook his head. 'No, you see, all the trips I've made before were unofficial. They don't have the same effect as a State Visit. And for far too long, I have been unable to travel freely in Europe.'

'It is too dangerous, sir,' Lansdowne objected. 'If you recall, there was an attempt on Your Majesty's life at Brussels.'

'It's not something you forget easily,' Bertie smiled. 'But don't you think it's worth the risk to find out if we still have some friends in the world?'

'That could be very valuable,' Balfour allowed, reluctantly.

'My nephew, the Kaiser, runs about all over the Continent as if it were his back garden,' Bertie said. 'Der Reisende Kaiser, his people call him. He does it in great style to show the smaller countries how much better off they'd be to support Germany. Some attention from us might help them to resist pressure.'

Balfour hesitated. 'Where precisely had you thought of going, sir?'

'Precisely, Mr Balfour, I'm not sure,' Bertie shrugged. 'I've promised the Portuguese Ambassador to visit his country. Then I thought I'd go to Gibraltar, cruise a little and maybe call in somewhere in Italy.'

'And that is all, sir?' Lansdowne asked.

'As I say, I'm not sure.'

Lansdowne was thrown by his casualness. He coughed. 'Well, I could ask my department to look into the feasibility of it.'

'Ask all you like,' Bertie told him blandly, 'but I'm going next month.'

Lansdowne gaped. 'That's impossible, sir! There will be arrangements to make.'

Bertie smiled. 'I shall make my own as I go along.'

'It gives us very little time,' Balfour pointed out.

'For what?'

'To prepare subjects for Your Majesty to discuss, to appoint a Cabinet Minister to accompany you.'

Bertie considered him. 'What do I need a Cabinet Minister for?'

'Uh—well, sir,' Balfour began. He could not say that he

did not trust the King's discretion. 'There are no problems with Portugal, but the new King of Italy is an unknown quantity.'

'Exactly why someone ought to go and have a look at him,' Bertie smiled. 'And then, I don't know that he'll even want to meet me. But that's the kind of thing I'd rather play by ear as I go along. Now. I take it you have no further objections?'

It was at once a question and a dismissal. Lansdowne was seething again, but stayed silent. He did not want another unseemly clash with the King.

Balfour had one last try. 'If you insist on going, sir, I must also insist that you take a representative of the Government with you.'

Bertie drew himself up, but managed to stifle his irritation. 'Very well, Prime Minister,' he said. He thought for a moment. A young man from the Foreign Office had just married one of Alix's ladies-in-waiting. He seemed capable and highly promising. 'I'll take Charles Hardinge. We shall communicate through him.'

Lansdowne had to protest. 'He's only an Under-Secretary!'

'It's Hardinge or no one,' Bertie said decisively, then smiled. 'Well, I don't need the President of the Council, do I? After all, I don't intend to sign anything. I'm only going visiting.'

Alexandra was in high anger. Once again, everything had been decided without her knowledge and she had just realised that she was to be left behind. She and Bertie were in the sitting-room with George and May. Ponsonby waited at the door, trying not to hear.

'Why can't I come with you?' Alix demanded.

Bertie did not like to hurt her but, for the trip he had in mind, her deafness would be a handicap, and he did not wish to have to stop at any time to consider her safety or comfort. 'All the arrangements have been made,' he said.

'Without telling me!'

'It had to be kept secret,' he explained. 'There's an element of danger involved.'

'All the more reason why I should be with you!' Alix insisted. 'You're taking everyone else.'

'Only Ponsonby and a few others,' he told her. 'Now I'm sorry, my dear. It's not possible. If you'll excuse me, I have a lot to do.' He moved towards the door which Ponsonby opened. Bertie looked back. 'George—speak to your mother.'

He went out and Ponsonby followed him, closing the door.

Alix caught her breath. 'You see how I am treated? . . . And it's not the first time. He won't share things with me.'

'He genuinely feels that the trip would be too strenuous for you, Motherdear,' George assured her.

'Nonsense!' Alix rapped. 'I'm as fit as a fiddle, while he puffs and blows all the time.' She moved to the piano, her back to them, touching the keyboard. She did not like the feeling of being neglected. 'I know what it is,' she muttered. 'He was supposed to come with me to Denmark. He has never cared for it. Anything to get out of visiting my father.'

'Oh, I don't think it can be that,' May said, then bit her lip. She sympathised greatly with her mother-in-law. If ever Georgie treated her in the way his father treated his mother, she would never forgive it. She did not approve of Mrs Keppel and the others, but at least none of them could go with the King on an official visit.

Alix turned. 'Why else would he choose to leave now? And why won't he tell me exactly where he's going?'

George shrugged. 'He hasn't told anyone.'

Alix frowned. 'Why does it all have to be so secret?'

Even the members of Bertie's staff were not sure where they were going, nor why. He had told each of them only as much as he needed to know to carry out his duties. All they were certain of was that the first stop was Lisbon.

Although this was an official foreign visit, he had brought surprisingly few aides, only Hardinge and Ponsonby, Major-General Sir Stanley Clarke as Acting Master of the Household, Sir Francis Laking and his favourite among the younger Equerries, the handsome Captain the Hon Seymour Fortescue. Also with them was the Royal Marine Painter, the Chevalier Eduardo de Martino, a volatile, vainglorious man who had no real function on the trip, except that his posturing amused the King and the Marquis de Soveral who travelled with him. It's a bit like a flying column, Ponsonby thought.

On the day they left Portsmouth on the Royal Yacht, they were all, including Soveral, paraded in full dress uniform for the King's inspection. The sea was rough and some of the suite felt distinctly queasy. It was worth it, however, to see the pompous Martino, green-faced, heaving inside his tight court dress, barely able to stand to attention. None of them had experience in paying a State Visit. Much depended on the first impression they created. It was the King's way of showing them that every detail must be perfect.

Ponsonby quickly became friends with Hardinge, with whom he would have to liaise closely. One or other of them should have been making all the arrangements. At their first meeting they discovered, to their mutual surprise, that the King was organising everything, himself. The Hon Charles Hardinge was not a difficult man to like. Tall, good-looking, with a diplomat's ease of manner, he was an Assistant Under-Secretary when he was plucked from the Foreign Office to accompany the King. He was ambitious and knew that it could be invaluable to his career. All the same, behind the cool exterior, he was slightly nervous. Suddenly to find himself Minister Plenipotentiary was unnerving enough, but Lansdowne had impressed on him the need to supervise the King minutely, to monitor his statements and actions and report back to the Cabinet. Failure to do so would be inexcusable. Yet all the King wanted of him was up-to-date information and a list of points the Foreign Office would wish to be mentioned in any speeches that were made. He had read through the drafts Hardinge gave him.

'Yes, well, that seems reasonable,' he said with a smile. 'I'll say something like that, though not perhaps in quite the same words or the same order.'

Before they had even reached Portugal, Hardinge realised that he was in the presence of a master of diplomacy. Far from instructing the King, he and the Foreign Office had a great deal to learn from him. For his own part, Bertie realised he had made the right choice. He was seldom wrong in his judgement of character. Hardinge was well-informed, but not biased or hidebound. He would not be afraid to improvise. In time, he could be another right hand, like Ponsonby.

When the Royal Yacht and its escort arrived at Lisbon, it was a perfect spring day. In the centuries-old state barge with a golden dragon's head at its prow, rowed by eighty men in red, the King of Portugal, Dom Carlos, came out to take his visitors ashore. Welcoming him on board, Bertie was struck again by the likeness between him and Soveral, who was reputed to be his natural son. Dom Carlos was a larger version of his ambassador in London, a vast jovial tub of a man with an infectious laugh, merry eyes and a gargantuan appetite. He was Bertie's firmest friend among his foreign cousins and, for many years, he had done whatever he could to help him hold together his tottering, nearly bankrupt country. Many times Portugal had been on the verge of revolution and it was not made easier by Carlos's personal extravagance. He adored England and invited himself as often as possible. His last stay, just after Wilhelm's disastrous visit, had lasted three weeks. Bertie and Alix had entertained him at Sandringham, show him the wonders of the redecorated Buckingham Palace and Windsor Castle, given a ball in his honour, a state banquet, taken him to the theatre and the opera. On the evening before he left, Bertie had asked him what had impressed him most during his stay. Without hesitation, Carlos said, 'English roast beef.' 'Yes, yes,' Bertie chuckled, 'but what next after that?' Carlos had thought for a little longer before deciding. 'English roast pork,' he beamed.

Carlos was touched by Bertie's tribute in wearing his honorary uniform as Colonel of a Portuguese cavalry regiment. He was delighted to have him as his guest for once and apologised profusely for the absence of his wife, Queen Amelie, who was on a yachting cruise somewhere in the Mediterranean. The visit had been arranged too quickly for her to return, he explained. Bertie reassured him. Since Alix was not with him, the Queen's presence was not essential. Privately, he thought that Carlos was relieved to have his wife out of the way in case the visit sparked off Republican demonstrations. After the suites were introduced, the two Kings walked together on the forward deck while their aides discussed the arrangements for the next five days. Carlos was most impressed by the appearance of his cousin's staff, their dress and behaviour had such style. He chuckled and sympathised when Bertie mentioned that he might change into Admiral's uniform like him before going ashore.

'Yes,' he twinkled. 'Short jackets and tight breeches are not very kind to gentlemen with majestic figures.'

The Admiral's uniform was already laid out in the dressing cabin next to the Royal state room. As his valet helped him out of the frogged, cavalry jacket, Bertie paused, looking out of the porthole across the Tagus at the distant white buildings of Lisbon, shimmering in the haze of the afternoon sun. All sound was muted. He could just make out a band playing on the quay where he would soon be landing. No one could guess how much this journey meant to him. All he had shown was smiling self-confidence, yet he realised that the course he had set could end in disaster and the ruin of his dearest hopes. Portugal was the first step and had been carefully chosen but, even here, nothing was certain. He was sure of Carlos's friendship but the reaction of his people and Government could be very different. No one knew how deep the hatred and distrust of the last few years had gone.

Chapter

12

With guns booming and bands playing, the visitors were rowed to the quay where Bertie replied to a formal address of welcome from the Portuguese Cabinet before joining Carlos in the first of a cortege of gilded, fairytale coaches, each drawn by six white horses, to drive to the Necessidades Palace. The streets of Lisbon were filled with thousands of people curious to see him. Their cheering was fairly warm but scattered and, in spite of a large cavalry escort, the police were afraid of anti-Royalist agitators. Riding in the last coach with Martino, Fortescue frightened him by pretending to look out for revolutionaries. The poor man's terror was complete when Ponsonby remarked that the floorboards of the ancient carriage were rotten and they might end up running along inside it like Charlie Beresford.

Seated in the second coach, Luis de Soveral prayed that the visit would be a success. Not only because he was Bertie's friend, but because he knew it was vital to prevent his own country from coming under the influence of Germany. During his years as Chargé d'Affaires in Berlin, he had realised that the enormous increase in the Imperial Army and the Kaiser's reckless attempts to bully and dominate the whole Continent would inevitably lead to a cataclysmic war unless sufficient nations combined to keep him in check. Created by similarity of taste, his friendship with Bertie had deepened when they recognised in each other the same clear, unbiased view of international politics and the same passionate desire to preserve peace. Soveral had already played his part. When the Kaiser had used the possibility of his intervention in the war in South Africa as a diplomatic lever against Britain, Soveral was Foreign Minister in Lisbon. He had drawn the teeth of the threat by refusing to allow German soldiers to pass through Portuguese Mozambique, the only route by which they could

198

reach the Cape. He had earned Britain's undying thanks, and the hatred of Wilhelm.

Soveral had helped to plan the whole secret strategy of this trip and knew how important this first lap was. Through the window of the coach he could see his countrymen, some smiling and waving to the Royal procession, but many of them merely watching, distrustful. Some of them had accused him of being a lackey of the King of England. If only they realised how much their future might depend on that one man. He glanced at Hardinge who sat behind him. He seemed balanced and intelligent. He hoped he would have the sense not to obstruct the King, to back him rather than be merely a watchdog for the Foreign Office.

Dom Carlos was most anxious for his arrangements to be effective. He could not force his people to be enthusiastic about the visit but at least he could give it the appearance of success by keeping them interested. Advised by Soveral, he packed each day with entertainments, receptions, sightseeing excursions, firework displays, dinners, visit to museums and the Taurada, the Portuguese version of bullfighting, a dazzling demonstration of horsemanship where the bull has blunted horns and is not killed. Each day the numbers in the streets increased, won over by Bertie's geniality. He moved so freely among them and with such obvious enjoyment, they began to be embarrassed by their mistrust. There were many who said: 'Whatever went wrong in the past, it is not his fault.'

Hardinge had to confess himself impressed. He had heard of the King's energy, but seeing it in action was incredible. At every moment of the day he was alive and alert, adapting himself to every event, to any company. No one had a greater gift of putting people at ease. He also realised that King Edward was a master of timing. A special point had to be made, yet the King avoided it in all his speeches, holding back until it was certain to make its maximum effect. The Portuguese were now sympathetic to him and proud that he had paid his first State Visit to their country, but they were more proud of their crumbling empire and still had a lingering fear that the whispers of the agitators might be true, that England planned to take over their territories in Africa.

On the last day, in reply to a speech by the President of the Chamber of Commerce praising the work of their two nations through the centuries in colonising and civilising foreign lands, Bertie said he was sure it would continue, emphasising his hope for the lasting prosperity and integrity of the British and Portuguese colonies. He stressed the word 'integrity' very slightly, just enough to make his meaning clear. For a few seconds there was no reaction, then as his words were understood, applause began which developed into a tempest of cheering. He had personally guaranteed the security of the Portuguese Empire. The news spread from the hall and it was as if a floodgate had opened. Huge crowds collected at once outside, cheering, clamouring for 'The Great King!' When he appeared, they surged round the Royal carriages, waving hats and handkerchiefs, shouting 'Long Live Edward!', 'Long Live Portugal's greatest friend!' All the way to the quay, the excitement was unending, the guns of the port roaring out in salute and people singing 'God Save the King'.

On the galley taking them to the *Victoria and Albert*, Dom Carlos brushed tears from his eyes and hugged Bertie, unable to express what he felt. They lunched together on board and Carlos presented decorations to Bertie's staff before saying an emotional goodbye. Bertie was more than pleased. He had dreamt of just such a start to his trip and his only regret was that Soveral had to stay behind in Lisbon. From now on, he was on his own.

Hardinge was encouraged by the triumph of the visit. He had never imagined anything quite like it, he told Ponsonby. Ponsonby smiled and nodded. If his suspicions were correct, the Minister Plenipotentiary had a few more surprises to come, not to mention the Foreign Office. Dealing with the King's despatches, deciphering the telegrams that poured in, he had begun to have a picture of what was in the wind, something more than a simple Mediterranean Cruise.

The *Victoria and Albert* reached Gibraltar the next day and anchored in the breakwater for the first visit to the fortress by a reigning monarch. Here from the beginning there was no restraint. The soldiers and sailors who garrisoned the Rock, their families and the people of the small colony flocked to see their King. With them were thousands of Moors from across the straits and so many people from the Spanish mainland that, finally, the police were forced to shut the barriers.

The harbour was filled with ships of the British Mediterranean Fleet. Hearing that the President of France, Emile

Loubet, was on his way to visit Algiers, Bertie ordered four battle ships to sail there, to be ready to salute him on his arrival. Hardinge agreed that it was a pleasant touch of diplomatic courtesy and would probably be appreciated.

Bertie stayed at Gibraltar for five days of inspections, receptions and sightseeing, ending with a review of troops in the plain, led past by the Governor, Sir George White, the defender of Ladysmith. The Royal salute was fired by all the guns of the fortress, starting at the top and carrying on down through each tier, the hidden galleries belching sudden flame and smoke, until the whole Rock thundered. There was only one jarring note, when the police reported they had arrested an Italian anarchist in the crowds waiting to see him. A dangerous man, he had been under surveillance in his own country, but had disappeared. His trail was picked up in France and he was traced through Spain to Gibraltar.

'And they arrested him? On what grounds?' Bertie asked. 'He might just have come here for his health.'

'A curious place for an anarchist to come for his health, sir,' Sir George White answered.

'He was in front of the crowd, sir,' Sir George said assume that he meant any harm.'

'He was in front of the crowd, sir,' Sir Geroge said quietly. 'He had a stabbing knife and a revolver.'

Bertie felt a momentary chill. Any crowd, he knew, might contain an unknown assassin, one silent man with fanatical eyes among all the smiling faces. 'It is a risk one takes,' he said. 'But without more evidence you'll have to release him—after I've gone.'

From Gibraltar, the Royal Yacht steamed on to Malta accompanied by six cruisers, three days of perfect, calm sailing. The escort was dramatically increased when they came in sight of Gozo, the small island to the north of Malta, and a squadron of destroyers raced to meet them, fanned out and fired a salute before turning about and leading the way in line abreast. Under the thundering guns of Fort St Elmo, the *Victoria and Albert* steamed into the Grand Harbour between the two battleships that guarded the entrance; their yards hung with flags and the decks lined with cheering sailors. The golden stones of the old city of Valetta glowed in the morning sun, the terraces were gay with waving flags and the bells of all the churches were ringing.

The reception in Malta dwarfed the memory of Gibraltar. It was another first visit by a reigning sovereign and another five days of spectacle, levees, inspections, banquets and reviews, ending with a gigantic water carnival in the Grand Harbour with the ships of the fleet illuminated and a fantastic procession of launches rebuilt to show the history of sail from Noah's Ark to the latest make of battleship. When the Ark passed the Royal Yacht, the sailor dressed as Noah set free a white dove. At the close of the carnival, all the men-of-war were outlined with red fire and Bertie signalled the release of a thousand rockets that burst in the night sky and dropped in showers of spangled colour to the water.

By now Hardinge knew that the next stop was Italy and that the King did not mean merely to cruise along the coast but to pay an official visit to King Victor Emmanuel. He was astonished by the Foreign Office's reaction. Even after the success of the stay in Portugal and the way the people of Malta had taken him to their hearts, the Cabinet attached so little importance to the King's influence that their only real concern was that he should not call on the Pope. Bertie had every intention of calling on the Pope.

'There are millions of Roman Catholics among my subjects,' he said. 'I will not insult them by ignoring the Vatican.' Balfour and Lansdowne's argument that a visit would infuriate the Protestants and look like a scheme to buy off Roman Catholic opposition in Parliament exasperated him. 'On the other hand,' he countered, 'it might prove that we're not all ridiculously prejudiced!'

'You are the head of the Church of England, sir,' Hardinge reminded him.

'In England we pride ourselves on being tolerant,' Bertie said. 'And despise as uncivilised those who are not. How can we presume to look down on them, if we do not set an example?'

Hardinge made the mistake of asking the Government's advice. Balfour replied that the Cabinet could not give its consent, while Lansdowne's secretary wrote to say that they trusted the King would read between the lines and pay an informal, not an official visit to the Pope on his own responsibility. Bertie was angered, with good reason, by the Government's timidity and double talk. They wanted to please the Catholics and at the same time, if the visit caused a storm of protest, they could publish the fact that

202

they had advised against it. He dictated a violently-worded telegram to Balfour, asking for a straight answer, yes or no. Hardinge gave it to Ponsonby to code and send off.

Ponsonby at once realised the message was too strong. It left the Government no alternative but to refuse their consent. It would also give the Prime Minister another chance to use his threat of resignation and weaken the powers of the King still more. He rephrased the telegram to allow the Government an opportunity to change its mind with grace and to keep the initiative with the King. Hardinge was furious when he discovered that the message which he had approved himself as Minister had been altered, but Ponsonby was unrepentant. If anything went wrong, he told him, he would take the blame.

The Royal Yacht steamed into the Bay of Naples. It now had an escort of four cruisers, eight battleships and eight destroyers which made a nonsense of Bertie's smiling assurance that he wished to be strictly incognito. Members of his staff who did not know of the many letters and telegrams were amazed by the stream of distinguished visitors who had obviously been expecting his arrival. Among them was the plump and charming Queen Amelie of Portugal, the wife of Don Carlos, whom he had missed at Lisbon. He was especially delighted to welcome his close American friend, Mrs Cornelius Vanderbilt. The following day, with her on his arm, he went ashore to go round the museums and explore the back streets of Naples. The previous King of Italy, Umberto, had been killed by a bomb only three years before and the Italian police were in terror. They wanted to close the museums to everyone but him and surround him by scores of detectives. Bertie laughed and refused to be protected. When Ponsonby and Fortescue tried to stay close behind him to guard his back, he sent them off in opposite directions. Seeing him walk through the narrow, teeming streets without bodyguards, the Neapolitans were honoured and treated him with great courtesy. That night, when he went to the Opera with Queen Amelie, it was filled with women wearing their most beautiful dresses and jewellery, angling to catch his attention. By the time he landed for the official reception, stories of his gallantry and courage had made him a popular hero and the crowd's welcome was full-hearted. He dismissed the Royal Yacht and its escort and took the train for Rome.

The young King, Victor Emmanuel, met him at the

station with an array of dignitaries. As they drove through the decorated streets to the Quirinal Palace, the enthusiasm of the city amazed even his host. Bertie's reputation, rumours of his wish to meet the Pope and the memory of the help Britain had given in the struggle for Italian unity had excited people's eagerness to see him. Throughout his stay the enthusiasm grew. His speeches in reply to civic and political leaders were models of choosing just the right words at the right time. The climax came at the State Banquet when his theme was the generations of friendship between the two nations, reminding his hosts of how they had fought side by side in the Crimean War. It was emotional and had his audience cheering, yet he stopped them by declaring that his sole ambition was to prevent them from ever having to bear arms together again. 'Our two countries,' he proclaimed, 'have one great principle in common—liberty; one great object in view—peace!' The response was tremendous.

Bertie had been sickened by his own Government's attitude but their reply finally came to Ponsonby's telegram. It had shamed them into agreeing officially to a visit to the Vatican, provided the first move was made by the Pope. After some diplomatic jockeying and a plea from the Duke of Norfolk, the foremost British Catholic, the Papal Secretary of State issued an invitation. Even then the difficulties were not over. The Vatican did not recognise the Kingdom of Italy which had seized the Papal territories and relations between them had been broken off. Bertie explained that although he was a guest of the King of Italy he would be coming from the British Embassy in the Ambassador's personal carriage. When the historic meeting between King Edward and the ninety-three-year-old Pope Leo the Thirteenth at last took place it passed off perfectly. They met in the Pontiff's private library and discussed international problems which concerned them both. Each was impressed by the other's tact and knowledge. As they parted, His Holiness shook Bertie's hand and thanked him for his courtesy and the liberty of creed and confession that existed in the Empire.

Instead of the threatened angry demonstrations, reactions in Britain and Italy were overwhelmingly favourable. Hardinge had the grace to apologise to Ponsonby. He only wished the Foreign Office would see what had happened and follow it up. In three days, by sheer personality and diplomatic skill, the King had made firm ties with both the Vatican and the Quirinal. Italy was bound to Germany and Austria yet, in that same short time, he had completely won over Victor Emmanuel and his people and cracked the Triple Alliance.

Lord Lansdowne's face was pinched with disapproval. He sat, stiff and erect, in the Prime Minister's study staring at Francis Knollys, who had asked for the meeting. He shifted his gaze from him to Arthur Balfour who lounged behind his desk.

'Well, at last we know!' Lansdowne snapped. 'The King has hoodwinked us. Not only has he visited Italy *and* the Pope, but now he proposes to pay a State Visit to Paris!'

'That was clearly his main intention all along,' Balfour agreed. 'The other countries were only a smokescreen.'

Francis Knollys smiled. 'I feel that I should point out that his visit to the Pope has had a great effect in Ireland, and that he has cemented a friendship with King Victor Emmanuel.'

'We have always had good relations with Italy,' Lansdowne said shortly. 'France is a totally different matter!'

'The salute by the English battleships at Algiers was deeply appreciated,' Knollys argued. 'President Loubet, himself, has invited the King to Paris.'

'He couldn't do anything else out of politeness,' Balfour observed drily. 'That's why the King sent them. The whole thing was completely calculated.'

'Are we just going to let him do as he likes?' Lansdowne asked. He was annoyed with Balfour for taking it so calmly.

'He is coming home by train through France,' Knollys said.

Balfour shrugged. 'Quite so.' He had begun to find the whole business of the Royal travels irritating. He could not see why there was all this fuss. The King could go where he pleased for all he cared, for all the difference it would make. If he wanted he could fly in a balloon to Timbuctu. 'Quite. It would look damned odd if he didn't stop at Paris.'

'But what's the purpose behind it?' Lansdowne demanded.

'Obviously, he's counting on charming the French as he did the Italians and the Portuguese.'

Lansdowne sniffed. 'We have tried every avenue of approach, worked unceasingly to establish a better relationship with France. Their Government wants it too, but the

205

French people will not stand for it! There is no means of bridging the gap between us. It is not possible.'

'His Majesty has many connections with Paris,' Knollys reminded him. 'In former times he had many friends there.'

'*Had* many friends,' Lansdowne repeated. 'Precisely, Sir Francis. That era has ended. He has been unable to visit any part of France for nearly five years because of the antagonism there. I presume you are aware of the obscene caricatures of King Edward—and his late mother—which appear every week in the French newspapers?'

'Not to mention the ones of ourselves,' Balfour drawled. He clicked his teeth thinking. 'Still—someone has to test the thickness of the ice. If it's on his own responsibility, it can't do us any harm.'

'Our Ambassador in Paris has sent a report on public opinion there,' Lansdowne said sharply. 'The situation is serious. There is violent hatred. The newspapers claim that a visit by the King of England would be an insult.' He paused and added unwillingly, 'I must admit his visits have improved our relations with Portugal and Italy. But that could be swept away if there were an unfortunate incident in Paris. The French Government is alarmed at the very prospect of it. They have warned us that their police cannot guarantee his safety.'

Balfour sat up, affected by Lansdowne's urgency. If the French themselves were worried, that put a different complexion on it. He tapped the desk. 'Obviously, then, His Majesty must be induced to cancel his visit.'

Francis Knollys leant forward, hunching his shoulders. This was the difficult part. 'He is already on his way,' he said.

The special train carrying the King and his staff crossed the frontier into France at night and sped on to the north.

Bertie lay awake and restless in his sleeping compartment. He had talked late with Hardinge and Ponsonby who were still excited by the visit to Rome. No one could have expected it would go so well. As Hardinge said, coming so soon after the reaction in Portugal, it would flutter all the Chancelleries of Europe. He smiled, remembering the boyish delight of Victor Emmanuel at being invited to London. He had sympathised with him and his beautiful Queen Helena in the difficult role they had to play in a young nation torn by the extremes of political opinion. Of the

206

quarrel between the State and the Vatican, Victor Emmannel had said that he honoured the Pope as head of the Church but could not allow him or his Cardinals to meddle in the country's internal policy. In the circumstances, it was the only correct attitude. Bertie grimaced, realising that to an extent he was like the Pope in his own country. He reached for a cigarette on the bedside table. As he struck a match to light it, he told himself this would be his last cigarette of the day. He had told himself so half an hour ago, and half an hour before that. He could not sleep.

All the time he had been in Rome, he had felt tired and unwell although he had concealed it. It was partly a difficulty in breathing and partly a depression brought on by his Government's attitude. If only they would give him just a little support the strain would be more bearable. He was ready to give them credit for any success he had. Why must they cover themselves so obviously and so continuously against his possible failure?

Bertie had no illusions about what he was doing. He had staked his whole reputation on this journey. So far the gamble had succeeded more spectacularly than he had dared to expect, but the real test would come in the next few days.

With all possibility of a real alliance with Germany gone, an understanding must somehow be reached with France. For the chance of achieving that, he was prepared to sacrifice himself if necessary. To him, France was not merely another Power. On his first visit there as a small boy, the kindness of the Emperor Louis Napoleon and the lovely Empress Eugénie had seemed almost miraculous. The warmth and gaiety of their court were such a contrast to his own strict life at Windsor and Osborne that he had never wanted to leave. On the last day, he had asked them shyly if he could stay, at least a little longer.

'Your parents will need you at home,' Eugénie had told him.

'They don't want me,' Bertie said.

Louis Napoleon smiled gently. 'They would miss you.'

Bertie hesitated. 'Not really. You see, there are so many of us.' He had lowered his head and the Emperor, sensing how starved he was for affection, held out his hand. Bertie had taken it. 'I wish I were your son,' he had whispered.

As he grew to manhood, Bertie has escaped more and more often to Paris where he enjoyed a respect and freedom denied to him at home. The Queen of Cities opened her arms to him as a born boulevardier. His perfect taste delighted French society and the Parisians, seeing his undisguised appreciation of rich food, attractive women and amusing company, accepted him as one of themselves. Stories of his love affaires were legion, from the passionate Sarah Bernhardt to the sophisticated singer, Jane Avril, and the elegant Princesse de Sagan who bore him a son. The world of Napoleon the Third had been smashed by the guns and bayonets of the Prussian army but in time Bertie had forged links of friendship with the new republic whose senators discovered to their surprise that he was not merely a Royal playboy interested only in gratification, but a skilled diplomat able to consider the needs of other countries while working for the good of his own.

Each year he slipped over incognito for a short stay with his current favourite—Lillie Langtry had been the first— and later returned en garçon with a few close friends like Carrington, Henry Chaplin or Francis Knollys, all equally at home as he was at an embassy reception or in the salon of a House of Pleasure. To entertain the Prince of Wales was the ambition of every leading courtesan and the piece of jewellery he sent round next day, usually a diamond and pearl brooch, was given pride of place over all the more fabulous gifts, the necklaces, studs, collars and bracelets lavished on them by lesser suitors. To the admiration of the gentlemen of fashionable Paris for Bertie's style and chic was added a certain envy of his stamina.

In addition to the shorter visits he came each year for a longer holiday in the spring when Alix went to Denmark, to lead the festivities at the Battle of the Flowers in Cannes or to stay more sedately in a hotel on the Atlantic coast at Biarritz.

Bertie grunted and flicked his cigarette. He had ceased his visits to France in protest against the attacks on his mother in the newspapers and the financial aid given to the Boers. When his anger cooled, he had realised the root cause of it all was again colonial rivalry. The French Republic was jealous of the Empire and desperate to protect its own smaller possessions. He also realised that there must be statesmen in France who could see the dangers to both their countries if the hostility continued. After the first Privy Council of his reign, he had sent Carrington to inform the French President of his accession and to find out discreetly if any members of his government were in favour of improving relations between their two countries. Carrington had done his work well, reporting back that both President Loubet and his Foreign Minister, Théophile Delcassé, were eager for a better understanding but reluctant to express their feelings too loudly in the face of public opinion. Through Paul Cambon, their ambassador in London, Bertie had established contact with them and satisfied himself of their genuine wish for a reconciliation. He had passed the discussions on to Lansdowne and there the matter had stuck. Neither side would risk taking the first step. The longer it was left, the more bitter public opinion on both sides of the English Channel became. Bertie saw that if a gesture was not made, it would soon be too late.

The collapse of the talks with Germany had decided him. He had kept all knowledge of his intentions from his own government until the last moment, knowing that they would think of a hundred reasons why he should not go, all valid. Through Cambon he had arranged that the announcement of his visit would also be left to the last moment in Paris to give less time for demonstrations to be organised. And with Soveral he had devised the strategy of the trip to Portugal and Italy so that he would be coming from the south and it would seem more natural to pass through France on his journey home. It concealed the importance he attached to the visit and the Kaiser would have no reason to object.

Bertie stubbed out his cigarette. A faint light was coming through the blinds of his compartment already. In a few hours his supreme test would begin.

The train stopped in the morning at Dijon for the British Ambassador, Sir Edmund Monson, and a group of French officials to come aboard. While Ponsonby dealt with the officials, Hardinge brought the Ambassador to the King. They found him in the dining salon finishing breakfast and were invited to join him for coffee.

Monson was an elderly career diplomat. He had handled the Paris Embassy during the recent difficulties with great ability and resented the intrusion of the King. He made no bones about it to Hardinge. Paris was a powder keg which one spark could set off.

'Don't think the mob will be flattered by a bit of

209

pageantry like they were in Lisbon and Rome,' he said. 'We've had stones through the Embassy windows. While the King is there, he'll be lucky if it's only stones.'

The closer Bertie came to a crisis, the more relaxed he seemed. He sat in a velvet smoking jacket, aware of Monson's disapproval and Hardinge's concern. As he spread more butter on his toast, he glanced at Hardinge who had had a private letter from the Foreign Office. 'Well, Charles, what do they say?'

Hardinge hesitated. 'There is great concern in London, sir. The Prime Minister and Lord Lansdowne feel that, in the circumstances, the visit is unwise.'

Bertie smiled. 'I can hardly order the train to turn round and go back at this stage.'

'I believe Sir Edmund has informed them what your Majesty's reception is likely to be.'

'It will be unfriendly,' Monson said bluntly. 'My Embassy is the only safe place for Your Majesty to stay. Even that has been threatened. The Nationalists are preparing protest marches and anti-British rallies.'

Bertie added orange marmalade to his toast. 'Well, we'll see.'

Monson glanced at Hardinge for assistance. Hardinge looked again at the letter. 'The Foreign Office is deeply sensible of the success of Your Majesty's trip so far, but they fear that all the good done will be ruined if we meet with disaster in Paris.'

'If I shirk going there now, the result would be the same,' Bertie shrugged.

Hardinge decided on the last try. 'This is difficult for me to say, sir—I have admired Your Majesty's handling of the situations we have met. It has been a lesson in diplomacy. But the odds against you here are too great. My own fear is of a loss in Your Majesty's personal prestige.'

Bertie heard the sincerity in Hardinge's voice and liked him all the more for his frankness, but he was fully committed. 'Well—the Government can always claim they advised me to turn back.' He smiled. 'If I fail, the only person to suffer will be myself. I am going.'

As he finished his toast, Ponsonby came in with a printed schedule. 'From the President's Chef du Protocole, sir,' he said, handing it over. 'It's fairly detailed.' Bertie glanced down the list of engagements and events. He paused.

'Detailed? They're even telling me what to wear!' he

muttered, incredulous. 'Evening dress . . . At ten o'clock in the morning?'

'It is the French official dress, sir,' Monson said quickly.

'But not mine,' Bertie growled.

'There is good reason for the choice, sir,' Monson told him.

Bertie looked at him, his eyes piercing. 'The reason being that the British uniform is hated and if I arrive wearing it, it could provoke a disturbance?'

'Partly that, sir,' Monson agreed reluctantly. 'And also . . . it makes an easier target.'

Bertie's eyes held his for a second longer, then he looked again at the schedule. He took his propelling pencil and drew a line down through the column of recommended clothes. 'I am too old to be taught how to dress,' he said. 'We'll be there in an hour. I must get ready.' He rose and moved towards the door of his state room which Ponsonby hurried to open for him. He paused.

'When we stopped at Dijon, some other people got on as well as Sir Edmund and the Head of Protocol. Who were they?'

'French officers, sir—and detectives.'

'Ah,' Bertie nodded. 'See that they're made comfortable.'

At the station in the Bois de Boulogne, President Loubet waited with the dark, intense Foreign Minister, Delcassé, and a group of officials, dressed in tailcoats and black top hats. The station had been searched and was cordoned by Police and soldiers. Journalists and press photographers were kept wedged together in a corner of the platform. Loubet, a short white-haired, bearded man, glanced tensely from them to the approaching train, conscious of the huge crowds that stood in silence outside the station. In spite of the decorated lampposts, the red and gold draperies, the military bands, there was none of the bustle and excitement of a normal State Visit, only that chilling silence.

The Royal train drew up at the platform, with a hiss of steam, perfectly positioned so that the red carpet was directly in front of the door of the state room. When Bertie stepped down, followed by his aides, there was a moment's consternation. He wore his scarlet Field-Marshal's uniform, sword and decorations with a white-plumed hat. Behind him, Hardinge and Monson were in diplomatic uniform and

211

the Equerries of the staff in red tunics with gold aguillettes.

President Loubet was not entirely certain how to greet the King, remembering the stiff, distant manner of Czar Nicholas on his arrival. He raised his hat and was slightly taken aback as Bertie came towards him smiling, holding out his hand. They shook hands warmly. 'Votre Majesté,' Loubet muttered. 'C'est avec une joie inexprimable que je vous acceuille en France.'

'Monsieur le Président, je vous assure que votre joie ne peut égaler le plaisir que j'éprouve à me trouver une fois de plus dans votre charmant pays.' Bertie spoke French as fluently as English and German, the deep, faintly guttural sound in his voice bringing an added resonance to his pronunciation.

They stood to attention for *La Marseillaise* and *God Save the King*, then the suites were introduced and the two groups moved out through the ranks of saluting soldiers to six open carriages. The King and the President went in the first, followed by Hardinge and Delcassé in the second, to drive to the Arc de Triomphe and down the Champs Elysées. If Bertie was aware of the cold antagonism of the crowds lining the route, he showed no sign. Smiling and affable, he raised his hat like Loubet to the few shouts of 'Vive le Président!' A heavy escort of French cavalry surrounded them and Loubet hoped that the sound of the hooves would muffle the other cries of 'A bas les Anglais!' and 'Vivent les Boers!' which he could just hear.

Riding in the last carriage with Fortescue and two French officials, Ponsonby found the procession an ordeal. Respect for the President restrained the mob's hostility as the head of the cortege passed but the sight of the two red coats in the last carriage infuriated them. They jeered, calling out mocking insults mixed with cries of 'Vive Fashoda!', 'Vive Marchand!' and 'A bas l'Angleterre!'

Both staffs were relieved when they reached the British Embassy at last. As they parted, Delcassé who had risked his career on the visit kept saying, 'Our people are delighted. Such enthusiasm!' but sporadic booing from behind the cordon of police robbed his words of any conviction. Hardinge had been less depressed by the shouting than by the sullen unfriendliness of most of the people they had passed.

Entering the Embassy he said to the King, 'Monson seems to be right, sir. They don't like us much.'

'Why should they?' Bertie answered quietly. 'We've given them little reason to.'

The Embassy was in a house formerly owned by Pauline Borghese, the sister of Napoleon the First, and was still furnished in her sumptuous style. Bertie inspected it quickly and announced, to Hardinge and Ponsonby's surprise, that he would leave in ten minutes to pay a courtesy call on his host and Madame Loubet at the Élysée Palace. He was tired from an almost sleepless night and his breathing was restricted by bronchitis from too much smoking but he had not come to Paris to rest. The crowds had not gone from the streets and on the journey to the President's Palace and back the earlier pattern of frigid silence broken by occasional shouts and catcalls was repeated. If they hoped to see Bertie disconcerted, they were disappointed. All the way he smiled and bowed as though he were being given the most cordial welcome.

A French officer attached temporarily to the staff shook his head wonderingly. 'Your King Edouard—he seems to be enjoying himself. Every time anyone shouts he just smiles and waves. He can't be hearing what they're saying.'

'Oh, he hears all right,' Ponsonby murmured. He could feel the tension and saw how the staring crowds were thrown off balance by the King's unruffled geniality. Only that and the memory of his former popularity stopped them from being more openly hostile.

That afternoon Bertie received a deputation from the British Chamber of Commerce in the Embassy salon and made his first speech of this visit. He told them of his belief that the days of conflict between the two countries were over and his hope that the years to come would only see between them a brotherly rivalry in the fields of commerce and industry. He told them he counted on them, as resident in the beautiful city and enjoying the hospitality of the French Republic, to aid and assist him in making his hopes a reality. 'A divine Providence,' he said, 'has designed that France should be our near neighbour and, I trust, always a dear friend. There are no two countries in the world whose mutual prosperity is more dependent on each other. It is my heartfelt wish that the friendship and admiration which we all feel for the French nation and their glorious traditions may, in the near future, develop into bonds of the warmest affection and attachment between the peoples of our two countries. The achievement of this aim is my constant desire, the establishment of a lasting Entente Cordiale.'

Monsieur Claretie, the administrator of the Théâtre Français, was a nervous man as he conducted the King and President Loubet to the State box. His theatre was packed with a distinguished, invited audience, yet he kept thinking of the many plain clothes detectives sprinkled among them. He hoped there were enough. He was terrified of a riot, even of an assassination attempt. He could still hear the booing of the Nationalist demonstrators outside.

When the official party made its appearance, the audience stood but did not applaud. Bertie took his seat in the same frigid silence that had greeted him in the streets. He was disappointed. The theatre was always a barometer of public opinion to him and he had hoped for some reaction, but none of his real friends had been invited. Everywhere he saw unfamiliar faces, except for the German Ambassador, Prince von Radolin, who was smirking with satisfaction. That night a mocking, jubilant telegram would be sent to Rome where Kaiser Wilhelm was paying a hurried visit in an attempt to counteract the sudden popularity of his uncle.

The scheduled performance had been Racine's *Phèdre* which Bertie had seen at least twenty times. He asked for something more modern, more Parisian, and Claretie had substituted a new comedy, *L'Autre Danger*. It was an unfortunate choice. Because it contained anti-republican remarks, the President refused to laugh or applaud. Neither could Bertie, as he had to follow the example set by his host. They sat in silence. Loubet with his arms folded, Bertie sucking lozenges to ease his bronchitis. The evening settled down to be a dull failure.

In the interval, the arrangement was that they should remain in the small salon behind the box but Bertie electrified the detectives by insisting on strolling in the foyer. 'Excuse me, sir,' Ponsonby said. 'The Police say we must not walk in the crowd.'

'Do they indeed?' Bertie growled, his voice dangerously low.

When the audience saw him appear in the foyer a moment or two later, a relaxed, smiling figure in evening dress

214

with the Grand Ribbon of the Legion of Honour across his white shirt front, they stiffened in surprise, then looked away to avoid having to acknowledge him, their conversation suddenly animated. Bertie paused to light a cigar, apparently unconcerned. Hardinge and Ponsonby stayed close to him as he had ordered the detectives to remain behind. They were distressed on his behalf, knowing how much the deliberate indifference of the fashionable audience must have upset him. Hardinge hated the thought of the report he would have to make to London.

'What do you think of the play. Fritz?' Bertie asked.

'Rather fun, sir. But very light.'

'And scarcely appropriate,' Hardinge added.

Bertie nodded agreement. He was using the technique he had developed of seeming to concentrate on one or two people, while in reality he was aware of everything that was going on around him. He saw no one but strangers. The interval was nearly over.

'There's someone I know . . .' he breathed.

A woman, slim, with dark hair, in a cream evening gown that left the delicate line of her shoulders bare, was talking to two older gentlemen near one of the gilded pillars. Strikingly beautiful, she was the actress Jeanne Granier. The crowd stilled and fell silent as Bertie moved through it towards her, smiling. She did not notice him approach and only the expression of the men she was with made her turn when he reached her. He bowed.

'Mademoiselle Granier, I believe.'

She curtsied slightly, surprised and a little distant. 'Votre Majesté?'

The crowd was deathly silent, listening, intrigued.

'We have not met,' Bertie said, 'but I had the pleasure of applauding you once in a play in London.' He was speaking to her but just loud enough for everyone to hear. She inclined her head at the compliment. Bertie smiled. 'And I see I was not mistaken.'

Jeanne was puzzled. 'Sire?'

Bertie smiled. 'It seemed to me then, as it does now, that you represented all the grace and spirit of France.'

There was a gasp of pleasure from the crowd and a murmur began. Jeanne Granier smiled. She felt herself thawing in the warmth of his admiration and was ready to repay the compliment. 'It is Your Majesty who is le roi charmeur —the charming king.'

It was a game that Bertie played very well. 'I see I must be careful,' he said, 'now that I am in a Republic.'

The depth of his voice and the smile that crinkled the corners of his eyes had a disturbing effect on Jeanne. She hoped she was not flushing. 'We are only a Republic, sire,' she murmured, 'because we do not have Royalty like you.'

There was a brief pause and the people around them applauded. Bertie's smile thanked her. He kissed her hand and bowed again before turning away. Now as he walked back through the foyer, the people bowed and curtsied. Hardinge and Ponsonby were staring at him. As he passed them to return to the state box, the look he gave them was inscrutable.

When the play began again, President Loubet could not understand the whispers that were running through the audience, nor the light laughter. But he was gratified at the end of the performance when they stood again for the National Anthem and, this time, were applauded. The applause increased as Bertie waved.

The next morning, the King and his staff attended a military review at Vincennes. There was no enthusiasm in the streets but neither was there any booing. Stories of his inimitable charm on the previous evening had begun to circulate and reports of his speech to the Chamber of Commerce. The first cheers came when he arrived later that morning at the Hôtel de Ville for his official reception by the Municipal Council.

Monson and Hardinge had both wished there were some means of having that visit cancelled. The Government of Paris was controlled by the Nationalists, the chief supporters of the campaign against England. He would face some of the most hostile critics of his life and Parisians were astounded themselves that he had accepted the invitation.

At the Hôtel de Ville Bertie behaved as though he were not with the people who had spearheaded the hatred of the past years but among responsible men who would receive him with civility. Again his attitude threw his critics off balance. They were already undecided how to react since, by this time, his earlier speech had been translated and published in the daily papers, making an excellent impression. The councillors listened to the Council President's

216

address welcoming the King as an old friend who had not been forgotten, and waited in suspense as he rose to reply.

He smiled, looking round them. Over the small spatter of applause, he said, 'I had not expected to speak today. But I am going to say a few words, personally, from the heart.' There was a stir of interest. 'How could I do otherwise? In a city which I first visited as a small boy with my parents and found there the first warmth of an affection which has stayed with me for the rest of my life.' He bowed to the President of the Council. 'Monsieur le President, Messieurs —I would like to say how deeply I have been touched by your friendly words. It would have been distressing to me, during my stay in your beautiful city, not to have been able to call at the Hôtel de Ville. Most sincerely, I thank you for the welcome you have given me today. I shall never— never forget this visit to your charming city and I assure you that it is with the most profound pleasure that I have returned to Paris where I always feel as if I had come home.'

His sincerity and perfect command of French had an immediate effect. The applause which began as he finished speaking built up as he stood still, smiling and relaxed, into an ovation. The people in the corridors outside were amazed and soon the words of his short speech were relayed to the crowds waiting in the street. When he came out, the cheers for the first time were genuine and unrestrained.

After lunch, he rode in his open carriage to Longchamps for a race meeting that his friends in the Jockey Club were holding in his honour. The stewards had been worried but the atmosphere was now completely transformed. On every corner, groups gathered to cheer him and many hurried to the track to see him for themselves. Their eagerness and his smiling good humour changed the race meeting into a party. They told one another stories of his past visits, of his private suppers at the Café Anglais with Cora Pearl and Hortense Schneider, of how he had converted the rabid Republican, Léon Gambetta, and how together they had prevented a pointless war between France and England, how he had sent money to feed the poor children after the horrors of the Siege of Paris, of how in his youth the leaders of Parisian society had lent him their mistresses, not knowing he had already entranced their wives. As his smile passed over the throng, the women felt a frisson of excitement, each one wondering if he had noticed her. The applause on his arrival lasted for over five minutes.

Hardinge and Monson were staggered and gave up any attempt to offer him advice. He was cheered again when the winning filly in the first race was Chrysothemis, the daughter of his great champion Persimmon, and a huge shout of laughter and delight went up when the second race went to an outsider called 'John Bull'. Seated in his box between the dowdy wives of President Loubet and the Governor of Paris, Bertie longed to escape and sent Ponsonby to arrange for the Jockey Club to invite him to inspect their new stand. Coming back, Ponsonby found himself cut off by the crowd and tried to push through. The people round him protested and he was stopped by a gendarme. When he explained who he was, they parted for him, laughing and clapping him on the shoulders. He would not let himself think what might have happened in the same situation the day before.

The King's appearance in the paddock was the signal for another prolonged burst of affection and his old friends who had been kept from him until now swarmed round to welcome him. They laughed with him when the Persimmon Cup was won by another outsider, The Tsar. 'I couldn't have asked for more,' he said. 'I've seen my own stables win with Persimmon's daughter, my people with John Bull and my family with The Tsar, who's my nephew.'

That evening when he drove to the Elysée for a State Banquet all Paris seemed to have turned out, jamming the streets and milling round his carriage so that the short journey became a conqueror's progress. Chanting, cheering, applauding, they shouted, 'Vive Edouard', 'Vive le Roi', 'Vive Teddy!' All thoughts of the Boers and Fashoda had vanished. He had taken the town by storm.

At the banquet, Loubet was unaccountably nervous and mumbled his speech which was propped up on the candlestick in front of him. Bertie's reply, a variation of his speech at the Hôtel de Ville, had most of the guests on their feet cheering. Loubet's nervousness increased and Bertie correctly guessed the reason why. Loubet was thinking back to the elaborate reception given to Nicholas when there had been no such enthusiasm. Bertie made a point of spending time with the Russian Ambassador, assuring him that he had no wish to drive a wedge between France and Russia but hoped for the friendship of both. He was also careful to be seen talking to Prince von Radolin. He almost succeeded in putting him at ease, but the German Ambassador knew he would now have a very difficult telegram to send to the Kaiser.

The thousands in the streets had waited throughout the banquet and the King's triumph was repeated as the official group drove to the Opera, where the audience, in total contrast to the night before, rose to their feet crying 'Vive le Roi!', 'Vive L'Angleterre!' Now Bertie saw many people he knew and recognised. His friends had turned out in force. Among them in the stalls, he caught the smile of the delightful cocotte, Liane de Pougy, who had begun her career as a singer at the Folies Bergère. A tiny, elfin-faced girl with petal-soft skin, she had appealed to Bertie to help her by being present at her first appearance. He found the little girl from Provence enchanting with her blend of delicious wickedness and fragile delicacy. When it was known that she was under the Prince of Wales's patronage, her fortune was made and she went on to become one of the most famous of les grandes horizontales. Seeing where Bertie was looking, Loubet stiffened. 'If my eyes are not mistaken, that is Madame Liane de Pougy,' Bertie said. 'That—that is who she is,' Loubet stumbled apologetically. 'I can't think how she got on to the list of guests. Would you like her to be asked to leave?' 'Good heavens, no,' Bertie smiled. 'Some things in Paris may have changed, but surely not the laws of gallantry?'

After another day, a Sunday, when he went to church, received his friends, had a private lunch with Delcassé, gave a garden party in the afternoon for the English colony and, in the evening, a reception and dinner at the Embassy for the whole diplomatic world, it was time for him to leave. As the carriages of the procession moved towards the Gare des Invalides, Loubet thought his people had gone mad. It was the only way to describe it. As if to make up for their hostility at his arrival, the people of Paris began to assemble before sunrise outside the British Embassy and all along the route. They greeted Bertie, who was again wearing his scarlet uniform, with a storm of love and affection singing, waving small Tricolours and Union Jacks. 'Vive Teddy!' they roared. 'Vive Edouard—notre bon Edouard! Vive notre roi!' Even the soldiers and police were cheering. In an incredible three days, the Entente Cordiale was born and the whole shape of European politics had changed.

Bertie said his last farewell to Loubet and his ministers on the platform, while the dense crowds pressed against the barriers, shouting and calling out his name. He climbed on board his train and stood saluting at the window of his salon until it left the station.

He turned, smiling. Hardinge and Ponsonby were behind him, standing very straight and proud. 'Well, gentlemen,' he murmured, 'the tide seems to have turned. Now what will the Government say?'

Chapter
13

Alix waited with Toria and George at Victoria Station to welcome Bertie back to London. In her excitement at his success, all her resentment over being left behind was forgotten. She was so happy for him that, when the train pulled in and he stepped out on to the red carpet, she had to fight the impulse to run to him. She made herself curtsey and flushed when he chuckled and kissed her. On the short journey to Buckingham Palace, he questioned her and George closely about the country's reaction to his tour. He had heard nothing yet from the Government and needed to know, at least, that public opinion was with him. He decided to tap his own barometer.

That evening when Alexandra and he appeared in the royal box at Covent Garden just before the overture of Wagner's *Das Rheingold*, the cheers of the audience gave him his answer. At supper after the opera, Carrington explained what lay behind the cheers. People were not quite sure what had happened, only that it was something tremendous. With mounting astonishment they had seen what looked like a pleasure cruise turn into a series of dazzling diplomatic triumphs, culminating in the King's conquest of Paris. For centuries, France had been the traditional enemy of England. Only in the past fifty years had the idea spread that their interests would be better served as allies and then, for the last five, the two nations had teetered on the brink of war. Now all that was over. They could not grasp the political implications yet but they could see that from being monarch of the most hated nation in the world, the King was suddenly hailed everywhere as a statesman, the Uncle of Europe. They had loved him before, in spite of his faults, for his warmth and humanity. Now to the love was added admiration and pride. His people discovered to their joy that they could be proud of him.

Incredulous at the reports from Paris, Balfour and his

Government waited until they were confirmed, until Monson assured Lord Lansdowne that 'the visit had been a success more complete than the most sanguine optimist could have foreseen' and the French Ambassador, Paul Cambon, called to ask when negotiations for a formal agreement could begin. Balfour and Lansdowne found themselves in the uncomfortable position of having to congratulate the King officially on an achievement they had pronounced impossible. They could no longer bypass or ignore him. He had come into his own.

Wisely, Bertie left the discussion of terms to the Foreign Office, smiling to see how Balfour and Lansdowne scrambled to claim credit for the Entente Cordiale. He was used to the ways of politicians. Unknown to them, in case difficulties arose, he kept a direct link through Cambon with Delcassé and the French Government. He had worked too long for the Entente to risk letting anything go wrong.

Unlike his staff who were exhausted by the travelling and nonstop round of engagements, he returned from the tour wound up and full of energy. He had several days of meetings with his ministers sandwiched between visits to Kempton Park Races and evening parties, before whirling Alix off on a State Visit to Scotland. At Edinburgh they held a Court in the long picture gallery of Holyrood Palace where Bonny Prince Charlie had held his reception in 1745, opened the new hospital at Colinton Mains and drove to the ancient Castle for the ceremony of the keys, attended by the King's Bodyguard for Scotland, the Royal Company of Archers in their dark green uniforms and wide bonnets plumed with eagles' feathers. When the Royal carriage halted on the esplanade, the Lyon King of Arms in his herald's costume strode forward with his trumpeters who sounded a challenge to the closed fortress. A sergeant and corporal of the Black Watch came out on the battlements, calling 'Who goes there?' The herald gave the parole 'Thistle', and commanded them to open in the name of King Edward. 'Advance the King, and all's well!' the sergeant shouted, the massive gates swung open and a company of the garrison doubled out with pipers and drummers to salute the sovereign. On the drawbridge the Governor presented the keys of the castle and the King and Queen passed in.

At Glasgow, Bertie laid the memorial stone of the new Technical College, knighted the Lord Provost and visited his old friend the Duke of Hamilton before travelling south again to open the bridge across the Thames at Kew and a new wing of the London Hospital and attend Ascot Races. Even in a younger man his vigour would have been remarkable. He had recovered all the zest for life that had been eroded by the sorrows and illness of the past few years.

Balfour learnt very quickly that he had a different and determined man to deal with. Bertie would surrender no more of the privileges of the Crown, one of which was the right to approve and appoint ambassadors, and had insisted on diplomatic relations with Serbia being broken off. A few weeks earlier, a group of Army officers had broken into the Royal Palace in Belgrade during the night and brutally murdered the young King Alexander and his wife, Queen Draga, dropping their bodies out of the window of their bedroom into the courtyard below. They had acted on behalf of an exiled noble, Peter Karageorgevich, who had now been proclaimed King. The colonel who died blowing open the door of the Royal apartments with a bomb had been hailed as a national hero and the other officers given positions of power. Bertie had recalled the British Minister to London.

Balfour came to a weekend party at Sandringham, hoping to change the King's mind. In spite of the outrage, the Foreign Office found it inconvenient not to have a representative in Belgrade. Russia and Austria, he pointed out, had recognised the new King Peter. Bertie was adamant. 'Russia and Austria are interested countries,' he said. 'There is no need for England to recognise a government made up of assassins.' The other guests warmly supported him. 'Well,' Bertie said. 'One does not throw Kings out of windows.'

Alix was slightly annoyed with him. She had insisted on their coming to Sandringham so that he could rest but he had brought Esher, Soveral and Carrington and spent the whole time talking politics. They met in the salon after the Prime Minister had left and she taxed him with it. 'We might as well have stayed at Windsor. I brought you down here to get some fresh air.'

'I was just thinking of that, my dear,' he smiled.

'Shall we all go for a walk?'

'Well, actually I was thinking of a round of golf.'

'Good!' Alix exclaimed, delighted. 'Charlotte and I shall play too.'

Charlotte Knollys was sitting with old Sir Dighton Probyn, the Keeper of the Privy Purse. A tall, kindly man with a long white beard that completely covered his tie when he wore civilian dress and his medals when he was in uniform, he had won the VC during the Indian Mutiny, accompanied Bertie as Equerry on his tour of India and stayed in his service ever since. Like Charlotte he was devoted to Alix and they were her most faithful friends. Charlotte looked from him to the Queen. 'But I don't play, ma'am,' she said.

'Nonsense,' Alix laughed. 'It's very easy. Come along—we'll go and change.' She took Charlotte's hand and hurried her off.

Bertie turned to the men. 'Anyone feel like a game?' The others hesitated. The King had taken up with enthusiasm but his playing was erratic and his temper inclined to be short. 'If you'll give me a stroke a hole, sir,' Soveral offered, smiling.

'Hanged if I shall,' Bertie chuckled. 'You're being modest, Luis. Let's get out there quick, before they ruin the course.'

The links in the park at Sandringham were fairly new. While the fairways were good and the nine greens small but adequate, there was a notable shortage of bunkers. The problem was that no one could agree on the correct site for them. Bertie had asked Ponsonby and Fortescue who were both keen players to help him decide, and the agent had a number of wicker screens made which could easily be moved from position to position as they indicated. Unfortunately, the King's swing was mighty but he was inclined to slice his shots and his ball invariably struck the screens, slamming from one to another up the fairway like an obstacle course. He would order them moved and, next time, hit them in their new positions. Finally, he blew up and ordered them all to be removed and real bunkers made. This was left to the head gardener who knew next to nothing about golf, and, to date, he had only made two, built like dugouts in a battlefield.

In his match with Soveral, Bertie started badly by foozling his first drive. 'Blast!' he muttered as his ball trickled forward a few yards. 'I was thinking of something else.'

'Do take the shot again, sir,' Soveral suggested.

'No, no,' Bertie said tetchily. 'Let it lie, let it lie.'

He stood back. Soveral teed up quickly, sighted and hit a

splendid drive straight down the fairway. He had not meant to hit it so hard. 'Good shot,' Bertie said, flatly.

Soveral won the first two holes, both under par. On the third, he was careful to pull his drive so that it turned into the rough, cursing himself loudly for being over-confident. Bertie's humour was restored and his own drive was magnificent. He chuckled as Soveral complimented him and they set off in search of his ball. Unerringly, it had found its way to the first of the two bunkers.

Bertie stared at it, thoroughly disgruntled. He snatched an iron from his caddy and clambered down into the pit. 'I knew they'd put these bunkers in the wrong place!'

'Very badly sited, sir,' Soveral agreed. Bertie glanced up at him sharply to see if he was smiling, but Soveral was impassive. Grumbling to himself, Bertie chipped at his ball and it flew out of the bunker in a flurry of loose sand.

By careful play, Soveral managed to draw the hole and, on the fourth, the King had recovered his form. His approach shot to the green was perfect and he only needed to sink a putt of about eight feet for a Birdie. Soveral's ball lay nearer the hole but he was two strokes behind. Bertie concentrated very seriously, lining up on the flag which his caddy held. As he positioned his putter, there was a burst of laughter from behind him. He looked round, annoyed, and prepared again to play.

Just as he raised his putter, another ball whizzed past and Alix ran on to the green, knocking his ball off to the side with her iron. 'What the devil——?' Bertie spluttered.

Charlotte Knollys rushed past him after Alix, laughing. They were both using their clubs like hockey sticks, dribbling their balls forward. Alix turned and called, 'Come on, Sir Dighton——! You'll get left behind!'

Bertie stared disbelievingly as old Probyn came running towards them doggedly, holding his hat on. He was also waving a club and laughing.

Alix whacked again at her ball and Soveral jumped out of her path. The caddy pulled the flag out as Alix dribbled her ball eagerly towards the hole and clunked it in. 'I've won! I've won!' she laughed, excitedly.

Bertie glared at her incredulously, then raised his putter and dashed it down on to the green.

Charles Carrington sat talking quietly to Lord Esher in the salon. He had never really taken to him. As a politician, he tended to distrust a man who busied himself in politics, yet claimed not to owe allegiance to any one party, and as Bertie's oldest friend he tended to resent the influence which the newer triumvirate of Esher, Cassel and Soveral had on him. He realised that his resentment was partly caused by jealousy and sensibly kept it to himself.

Esher was quite aware of Carrington's resentment. It was a reaction he was used to. Privately, it amused him to see how the King's men friends, while forming a pretty close circle, each had a touch of jealousy for the others. Once when Soveral was asked if he had seen *The Importance of Being Earnest,* he had replied mournfully, 'No, but I've seen the importance of being Ernest Cassel.' And Cassel sometimes referred to the Marquis as 'Soveral overall'. For himself, Esher made no pretence. He gloried in his nearness to the throne. Being one of the King's intimate advisers perfectly suited his love of power without responsibility. He had not found being in business with Cassel fully satisfying. It was profitable but he missed the sense of behind-the-scenes intrigue and had responded readily when the King asked him to make a study of the state of the country's armed forces. Bertie knew that, although no military alliance was to be discussed, the French were anxious for reassurance that Britain was capable of supporting them in case of attack. That attack could only come from Germany whose army was easily the largest and most efficient on the Continent while Britain's army was under-manned and still commanded by out-of-date generals.

'The other thing that troubles the King is Ireland,' Carrington said. 'He's thinking of going there.'

'Surely not,' Esher objected. 'It could be dangerous after that Serbian business. Agitators imitate each other like monkeys. Someone's thrown a bomb at the Shah of Persia already.'

'You know the King,' Carrington answered. 'If he's told something is dangerous, it makes him all the more determined to do it. He'll take the risk if there's a chance of a visit having any effect. He says, what's the point of him healing the breach with France, if he can't do the same inside his own country?'

They sat for a minute in silence, then Esher smiled. 'I must say I was pleased to see how happy he and the Queen still are together. Too many people were saying they had grown apart, that he doesn't have any time for her any more.'

'He spends more time with her than anyone else,' Carrington said. 'But their interests are very different. She likes a simple life, with her family. She'd be content never to leave here.'

Esher nodded. 'Yes. And her deafness makes going about in society an ordeal for her. We often forget that.'

They broke off and rose as the door opened and Bertie strode in. Alix was following him. 'You're a bad loser,' she laughed.

'Loser!' Bertie snorted. He marched to the drinks table and poured himself a brandy and soda, fuming. Esher and Carrington looked from him to Soveral who had appeared behind Alix with Charlotte Knollys. He seemed to be having difficulty restraining his laughter, as did Probyn who followed him in, combing his beard with his fingers.

'You can't deny it.' Alix said serenely. 'I got my ball into the hole first every time.'

'That is not the object of the game!' Bertie protested.

'Nonsense.'

He sighed. 'Well, if you won't believe me, will you listen to Luis?'

As Alix turned to him, Soveral smiled. 'The winner of the game, ma'am is not the one who knocks the little ball into the little hole first—but the one who takes the least number of shots.'

'How ridiculous!' Alix commented. 'I think my way is much more fun.'

Soveral laughed. 'It may well be.'

She turned back. 'Well, I don't want you to sulk, Bertie. We'll play it your way after lunch.'

Bertie set down his glass. 'I'm afraid not, my dear. I have to run up to London for a few days.'

Alix paused. She did not notice the others' slight start of surprise. 'London? That's very sudden.'

'The Prime Minister wishes to see me,' Bertie said.

'Why didn't Mr Balfour mention it when he was here?'

Bertie looked at Esher who had recovered his poise. 'It is a diplomatic matter requiring His Majesty's presence,' he explained. 'In case a Privy Council has to be called.'

Alix shrugged, disappointed. 'Well, I hope you don't expect me to come with you? I cannot abide London out of season.'

Bertie picked up his glass again. He sipped it, aware of the others watching him. 'Of course, my dear. It is very inconvenient. And if you don't wish to accompany me, I shall not insist on it.'

The others were still watching him. Only Charlotte saw the depth of sadness which showed for a moment in Alexandra's eyes.

Late that afternoon, Bertie called on Daisy, Countess of Warwick, at her London home. Lately they had not met very often and she was overjoyed. He was struck again by how much she had altered. Her superb figure had thickened, the firm flesh grown soft and billowy. She was still a beautiful woman, but more than a suggestion of a double chin spoilt the elegant line of her profile. The days when she had been his 'dear little Daisy wife' were gone, the days when he had been besotted with her and their time together had been one long, magical honeymoon. Since then she had almost ruined her husband by her extravagance, championed more and more loudly the cause of Socialism and taken many lovers, always carefully chosen from her own class. Most upsetting of all, in her vanity she saw their former closeness as giving her the right to interpret Bertie's thoughts and speak in his name.

He could not fully forget the past and always thought of her affectionately but her boasting about his feelings for her and her self-publicising commitment to radical politics, in which she tried to involve him, hurt Alix, which was the one thing he would not allow. The main reason he had come to London was to beg her to be more discreet.

Having him with her, charming and sympathetic, Daisy miscalculated her power. She reminded him artfully of their old tenderness and gossiped of mutual friends. She was paying particular attention just then to Winston Churchill, the Unionist MP for Oldham. The Unionists were a breakaway section of the Liberals, who had split from the main party over Home Rule for Ireland. They were led in the House of Commons by Joseph Chamberlain and, in the Lords, by the Duke of Devonshire and allied to Balfour and the Conservatives. Bertie had always been interested in Winston, not only because he was Jenny and Randolph's son, but for himself. He had helped his career whenever he could, seeing the great promise in the aggressively brilliant, ambitious young man. He was radically-inclined and amused

Bertie by his scathing attacks on Balfour and his own party, though it made the chance of his promotion to the Government remote. Bertie was disturbed when he saw that Daisy's chief interest in Winston was to get him to change parties, which she felt would be a victory for the Left.

To distract her from the subject, he told her of his diplomatic reception in Paris, in the embassy which had once belonged to Napoleon's sister. Monson, the stuffy Ambassador, had been paired with an equally stuffy member of the French Cabinet. In an effort to make conversation, he had said brightly, 'Did you know that I'm sleeping in Pauline's bed?' To which the French official replied glacially, 'Your Excellency's private life is no concern of mine.'

Daisy laughed but used the story to raise the point she had promised her comrades she would take up with him. Why had he gone to Paris at all? she asked. Why do we need an agreement with France? It would be better to identify ourselves with our natural allies, the Germans. Then the march of the British working man and the advance of Trade Unionism would be an example to the German proletariat, an inspiration to them to win their freedom and an end to colonialism and capitalism. France was allied to Russia, the hated home of Czarism. If only Bertie and she could be as close as they once were, she was sure she could make him see. Bertie listened and nodded without replying as she smiled, laying her hand on his thigh to reinforce her argument. She still thought she could convert and use him. She did not realise that she was saying goodbye.

Two evenings later, Bertie gave a small dinner party for a few friends. Among them were Alice Keppel and Lord Esher. Afterwards he led them into the green drawing-room at Buckingham Palace, furnished with the choicest pieces from the Prince Regent's Pavilion at Brighton, and Esher again talked to Alice Keppel.

'You'll know I speak in confidence,' he said, 'when I tell you that yesterday I was sent with a letter to Lady Warwick.'

Alice tensed. She had learnt to be wary of Esher's oblique approach. She made herself look away from him, as if to admire a tall Chinese vase behind her. 'Indeed?'

'She wished to resume her . . . special relationship with His Majesty,' he went on. 'I had to tell her that her attempts to associate him with her extreme political opinions, and her tactlessness, caused distress to the Queen. And that she must have no further connection with the Court.'

Alice hesitated. This was news. She did not care for Daisy Warwick. But why had he told her? 'Am I to take it that my own "special relationship" is to be ended?'

'There's no suggestion of that,' he assured her quickly. 'On the contrary—your devotion to the King and lack of self-interest can only be admired.'

Alice ran her fingers down the slope of the vase, feeling the cool, delicate texture of the porcelain. 'My feelings for His Majesty are of interest only to myself, Lord Esher,' she said levelly. 'And not a matter for discussion.'

Bertie was talking to another guest, a leading Irish Catholic, Sir Anthony MacDonnell. His attitude to Ireland was simple. It was part of the United Kingdom and those Nationalists who tried to say otherwise were deliberately ignoring eight hundred years of history. He did not believe Home Rule was the answer to the chronic poverty and discontent, a discontent kept alive by religious quarrels. He urged the Government to cure the poverty and wanted to strengthen the tie between the Irish people and the Crown. So far he had been persuaded from paying an official visit. If he were received with antagonism or even ignored, it could do untold damage. MacDonnell promised him that the Irish people were not themselves disloyal. It was their political leaders, some fanatics, others seeking power, who stirred up the unrest when all the people wished was peace and some of the prosperity the other parts of the kingdom enjoyed.

'What do they most want?' Bertie asked him.

'Education,' MacDonnell answered. 'Education and security in their land.'

Bertie smiled, decided. 'Then I shall come to Ireland with an Education Bill in one hand and a Land Bill in the other.'

It was not an empty promise. After entertaining President Loubet in London on a return visit and giving a dinner at Buckingham Palace for Rear-Admiral Cotton and the officers of the American Naval Squadron, King Edward and Queen Alexandra sailed in the Royal Yacht for Dublin. On the day they arrived, the Irish Land Purchase Bill was passed by Parliament. This was a farsighted reform, designed by Balfour to allow peasants to own farming land which they could buy with no-interest loans at below market value, at a cost to the British taxpayer of £112,000,000.

Its announcement halved the flow of emigration to the United States and Australia almost at once.

The omens for a state visit by Bertie and Alix were not good. The Corporation of the City of Dublin voted against giving them an address of welcome. The Nationalists saw the danger of increased prosperity to their dreams of independence and denounced the Land Bill and the King's presence as a Conservative plot. News came of the death of the venerable Pope Leo. More trivially but more personally, Bertie had brought Caesar and his Irish Terrier, Jack, with him. On the first evening at the Viceregal Lodge, the Irish Terrier died suddenly of no apparent cause. To the superstitious it was a sign.

George Wyndham, the secretary for Ireland, strongly doubted the wisdom of the visit. He could see no good coming from it. Like the Corporation he had underestimated the almost mystical appeal of the King's personality. No welcome from them but an unprecedented eighty-two loyal addresses were presented to him at Dublin Castle by other groups. For four crowded days, the King and Queen went everywhere, holding receptions and dinners, inspecting Trinity College, Alexandra College and Maynooth, exhibitions, libraries and the Guinness Trust Buildings. Bertie walked, as always without bodyguards, in one of the poorest districts, accepting invitations into people's houses and talking to them, while Alix visited the patients in the Hospital at Harold's Cross. Their ease and sincerity won them immense popularity. Bertie had been genuinely impressed by the heroism of the Irish regiments during the war, and said so. He was genuinely moved by the death of the Pope, and said so in a letter of condolence to Cardinal Logue.

At the climax of the visit, a review of fifteen thousand troops commanded by the Duke of Connaught in Phoenix Park, with Lord Roberts in attendance, the whole populace of Dublin seemed to turn out, shouting for the King of Ireland. Wyndham wrote back to the Cabinet amazedly that they were 'in a frenzy'. For the journey back to the Castle, Bertie changed to horseback and rode alongside the open carriage in which Alix sat. It looked as if they would be mobbed. The fluttering of flags and the wildness of the cheering panicked the horses of the cavalry escort and they cannoned into Bertie's. Women and children dodged under the hooves and swarmed round him and the Royal carriage. Unlike their staff who were alarmed, Alix laughed and

231

bowed. Bertie shook hands with some of the people who reached up to touch him and, to show his confidence, lit a cigarette and smiled, waving to others who had climbed the trees at the side of the road.

From Dublin, they went to Belfast and on to Londonderry, Galway and Connemara and everywhere the welcome was the same. In Cork, the Nationalist stronghold, Bertie presented colours to the Royal Munster Fusiliers and the Royal Irish Regiment, cheered by everyone except the politicians whose attempt to lead a boycott of the visit had been ignored. It was the last stop and here, as everywhere, people sobbed and shouted, 'Come back! Say ye'll come back!'

Once again, Balfour and the Cabinet found themselves having to congratulate the King on achieving the impossible. It was all the more galling as their government was under attack and showing signs of splitting up, stung by the Liberals and internal disagreement. The certainty with which Balfour had assured himself that he did not need the King's support had vanished.

After the jostling and staring of the crowds at Homburg, Bertie decided to take his annual cure this year at Marienbad in Bohemia, a fashionable, classically beautiful town famous for its mineral waters and baths. He booked the comfortable suite of rooms at the Hotel Weimar which he had used before and brought only Ponsonby and Stanley Clarke as staff and a few servants. To his annoyance, the Government insisted on his being accompanied by two Scotland Yard detectives but they proved to be inconspicuous and were useful when the crowds turned out at first to be worse than at Homburg.

Everywhere he went, hundreds of people followed him, excited, photographing him with small Brownie snapshot cameras. Then Ponsonby discovered that the Burgomaster had hung up placards everywhere asking visitors to the town to respect the King's incognito which, of course, had exactly the opposite effect. When they were removed, people behaved better and Bertie was able to relax. He found he needed the rest, and the cure. He had put on weight again.

The holiday started on a sombre note with news of the death of the Marquess of Salisbury. The Tory elder statesman had not lasted long in retirement. One more link with the past was cut. To Bertie, it was a symptom of the change that accelerated with each year of the new century. It depressed him for a time. Salisbury had left the Government secure and the country settled. Now the Government was breaking up and there was industrial unrest in the Midlands and the North, the worst for many years, fanned and encouraged by the Liberals as they struggled to climb back into power. Yet Bertie had always championed change himself, improvement, provided it was controlled and positive. And he had always been able to counsel restraint before. He could not remain depressed for long.

Clarke and Ponsonby were good company. Although they were both younger than him, and fit, he was touched to see how they stuck manfully to the cure themselves to help him. Under the doctor's instructions, with strict dieting, walks and the daily ritual of drinking the waters, he soon had the pleasure of ordering his valet to have all his suits taken in. It was the moment of the cure he liked best. Years seemed to slip away from him with the lost pounds and he began to take an interest in his fellow visitors. It was almost as if the new jauntiness in his step acted as a signal. Pretty ladies stationed themselves where they could catch his eye as he strolled in the mornings after going through the mail and despatches with Ponsonby. In his grey pin-stripe suit and grey felt hat, he would offer his arm to one he recognised and stroll on, murmuring to her while her heart fluttered and she felt the eyes of all the other women in Marienbad burning her with envy.

The two detectives would follow them at a discreet distance. They had learnt discretion one day when they had followed him as he walked with his companion into the woods. The green forest came close to Marienbad, old trees and scented bushes with a carpet of lush grass and ferns and quiet paths wandering through, dappled in sunlight. The detectives lost the King and beat about in a panic until they suddenly came on him, taking his ease in a clearing with the little American widow who was with him, perched above him, half-naked and ecstatic. Mercifully, they had been able to retreat out of sight and hearing without being seen. The detective sergeant's face was scarlet.

'Well, my lad, that's a right royal lesson for you,' the Inspector said solemnly, with only a trace of a smile.

When the King of Greece broke off his journey to Denmark to join his brother-in-law, the pace quickened and Marienbad preened itself over all other resorts. Bertie also made a surprising discovery. Henry Campbell-Bannerman, the leader of the Liberal Party, was an habitué of Marienbad, coming every August. He was a wealthy, elderly Scotsman and, on previous occasions, Bertie had carefully steered clear of him, convinced he would be censorious and boring. This year they met and Campbell-Bannerman turned out to be interesting and amusing, a shrewd man of the world with a pawky sense of humour. It tickled the King to realise that the old politician had been avoiding him too, expecting him to be pompous and distant. They got on very well.

The sensation of the holiday came when senior members of Bertie's staff arrived and he announced that he was to pay a State Visit to Vienna, capital of the Austrian Empire, third member of the Triple Alliance. Kaiser Franz Joseph sent the Imperial and Royal train to bring him and met him at the station with a host of Grand Dukes and Court dignitaries. By Bertie's special request the streets were not lined with troops and the people of the gayest city in Europe laughed and appreciated the point, cheering and waving to him as the procession of the two King-Emperors drove to the Hofburg Palace. Kaiser Wilhelm always insisted on full military honours, coming with his own escort of immensely tall Prussian Grenadiers and jack-booted Staff Officers, with soldiers posted three-deep along the route from the station. Czar Nicholas, on his visits, left the Imperial train some distance outside Vienna and was smuggled into the city in a guarded, closed carriage. Wilhelm came as a War Lord, Nicholas as a frightened, suspicious despot and Bertie, openly, as a friend. That evening at the State Banquet, when he proclaimed that he had made the Emperor Franz Joseph a Field-Marshal in the British Army, the guests beat on the tables, shouting 'Hoch! Hoch!' and the German and Russian Ambassadors realised that the conquest of Paris was being repeated here.

Bertie had many friends and relatives in the Austrian court and they helped him to keep the atmosphere of the visit informal. It was hard for him to adjust to the seventy-four-year-old Emperor's routine of rising at 4 am and working till breakfast, lunch at midday, dinner at 5 pm and going to bed at 7.30, but he forced himself and built up a new intimacy between them. He liked Franz Joseph and was sorry for him. His strange and beautiful wife, Elizabeth, had been stabbed to death by an anarchist on a landing stage on the lake of Geneva six years earlier. Since then, the lonely old man had withdrawn more and more from the world, growing apart even from his effervescent and understanding mistress, the actress Katherina Schratt, who had been protected from publicity by Elizabeth's tact. He had never fully recovered from the suicide of his heir, Crown Prince Rudolph, who had shot himself and Marie Vetsera in the hunting-lodge at Mayerling. He welcomed Bertie initially as a friend of his dead son. As Bertie laid a wreath on Rudolph's tomb, he thought how little his father had really known him, the high-spirited young man who had secretly been so afraid of succeeding to the throne and tried to forget his fear with drink and drugs. He had not even really loved poor, pretty Marie Vetsera. She was only one of a number of girls he had begged to join him in a suicide pact.

The talks Bertie had with Franz Joseph and the Austro-Hungarian Foreign Minister were the first significant contact between their two countries for years and they agreed on the need to stay in closer touch. It was an important step in his policy of personal diplomacy. He was also able to enjoy himself and, more usefully, to be seen to enjoy himself. He gave a reception, hunted on an island in the Danube, lunched at the Jockey Club and, after his host had gone to bed, changed into ordinary evening clothes and went out to the theatre and the nightspots. Seeing him among them, unfearing, amused and amusing, the Viennese quickly thought of him as one of themselves. 'No, no, I have no political purpose in coming here,' he assured the German Ambassador. 'It is just a friendly visit.'

'No political purpose! . . .' Kaiser Wilhelm muttered thickly. He was pacing between his desk and the window of his office in the Neues Palais. The muscles of his stomach cramped with anger and he swallowed to clear the sudden taste of bile. He looked again at the telegram. 'He is Satan . . . No one can tell me he is not Satan!' He crumpled the telegram and threw it violently across the room.

Eulenberg had brought it and closed the door as he began to pace again. 'He has visited everyone but me! Why?'

Wilhelm demanded. 'Paris, Rome, Vienna . . . The Italians and Austrians are our allies. He is trying to win them away from us—to dispute the natural leadership of the Reich! To humiliate me!' He was conscious of Eulenberg's eyes, sympathetic and concerned. He stopped and drew himself up. He must show firmness. 'Well, he shall not, that strutting peacock! Let him lead them all against us. We Germans have always been best with our backs to the wall. I shall tell my people to be on guard—to be prepared!'

When he was like this, Eulenberg adored him. Indecisive or tearful at his uncle's lack of affection, he was less than himself. Now he was glorious. Yet the feminine streak in Eulenberg advised caution. 'The greatest victories are diplomatic, All Highest,' he said, almost in a whisper. 'You could follow him to Vienna as you did to Rome.'

'Yes,' Wilhelm breathed. Once he had been embarrassed by the intensity of his friend's admiration, so like a caress. Now he needed it as approval. 'I shall show those mincing Viennese how a true Emperor behaves. They shall not waltz with Edward, but fall into step with me!'

Arthur Balfour arrived at Balmoral to find his fellow guests were Admiral Fisher and Lord Esher. He was a troubled man. This split in his Cabinet had become a chasm, over proposals for tariff reform. He had to report a series of resignations, including the Duke of Devonshire and Joseph Chamberlain, the Colonial Secretary. It had rocked confidence in the Government. Although he had enough votes to carry on, he was also under fire for failure to improve the efficiency of the Army and Navy. First concern was the Army. He had agreed with Esher's findings on the War Office. It galled him to admit, but he knew he should have listened to the King earlier. 'Yet to build up our land and sea forces, we should have to increase taxes, sir,' he explained. 'Campbell-Bannerman' and the Liberals would set up a howl from one end of the country to the other.'

'Greater efficiency does not necessarily mean greater numbers,' Bertie said. 'Cleaning out your stables doesn't make them bigger.'

When Balfour left to change for dinner, Bertie had Esher called to his study. 'The Kaiser has ordered an immediate expansion of his forces,' he told him.

'I suppose it was inevitable,' Esher said. 'Will he attack?'

'Not if we stand up to him. He'll back down, like all bullies.'

'What do we oppose him with, sir? An antiquated navy and a pitifully small army, still staffed by generals who proved their incompetence in the Boer War? I thought Balfour was aware of the problem but he's taken no action.'

'It's the same old story, Reggie,' Bertie said. 'Party politics come first—local issues. But if our very existence is threatened, they must take second place. France looks to us. The small nations depend on us and Balfour has no choice any more. There must be reform.'

'Total reform, sir? Including the War Office?'

'Yes,' Bertie nodded. 'The mutual admiration society at the top must be removed. We must have a new General Staff and an office of Imperial Defence. Without that, there can be no progress.'

'It is essential, sir.'

Bertie looked away from him. 'Mr Balfour and I have agreed that the present Secretary of State for War must resign. He intends to offer the post to you.'

Esher was glad the King had given him a moment to think. He was excited at the thought of stepping straight into a position of such importance, but the more he thought, the more reluctant he became. 'I am flattered, sir,' he said carefully. 'However, there are other considerations.' The King's head turned to him. 'Chief among them—if I were a Minister, I would be liable to pressure from the Government. Whoever does this work should be independent.'

Bertie fought down a spasm of anger. He had worked hard for this appointment. He would have liked a friend in the Cabinet at last. Even so, he had half expected the refusal. He was fond of Esher but had no illusions about him. The other considerations were his addiction to intrigue and more indirect power and his profitable business association with Cassel which he would have to give up. All the same, Bertie needed him as the one man both Parliament and the Army would accept. 'In that case,' he said pointedly, 'I would like you to head a committee to advise on the reconstruction of the War Office, appointed by the Prime Minister.'

'I should be honoured, sir,' Esher answered. He hesitated. 'But it would have to be known that any recommendations had Your Majesty's complete backing for them to have a hope of being approved.'

'I would insist on it,' Bertie murmured. He smiled. This time, the Government would have to acknowledge the part he played. And he had ensured the proper defence of the Empire. Almost too late, but he had done it.

Chapter

14

Charlotte Knollys woke herself coughing. She was in her third floor bedroom at Sandringham. Her throat felt raw and her lungs congested. For a second she wondered if she had caught a cold. Then she smelt burning.

She sat up quickly, peering across at her iron stove. It was very early on a dark December morning but it was not only the dimness of the light that made it difficult to see. The room was full of smoke. Even as she looked, a tiny tongue of flame licked up and ran along the line between two floorboards and the fringe of the carpet caught fire. She had a moment of panic which ended abruptly as she realised that the bedroom below hers was Queen Alexandra's.

She swung her legs out of bed and hurried to the door. She ran along the passage and down the stairs to the lower corridor, switching on the lights and shouting, 'Help! Fire!' Wisps of grey smoke drifted from underneath the door of the Queen's bedroom and, in the distance, she heard the footmen on night duty calling. She was breathless and weak with shock but knew there was no time to wait for help.

She opened the bedroom door. A cloud of smoke billowed out. Through it, in a single, horrified glance she saw the Queen asleep or unconscious on her fourposter bed and above her a wedge of small flames spreading and eating their way across the ceiling. She hurried into the room, calling out, but Alix did not respond. Charlotte ran to her and touched her shoulder, gasping and coughing. She sobbed with relief as Alix woke, startled, coughing also. With the fresh air from the open door, the flames above them suddenly blossomed, crackling as they burned through the moulded plaster.

Because of her deafness, Alix had heard nothing. She was dazed, choked by the smoke. Charlotte snatched up her dressing gown from the couch at the foot of the bed and, pulling her up to sit, wrapped it round her shoulders. She helped her out of bed and, holding each other, coughing, they stumbled to the door. As they reached it, a section of the ceiling cracked and fell, smouldering, through the velvet hangings on to the bed. Almost immediately it was blazing.

As Charlotte helped the Queen out into the corridor, Dighton Probyn came running in his dressing gown and slippers. An Equerry and a footman were behind him. He closed the bedroom door and took the Queen from Charlotte, half-carrying her along the corridor and down the main stairs to a sitting-room as far from the fire as possible. The Equerry brought Charlotte. Others of the Queen's ladies began to appear, worried and frightened. When one of them started to wail, Probyn told her brusquely to stop her caterwauling and sent the Equerry to fetch some brandy. He had already sounded the alarm and he could hear the clanging bell of the estate fire brigade as the engine raced up to the house.

He had laid Alix on a sofa and she recovered in the clear air, sucking it in gratefully. Charlotte was in a chair near her. Probyn went out and came back with a man's overcoat which he tucked round her. She was shivering. When his ailing wife had died, many people thought he would marry Charlotte. There was no chance of that, but now, in spite of her plainness and red, watering eyes, Probyn could have kissed her.

The Equerry returned with a decanter of brandy and glasses. Just as the fire brigade arrived, he told them, the whole ceiling of the Queen's bedroom had collapsed. Alix insisted on Charlotte being given the first glass.

'She is the heroine, not me,' she said. She rose unsteadily and handed her the glass herself, kissing her. 'Dear, dear Charlotte . . . how can I thank you for saving my poor life?'

Bertie was on a weekend shooting party at Elveden Hall in Suffolk with Alice Keppel, and heard the news later that morning. He came to Sandringham the next day, not alarmed since they had told him the firemen had managed to contain the blaze. Then he saw that the two rooms had been totally destroyed. The heat of the stove in Charlotte's bedroom had ignited the wooden beam under the floor. It a miraculous escape and he hurried to find Alix. He had not realised she had been in such danger.

She was in the main salon with Charlotte and Probyn, sitting on a couch near the fireplace with Charlotte, holding her hand. She had quite recovered, although Charlotte was still pale. She was touched to see that Bertie was trembling and rose to kiss him. 'You mustn't worry, my dear,' she told him. 'We are perfectly all right.'

'I should have been here,' he muttered. 'I—I can't thank Charlotte enough.'

'Yes, she was very brave,' Alix said, and smiled. 'We were just saying, isn't it appropriate that I was saved by my Woman of the Bedchamber?' He tried to laugh and Alix took his arm. 'Come and sit down, Bertie. You look as if you need to. What a pity you missed our second house-warming!'

The ball at Buckingham Palace was in honour of Princess Maud and Prince Charles of Denmark who had had their first son, Olaf, a few months before. Maud was Bertie's youngest and dearest daughter. Like her two sisters she had not inherited Alix's beauty but her long, heart-shaped face was appealing and her figure slim and graceful. Bertie had wanted her to marry a king at least, but she had fallen in love with her cousin, Prince Charles, a tall, serious young man with little to offer except his salary as an officer in the Danish navy.

George was talking to them and his wife May in the recess at the end of the white and gilt ballroom, smiling as May sympathised with Maud. She had known what it was like to be a young wife and mother and have her husband away at sea much of the time. George turned to his father who was watching the dancers. He was in his full dress uniform, relaxed and happy.

'There's not another woman who can hold a candle to your mother,' Bertie said quietly.

George looked down the hall. Through the glitter of court uniforms and ballgowns, he could see his mother dancing with the Marquis de Soveral. Her hip was quite painful at times, but there was no trace of her slight limp when she was dancing. She was laughing and her gaiety seemed to brighten the air around her. She was dressed in gold, a close-fitting gown cut very simply and elegantly, with hardly any jewellery, except a diamond choker and tiara.

'She turns every ball into a personal triumph,' his father added, admiringly.

'Yes, Father. But this whole year has been your triumph.' Bertie was pleased. 'You think so?'

Although his father treated him with great understanding and kindness, George found it difficult to be at ease with him. His own more reserved nature prevented it. He was proud of him but paying a compliment made him even more stiff. 'One of—one of the papers called it your Annus Mirabilis,' he faltered. 'You have changed the whole feeling of Europe towards us.'

'Not quite all of it, George—but we'll see,' Bertie murmured. He turned to the others, raising his voice. 'Now then, Maud, why aren't you dancing?'

She smiled. 'Because my husband hasn't asked me, Papa.'

Charles was embarrassed. 'We have danced three waltzes, two polkas and a quadrille. I thought you would like to rest.'

Bertie scoffed. 'Rest? We didn't know the meaning of the word when I was your age.' They laughed. 'Whatever the next item is I want to see you all out there. Oh, not you, George. Forgive us, May—I'm taking him away.' When May glanced at her husband, surprised, he chuckled. 'We're only going to circle a little.' He beckoned to Ponsonby who stood by one of the side pillars in his scarlet Equerry's uniform with gold aiguillettes. He came to the King and bowed. 'I have commanded the Princess of Wales to dance, Fritz.'

'Yes, sir,' Ponsonby replied blankly.

'So see to it.'

May laughed and Ponsonby bowed to her, thinking it was a pity she was normally so solemn. She really looked rather pretty when she smiled. Bertie took George's arm and moved slowly round the side of the ballroom with him. The people who were sitting out rose and he nodded affably, saying a few words to each one as he passed.

Alice Keppel was standing with Esher, Cassel and Admiral Fisher nearer the orchestra.

'The King's making his rounds,' Cassel said. 'He's taking young George with him. That's unusual.'

'Not really,' Alice commented. 'He treats him more like a brother in many ways, than a son.'

Fisher had become an intimate of Esher, who had asked him to join his War Office Reconstruction Committee. As Naval Commander-in-Chief at Portsmouth, he had made things hum by concentrating on technical training for cadets and junior officers and on the development of the submarine. He was puzzled. 'How can a walk round a ballroom help him?'

'It's the King's style,' Cassel explained. 'He doesn't have the kind of mind to read complicated reports. But he can read people.'

'He likes to catch them relaxed and off duty,' Esher added. 'Then he can usually tell what they're really thinking.' As Fisher grunted, Esher smiled. 'Ah—I thought so.'

Arthur Balfour and Lord Lansdowne bowed as King Edward and Prince George approached them. Bertie was smiling, partly because he had noticed that both Lady Mary Elcho and Ettie Desborough were present. So here was bachelor Balfour on the horns of a dilemma, caught between his two mistresses and having to spend the evening with Lansdowne. 'A most enjoyable ball, sir,' Balfour said.

Bertie's smile deepened. 'Then why are you both looking so solemn? I've just been speaking to the French Ambassador. He tells me his government is very happy with the terms of the treaty between us.'

Lansdowne glanced round warningly and lowered his voice. 'Its existence is not generally known yet, sir.'

'Then shouldn't it become so?'

'Public opinion must be conditioned before the announcement,' Lansdowne stressed. 'Not to mention the reaction . . . in other quarters.'

'By "other quarters", I presume you mean Germany and Russia,' Bertie murmured. 'Then perhaps I should say that my Russian nephew will already know of the treaty.'

'How can the Czar know, sir?' Lansdowne asked, surprised.

'Because my nephew, the Kaiser, will have told him. He will try to use it as a way of loosening Russia's own link with France.'

'How had he heard of it, sir?' Balfour wondered.

Bertie motioned to George. '. . . Diplomatic sources would be the polite name,' George said.

'Precisely,' Bertie agreed. 'He had learnt of it by the time I was in Marienbad.'

Balfour was worried. 'Have you discussed the terms with him, sir?' he queried.

Bertie's eyes narrowed. 'Of course not. But I have assured him there is nothing in it harmful to Germany. His reply was—if that is so, why was it hidden from me? That is why I say it should be made public.'

The schottische the orchestra had been playing ended

243

and the dancers bowed and curtsied to one another. There was a light ripple of applause for Alix as she headed for Bertie with Soveral in attendance. The gentlemen bowed. 'That was delightful,' she told Bertie. 'Luis dances as well as you used to.'

'I am greatly honoured, ma'am,' Soveral smiled.

'Have you come to look for another partner, my dear?' Bertie asked playfully. He indicated Balfour and Lansdowne and, a short distance away, the stocky, grey-bearded Henry Campbell-Bannerman who stood with Charles Carrington. 'Here we are poised between the Government and the Opposition. So you must choose carefully.' They laughed.

Alix raised her hands. 'Oh, no—my next partner is already decided. Here he is—Admiral Jack.' Fisher came towards them and bowed, smiling. 'I have only promised to dance with him on condition he doesn't make me laugh too much.'

One of Fisher's most endearing qualities was a boyish and unpredictable sense of humour, which she found irresistible. Seeing the others amused and occupied, Bertie moved to the side. It was an effortless technique he had developed for meeting as many people as possible in the shortest time. He would engage one small group in conversation, draw in the next and move on to them.

Standing next to Carrington, Princess Daisy of Pless caught her breath as she saw the King coming towards them. She wore a daringly lowcut balldress from Worth's, of peach-coloured poplin with flounces of peach-tinted lace on the skirt and miniature flowers made of clusters of topaz on the bodice. A rope of pearls, the celebrated Pless pearls seven yards long, was wound round and round her throat to make a lustrous, close-fitting collar. It was ridiculous to feel so flustered, she scolded herself, a married woman in her twenties should be able to control herself. A tall, blue-eyed blonde with a superb figure, she was the sister of George Cornwallis-West, the daughter of Patsy, the lovely Mrs. Cornwallis-West whose intimacy with Bertie had been the talk of the town until it was ended by his liaison with Lillie Langtry. Daisy had known the King since she was a madcap little girl. He had even sponsored her marriage to the rich young Prince Hans and come to her wedding at St Margaret's, Westminster. He had always been kind, like a charming uncle. She had gone off to live in Hans's palace in Silesia and learn to be a princess. After suffering the rigours of Court etiquette in Berlin, she came back gratefully as often as she could to visit England.

Grown into a stunningly attractive and vivacious woman, she was invited everywhere and naturally kept meeting the King. That was what disturbed her. He had been as kind and charming as ever but she became aware that he was no longer avuncular. He did not speak to her nor look at her as a girl any more, but as a woman. It was not that he flirted with her, pressed his knee against hers under the table or tried to hold her hand as some men did. She knew how to deal with *them*. There was a warmth, an inflection in his rich, deep voice when he spoke to her that made her feel insecure and very feminine. It was unseemly—he was old enough to be her father, yet she forgot that when she was with him and, afterwards, was left bothered and unsettled and still vaguely excited. And, somehow she was sure that he knew, which made it worse. She was proud of her figure, yet when his perturbing, heavy-lidded eyes turned to her, she felt he could tell exactly how she would look without her long, S-shaped, French corset and wished that the fashion was not so decolletée and her breasts so high and impudent. Gentlemen, of course, did not look. But the King was a gentleman, and he always looked.

She curtsied as he reached them, keeping her back straight so that her front would not dip and reveal more of her cleavage. Bertie almost laughed aloud. She really was tantalising. The wide blue eyes and full lower lip, combined with the sensational figure, gave her an air of innocent sensuality. He doubted if Hans had tapped a quarter of the passion that was so obviously latent in her. One would not have to seduce her. She was so high-mettled and defensive, she would seduce herself. It would not be fair, and she could not replace Alice. 'You are très en beauté this evening, Daisy,' he murmured. 'That gown is exquisite.'

Daisy curtsied again and was relieved as Alice Keppel and Lord Esher appeared beside them.

Bertie smiled to see them and wondered if Alice had been able to read his thoughts. Probably. However, their coming had made his chance of a moment or two alone with Campbell-Bannerman more unlikely and that was what he had aimed for. He looked at him. 'I was sorry I didn't see more of you at Marienbad this year, C.B.'

Campbell-Bannerman bowed. 'I was just saying the same to Lord Carrington, sir.'

'Do you think the waters did you any good?' Bertie joked. 'You don't seem to have lost much weight.'

'I've noticed that most people seem to put it on again quite quickly, sir.' C.B.'s eyes were humorous, watching for the King's reaction.

Bertie glanced at the others. They were waiting, but Alice smiled. He chuckled. 'Very true. Every year I tell my valet to have my suits taken in. The rascal never pays any attention—and a month later they all fit again.'

As the group laughed, the orchestra played a chord to signal partners for the start of the Lancers quadrille. Alexandra was the first to move out, with Fisher. They were followed by Ponsonby with May and Prince Charles with Maud. Bertie smiled to Alice and looked at Carrington, who bowed to her and led her on to the floor. Esher had also understood and bowed to Princess Daisy. When she hesitated, he took her hand and drew her out to join the others as the sets quickly formed.

'You're not a dancing man, C.B.?' Bertie asked.

'In former times, sir.'

'So were we all,' Bertie murmured. The orchestra played another chord and the dancers bowed and curtsied. Bertie watched the first set of the Lancers begin. 'No, I was going to Paris,' he said casually, 'but I'm concerned about this industrial trouble in the Midlands.'

'A direct result of the Government's policies, sir,' Campbell-Bannerman commented. He was just as casual, also watching the dancers.

'But I trust the Liberal Party will not encourage these disturbances. It is a small step from violent protest to revolution.'

'Not one that my Party would ever take, sir.'

C.B. was considerably less extreme and more balanced than Bertie had expected, but then he had been trained by Gladstone. It was reassuring. However, one development perplexed him. Jenny's son, Winston, had been disowned by his constituents and had crossed the House to join the Liberal Opposition. Bertie hoped it was a sincere conversion, at least, and that he would not live to regret it. 'Young Churchill's made some pretty inflammatory speeches. Under the influence, no doubt, of his Welsh friend.'

'Churchill and Lloyd George are young men, sir,' Campbell-Bannerman said. 'They are passionately concerned about the plight of the labouring classes in this country.'

Bertie looked at him. 'They are not alone. But do not let them trap you into making promises which your Party will be unable to fulfil—after the next election.'

Campbell-Bannerman tensed. 'Do you predict that we shall win, sir?'

'It was merely an observation,' Bertie said mildly. 'These are times of change, both national and international. It is easy to be radical. The country needs men of common sense and moderation.'

Campbell-Bannerman bowed. 'I shall bear that in mind, sir.' He had wondered how the King would react to a change of government and under what terms he would co-operate. He had just been given them.

The world had turned over for Arthur Balfour. From a position of Olympian detachment he had been dragged down to a mundane struggle to keep his government in office. It had been seriously weakened by the controversy over his great Education Act and the resignations over whether or not to give preferential trade terms to the colonies. At least Esher's brilliant proposals for the reform of the army and War Office had been accepted by the Commander-in-Chief, Lord Roberts, whose post was to be abolished in favour of an Army Council, and that had taken the sting out of the agitation over defence. But now Russian expansion and threats in Korea and Manchuria had goaded the Japanese into attacking and there was full-scale war in the Far East. Almost at once, the Russian commanders who had dismissed the Japanese as primitive barbarians discovered that they had developed in an incredibly short space of time from a medieval state into a frighteningly efficient, modern industrial and military power. The Japanese had smashed the Imperial fleet at Port Arthur and were rolling back the Russian armies from the Yalu River. As the disasters continued, Russian fury turned on Britain which was Japan's ally. As Russia was allied to France, the whole question of the Anglo-French agreement was put in jeopardy.

Bertie sat behind the desk in his study at Windsor, listening patiently to Balfour's fears and uncertainty. He had expected it, but he felt compassion for him. Scholarly and able, even brilliant, Balfour was gradually showing himself unfit to lead. George stood at the corner of the desk and marveled at the difference in the Prime Minister's approach to his father.

'I have explained the situation over and again,' Bertie said. 'Our agreements are designed to restrict war—that is their whole purpose! Consider what would happen without them. The Russians would scream for France to come to their aid. Germany would see its chance to profit and either join them or harass them until it, too, was involved. One incident in the Pacific would bring in the United States. But because we are committed to ensure the neutrality of other nations, France will not move and Germany cannot. And the war is restricted to the only two countries it concerns.'

'Yes. Yes, of course, sir.' Balfour nodded.

'If the Foreign Office explains our attitude carefully to the French, I assure you they will respond. But it must also be explained to the Czar.'

'And what about the Kaiser, sir? He still complains that you do not visit him.'

Bertie sighed. 'First let us sign the agreement with France. Then I shall visit him. Now if you'll forgive me, Prime Minister, it's my grandson's birthday and we are late already.' He rose and, brushing aside Balfour's excuses, led them through into the sitting-room.

The din was fairly deafening but it dropped in volume as they came in. In all, there were about eleven or twelve children of the Royal Family and their governesses. Alix was playing a noisy game of charades with Louise, Toria and the older boys and girls, while May presided at the large table set for a birthday tea at which the smaller children were seated. Her youngest son, Prince George, aged three, sat beside her and a decorated cake with four candles was in front of Prince Henry, whom Alix insisted on calling Bobs, after Lord Roberts. The game stopped and May rose to curtsey.

'Good afternoon, children,' Bertie chuckled.

Bobs jumped up and ran towards him. 'Kingy!' he shouted, thrilled. Little Prince George eluded his mother, scrambled to the floor and hurried after him.

Bertie smiled and stooped to let Prince Henry hug him. 'Hello, Bobs—and Georgie.' He turned to Georgie who, instead of kissing him, held out his hand. Bertie bowed very formally and they shook hands.

Alix was laughing. 'Bertie—what are you wearing that old thing for?' He had on an old fashioned, black frock-coat, with a waistcoat and grey, striped trousers. 'It's a party, not a committee meeting.'

'Well, I thought I would dress up,' he said. 'Don't you like it, children?' He held the skirts of the frock-coat out at the sides and revolved slowly, displaying it. The children laughed, shouting, 'Yes! Yes, Gran'pa!' Bobs and little Georgie caught the skirts and tried to spin round with him.

May saw Balfour's eyes widen. 'Children,' she called, 'leave Grandpapa alone.'

'They're fine, they're fine,' Bertie laughed. He scooped Bobs and Georgie up, one in each arm, and carried them to the table which was set with toast and scones and jams, iced cakes and chocolate cakes, sugared biscuits and trifles. 'Ooh, look at that!' he marvelled. 'Are we going to eat it all up?'

'All of it!' Bobs promised him.

'Just us!' Georgie added.

May was smiling. 'You spoil them, Papa.' Bertie sat at the head of the table with one on each knee. 'Not a bit,' he panted. 'Not a bit.'

Balfour had moved round with George to Alix. He bowed and kissed her hand. 'How lovely to see you, Mr Balfour,' she smiled. 'How good are you at charades?'

He was thrown. 'Not . . . very good, ma'am.'

'What a pity!' Alix pouted. 'I was hoping you could help us. We've run out of ideas. But after tea we're going to play Hunt the Slipper and Rounders. I'm sure you're much better at these.'

As she smiled up at him, Balfour melted. 'I shall be delighted, ma'am.'

They looked round at a loud protest from May. 'Children! what are you doing?'

She was peering over the table. Bertie had turned sideways and the two small boys were out of sight. 'Papa . . . !' May exclaimed, scandalised.

Balfour was almost reluctant to follow the others as they moved to see. The King was sitting with his legs stretched out in front of him at a rather steep angle. Bobs and Georgie were kneeling on either side of him and pieces of toast lay scattered on the floor. From the knees down his trousers were stained. 'What on earth are you doing?' Alix asked.

'Playing races,' Bertie confessed. He looked rather like a little boy himself, caught out.

'But your trousers, Papa!' May blurted.

'It's only butter,' Bertie grinned and the children laughed.

Alix moved in closer, intrigued. 'How do you do it? I want to see.'

Bertie smiled. 'Very well.' He took two slices of hot buttered toast from the table and gave one each to Bobs and Georgie. 'Get set, children.' They placed the slices of toast, butter side down, one on each of his knees. Balfour glanced at Princess May and thought he had never seen such an expression of disbelief.

The King was holding up the index finger of his right hand. 'They have to stay on the stripes, mind,' he warned. 'Now . . . ready—steady—go!' Bobs and Georgie tipped the slices of toast over and they slid oozily down the front of his striped trousers, gathering speed.

When the first one reached the bottom and toppled off on to the carpet, everyone cheered and applauded. Except May who looked from her father-in-law, who was laughing, to her husband who smiled to her, apologetically.

Bobs jumped up and down in excitement, clapping his hands. 'I've won, I've won! I've won!'

Old King Christian of Denmark sat in a leather armchair in the family drawing-room of the Amalienborg Palace, at eighty-five still sprightly and alert. Alix sat with Minny, the Dowager Empress Marie Feodorovna, on a gilt and brocade sofa near him. Alix smiled to her daughter Maud who was sitting on his other side with Charlotte Knollys. Prince Charles stood behind them. 'I wish I could have seen it!' the old King laughed. 'That's the kind of grandsons to have.'

'I think George and May were shocked,' Alix confided. 'They say we spoil them, Papa.'

'Why not?' Minny said flatly. 'Spoil them, enjoy them while you can. When they grow up, you never see them again.'

Her bitterness brought a momentary chill. Alix took her hand and pressed it. 'I'm sure Nicholas is devoted to you, Minny.'

'Dutiful. No more than that,' her sister answered. Though attractive and almost as unageing as Alix, in her soreness of spirit she had become prickly and discontented. She had lost most of her power in Russia and saw the country, which had been mighty and prosperous in her youth, being mismanaged by her son under the influence of his wife, ripped apart by the people's unrest and humiliated by Japan.

'As Czar, he has so many things to attend to,' Christian explained soothingly.

'It is not that, Papa.' Minny's face hardened. 'It is Alexandra who stops me from seeing him and the children.'

Alix was upset. 'She was such a gentle, loving girl.'

'Not any more,' Minny said. 'She is cold and distant. To please her, Nicky has cut himself off from everyone. Now that she is to have another baby, all her time is spent with those . . . magicians who promise her a boy.'

'If only Bertie could speak to him,' Alix suggested.

Minny shook her head. 'He would not listen. No Russian would listen to the King of England.'

But Minny was mistaken.

Bertie had accompanied Alix on her spring visit to Denmark and stayed for the full three weeks, making the time-honoured round of museums, historic buildings and the farm that produced butter for export. He brought Ponsonby and Fortescue with him and invited Charles Hardinge whom, after his assistance on the previous year's tour, he had knighted. He had also insisted on his promotion to one of the key diplomatic posts, Ambassador to St Petersburg.

Bertie had no objection to Ponsonby spending some afternoons at the new golf links out by the racecourse of Copenhagen. In fact, he encouraged it and came with him when he was to play against Prince Demidoff of the Russian Legation. The Prince was also a Bridge enthusiast and gladly accepted an invitation for that night. After King Christian and the others had gone to bed, he came to Bertie's private rooms in the palace for a few rubbers with him, Ponsonby and Fortescue. A keen traveller and sportsman, he had much in common with Bertie, who convinced him of his wish to heal the breach between himself and his nephew, the Czar, and the Bridge parties were repeated on many other evenings. Through Demidoff, Bertie met Alexander Isvolsky, Russian Minister to Copenhagen, the fish for whom he had been angling. According to Hardinge and other sources, he was very much the man to watch. With no fortune or influential family to help him, he had risen by his own talents and, in Vienna, Bertie had even heard a rumour that he might become the next Russian Foreign Minister.

Isvolsky was ambitious and intrigued by Demidoff's reports of King Edward's desire for a reconciliation between their two countries. A devious man, himself, he was flattered to realise that the statements were aimed at him. In their conversations, sometimes alone, sometimes with Hardinge, he was first impressed by the King's knowledge and then completely charmed. The Anglo-Japanese alliance was the main barrier between them but the King's explanation of the motives behind it was illuminating. He, himself, warned the King that his motives were constantly being misinterpreted by the Kaiser who was now trying to arrange an understanding between Germany and Russia, claiming that France was abandoning its alliance with Russia in favour of Britain. During Bertie's stay in Denmark, the Anglo-French agreement was at last signed. He at once arranged a meeting with Isvolsky and told him its terms. By a system of barter, France and England had settled their old disputes over West Africa, Madagascar and Siam and arranged for joint control of the New Hebrides, for which France gave up her fishing rights in Newfoundland. Most important, in return for the French agreeing to Britain's total possession of Egypt, the British recognised France's controlling interest in Morocco. There was no military alliance, nothing which could affect France's relationship with Russia. Isvolsky was excited. The King had proved he spoke the truth and he, himself, could increase his prestige by reporting the terms immediately to St. Petersburg.

Bertie returned from that meeting with Ponsonby and met Hardinge outside the salon just as King Christian, Alix and Minny were speaking. He described Isvolsky's reaction to Hardinge. 'It's a heaven-sent opportunity. Through him, I know I can make a rapprochement with the Czar.'

Hardinge was torn. That morning he had had his own instructions from London. 'The Government feels it would be unwise, sir.'

Bertie stared at him. 'Why?'

'At this juncture, sir. Any direct approach to a nation at war with our ally might be taken as giving encouragement to the enemy.'

'My intention would be to show that we have no enemies,' Bertie said quietly. At that moment, King Christian saw him sanding in the doorway and waved. 'I presume I may speak to my sister-in-law, the Dowager Czarina?' Bertie growled and moved into the room.

Hardinge was uncomfortable. He owed his advancement to the King but his livelihood depended on the Foreign Office. He made up his mind that if the King asked him to follow up the opening he had made privately, he would do so. Ponsonby felt the same concern. 'Don't they trust him?' he asked. 'Why do they still treat him like this?'

'Sheer, damned jealousy, Fritz,' Hardinge muttered. 'Sheer, damned jealousy.'

As Bertie reached them, Maud and Charlotte rose to curtsey and he motioned them to stay seated. Alix thought he looked very smart in his blue blazer and light trousers, very modern. 'What are you whispering about?' she said.

Bertie glanced at Hardinge and Ponsonby who had followed him in. 'I was asking them not to tell how badly I'd done on the golf course today.' They laughed and he sat in the chair next to King Christian's.

'You shouldn't play at all, with your chest,' Christian said.

'I'll give up when I'm your age, Papa,' Bertie promised.

The atmosphere had lightened again with his arrival. Alix smiled fondly at her father and he nodded contentedly. 'Eighty-five—it's not bad. I've seen many things.'

'Is it true you nearly married Queen Victoria, Grandfather?' Charles asked, teasing.

The old King chuckled. 'I was never really in the running. Though I had hopes.' As they laughed, he shrugged. 'But I had no prospects—nothing to offer. Now one son is a King, two of my daughters are Empresses and, through Victoria's own son, I am related to most of the crowned heads of Europe. You could say our family has done very well.'

Bertie could see his son-in-law, Prince Charles, laughing with the others, but wth more reserve. He knew what troubled him. Once part of Denmark, Norway had been annexed by Sweden nearly a hundred years ago. Now the Norwegians were demanding independence as a separate country, either as a monarchy or a republic. Remembering their history, those who were in favour of a King called for a Danish prince. The most likely choice was Prince Charles and he had already been named. Bertie was delighted at the prospect of his favourite daughter so unexpectedly becoming a Queen. He also knew that Kaiser Wilhelm was trying to induce the Norwegian Assembly to choose a German prince.

Alix brought it out into the open. 'You've left out Charles,' she smiled. 'You may soon have a grandson who is a King.'

Maud was holding her husband's hand and felt it tighten. 'It is not certain, Motherdear,' she said quickly. 'The Norwegians may vote for a republic.'

'True,' King Christian sighed. 'More and more, people ask—what good are we?'

Bertie was looking at Charles. 'If you are elected, you will accept?'

Charles hesitated. 'I have not fully decided, sir.'

'You must, Charles,' Bertie told him. 'It is a God-given responsibility.'

'That is why I am uncertain,' Charles said. 'I am not sure—not sure that I could do it, what it would mean.' He was a sincere and conscientious man. His ambitions were for his wife and son, not for himself.

Bertie could see that his hesitation came not from fear but from a desire to do what was right. 'It means a lifetime of service,' he said gently. 'None of us knows we are up to it till we try. Make up your mind to do your best. Whatever you do, think always of your country first.' Charles nodded, listening. The others had all fallen silent as Bertie went on. 'Give your trust to as many as deserve it. Let your people know you and always be honest in any dealing with your Government, so that they may respect your advice.'

'Yes,' Charles said.

'There are some who say the days of the Kings are over. Do not listen. If a President is elected, he will only have learnt his duties when it is time for him to be replaced. If the State itself is King, when either there is no one to take personal responsibility or small men struggle for power, great crimes may be committed against the people. We are the people's shield against dictatorship of the Left or Right. We are the members of the smallest Trade Union in the world—and its rules are tolerance, duty and love.'

Listening to him, Minny realised she had never really known her brother-in-law before. She saw the effect his words had on Charles and suddenly wished Nicholas had been with her to hear them.

* * *

That evening, Bertie went to the theatre with Alix and Minny and their brother, the Crown Prince Frederick. The play was a symbolic drama in Danish and, after an hour, he excused himself, saying he was tired and going home to bed. He would not hear of any of his staff leaving with him. Round the corner from the theatre, he stopped his carriage and got out, telling the coachman he had decided to walk.

One of his greatest pleasures was to mingle with ordinary people, unrecognised, and as he strolled through the picturesque cobbled streets he smiled, fancying himself as a latterday Haroun al Raschid in a Scandinavian Baghdad. His energy demanded release after the enforced rest of past weeks. He was not in the least tired and had, in fact, promised to call on one of the King of Greece's two friends, the Countess de Hagen, if he could slip away. He found her town house in its discreet, little side street and rang the bell. The butler showed him up to the salon. Unlike most of the Danish houses he had visited, which were solidly old fashioned in the style of the Amalienborg, hers had a chic, somehow Parisian air.

The Countess seemed surprised to see him at first and, almost at once, Bertie realised his mistake. The invitation had come from Willy's other friend, the Countess Roben. However, his involuntary hostess made him welcome, overcome by the unexpected honour. Although it was hardly something she could boast about, she felt that his calling on her so impetuously singled her out above all the other ladies of Copenhagen. She was tall, slim, elegantly attractive in a black dress trimmed with jet and black-dyed swansdown that moulded her slender figure. Her flame-coloured hair and green-hazel eyes gave the lie to her fashionably languorous manner and Bertie quickly decided that fate had made the mistake, not him. It would be ungallant to explain what had happened and leave. Her skin was milk-white and, as he sat beside her on the divan, her high breasts trembled in their swansdown cups like doves nestling, her arms in their long, black satin gloves reaching for him.

When he left two hours later, he was still slightly bemused at the suddenness with which everything took place. He had scarcely said ten words to her. His impression was of blackness. The black dress and gloves seeming to dissolve, then filmy black underskirts, black silk stockings and garters. Black sheets even on the bed, backed by an ebony bedhead carved in the shape of a shell, and on the bed that white body, writhing and slender, and the sudden, vivid red of her loosened hair.

The night air revived him and, since it was only just after ten, he decided to make his apologies to the Countess Roben if she were still up. The lights were on in her second floor apartment in one of the old mansions near the Rosenborg Palace. She opened the door herself as she had dismissed her servants for the evening. She had no longer been expecting him and had already changed into a lacy, baby-blue negligée that matched her eyes. Masking her confusion, she showed him into the drawing-room. Through a partly open door he saw a table in the small dining-room still laid for two with cold meats, salmon, sorbets, mousse and cheeses on the sideboard. He was touched and, to please her, suggested that he at least open the bottle of Pol Roger that stood beside it in its ice bucket. As he opened the champagne, he discovered that he was starving.

This second Countess was gentle and appealing, with lint-blonde hair and silken skin flushed with gold. Her figure was soft and curving and her hands moved restlessly as she thanked him breathlessly for sparing even ten minutes out of his crowded life, the fingers of her delicate hands touching herself lightly and moving on as though to draw attention to her plump shoulders, pouting bust and the swell of her hip. Bertie understood all at once why Willy was always so keen to visit his relations in Denmark. He smiled into her melting blue eyes and when he murmured that, if it was not too late, he might join her for a slice or two of salmon and perhaps a sorbet, her gratitude overwhelmed him. Her lips tasted of iced champagne.

Tomorrow, he knew, he would be exhausted. 'Ah, well,' he added to himself, 'it makes a change from the museums, the historic buildings and the farm that produces butter for export.'

Chapter
15

For generations, London had been the Queen of Cities, a huge, ever-spreading metropolis, greater than any other on earth, unequalled as a shipping port and business centre, the seat of government of the United Kingdom and pivot of a vast and prosperous empire. It was a city full of contrasts, from the narrow streets and tenements of Limehouse and the East End to the Georgian elegance of Piccadilly and Mayfair, teeming with history, from Greenwich Palace and the Tower to Westminster Abbey, and touched with a unique beauty, the changing views of her river from the Embankment, the spires of the little Wren churches and the space and freshness of her parks. She had always been important, although she could not rival Paris for grace, Vienna for lightness, Berlin for grandeur nor Rome for the sense of times past. In the old Queen's days, her official face had been solemn, aloof, reflecting the deliberate distance she kept between herself and her neighbours, but now it was as though she had been rejuvenated and admirers flocked to her door.

The critics of King Edward who had scoffed at his tours as pleasure trips of no real significance were silenced as London became the diplomatic focus of the world. Even Lansdowne and the Foreign Office were forced to acknowledge the triumph of the King's personality as foreign governments jostled to reaffirm half-forgotten understandings and open negotiations for new agreements. Diplomatic difficulties, the problems of international co-operation which had seemed insurmountable, simply disappeared. To the fashionable London Seasons in the spring and the month before Christmas, over which Bertie and Alix presided, came the wealthy, influential and famous of all countries to see and be seen. The beautiful daughters of American industrialists joined the debutantes of the Dominions and the Continent in the nervous lines waiting to be presented at Court, all wearing the regulation white satin dress with its full train, the tiara and ostrich feathers for the long-rehearsed curtesy and agonising retreat backwards from the thrones. And throughout the year, deputations, couriers and Foreign Ministers came on official or private visits, each new arrival calling on the King, while the length of his conversation or the warmth of his greeting caused intense speculation.

The people of Britain who had become accustomed to seeing events abroad as of limited interest, except where British citizens were directly involved, gradually realised that their destiny was linked to that of other countries. The days of isolation, when Britain was feared and distrusted, were over and she had taken her place as the head of a consortium of states which looked to King Edward as the guarantor of peace and international friendship. In a few years he had passed from being an observer whose comments on foreign affairs were grudgingly or negligently considered by the Government to a position as leading world statesman whose advice was eagerly sought and carefully studied. His prestige and popularity had become incalculable.

Ordinary men and women followed his success with mounting pride in the newspapers and illustrated magazines. Nowhere was it more obvious than in the constant parade of rulers and princes who hurried to London to return his visits and receive his hospitality. President Loubet of France, King Victor Emmanuel and Queen Helena of Italy, King Carlos and Queen Amelie of Portugal, the Khedive of Egypt, young King Alfonso of Spain, Prince Arisuyawa of Japan and King George of the Hellenes were among the first to be welcomed as guests at Buckingham Palace and entertained at Windsor. As hosts, Bertie and Alix could not be matched and the unforced friendliness of the London crowds was a revelation to visitors brought up on stories of English coldness and reserve. They were impressed by the impeccable service and astonished by the new taste and comfort of the guest apartments, all except the ex-Empress Eugénie. Sentimentally, Bertie had not touched the curtains and hangings in the rooms at Windsor specially decorated by his parents for the State Visit of Eugénie and her husband, the Emperor Napoleon. Shown in to them nearly fifty years later, the aged Empress was heard to sigh, 'Toujours ces affreux rideaux!'

There were two Kings whom Bertie would not invite and whose overtures he refused. One was his cousin, Leopold the Second of the Belgians, who had taken over the Congo and administered it as his personal estate. By permitting atrocities and gross mistreatment of the natives, Bertie held that he had betrayed his duty to humanity and would not meet him. The other was King Peter of Serbia who had come to the throne after the barbaric murders of King Alexander and his Queen in the palace at Belgrade. In spite of pressure from Lansdowne and pleas from Belgrade, Bertie refused to renew diplomatic relations while the assassins were still serving in the Serbian army and Government. King Peter was supported by Czar Nicholas and his sister-in-law was the lovely Queen Helena of Italy. He appealed to them and the Russian and Italian Ambassadors came to Windsor to plead his case. Bertie listened to them courteously.

'I wish his people peace and prosperity,' he said, 'but I cannot change my mind.' To the argument that other countries had recognised Serbia, he replied, 'That may be. However, here we have longer memories and a different political morality. Public opinion would not approve of my granting your request.' As he rose to end the interview, he saw their disappointment. 'Besides,' he added, 'I have another and, so to speak, more personal reason. Mon métier à moi est d'être Roi. King Alexander was also, by profession, a King. You see, we belonged to the same guild, as workers or professional men may be said to do. And I cannot be indifferent to the assassination of a member of my guild— or if you like, a member of my Trade Union. We should be obliged to shut up business if we, the Kings, were to consider the assassination of Kings as of no consequence at all. I am sorry, but you see that I cannot do what you ask me.'

The stream of visitors being met by members of the Royal Family, the State Banquets, balls, receptions, gala nights at Covent Garden Opera and processions to the Guildhall for the official welcome by the Lord Mayor and citizens of London were the outward and visible signs of the new diplomatic activity, but people realised that its significance went far deeper than the pomp and show. The foreign policy which Bertie made a reality had already proved its value by its first dramatic success.

In October 1904, the Russian Baltic Fleet under the

command of Admiral Rojdestvensky sailed for the Far East to join in the war against Japan. Steaming through the North Sea, it passed the Dogger Bank early on the morning of the 22nd. Through the mists in the half light, the look-outs spotted a cluster of small craft off to starboard. They were fishing boats from Hull, but the Admiral, in his alarm not pausing to check, took them for Japanese torpedo-boats and ordered Battle Stations. Searchlights stabbed out across the water and, as the Russian warships fled south in panic, their quick-firing guns pounded the little trawlers, crippling two and sinking a third. Rojdestvensky did not stop until his fleet had reached the safety of the Spanish port of Vigo. By that time, Europe was in an uproar.

Miraculously, only two fishermen had been killed, although many others were wounded, but the Russian action in continuing the bombardment and not stopping to give assistance when their fire was not returned caused anger and resentment. The newspaper headlines screamed 'North Sea Outrage!' and excitement in all the capitals of Europe was intense. The Cabinet demanded apologies and redress from St Petersburg. The day before, Jacky Fisher had become First Sea Lord and he placed the British Home Fleet on immediate alert.

Bertie was sickened. He had just congratulated Czar Nicholas on the birth of his long-awaited son, Alexis, and accepted an invitation to be the boy's godfather, another step towards bringing their countries closer together. Now, overnight, they were on the brink of war. He sent a strong telegram to Nicholas expressing his horror at the incident, yet to his Government he advised restraint. There was little danger in a war with Russia, already half beaten by Japan. However, if Britain entered the struggle, Russia would call on the aid of her ally, France, and the Entente Cordiale was more important than humiliating Russia over the fear and stupidity of one admiral. Urgent messages from Delcassé and President Loubet assured Bertie that they had no wish to take up arms against England and he pressed them to counsel the Czar also to show restraint before it was too late. Russia agreed to pay compensation to the trawlermen and their families, the amount to be decided by a commission of four naval officers appointed by Great Britain, the United States, Russia and France. Only a year before, with national feeling so high, war would have been inevitable, but by using the Anglo-French agreement

Bertie had managed to avert it and establish a common sense principle of arbitration.

As the grief and the fury died down, the Cockney music hall favourite, Pelissier, made up a jingle that he sang to cheers on the stage. Soon people were singing it in the streets.

> 'There'll be no waw-er,' it went,
> 'There'll be no waw-er,
> So long as we've a King like good King Edward.
> There'll be no waw-er
> For 'e 'ates that kind o' thing.
> Mothers won't worry as long as we've a King,
> Like good King Edward.
> Peace wiv' honour, that's 'is motter—
> Gawd Save the King!'

In Berlin, the Kaiser fumed. Everywhere he heard nothing but praise of The Peacemaker. Officially, he joined in the praise, but privately he saw his uncle's increased prestige as diminishing his own.

'Yes, my uncle wants peace,' he sneered. 'Peace through everyone becoming an ally of England's, everyone dancing to his tune!'

He cast about for some means of breaking up the Anglo-French Agreement and of splitting the alliance between France and Russia, so that Germany would regain her dominant position and he would be revealed as the master diplomat of the age.

Bertie was very aware of his nephew's resentment and always took care to meet him on his way to or from Marienbad. He even proposed to visit Berlin, but Wilhelm invited him, instead, to the regatta at Kiel. Bertie soon found out why. The *Victoria and Albert* was surrounded by massive warships of the German navy. Even Wilhelm's Imperial Yacht, the *Hohenzollern,* was a converted battleship. His Treasury had poured enormous amounts of money into naval ship-building and, as the ironclads passed in review, he could scarcely hide his exultation.

'Ever since dear Grandmama showed me the torpedo-boats at Portsmouth, I have dreamed of having a fleet as large as England's,' he smirked.

'Yes, my dear Willy,' Bertie murmured, 'you have always been fond of yachting.'

It was a bewildering visit for Ponsonby. The Kaiser had somehow conceived it as his fault that King Edward had not paid a State Visit to Germany and deliberately snubbed him. At the same time he was overwhelmed by attentions from Count Eulenberg who hoped he would persuade the King to present British decorations to all his friends. Bertie advised Ponsonby not to notice the Kaiser's insults and to beware of Eulenberg's charm. He had seen the Count's influence on his nephew and considered it unhealthy. He had heard from various sources of the White Stag Club, the secret male club headed by Wilhelm and Eulenberg, where new members were initiated by kneeling on a chair and telling a dirty story which they had to finish without faltering, although throughout they were being spanked on the buttocks by the flat of the Kaiser's sword.

Bertie, himself, made light conversation with Wilhelm and kept more serious talks for the Chancellor, Count von Bülow, a cautious man whom he relied on to balance the militarists whose control of German affairs was growing stronger. Wilhelm asked bluntly why Britain had signed a treaty with France and not with Germany.

Bertie smiled. 'We have fought wars with France off and on for hundreds of years, that's why a written agreement is absolutely necessary. On the other hand, the English and the Germans are such good friends that that sort of precaution would be utterly pointless.'

Afterwards, von Bülow described it as like watching a mischievous tomcat play with a mouse. He agreed with the King that relations between the two countries had been poisoned by the newspapers and Wilhelm assured his uncle that he had only affectionate feelings towards England.

The following spring, Wilhelm revealed the extent of his affection and of von Bülow's reliability. The Kaiser was cruising on holiday in the Mediterranean and landed unexpectedly at Tangier in his most splendid uniform as if on a visit of State. Morocco was on the point of financial collapse and France preparing to take over the administration of the country from the Sultan. To the amazement of the world, Wilhelm suddenly declared that the German Empire had great and growing interests in Morocco which he would defend and that his visit was a recognition and guarantee of the Sultan's independence. It was a direct challenge to France and the Anglo-French Agreement.

Bertie was preparing to take Alix on a Mediterranean cruise himself, and hurried to Paris to urge President Loubet and his Foreign Minister, Delcassé, to stand firm and go ahead with their plans for Morocco. Throughout his cruise, he kept in touch with them and returned to Paris when it was over. He found Delcassé under attack from other members of the French Government who were panicking, including the nondescript Prime Minister, Rouvier. Bertie had no sooner returned to London than von Bülow announced that Germany backed the Sultan of Morocco in calling a conference of leading Powers to decide the future of the country. Delcassé was opposed to France attending a conference which he realised was aimed at demolishing the Entente Cordiale. Great Britain also refused to attend unless France agreed to it. To Wilhelm's fury, Italy and Spain followed Britain's lead. He was even more incensed at the reaction of the United States. For some time he had been wooing Theodore Roosevelt, writing letters to accompany elaborate gifts, sending his son, Prince Henry, on a goodwill tour. However, Roosevelt had continued his private correspondence wth Bertie and a respect had developed between them. He replied that the States, too, would follow the decision of the British Government.

A number of French politicians and financiers had been bought by Wilhelm's agents. He ordered them to increase their agitation and sent Prince Radolin, his Ambassador in Paris, to tell Rouvier that unless Delcassé, the chief advocate of the Entente Cordiale, was removed from office and his foreign policy repudiated, Germany would break off diplomatic relations. It was dangerous but he was gambling for high stakes. Delcassé knew that France could expect no help from her Russian ally and appealed to the British Government for a clear statement of how far they were prepared to go in resisting Germany's aggression. To Bertie's disgust, Balfour and Lansdowne hedged their answer so carefully as to make its promise of support meaningless. Scenting victory, Wilhelm ordered Radolin to put more pressure on Rouvier. The Ambassador informed the terrified Prime Minister coldly that, if France did not consent to attend the conference at once, the German Army would be at the gates of Paris within two days.

Delcassé was forced to resign and the Entente lay in tatters.

Wilhelm's stratagem had succeeded brilliantly and he glowed as he received the thunderous salutes of the Reichstag and his Generals. At one blow, he had humbled France for preferring Britain's friendship to Germany's and badly damaged his uncle's prestige. The German Empire stood disclosed as the master of Europe, with the smaller countries at its mercy. As Kaiser, Wilhelm was poised on the topmost pinnacle of power. In gratitude, he made von Bülow and Eulenberg Princes. He told himself that, in his triumph, he would be magnanimous, yet he gloried in the knowledge that all other nations trembled as they looked at him.

'It is the most thoughtless and irresponsible action he has ever been involved in,' Bertie muttered. 'He thinks he is seen as a new Caesar, but he has revealed himself to the world as a political *enfant terrible* in whose assurances one can have no faith.' He was speaking to Agnes Keyser in her drawing-room at 17 Grosvenor Crescent.

It was a secret known to very few that when he was in London, King Edward dined with her once a week in the small apartment she had kept for herself on the top floor of her house after turning the rest into a Nursing Home for Officers. Now in her fifties, Agnes Keyser was still an attractive woman, but her intimacy with the King was more than physical. She was a mature, balanced woman and her matter-of-fact attitude soothed him when he was depressed. The meals she gave him were simple and, on her advice, he cut down on rich foods and the number of courses served at his own table. Through him, the example was followed by the rest of society and, at private dinners, elaborate meals of fourteen to eighteen courses became a thing of the past. The only thing which she could not induce him to cut down was his smoking, although she warned him that his breathing was endangered and that it put an undue strain on his heart. His physical strength had enabled him to recover quickly so far from his recurrent attacks of bronchitis and he ignored her advice.

Sister Agnes to her patients, she was like an actual sister to him and he enjoyed her plain-speaking and lack of ceremony when they were alone together. For her part, she, whose life was devoted to the care of others, loved him very dearly. No one suspected how much his sympathy and affection meant to her, yet she did not ask for more than the few hours of those few weeks in the year they spent together. She could tell now that he was deeply troubled. His dejection over Delcassé's forced resignation, the apparent submission of the French Government to Germany and his own Cabinet's weakness was greater than he would admit.

'Sometimes I wonder if it is worth going on,' he told her. 'And then I know I must or Europe will be torn apart through the folly of my Imperial nephews. They goad each other on, while one is heading straight for revolution and the other seems intent on war.'

In Russia the situation was critical, with assassinations, massacres of Jews and riots in the cities, and uprisings on the land. Workers and peasants were crippled by taxes made necessary by the disasters of the war and widespread corruption. In the early part of the year, a large body of strikers led by a priest, Father Gapon, marched to the square beside the Winter Palace in St Petersburg to present a petition to their Little Father, the Czar, begging him to consider their grievances. Nicholas refused to meet them and the workers under their crosses and religious banners were shot down by the Cossack Guards. Hundreds were killed and street fighting broke out in the capital and in Moscow, with strikes in every major town and mutiny among the sailors of the Black Sea Fleet. What the strikers wanted was representation in the government of the country, an elected Parliament to advise the Czar, but Nicholas refused to give up his autocratic power.

'No one can help Russia,' Agnes said, 'but surely you could speak to the Kaiser? He has listened to you before.'

'He will not, this time,' Bertie shook his head. 'He hears only the sound of drums and sees himself riding in the victory parade through Berlin with laurel leaves round his helmet.'

Agnes felt chill. 'Then war is certain?' she whispered.

'No . . . No,' Bertie said, 'because I will not let it happen. I shall not try to reason with Willy nor offer to meet him, because at the moment he would take it for cowardice. Neither shall I react publicly to any of his threats and boasting. He'll soon grow tired of beating the air with his fist.' He coughed on his cigar which had gone out. Agnes raised an eyebrow as he dropped it into the ashtray of the

265

armchair and took out his cigarette case. 'Yes, I know,' he muttered, 'I smoke too much. The problem is, we have embarked on a policy of ensuring peace through alliances. In a strange way, as a legacy from my sister and her husband, Willy also believes in peace, but his method of achieving it is through intimidation. It serves his obsession with establishing the supremacy of Germany. It is a dangerous course and one that can be effective only as long as no one calls his bluff. Half of his ranting is pure nonsense, yet unfortunately there are people behind him who take it seriously. That is the real danger.' He lit his cigarette. 'Well—he insists on this Conference at Algeciras. Since France has agreed to it, we'll all go. He is expecting to bully us into giving him a footing in North Africa and a port on the Mediterranean. We'll see.'

Agnes poured a glass of the brandy she kept for him. 'Arthur Balfour seems to think that France is finished as a political force,' she said carefully. 'He is glad we were not drawn into a military alliance.'

'He's right to an extent,' Bertie nodded. 'However, Wilhelm was encouraged to make his demands because he knew we were not fully committed. Our philosophical Prime Minister has a great deal to learn. There are people in France who are not so timid as some of the members of its present Government. And the Kaiser is not the only one who can make theatrical gestures.' He paused and toasted her, smiling. 'Jacky Fisher and I have invited the French Fleet to visit Portsmouth. In return, President Loubet has invited our Channel Fleet to Brest. Seeing them together may give Wilhelm pause to think. It should keep him occupied till the Conference.'

There were those in the navy who could not forget that Admiral Sir John Fisher had no real background or breeding. A poor boy who entered the service at the age of thirteen, he reached his position as First Sea Lord through sheer hard work and outstanding ability. He had no patience with inefficiency and the career officers, who were complacently satisfied with an organisation which had stayed virtually unchanged for a hundred years, were incensed by his demands for modernisation and increased proficiency. It was outrageous to expect the sons of gentlemen to undergo technical training like Grammar School boys. His interest in submarines was understandable but his

266

ideas on the design and armament of new types of warship were too revolutionary.

With a far-flung empire to protect, the British navy had been run on the Two Power Standard, by which is was maintained at the strength of the next two most advanced naval Powers combined. In theory, it made certain that Britain kept her command of the seas. In practice, it meant that many obsolete vessels were retained and constantly refitted at great expense and others, almost totally unfit for service, were of use only to police some remote protectorate. Fisher was determined to streamline and rationalise the forces at his disposal and met fierce opposition from enemies inside the navy itself, and their friends in both Houses of Parliament. It happened, however, that the King agreed with his ideas.

Bertie worked to maintain peace but he was not a pacifist. He knew one had to speak from strength to make one's presence felt. Britain had to be ready to defend herself and able to give positive assistance to her allies. He was disturbed by the vast increase in the German navy and by Fisher's report that the fleet was as unprepared for a major conflict as the army at the start of the Boer War. The army reforms were under way, thanks to Lord Esher, on whose committee Fisher had served with distinction. Bertie was not impressed by the arguments of his critics. He listened more to Esher's praise of the Admiral's drive and brilliance, his clarity of vision and single-minded devotion to duty. Besides, he liked the man for himself. Fisher was an interesting and amusing companion, with an unpredictable sense of humour. They became firm friends after a lunch party at Balmoral which had been unaccountably dull. Fisher had asked the King if he would mind him livening it up. To the astonishment of the guests and delight of the King, he got to his feet, called for silence and sang a rollicking comic song.

Bertie summoned him for a private discussion after he heard from Alice Keppel that Fisher's outspokenness and blunt criticism had hardened the opposition against him. His enemies, led by Admiral Lord Charles Beresford, sneered at his capabilities and, hinting that his dark complexion proved he was part coloured, nicknamed him 'The Kaffir'. Determined to ruin him, they spread rumours that he was half mad.

'Unless someone advises him, he could be in trouble,'

Alice warned. 'You are the only one he'll listen to.'

She was puzzled when Bertie smiled and said, 'It may be his opponents who are in trouble.'

Francis Knollys showed Fisher into the King's private sitting-room at Buckingham Palace and left them together. As Fisher bowed, Bertie waved to a chair opposite him at the fire. 'Take a pew.' Fisher sat, a stocky figure full of suppressed energy, his hands lying curled on his thighs. 'Well now, Jacky,' Bertie murmured, 'what's all this argument between you and the Admiralty?'

'Not the whole Admiralty, sir,' Fisher said. 'But more that half the senior officers, hang 'em! There are some who cannot see the dangers in this expansion of German naval building. I say, look at the estimates, more than three times ours. But we've been masters of the seas for so long, they can't believe we're threatened.'

'It is disturbing,' Bertie nodded. 'Do you have a solution?'

Fisher paused. 'There's a simple one, sir. Before the arms race develops any further, before the whole thing gets beyond our control, we Copenhagen them.'

'We do what?'

'Do like old Admiral Gambier did once at Copenhagen. Steam the Home Fleet up the North Sea, swoop in on Kiel and smash the German Navy at its base.'

Bertie stared at him, horrified. 'Without warning? . . .'

'A surprise attack, sir. We could occupy Schleswig-Holstein and give it back to Denmark. Her Majesty would like that. It would solve the problem.'

'It's barbarous,' Bertie breathed. 'I hope you're joking?'

It was a moment before Fisher smiled. 'Not entirely, sir.'

'Then for pity's sake, Jack,' Bertie protested, 'be careful who you suggest it to. Though—mind you—I'd like to see my nephew's face if he heard.'

He chuckled and Fisher relaxed slightly. All the struggles of his career, the secret campaigning and manoeuvring to gain acceptance of his ideas which he knew were right and necessary had brought him to this point. He waited, conscious of the King's eyes on him, amused but shrewd. 'Do you have any other proposals?' Bertie asked. 'Apart from blowing up the German High Command. Anything practical?'

'There is only one other way, sir,' Fisher said seriously 'Balfour and the Government won't give us any more money for the Navy, so we must make more efficient use of what we have. First, we must reorganise naval command.'

'Agreed,' Bertie nodded.

'Russia's as good as beaten by Japan, so she's out of the running. Our only potential enemy in the world is Germany. It would be foolish not to accept that and ridiculous to have the most substantial part of our forces scattered over the oceans. We must reconstruct the Home Fleet so that we have sufficient battleships to defend these islands and also to go instantly on to the offensive if we are attacked.'

'Agreed.'

Fisher leant forward, encouraged. Esher had advised him that, if he found the King receptive, he should not go into too many details but stick to essentials. He knew them by heart. 'Then we need an efficient Reserve Fleet. We can find the personnel by scrapping all out-of-date warships that are kept merely for showing the flag. We must increase efficiency and enthusiasm within the Service by making promotion due to merit and not just by length of service. Every penny we save must be spent on technical training, for senior officers as well as new entrants. And above all, we must build bigger, newer battleships and cruisers, all big guns, fully armoured. I know exactly how they should be designed.'

'What would be their value?' Bertie asked.

'They would outrange, outshoot and outdistance any other warship in existence, sir. I call them Dreadnoughts.'

Bertie sat for a second or two in silence. He saw what Esher meant. Fisher's dedication and conviction were inspiring. He had felt the lift of excitement, himself. 'Yes,' he said. 'We'll see the first of your Dreadnoughts laid down this year.' Fisher rose to thank him, but was speechless. 'Would you be prepared to carry out these reforms?'

Fisher controlled his elation. 'Given the authority, sir,' he promised. 'But I do not delude myself. I shall need your support.'

'You have it,' Bertie said. 'I have written to the Government and the Admiralty to insist that you are appointed principal naval ADC to the Palace. Everything you do will be also in my name.'

'I don't—there are no words to thank you enough, sir,' Fisher stumbled, thrown for once. The King's confidence

269

and being given the opportunity at last to fulfil his greatest ambition overwhelmed him.

Bertie grunted and waved his thanks away. 'Do things as you wish, but you must remember that it will be easier if public opinion is on your side. You are Jekyll and Hyde, Jacky. Jekyll with the men who serve under you in the navy, and Hyde in society. You've worked with Esher. I want you to take advice from him.'

Fisher bowed. 'Willingly, sir.'

'Reggie's a political animal. He'll stop you antagonising the wrong people.'

Fisher smiled. 'He once told me I should learn to play on the delicate instrument of public opinion with my fingers instead of my feet.'

Bertie smiled briefly, but his smile was serious. 'He was right. We can do very little if the people are against us. I depend on you. I am determined this country shall not be left unprotected—but there will be fierce opposition from the pacifists and the enemies of change.'

Fisher drew himself up. 'We shall win, sir,' he assured him.

'We must,' Bertie said, very quietly.

It was a clear, sunlit morning in July when the Kaiser's *Hohenzollern* drew up alongside the Russian Imperial Yacht, *Standart* off the island of Björkö in the Gulf of Finland. Their guns had fired salutes and their Marine bands were playing each other's National Anthem. As he waited to go aboard the *Standart,* Kaiser Wilhelm almost regretted that there were so few people here to witness this historic moment. But until everything was settled, it could not be made public. Nicholas and he must appear to meet casually. For months he had planned this meeting as his final victory over his uncle, sending Nicholas letters and secret telegrams, playing on his insecurity.

'How can we stop the whole world from becoming John Bull's private property?' he asked. 'He is setting us all against one another for his own benefit. He encouraged Japan to attack you, and all he wanted was to take Tibet. Now he is scheming against us both with France.'

Nicholas was torn, not knowing whom to trust. He was distraught over his troubles at home, the desperate situation of the war, hardly able to eat through fear of being poisoned. His cousin's strength and the warmth of his

270

sympathy gave him brief periods of comfort. Reading his letters, he began to see that what Wilhelm said was true, all his suffering was due to their uncle's intrigues. He was a fool not to have accepted Germany's offer of a defensive alliance before. As he still hesitated, terrible news reached him from Korea. His huge land armies had been routed by the Japanese in every sector of the war, with appalling losses in men and materials. His last hopes had been fixed on his Baltic Fleet, under Admiral Rojdestvensky, winning back control of the China Seas. But, incredibly, Rojdestvensky had taken seven months to reach the Far East. Sending some of his ships through the Suez Canal and others round the Cape of Good Hope, he rendezvoused and wasted more precious time at Madagascar. Finally on his way to Vladivostok to obey his orders and cut supplies to the Japanese armies in Manchuria, he was intercepted by a Japanese flotilla under Admiral Togo and smashed in the greatest naval victory in history. Of the thirty-six Russian warships who joined in the battle, only two escaped to reach Vladivostok. Twenty-two were sunk and the rest captured or forced into internment in neutral ports. In his despair, Nicholas begged Wilhelm to help him now that he was at the mercy of 'English and Japanese arrogance and insolence'.

In spite of the brightness of the day, the curtains in the state-room of the Russian Imperial Yacht were drawn and the light came from shaded electric lamps. Wilhelm was wearing his green uniform and military cap as he entered, flanked by two high-ranking aides. He swept off his cap and advanced, smiling, to meet Nicholas who stood with one of his naval officers. They shook hands and Wilhelm kissed his cousin on both cheeks.

'It has been too long since we met, Nicky,' he said.

'Far too long,' Nicholas muttered.

Seeing him clearly, Wilhelm was shocked. Nicholas was strained and nervous, his body wasted under the white tunic of his uniform. Wilhelm grimaced. Amongst themselves, members of the Family always spoke English. It galled him, but the habit was too entrenched to break.

'Time has not been kind to you, Nicky.'

Nicholas's shoulders twitched. 'We both suffer from the same disease.' He wanted to touch Wilhelm, needing the contact of his vitality and certainty, but he was disturbed. Willy had insisted their discussion should be private, without any Government official present, yet Nicholas recognised one of the two men he had brought with him as von Tschirschky, German Minister for Foreign Affairs. 'We were to talk alone,' he said.

Wilhelm realised he had nearly made a serious blunder. 'Leave us, gentlemen,' he directed. They came to attention and moved to the door. Nicholas nodded to his naval attendant who showed the Kaiser's aides out, closing the door. Wilhelm smiled. 'Now we can speak freely.' He watched as Nicholas crossed to a sidetable and took a cigarette from an ivory box.

Nicholas used the cigarette to steady his hands, concentrating on it. His voice was toneless. 'The war is virtually over. My forces are defeated on land and sea.'

Wilhelm moved closer. He already knew of the annihilation of Russia's fleet and the rout of her armies. The timing was perfect. Nicky would be at his utmost susceptibility. 'Tragic,' he murmured. 'Will you sue for peace?' As Nicholas nodded, Wilhelm slapped his open right hand against his thigh. 'To think of victory going to those creatures! When Uncle Bertie was with me in Kiel, I told him we would all have to unite one day against the Yellow Peril. Do you know his reply? "I refuse to condemn a brave and chivalrous people, distinguished from *us* only by the colour of their skins".'

Nicholas flushed. 'Japan would never have dared attack us if they had not been encouraged by England.'

'England?' Wilhelm repeated. 'You mean Uncle Bertie. It is his policy!'

'I have read your letters and thought over all you have said,' Nicholas muttered. 'I agree. He pretends to want friendship with all countries, but his real ambition is to be the secret ruler of Europe! Why didn't I see it before?'

'Because you have been blind—like I was for so long.' Nicholas glanced round, tensing, but was silent as Wilhelm went on, speaking softly to intensify the atmosphere of conspiracy. 'For years he has been behind every plot, every intrigue, with his legion of women. First my own mother, his sister—every move she and my father made was dictated by him. Then—you will forgive me—your mother.'

'Yes,' Nicholas said tautly. 'She is a creature of his.'

'His sisters and daughters, his mistresses,' Wilhelm continued. 'They carry his influence into every Court, spy for him, support his interests.'

272

'He is a devil . . .' Nicholas whispered. 'The Arch-intriguer!' The gold-tipped cigarette broke in his fingers and he threw it agitatedly into an onyx ashtray on the table. 'And now he resents us! He still thinks that he is the uncle and we should be little children, eager for his praise, taking his orders.'

'He shall never give me orders!' Wilhelm rapped.

Nicholas turned. 'What can we do?' In his voice was frustration, rage and despair.

Wilhelm savoured the moment. The Czar had surrendered to him and the shape of the future lay in his hands.

'Russia and Germany must be allowed to claim their true place in the world, he said solemnly. 'The time has come for a firm treaty of alliance between us.'

Nicholas desperately wanted to agree, but hesitated. 'How will that affect my alliance with France?'

'France?' Wilhelm laughed. 'The French will have no choice. When they see us united in each other's defence, they will be forced to join us—isolating England.'

'Yes . . .' Nicholas was excited and bit his lower lip, smiling for the first time. Yet he was still nagged by doubts. 'Won't the British protest? They might attack us straight away.'

Wilhelm controlled his irritation. 'They are in no position to fight,' he said soothingly. 'Their Government is collapsing. Before they could be ready, they would find themselves facing a Continental Fortress!' His voice rose. 'Austria and Italy are with us. With France would come Spain, all the smaller nations clustering for our protection. America will be forced to acknowledge us as the dominant Power in Europe. In time, we might even include Japan— a World Combine!'

Nicky's body was straighter, his eyes alight. He held out his hand and they clasped each other by the wrists. 'You have my word. This pact between us shall never be broken.'

The Treaty of Björkö was signed the next day, witnessed by von Tschirschky and by the Czar's naval attendant, Admiral Birilew. It was to be kept strictly secret between them until the official end of Russia's war with Japan.

'This is a turning-point in history,' Wilhelm said jubilantly. 'We have locked the English bulldog back in his kennel—snarling, but unable to get out!'

*   *   *

273

The existence of some form of treaty did not remain secret for long, although its details were unknown. Those which Bertie was able to find out were sufficiently alarming. An envoy came from King Christian whose daughter, the Dowager Czarina Marie, had written to warn him that, in the event of either going to war with Great Britain, Russia and Germany had agreed not to object to the other occupying Denmark. Bertie calmed the Danes. He also calmed his own Government and the French. There must be no panic, he told them, no action until the Conference at Algeciras on the status of Morocco. That's when we'll see whether Germany is going to dominate Europe or not.

It was a time of hectic activity for him .He wrote to Hardinge in St Petersburg and to Lamsdorff, the Russian Foreign Minister. He invited the Russian Ambassador to join him on his yacht at Cowes. To all of them he said the same, 'People can talk if they like of Perfidious Albion, but can there really be anything more perfidious and more stupid than the present policy of the Kaiser?' He resumed his correspondence with President Roosevelt who had offered to mediate between Russia and Japan and was conducting the peace talks at Portsmouth, New Hampshire. He cruised again with Alix in the Mediterranean and called on the Kings of Italy and Spain. He made several trips to Paris, staying incognito at the Hôtel Bristol as the Duke of Lancaster, for meetings with Loubet and the dismissed Delcassé. He also made a point of holding discussions with Clement Fallières, President of the Senate, an influential statesman largely responsible for France's alliance with Russia.

His activity had its effect. Wilhelm's exultation faded as the date for the publishing of the Treaty of Björkö passed with no announcement from St Petersburg. Unbelievably, the Czar's Ministers had refused to ratify it. They had been told that France, on whom Russia depended for urgent financial aid, would not accept it. And they had read the reports of the combined British and French fleets celebrating together in their home ports. Wilhelm cursed the Czar and wrote to him, denouncing his Ministers as being in the service of England and informing him that the spirits of their ancestors approved the treaty, that it had been duly witnessed and that 'what is signed, is signed. God is our testator!' Insulted, Nicholas replied, defending his Ministers and saying that Birilew had witnessed the treaty

without even reading it. He, himself, had not fully understood its implications, so could not be held to it. His Ministers had convinced him it was neither honourable nor in
his country's best interests. Across his quibbling, apologetic
letter, Wilhelm scribbled, 'The Czar is not treacheorus, but
he is weak. Weakness is not treachery, but it fulfils all its
functions!' Only by a spectacular success at the Conference
of Algeciras, only by demonstrating the subjection of
France, could he now win back Russia. The Old Peacock
had called his bluff.

Bertie would not see Wilhelm on his way to Marienbad.
To the emissary sent to suggest the meeting, he said, 'As far
as I am concerned, I have no quarrel with the Kaiser of
any sort, but I have more important things on my mind.'

In addition to his other concerns, he was involved in the
problem of Norway where the elections to choose between
a republic and a monarchy were to take place shortly.
Bertie had removed Swedish opposition to his son-in-law,
Prince Charles, by consenting to the marriage of his niece,
Margaret of Connaught, to the King of Sweden's second
heir, the Duke of Skania. But Charles was still proving
reluctant to assert himself, although Bertie urged him to
go to Christiania, the Norwegian capital, and show himself
to the people. Kaiser Wilhelm was canvassing support for
one of his own sons to be named as King. Bertie threw the
weight of his influence and prestige behind his son-in-law.
For once, he had a comparatively free hand, as Lansdowne
had apparently given up interest in the day to day work
of the Foreign Office, which he might soon lose.

Balfour's Government was in disarray. There were more
and more defections from the Unionist Party over the question of Imperial Preference, pereferential trade terms for
the Empire. The Government had even been defeated once
in the House of Commons and Bertie stood by to dissolve
Parliament, but Balfour would not resign. It was not ad-
ministratively convenient, he told the House blandly. It was
clear to Bertie that the Prime Miister had forfeited the confidence of his Party and the country, but, as a constitutional
monarch, he could not dismiss him.

He discussed the situation at Marienbad with Campbell-
Bannerman, whom he had knighted. The Liberal leader
had come to the spa as usual with his ailing wife to rest
and have treatment. He himself was in poor health, but he

welcomed his conversations with the King, which covered an extraordinary range of subjects from domestic matters to closer links with America. C.B.'s respect for him increased. For his part, Bertie was heartened. Campbell-Bannerman had denounced the Boer War as unnecessary and barbaric, but he did not believe in appeasement and would fight to defend the French Agreement. In London again, Bertie found Balfour still determined to carry on, although every day in the House the Opposition shouted 'Resign! Resign!' He took Alice Keppel to stay with the Saviles for Doncaster Races, then on to visit friends in Scotland, coming back to London to meet Alix on her return from her annual holiday in Denmark. He attended the funeral of the great actor, Sir Henry Irving, whose knighthood he had influenced his mother to grant. Recognition of the leading actor by the Sovereign had given his friends in the theatre status as members of a Profession, no longer to be classed with rogues and vagabonds. With Alexandra, he opened two new main thoroughfares connecting the Strand and Holborn. The most extensive improvement in the capital for a hundred years, the two new streets, named Kingsway and Aldwych, cleared away many of the stinking alleys and unhealthy tenements which had so horrified him on his visit with Carrington in disguise two decades earlier.

The duties and functions continued, increased by the arrival of the King and Queen of Greece. All the time, Bertie was conscious of waiting. The political state of the country was tense. Not only the Conservatives, but the Liberal Opposition was split, with fierce arguments between the Liberal Imperialists, led by Herbert Asquith, the Radicals under Lloyd George and Churchill and the Socialists led by Keir Hardie and Ramsay MacDonald. All clamoured for reform but, while the bulk of the Liberal Party urged moderation, the Radicals and Socialists demanded an all-out-attack on property and privilege. With no warning, at the height of their argument, Balfour resigned in early December without calling a General Election. He hoped to catch the Liberals divided and unable, without a majority, to form a Government. Bertie sent immediately for Campbell-Bannerman.

In the Red Audience Room at Buckingham Palace, C.B. was unaccustomedly nervous as he faced the King, very aware of the difficulties ahead. Apart from anything else, he had only had brief periods in office and few of the other prominent Liberals had any experience of administration. He felt his years and that his own leadership was under attack.

Bertie was sympathetic and tried to put him at his ease. Custom decreed that they stand for the interview and he hid the fact that he himself was unwell. The winter fogs had brought on his bronchitis and he limped painfully on the right foot from a bad fall while shooting at Windsor. He would not add to C.B.'s discomfort by showing it. He knew the problems. Rosebery had flatly refused to serve under Campbell-Bannerman, to Bertie's disappointment. Asquith and his followers were also reluctant, considering him unfit and, at seventy, too old to lead. Lloyd George thought him mediocre with not enough fire. Much as he liked Campbell-Bannerman, Bertie was positive that a Cabinet with him at its head, without the moderates, would be a disaster for the country.

Campbell-Bannerman handed him a typewritten list. 'I expect to have the names of the other members of the Cabinet for you by the weekend, sir,'

Reading down it quickly, Bertie was relieved. It did not include Rosebery, but it had Asquith as Chancellor of the Exchequer, Haldane as War Minister and several others of whom he strongly approved. 'This is a very able list, Sir Henry,' he said.

C.B. bowed. 'I believe it contains a fair sprinkling of moderates, sir.' He smiled very slightly. 'I remembered what Your Majesty once told me. It was on hearing of your views that they agreed to serve under me.'

Bertie was pleased and returned the smile, then winced as he saw David Lloyd George's name as President of the Board of Trade and, further down, the Socialist John Burns as President of the Local Government Board. 'You will need them, to keep some of the others in check,' he commented drily.

'Perhaps so, sir.'

Bertie nodded. He had spoken to Dr Ott, who treated them both at Marienbad and doubted if Campbell-Bannerman could stand the strain for long. 'Once more question, Sir Henry.' He paused. 'I am sure of your ability to lead the House of Commons. But is your health up to it?'

It was a question C.B. had expected and had asked himself. 'I know there are doubts, sir,' he said simply. 'People say Campbell-Bannerman's too old, he hasn't the stamina. But the Liberals have been out of power for most of the last thirty years. I have waited a long time for this—and I am determined to lead my Party.'

'That is a feeling I understand very well,' Bertie answered quietly and held out his hand for Campbell-Bannerman to kiss as Prime Minister. 'You will have my support.'

C.B. straightened. 'I shall need it, sir,' he admitted sincerely. 'I shall try to keep you informed of developments as they occur. The Under Secretary for the Colonies has offered to make abstracts of Cabinet Meetings to send to Your Majesty.'

Bertie glanced at the list he still held. 'Mr. Winston Churchill,' he murmured. So Jennie and Randy's son had won his gamble. He chuckled. 'Well, at least they should be lively.'

The Christmas season as Sandringham opened with a party for Bertie and Alix' personal friends. After dinner they lit the hundreds of candles on the huge, decorated tree in the hall and Alix insisted that she and Luis de Soveral be taught the Two Step which Lady Paget had learnt on a visit home to New York. The atmosphere was gay and lively and soon she had all the younger guests joining in, humming the tunes to dance to as the orchestra had been allowed to dismiss for supper and she did not wish to spoil anyone's enjoyment. Jacky Fisher danced enthusiastically with the handsome Gladys de Grey. Ponsonby partnered his attractive wife, Ria, who was thrilled at being invited.

In the sitting-room, Bertie talked to Alice Keppel and Louise, Duchess of Devonshire, one of his oldest friends. His breathing was laboured and Alice was concerned to see him light another cigar. 'Now, don't forget,' the Duchess was saying. 'You're coming to us at Chatsworth for Twelfth Night.'

'When have I ever failed, Lottie?' Bertie asked. She laughed like a girl still, although, at over seventy, there was little left of the sensational beauty that had captured first the wealthy Duke of Manchester and then the multi-millionaire Hartington, Harty Tarty, now Duke of Devonshire.

He stood near them with Ernest Cassel and Lord Esher, a tall bearded figure, as relaxed and negligently dressed as ever. Somehow, he managed to make the best-tailored evening clothes look secondhand. Charles Carrington had just joined them and Alice looked up. 'I haven't congratulated you, Lord Carrington, on your appointment to the Cabinet.'

Carrington smiled. 'Thank you, Alice.' He was now President of the Board of Agriculture.

'When I was in the Cabinet,' the Duke drawled, 'I dreamed once that I was asleep on my feet, making the most utter nonsense of a speech in the House of Lords. D'you know? I woke up and found it was true.' As they laughed, he added, 'Mind you, Charlie—you've got some strange company.'

It was a subject that engrossed Bertie, and troubled him. Harsher, more strident voices were being heard in politics. 'Perhaps it's time there were working men in the Government,' he coughed.

Carrington smiled. 'I'm not quite sure how to take that, sir.'

Bertie laughed with the others, then nodded to Alice and moved away. He was tired and reflective and did not wish to dampen the others' pleasure. He walked out into the hall and past the dancers, almost unnoticed. The small orchestra was reassembling. In the corridor the sound of the chatter and laughter was muted and he paused, leaning forward slightly to ease the constriction in his chest. The door of the blue and cream drawing room was open and he went inside, shutting the door behind him.

Here, the air was cooler and the only light came from a shaded standard lamp. He crossed and sat heavily, just out of the pool of light. In the distance he could hear very faintly a *valse lente* which the orchestra had begun to play. He relaxed, feeling a tiredness he could no longer fight take hold of him.

His head drooped, although he could not stop thinking. He started and looked round as he heard the door open. Alice Keppel stood framed against the brighter light from the corridor, her shoulders gleaming above the dark rose of her dress. 'Oh, it's you, Alice,' he muttered.

She had followed him, conscious of his unrest. 'Would you rather be alone?'

'With you,' he smiled. 'Yes.'

She closed the door and came to sit in a chair near his. For some minutes they sat without speaking, listening to the far-off music, a companionship more complete for its silence.

'I've been thinking . . .' he said, after a while. 'All the effort, all the striving and urgency—how pointless they are. Most of the time you work for one thing, and another happens. They congratulate me on influencing the Czar's Ministers to abandon his treaty with Germany—driving a wedge between my nephews.'

'It was a triumph.'

'Hollow triumph. People call me the Peacemaker. That is what I have worked for, hoped most to do in my life. And yet—now I spend most of my days preparing my country for war.'

'It must be done,' Alice said quietly.

'Yes. Yes, I agree. Change . . . reform . . . The whole world is changing. New men, new ideals, new thoughts everywhere. I've encouraged them. I've helped to give them being. But sometimes I feel caught in a tide that will sweep away everything I know.' He was very tired, almost exhausted. 'And I'm growing old, Alice. Old and tired. I am only a man and there's only so much one man can do. I have tried . . . to stand for something. Values—the human things that should not be forgotten. But I'm tired. And there's always more to do . . . Always more . . .'

As he spoke, his eyes closed and he fell asleep, his chin resting on his chest. Alice sat watching him, her eyes moist. She saw that he still held the cigar loosely in his fingers. She leant towards him and took it gently from his hand. Leaning close to him, she hesitated, then raised his hand and kissed it, very softly.

Chapter

16

Alix had just heard the news.

It had been one of the most magical Christmases and
New Years she could remember. With George and May off
on another official visit to India, she had had her grandchildren all to herself again at Sandringham. They had
helped Bertie and her to hand out the presents at the party
for the tenants on the estate and Bertie had taken David
and Little Bertie riding and on their first day's shooting,
while she played with their sister Mary and brothers Bobs
and Georgie and nursed Baby John, born the previous
summer. She especially loved bathtimes with the smallest
ones. At eleven, David was a laughing-eyed, independent
boy, very much the leader, and Mary was by far the
prettiest of her granddaughters, intelligent and already
daring on horseback. Yet her special favourite was shy and
retiring Prince Albert, Little Bertie.

It hurt Alix to see how afraid he was of George and
May, his own parents, who compared him unfavourably
with his elder brother and precocious sister. Naturally left-
handed, George had forced him to write and work with his
right hand, to hide it as though it had been a disfiguration.
Through that and being always in his brother's shadow, he
had developed a nervous stammer which only increased
his father's irritation with him. She could not understand
George's harshness; he had been brought up with so much
love, himself. And May was so stiff with the children, keeping them at a distance. Alix had to restrain herself, for they
saw advice as criticism, and was glad that Bertie took such
care to encourage his namesake, Little Bertie, and give him
confidence. As a boy, Bertie had been constantly compared
adversely with his elder sister, Vicky, and had also developed a stammer, so understood and sympathised with his
grandson. Like Alix, he did not want to criticise his son
and daughter-in-law, but pointed out to George that, when

he became King in his turn, if anything happened to David, Little Bertie would be next in line for the throne. George's answer was to apply stricter discipline and Bertie could only do what he could, treating the boy as his special friend, taking him to Balmoral where he could run free in the woods and fish the River Dee with the ghillies. But afterwards he had to return to the coldness of York House.

These months had been a pure joy and, at the end of January, they brought the children to Windsor for the annual remembrance of Victoria's death, and the games had continued in the nursery and the long corridors. On this day, Alix had taken the four eldest for a drive in her Wolseley, amusing them very much by the habit she had of jabbing the driver in the back with the tip of her umbrella when she thought he was approaching a corner too fast or had not seen a child or dog who might wish to cross the road. In spite of a light rain coming on, it was exhilarating and they returned to the castle laughing and excited. They were sorry their Grandpapa had not come with them but he was not well, suffering from an attack of bronchitis. While Alix was leading them to change for tea, Francis Knollys met her and told her the King was waiting for her in her private sitting-room.

Toria was with him and, from their seriousness, Alix thought he had come to scold her for being late. She laughed and reminded him that at Sandringham the clocks were always kept half an hour fast for her sake but not here, hence the confusion. She was wearing a dress of heliotrope velvet trimmed with lace and a matching toque, with a cream-coloured coat, and was enchanting. Seeing her like this, her cheeks still flushed with the rush of the wind and the rain, Bertie wished others could see her, the envious who whispered that her unfading youth and beauty were a fiction, her face an enamelled mask. She was excusing herself so charmingly, was so happy, he scarcely had the heart to end it. Very gently, he told her that her father, King Christian, had died suddenly, after only an hour's illness.

Alix was stunned. He had to repeat it. She swayed and he held her, helping her to the sofa, but she did not collapse as he had feared. She looked from Toria to him, dry-eyed. 'I can't,—can't believe it,' she breathed. 'He was old. But he seemed so well when we were last there.' Toria sat beside her and took her hand.

'It was mercifully quick,' Bertie said.

'Yes. For that—for that I am thankful.' Alix started to rise. 'I must let Minny know.'

Toria drew her back. 'She will have been told, Mother-dear.'

'Yes. Yes, of course.' Alix shook her head. 'I cannot believe I shall never see him again. I loved him so much.'

'And he loved you, all of us very dearly,' Bertie said. 'We must be grateful he was spared to us for so long.'

Alix nodded. 'Nearly ninety. Never ill for a day, he was proud of it . . . Minny will be so upset. We must go to Copenhagen at once.' Toria tensed, looking at her father.

'Yes,' Bertie agreed. 'You and Toria must leave at once.'

Alix gazed at him. 'And you. You will come, too.'

'I cannot,' Bertie said reluctantly.

'Why?' Alix was stricken. 'You said you loved him. He was my father!'

'I have important meetings with the Russian Ambassador. And this conference is beginning in Algeciras. I must talk to the French and Americans.'

'That is an excuse.'

'It is a necessity. I must also stay to open the new Parliament. And—and I am not certain that I am well enough to travel.'

Alix could not see that he was distressed, only that he was abandoning her in her sorrow. He would not even help to bury her father. 'You will be well enough to go to Biarritz,' she whispered.

Bertie knew she was being unjust, but he had not expected her to understand. 'There are things I must do.'

For a long moment, Alix still gazed at him, then she looked away. 'Very well—I shan't insist. I know that you will not listen anyway.' Her voice was breaking. At last, the tears came and she turned to her daughter, burying her face on her shoulder, crying bitterly.

Toria held her mother comforting her. She wished there was some way she could show her father how much she sympathised with him, too.

He was looking at them, helplessly. 'I'll fetch Charlotte,' he muttered.

The weeks when Alix was in Copenhagen for the funeral were a long struggle for Bertie. He had not let her find out how ill he was. The heavy winter air clogged his lungs and brought on spasms of coughing which left him breathless and exhausted. It was made much worse by sleeplessness and anxiety over the political situation. Laking urged him to get away from the fogs of London but he had to stand by to swear in new Ministers and to read the speech from the Throne at the opening of Parliament.

Balfour's political gamble had not paid off. In the General Election which was fought throughout January, the electorate revealed what it thought of his leadership of the country, his nonchalance and contempt for public opinion. From being a minority party, Campbell-Bannerman's Liberals swept in with an unprecedented majority of 356. It was a landslide. Balfour, himself, lost his seat in Manchester. 'What a pity,' he said. 'Just when it looks like becoming interesting.' Bertie, like the voters, had wanted the Conservative Unionists to be taught a lesson, but no one had imagined an upheaval like this. Such a majority had its own dangers and already the extreme Radicals and the new Labour members were clamouring for an all-out attack on property and privilege. The voice of moderation had gone. Bertie believed in evolution, not revolution. In the long, slow ascendancy of the middle classes, with men like Chamberlain and Dilke on either side of the House, social conditions and living standards had risen steadily, with free education and equal opportunities for all. He saw improvement as a continuing process, regular and controlled, but now there were politicians who had reached power for the first time by promising to exploit the country for the benefit of one section, the lower paid workers. Many of them were sincere and dedicated men but their passion could only set class against class, provoking a class war that had never been known in England. They were demagogues counting on agitation to keep them in power, threatening the investment and capital on which industry depended. They had a strong grasp of radical theories, but little of economics, and no interest in international politics. Among them were some who even called for the giving up of the colonies, seeing the Empire only as serving the aims of capitalism. They were impatient for change.

As a constitutional monarch, Bertie had to be bound by the dictates of Parliament, but he intended to make full use of his right to warn. He had always been in favour of the granting of self-government to the dominions and colonies when they were ready for it. The stability of those to which it had been given proved the success of that method, but if Britain were suddenly to relinquish her obligations to the others it could lead to the dissolution of the Empire and the inevitable end of her prosperity and influence in the world. The attacks on wealth and the structure of society might please a section of the community, might even seem fair, but would result in bitterness for many. The traditional way of life depended on balance and long-established customs and attitudes. Once shattered, like Humpty Dumpty it could never be put back together again.

In one area, Bertie was happier than he had been for many years. The new Foreign Secretary, Sir Edward Grey, was an astute and reasonable man. The son of a favourite equerry of Bertie's who had died at Sandringham of influenza, he acknowledged that he had much to learn. He did not speak a word of French or German or any other language except English and had little knowledge of foreign diplomats. Reading through the department's records, he was struck by the number of important steps initiated by the King and was happy to take advice from him. Although internal affairs were explosive, the continuation of Bertie's foreign policy was assured. With a less prejudiced Foreign Secretary, his ideas were more readily accepted and more quickly put into operation. At his urging, Grey instructed Sir Charles Hardinge in St Petersburg to reopen the delicate negotiations for an agreement with Russia. Whether an approach would be welcomed or not depended on the outcome of the Algeciras Conference, which had become a contest between Germany and the Entente Powers, with the other delegates looking on, uncommitted. For months the Kaiser's Ministers and agents had been at work, convincing the French Premier, Rouvier, that Britain would desert France, threatening Spain which also had a stake in Morocco and trying to sign commercial contracts to establish German industries in Morocco, itself. Bertie wanted the best possible representative in Algeciras and the right man was found in Arthur Nicolson, a rising young career diplomat of the same mould as Hardinge.

The new British Government contained many avowed pacifists and the French were worried in case the British were no longer so determined to back them. Their Ambassador in London, Cambon, was sent to see Bertie who reassured him. 'Tell us what you want,' he said, 'and we will support you without restriction or reserve.'

With Sir Edward Grey harrowed by the tragic death of his young wife in a carriage accident, Bertie threw off his illness and exerted himself to display all the firmness that was needed at this time. By good fortune, aided by planning, the *Dreadnought*, first of her class, was nearing completion. He launched and named her at Portsmouth with full publicity, a clear statement of Britannia's determination still to rule the waves. As soon as possible after the State Opening of Parliament, he travelled to Paris where he met the Premier, Rouvier, and tried to put courage into him. Loubet had just retired. Bertie dined with him and Delcassé and also with the newly elected President of the Republic, Clement Fallières, whom he urged to leave the bulk of the negotiations at Algeciras to Nicolson. Three days after his visit, Rouvier and his supporters were removed from office. His fall was a vindication of Delcassé, an affirmation that France would not yield. Simultaneously, a telegram was sent by the Foreign Office in London to all the delegates at Algeciras, stating that Britain supported France 'without restrction or reserve'. Grey had repeated the very words of the King.

Bertie also had another purpose in coming to Paris. He had arranged to meet there his youngest sister Beatrice and her daughter, Princess Victoria Eugenie of Battenberg, a genuinely beautiful girl, known in the family as Ena.

Alix followed her sister Minny into their apartments in the Amalienborg Palace and signed to Toria and Charlotte Knollys to leave them alone. She joined Minny as she stood by one of the windows of the second floor drawing-room, gazing down at the square where the snow had been pressed flat in a broad avenue by the cars and carriages and the trampling feet of the funeral procession.

They were both in full mourning with their veils pinned back. The death of their father had drawn them even closer together. From the days when they had shared a bedroom as girls, they had never had a moment's disagreement. They had no secrets from each other, no barriers between them, only a complete trust and affection. In her own grief, Alix was borne up by the need to comfort her sister, seeing her pallor and the effort at control which pulled the skin of her face tight, like a mask.

'I always knew I could come to him,' Minny said dully. 'Now there's nowhere for me.' Alix touched her arm and she moved away, afraid of the effect of sympathy on her command of herself. 'My son and his wife only tolerate me in Russia. My usefulness is over, Alix. You cannot know what it is like.'

'But I do,' Alix told her. Something in her voice made Minny look at her. Alix shrugged. 'Oh, my children love me—that is true. But I do not share Bertie's life any more.'

Minny remembered them in previous years, laughing and teasing, and Bertie so attentive. 'You seemed so happy.'

Alix smiled faintly. 'Happy enough. But it's a remembered happiness. We have grown apart.'

'If only there was somewhere we could live with memories,' Minny sighed. She turned, looking at the room which had so often been used for parties or family conferences, where her mother had sat with her and Alix, laughing at their stories of the children. 'Nothing else. But even here, everything will change now that Papa has gone.'

They were silent for a time. Alix knew what Minny said was true. It was their father who had held the family together. Their elder brother, Frederick, who was now King, was dear to them but had never been as close as Willy or their sister Thyra, Duchess of Cumberland. With his stiff, Swedish wife as Queen, the whole atmosphere would be different. The twice-yearly holidays to which they looked forward so much could never be the same. Almost without thought, as if the idea had come from outside herself, Alix said slowly, 'Why don't we make somewhere? . . .' She moved towards Minny. 'We could find a house, here in Denmark. A place of our own.'

Minny's eyes widened, but she was doubtful. 'To live there?'

'Not all the time,' Alix answered. The idea, now she had thought of it, took hold of her. She saw it had excited Minny, too. 'No, that would not be possible. But every so often, we could go there—just the two of us.'

'Oh, yes, Alix,' Minny pleaded. 'Yes . . . please.' In her relief, tears came and she sat on the small, brocaded sofa near the window. She was shaking.

Alix sat beside her. 'We'd tell the world to stay away.' She took Minny's hands, crying too and smiling.

'And we'd play music and grow flowers,' Minny sobbed. 'And forget all about courts and palaces.' She gave up

287

trying to hold back her tears and Alix held her, rocking gently as they planned their house by the sea.

Travelling abroad was a heady experience for Alice Keppel. At home she had to behave with so much discretion and was virtually unknown to the general public, her closeness to the King only acknowledged by a few intimate friends. The moment she landed at Cherbourg all was different. In France, her position was respected and she was treated almost like royalty. Her trunks and boxes were shown straight through customs and she, herself, escorted ceremonially by railway officials to her train for Biarritz, while crowds gathered to admire *La Maîtresse du Roi.* Her sleeping-car was filled with flowers and the attendants contended for the honour of serving her, for the reward of a few words in her husky voice and a glance from her violet eyes.

In Biarritz, the bracing and fashionable resort on the sunny, Atlantic coast of France near the border with Spain, she stayed at the Villa Eugénie which was rented by Sir Ernest Cassel. It was spacious and sumptuously furnished and had the special merit of being only a short walk from the rear door of the Hôtel du Palais on the seafront, where Bertie kept his permanent suite of rooms.

Alice was not alone in coming every year to Biarritz in March at the same time as Bertie. Others of his favourites also took villas, Lady Paget and Mrs Willy James among them. And the beauties of French Society, Hélène Standish, the Princesse de Sagan and the delicious Duchesse de Mouchy, no longer young, arrived to surround him with a Court of Beauty. He divided his days for three to four weeks among them, calling to pay his respects, to reminisce or make love as the moment suggested, but his most constant companion was Alice. With her and Caesar, he would walk on the splendid promenade or drive out into the country, to Pau or Bayonne, for picnics with visiting friends like Soveral and Cassel, while the fresh air and sun revitalised him and cleared the congestion from his lungs.

His arrival this year with his sister and her eighteen-year-old, golden-haired daughter caused great speculation. The rumours were confirmed the next morning when the twenty-year-old King Alfonso of Spain drove in his brand new motor car across the frontier and had a long conversation with Bertie before calling on the royal ladies.

The previous year Alfonso had paid a State Visit to England. A dashing, slim, not unattractive young man with rather prominent ears, he had just survived an anarchist bomb attack in Paris. He relaxed in the safety of London and Windsor and applied himself to the main reason for his visit, the finding of a bride. One of the daughters of Arthur, Duke of Connaught, had been proposed for him and he liked her very much. To his amazement, she took not the slightest interest in him, ignoring him so pointedly that he asked the sympathetic Duchess of Westminster, 'Am I so ugly? Do I not please?'

Bertie had been delighted at the prospect of a Spanish marriage for one of his nieces, but explained that he could not force Arthur's daughter to marry a man who did not appeal to her. His concern over Alfonso's disappointment was shortlived, for the young King announced that he had fallen utterly and irrevocably in love with a girl he had only seen twice among the guests at Windsor, whose name he did not even know. It was Princess Ena, who had positively no thoughts of marrying. When a meeting was arranged between them, he behaved like a knight of medieval chivalry and vowed that he would renounce the company of women, living chaste and celibate, unless and until she became his wife. From what Bertie had learnt of Alfonso, that was a very noble gesture. It had its effect on Ena.

There were difficulties. Chief among them, to become the wife of the King of Spain she had first to become a Roman Catholic. The very thought roused a storm of protest both among British Protestants and Spanish Catholics. But Bertie talked to Ena and guessed correctly that she had fallen in love, herself, with the romantic King whose adoration had at first disconcerted her and whose ears had not proved to be such a drawback. Advised by Bertie, she drove with her mother to San Sebastian where she was received into the Church of Rome by the English Bishop of Nottingham, who brought her a letter and a collection of rich gifts from the Pope. Afterwards, she and Alfonso, both radiantly happy, returned to Biarritz for Bertie's blessing and their betrothal was announced, the wedding to take place at the end of May.

Throughout his stay, Bertie kept in touch with Alfonso,

who was not only grateful to him for his help and kindness, but also hero-worshipped him as the ideal monarch, diplomat and man. The fateful conference of the Powers was being held on Spanish territory and Spanish interests in North Africa were strongly involved. Like France, Spain stood to lose part of its empire to Germany. Bertie kept him informed of the developments at Algeciras where the Kaiser's representatives, the blustering Count Tannenberg and the devious, twisting Radowitz, had succeeded only in alienating all the other delegates. They had intrigued, bullied and blocked sensible proposals until Nicolson judged the moment was right and, with the utmost finesse, bypassed and outmanoeuvred them so that they found themselves isolated, without even the support of their nominal allies, the Italians.

In Berlin, Kaiser Wilhelm fumed. He had lost all hope of breaking up the Agreement between Britain and France and the alliance between France and Russia. Not only that, he had strengthened them. Too late, he realised that if he had been more reasonable, the Conference might have allowed Germany part control of Morocco, giving him the base he desperately wanted in the Mediterranean. Instead, at the close of its two months session, it awarded joint responsibility for administering the country to France and Spain, and Germany received nothing. His attempt to demonstrate to the world how he dominated Europe had ended ignominiously.

From London, Grey in his excitement suggested that now was the time for the King to pay an official visit to Russia. Bertie refused. Russia was in too unsettled a condition for a State Visit to have any effect. Nicholas, himself, was too preoccupied. He had been forced at last to listen to the demands of his people and the first Duma, a form of parliamentary assembly, was in the process of being elected. Great suspicion of Britain's motives would have to be allayed before any understanding could be reached and only then would a personal visit by the English King have any real value.

In the meantime, steps could be taken to ensure that the negotiations would be handled faultlessly at both ends. Hardinge, who now knew Russia and was trusted by the French, was brought back to London and made Permanent Head of the Foreign Office, second in importance only to the Foreign Secretary. And Arthur Nicolson, who had proved his consummate diplomatic skill at Algeciras, was given the post of Ambassador to St Petersburg and the key task of reaching an understanding with the Czar and his Ministers. Hardinge was now in Biarritz, happy to be part of the team again, the King, himself and Ponsonby. Bertie called Nicolson to join them and brief him on the specific problems he would find in St Petersburg, on whom to trust and where he would meet the most difficult opposition, open and concealed.

When Nicolson travelled north, Bertie said goodbye to Alice and went by train with Hardinge and Ponsonby to Marseilles, where the royal yacht and Alexandra waited for them to begin a month's cruise, which included a State Visit to Greece.

Admiral Lord Charles Beresford, Charlie B., was no longer the handsome figure who had been the darling of society, the daring young naval officer who had run his small ship, the *Condor,* right under the muzzles of the guns to destroy the most dangerous shore battery in Alexandria during the Nationalist revolt. His fair hair had receded and turned grey. His cheeks had grown pouchy and his body had thickened. His carefree, unceremonious manner had hardened into pure arrogance. Yet he knew how to win and keep the devotion of those subordinates whose support he needed and he was careful to maintain his friendly contacts in Parliament and Fleet Street, having used political pressure and publicity throughout his career as a weapon and an aid to promotion.

He was in the best of spirits, buoyant and expectant. As Commander-in-Chief of the Mediterranean Fleet, he had brought his battleship squadron to Corfu to salute the King and Queen and escort them on to Athens. His quarrel with Bertie had long been patched over but their former intimacy had never been restored. He counted on his charm to win himself back into favour and on the immaculate appearance and efficiency of his ships and men to add weight to his criticism of the naval reforms begun by Jacky Fisher. If he could shake the King's confidence in them, he could use it in his campaign to discredit Fisher and have the reforms scrapped.

Fortune favoured him. At Corfu, Bertie and Alix rendezvoused with the Prince and Princess of Wales who were on their homeward journey from India and Beresford knew he could rely on Prince George's aid in the arguments he intended to present. George was firmly on the side of those who distrusted innovation and saw nothing wrong with the navy as it was. As long as Beresford was subtle in the manner in which he impressed and flattered the King, he was sure of a sympathetic hearing when his words could do most damage.

But his arrogance betrayed him. The King of Greece was acting as host to his sister and brother-in-law on the island and arranged to pay a courtesy call to the Admiral's flagship. He arrived with all ceremony but Beresford had seen no need to show him any particular honour and had not even bothered to wear full dress uniform. His offhand, patronising manner to her brother upset Alix when she heard of it and confirmed Bertie's dislike of Beresford, whose vanity and self-importance had caused the original quarrel between them. He instructed Hardinge to inform the Admiralty of Beresford's insulting behaviour, refused, himself, to have any private conversation with him and ordered the fleet to return to Malta. Charlie B.'s opportunity was lost.

Bertie had heard all his objections to Fisher's plans already. He would have taken them more seriously if he had not known that the main cause of them was jealousy. Charlie B. was next in line behind Fisher for promotion. In January, Jacky had reached sixty-five, at which age he should automatically have retired. Beresford would, then, have become First Sea Lord. Instead, to allow him to complete his essential work, the Government had appointed Fisher an extra Admiral of the Fleet, a post which let him stay on the active list till the age of seventy. Charlie B. could never catch up with him.

Bertie was troubled by Alix's decision to take a holiday home in Denmark. She had changed her original idea and now saw it as a place he could come, too, where they could live simply, with few attendants. He knew that he could not stand the inactivity for a week, let alone a month at a time, and would seldom accompany her. Instead of them seeing more of each other as she hoped, they would spend more time apart. But she was so eager, he felt he had no right to stop her going ahead. He was also concerned about Wilhelm. To defeat his schemes was one thing, but to alienate him completely was another. It would be dangerous to rub his nose in it. Bertie still had to be able to reach him, but it was too soon to suggest a meeting. He wrote him a friendly, conciliating letter for his birthday. Wilhelm snatched at the opportunity he had been given. He wrote back, 'Your letter breathes such an atmosphere of kindness that it constitutes the most cherished gift among all my presents.' He offered to let bygones be bygones, in the spirit that united them in the last days of his dear Grandmama, 'the silent hours when we watched and prayed at her bedside. I feel sure that from the home of Eternal Light she is now looking down upon us, and will rejoice when she sees our hands clasped in loyal and cordial friendship.' Bertie took it at its face value.

He let none of his concerns show. The visit to Athens was enjoyable and he was able to give the Greek Government some assurance of support in their dispute with Turkey over the possession of Crete, the reason for which he had included Hardinge on the cruise. Afterwards, he sailed with Alix for Naples where the countryside for many miles around had been devastated by a violent eruption of Mount Vesuvius. In the same month, on the other side of the world, large areas of San Francisco had also been destroyed by a severe earthquake, followed by fire. With more earthquakes in Chile and typhoons ravaging the southern coast of China, to the superstitious it heralded the Day of Judgement. Bertie wrote to President Roosevelt, expressing his sympathy, and toured the shattered villages round Vesuvius, going on foot with Alix and Toria over the litter of volcanic ash to the front of the irresistible tide of lava. It felt strange to visit ancient Pompeii, obliterated two thousand years before, but, on this eruption, completely spared. Their hosts were the Duke and Duchess of Aosta, a poignant meeting for Alix as the Duchess was the Count of Paris's daughter, Hélène, who had been so in love with her dead son, Eddy, and whose wreath of immortelles still hung on his tomb at Windsor.

Monsieur Lépine, the head of the French police, was worried. King Edward had arrived at the Hôtel Bristol in the Place Vendôme, ending his cruise as usual with a short stay in Paris. He had arranged to dine with President Fallières. Apart from that, he was here unofficially, to lunch at the Jockey Club and see a few private friends, and had announced that he wanted no nonsense of police bodyguards, which would only draw attention to him. Lépine could understand. The King was very popular and people naturally applauded and cheered when they recognised him. Very gratifying, but not while he was trying to carry on an intimate conversation.

At the same time, Lépine was responsible for the King's safety. In these crowded city streets, it was so easy for someone to pull out a knife or a revolver, and Paris had at least its share of madmen and fanatics. Lépine had checked out the Hôtel Bristol as he did every year, and had duly noted that Mrs Keppel had also arrived and booked her fittings at Worth's for the new season's gowns. He had a list of persons His Majesty would most likely wish to see, some fairly surprising. In fact, over the years, his dossier on the King's movements, interests, friends and acquaintances was extraordinarily complete and contained many secrets, but Lépine guarded it more closely than the State archives. When he set off in any direction, it enabled Lépine to guess where he might be heading, perhaps to call on the aged Empress Eugénie, living at the Grand Hotel as the Comtesse de Pierrefonds, or to take morning chocolate with Mme Sarah Bernhardt in her town house. Yet whenever the King spotted detectives following him, he waved them away.

Lépine asked for an appointment at the Bristol with Major Ponsonby. He found him snowed under with official despatches, telegrams and private correspondence, plus the deluge of letters, petitions and invitations which poured in from all over France. Ponsonby explained that he was too busy to accompany the King always and, besides was not always asked. Then again, one of King Edward's chiefest pleasures was to mingle with ordinary people, to go to a restaurant or a theatre like anyone else, without the feeling he was being spied on. In London, for example, when he could not sleep he would rise as soon as it was light and ride his tricycle round St James's Park. When he felt he was under observation all the time, he became irritable and when *le Roi* was irritable, it made life exceedingly uncomfortable for everyone. That, Lépine also understood. He had no wish to make Major Ponsonby's busy life uncomfortable, nor to spoil his Majesty's pleasure but, since the bomb attempt on King Alfonso, he had become nervous. 'I have a profound respect for His Majesty,' he said, 'but if I am not permitted to take the necessary measures, I cannot accept responsibility for his safety. Perhaps, Major, you would give me a piece of paper, signed by yourself, instructing me that the King is not to be given protection?'

Ponsonby smiled, admitting defeat. As Lépine intended, he had been put in an impossible situation. He agreed to give the head of police notice of each day's appointments, provided plain-clothes men were used whom the King had not seen before. He had a remarkable memory for faces, even for people he had only once noticed in a crowd. The officers would have to be constantly changed.

The bargain worked perfectly for a time, until Bertie was lunching one day with Alice and a group of their French friends in the garden of a restaurant at St Cloud. It was a warm, sunny day and tables were set in the arbours down either side of the garden, filled with well-dressed people. Ponsonby was with them, listening to the King tell Hélène Standish of how impressed he had been by the New York Fire Brigade during his visit to America when he was a boy, so impressed that up till recently he and the Duke of Sutherland, another enthusiast, had kept suits of firemen's clothes in a room rented above a butcher's shop in Watling Street and raced to put them on and join in whenever there was a spectacular fire in London. The Fire Chiefs had known but none of the men fighting the flames alongside them. As Ponsonby supported the King, assuring Mme Standish that the story was quite true, Alice caught his eye. She was the only one he had told of his secret arrangement with Lépine and it had made her extremely anxious on Bertie's behalf. He was so reckless. She had become aware of the party at the table on their right, which looked just like a group of gangsters with their women. One, who was clearly the leader, with baleful eyes set in a lean, villainous face, kept glancing at Bertie. She was sure he had been recognised. If he were attacked here in the open, the gangsters could make their getaway through the garden gate with no one to stop them. At last Ponsonby made an excuse to leave the table, disturbed that the police had let in such obvious criminals. He went into the hall of the main restaurant, to find a telephone and, to his relief, saw Lépine himself sitting in the dining-room. When he told him Mrs Keppel's suspicions, Lépine laughed. The 'gangsters' were a group of his men who had brought their wives to help them appear less conspicuous and the leader was one of his best young Inspectors. The gentlemen in the arbour to the left of the royal table were also his men, as was the gardener sweeping leaves by the gate.

The King appeared to notice nothing but, next morning on his way to Cartier's, he told his driver to go to the Eiffel Tower, instead. At the base of the Tower, he waited until the two cars which had doubled round after him arrived, raised his hat in the style he had made fashionable and asked the embarrassed detectives inside if they were enjoying their outing. That afternoon, he ordered the car for four o'clock. As the police relaxed, he suddenly sent for it at three, drove off and vanished. Lépine put the police drivers on permanent stand-by. Next morning they waited. When the King did not emerge, they discovered that he had expressed a desire to see the hotel kitchens, looked around, shaken hands with the chef and gone out the rear door. From then on, the Hôtel Bristol was ringed by plainclothes detectives dressed as everything from windowcleaners to beggars. It was a game which Lépine quite enjoyed and, by his vigilance, he was able to save his distinguished quarry from an embarrassing scandal.

For some time, Bertie had taken an interest in a young singer and dancer, Jeanne Marie Bourgeois, who had first appeared as 'La Môme Flora'. She was not really beautiful but had a bewitching, urchin face, a neat figure and the most perfect legs in Paris, sheathed in silk and shown almost to the knees by her scandalously short stage costume. During the years that Bertie had denied himself his visits to France, she had become one of the stars of the Alhambra under the name of Mistinguett. On his second evening, Bertie dined with her after the show at Maxim's. He was captivated by her huge eyes and toothy smile, and her teasing, mischievous manner which stopped just short of being impudent. For herself, Miss was thrilled to be seen dining with the most famous man in Europe, the monarch of la Belle Epoque. Part of the thrill was to think of all the queens of the theatre, the celebrated actresses who had been in love with him, Hortense Schneider, Sarah, Jane Avril, Gaby Deslys and, as some said, Jeanne Granier. She had expected him to be an old man. He was old, rather stout and his beard was grey but his smile was young and his eyes crinkled with laughter and the way he spoke to

296

her in his deep, cosy voice made her feel they had been intimate for ever.

The first day he had given Lépine's man the slip, he had gone to meet her. Not at her own apartment but at that of a married friend, who was very discreet. Bertie discovered that her vivacity and talent for improvisation were not confined to the stage. The beautiful legs were astonishingly strong and agile. And Miss learnt that, while age prohibits athleticism, agility can be more than compensated for by experience. Both were so delighted that another meeting was arranged for a few days later but, on this occasion, Bertie inadvertently left his monogrammed walking-stick in the friend's bedroom, where it was found by the lady's husband. Recognising the monogram, he flew into a jealous passion, refusing to believe that she had merely given the keys of the apartment to someone else. Fortunately, Lépine intervened as he stormed off to demand redress from the King, confiscated the incriminating evidence and chided him for abusing his wife instead of honouring her for doing her bit to maintain the Entente Cordiale.

The walking-stick reappeared with no explanations in Bertie's rooms, just after he had realised he had left it behind, and where. His staff, quite truthfully, denied any knowledge of it, so he knew it must have come from Lépine. He told Ponsonby to send the head of police one of the special presents they always kept in readiness. Ponsonby ventured to suggest that a gold cigarette-case with his cypher in diamonds seemed a fairly extravagant way of saying thank you for returning a walking-stick. Bertie considered him for a moment. 'Well, he's a good fellow, very conscientious and efficient,' he said and smiled. 'His only trouble is, he sees anarchists hiding behind every tree in the Bois de Boulogne.'

The marriage of King Alfonso and Princess Ena was the most splendid royal wedding that Europe had seen for generations, the long list of guests a roll call of all the Royal Houses from Great Britain to Russia. Excitement in Madrid was high and, on the day, jostling, noisy crowds jammed the flag-hung streets and had to be pushed back by cordons of soldiers and police to make a passage for the bands and carriages with their colourful escorts.

Matteo Morales was bitterly disappointed. By pretending

to be a journalist, he had hoped to get himself a ticket for the Press gallery in the Church of San Jeronimo where the wedding was to be held. He had even been promised the seat of an American reporter who was ill, and had made a specially large and beautiful bouquet to take with him but, at the last moment, the American recovered and claimed his ticket. In his best suit and carrying his bouquet, Matteo had to content himself with seeing the parade after it left the church.

In his resplendent uniform covered with orders and decorations, Alfonso waited at the altar. With so many eyes on him, he tried to appear calm, but Ena was late and he was anxious for her. It was the anniversary of the bomb attempt on him in Paris and there had been many anonymous threats and warnings. He glanced back down the narrow nave of the ancient church at a louder burst of cheering from outside and was relieved as the ladies heading his bride's procession appeared. Then he forgot all his fears for her as the distinguished audience rose and he saw Ena coming down the aisle toward him to the joyous singing of the choir, smiling shyly and inexpressibly beautiful in her dress of white satin and cloth of silver, trimmed with rosepoint lace and loops of orange blossom. She joined him and the pageant of the nuptial mass began.

By desperate bargaining, Matteo Morales managed to get himself a place on a balcony overlooking the return route of the bridal cortege from the church to the royal palace, four storeys up in a house in the narrow Calle Mayor. He waited patiently, clutching his bouquet and smiling to himself from time to time. He was not an attractive man and, suffering as he did from syphilis, he sometmes had strange ideas. The others on the balcony were scarcely aware of him, waving to the people across the street from them, gazing down at the sea of heads and fluttering Spanish and British flags below. Then they heard the detonation of the guns proclaiming the end of the ceremony and, a little later, the welcoming cheers as the royal couple appeared on the steps outside San Jeronimo and Alfonso handed his bride into their gilded barouche.

The cheering came nearer and nearer and, at last, the gorgeous procession with its carriage after carriage filled with illustrious guests turned into the Calle Mayor. After outriders and cavalry came the carriage of George and May, Prince and Princess of Wales, representing King

Edward, followed by the carriage of the Dowager Queen Christina of Spain and Princess Beatrice, mothers of the bride and groom. Behind them came the newly married couple. Ena was flushed and radiant and Alfonso kept glancing from her to the clamouring, laughing crowds. He loved her to distraction and was overjoyed that his people, who had received her coldly at first, had now so clearly taken her to their hearts.

A group of British officers of the 16th Lancers, of which Alfonso was honorary Colonel, stood on the first floor balconies of a house just ahead. They raised a specially loud shout. From his balcony three storeys higher across the street, Morales tossed down his magnificent bouquet. Looking up, Ena saw it and waved. It should have landed in the carriage but the coachman slowed the horses so that Alfonso could respond to the cheering and congratulations of the Lancers. The bouquet landed between the wheel horses and the massive bomb inside it exploded at once, blowing the horses and one of the grooms to pieces, killing twenty people and maiming sixty more. By a miracle the bridal couple were untouched. Ena's dress was spattered with blood. For several heartbeats, she sat stunned, gazing at the road where she saw a man lying without his legs, a headless woman sitting on the pavement. When her husband put his arms round her, she told him calmly that she was unharmed and that he should think of the others. He rose to his feet, staring round at the hideous destruction.

Ahead of them, their mothers and George and May sat in their carriages tensely, waiting for the next attack, yet refusing to go on without them. There was blood and flesh everywhere, but only those nearest knew what had happened. The police in front and behind thought it had only been another salute of cannons. The officers of the Lancers raced down from their balconies and fought through screaming, struggling people to rescue Alfonso and Ena from their shattered carriage. They found them perfectly controlled, both rejecting any idea of taking refuge in one of the houses. 'I'm damned if I'll be driven off my own streets,' Alfonso said, and gave orders for the care of the wounded.

Behind them was the empty Coach of Respect, kept by tradition to be offered to any priest that was met on his way to administer the last rites. The Lancers helped the young King and Queen into it and, guarding them, drove on to the palace, continuing the procession.

Matteo Morales had left his balcony at once, becoming just another onlooker in the street. By the time he reached the scene of carnage, he realised that he had failed in the act of revolution for which his anarchist comrades had chosen him. He ran towards the Coach of Respect fingering the revolver in his pocket, but the Lancers were round it and, when he tried to follow it, the press of people was too great. He disappeared into the crowd. Three days later, a policeman recognised him in a village near Madrid from his description and tried to arrest him. Morales shot him dead, then killed himself.

Chapter

17

Alix thought of Ena as she cut back the autumn roses in her garden. They had always been her niece's favourites and, when Ena had whispered to her that she was to have a baby, Alix had gone out into the rosery at Sandringham and cut her a whole armful of them. How quickly the year had gone since then, and now Ena had given her Alfonso an heir. And Spain was more settled too, after the rash of outrages that had blasted towns in the north. Bertie had said, in politics, only people with no arguments resort to bombs. Alix often thought that what Bertie said was very clever, and wished that his own Government would listen to him as seriously as foreign politicians did. The whole thing was, his own Government didn't want him to be proved right too often. Like the way he had seen that that M. Isvolsky whom they had met at Copenhagen would one day be Nicky's Foreign Minister. It had changed Russia's attitude so much that, for the first time in thirty years, Minny had been able to visit her in England and they had travelled together from London to the holiday home they had taken in Denmark.

It was quite small, a charming, white-pillared country house on the sea at Hvidore, not far from Copenhagen, where they could sit under the trees and watch the ships go by. Alix was cutting back a bush of plump, yellow roses at the side of one of the paths. Toria was with her, picking up the pieces and putting them in a handbasket, and Minny sat on a bench near them, watching. She was more contented now they had bought this house, an oasis of peace after the strain of St Petersburg where her son had dismissed the Duma, the first attempt at a parliament. She was considering Toria. Alix's daughter was thirty-seven, no, thirty-eight. It was unlikely she would ever marry now. A pity, but Alix was strange like that. So warmhearted and generous with everyone else, with her own daughters she was quite possessive, never wanting them to leave her. It had been a struggle for the other two to get her permission to marry and now Toria had become a kind of constant, unpaid companion, an old maid before her time.

Toria loved her mother. Although her restless, intelligent mind sometimes rebelled, and she wished passionately that she had defied her and married the widowed Lord Rosebery whom she had loved and still cared for, she accepted her quiet life for the most part with resignation. She had been standing, holding the basket patiently for twenty minutes. 'That's too much, Motherdear,' she said. She realised her mother had not heard and tapped her on the arm. 'Mama!' Alix looked at her in surprise. 'You'll cut them all away.'

Alix smiled. 'Yes, dear. Clear it all away. I'll have more for you shortly.'

Toria gave up. She was about to reply waspishly when she heard her Aunt Minny laughing and was forced to smile, too. Alix glanced from one to the other and laughed also, although she was not sure why. Toria took the laden basket away to empty it.

'That's enough, Alix!' Minny called. 'Leave some for the gardeners.' She patted the bench beside her and Alix came to join her. 'You should have let that girl marry,' Minny said.

Alix's eyebrows rose. 'Toria? . . . She's not the sort.' She sat beside Minny, changing the subject. 'I do adore our little house. I only wish Bertie would come sometimes.'

'Why doesn't he?' Minny asked.

'He gets bored when he's not surrounded by people. I can't bear that any more.' She shook her head. 'I stand in a room full of our guests, all talking at once, and I can't hear a word any single person says to me. And I know they're all thinking—what a stupid woman to be a Queen. So I smile and say something to make them laugh and move on. Even when I go to the Opera, I can't hear it. I can hear you and Toria, Bertie sometimes, one or two others. Nobody else.'

'Bertie should spend more time with you,' Minny insisted.

'I wouldn't want him to. He likes rushing about, and it really does a lot of good. I couldn't ask him to come here, instead of Marienbad.' In Alix's voice there was a touch of sadness, then she smiled. 'Well, at least if he

302

won't come here, I don't have to go with him to Germany. Still, he can relax there—and he needs the rest.'

On the stage, the can-can was nearing its climax, the dancers twirling and squealing, shaking their flounced petticoats in a semicircle as the leaders of the troupe showed off their specialties, two of them crisscrossing in a series of cartwheels while one in the centre held her right foot above her head and spun on her left like a top. The girls' batiste pantalettes were slick with the perspiration that made them almost transparent, sticking to the skin, revealing the gartered tops of their black stockings and the pink flesh above. The audience laughed and cat-called.

In the stage box, Bertie sat low in his chair, watching them expressionlessly. Ponsonby was with him. They had come to the small theatre in Marienbad for the performance by this Viennese company expecting from the title. 'The Underworld', to see a lowlife melodrama. Instead, it turned out to be a cheap revue, made up of crude sketches, poor comedians and worse singers. Even the girls were unattractive, their costumes tawdry and stained, their faces overpainted and their flaccid breasts jiggling, as if to substitute display for talent. Ponsonby could see the King's blunt fingers drumming incessantly on his knee, the sure sign that he was bored.

The specialities finished, the girls turned their backs on the audience and bent over, flicking up their dresses to show their rumps protruding through the split in their drawers. The curtain fell to scattered applause. When it rose again for yet another appearance of the large blonde lady who sang sentimental ballads while a baggy-trousered comic mimicked her in witless counterpoint, Bertie nodded. Ponsonby and he picked up their tophats and gloves, rose and left the box. There was a murmur of consternation in the auditorium. Some people applauded.

Coming out of the theatre, Bertie murmured, "Reminded me a bit of Princess Daisy, that singer.' Ponsonby smiled, but Bertie corrected himself. 'No, I take it back. Daisy's really very good.' It was a reference to the amateur theatricals at the Duke of Devonshire's home, Chatsworth, the previous January, when Daisy of Pless had sung folk-songs with costume changes in between and been the hit

303

of the evening. For the men, the main pleasure was just to sit and watch her.

It was not yet fully dark and the September air was warm. They strolled down towards the fountain, remembering that house-party, the snow that had made shooting difficult and the hundred workmen from the Duke's estate who had lined the carriage-drive waving flaming torches on the night the royal guests arrived. Alix had been there, and Alice Keppel. Soveral, and Arthur Balfour, more relaxed and agreeable now he was out of office. With the enormous number of guests, each with several servants, they tried to work out how many Chatsworth had been called to accommodate. It came to several hundred. The Duke was so wealthy, four or four hundred under his roof made no difference.

Bertie was looking better. Over this past year, the bronchitic attacks had grown fiercer and more frequent and, at times, to hear him struggling for breath was alarming. It intensified his moods of depression and irritability. Ponsonby remembered one awful moment at dinner in Buckingham Palace when the King helped himself to creamed spinach from a salver held by a footman and had splashed himself slightly on his shirt. He had snatched the salver and the guests froze, waiting for him to hurl it at the trembling footman. He had just managed to stop himself and, instead, grabbed a handful of the green mess and smeared it all over his starched white shirtfront, saying 'Might as well make a good job of it!' But as always, a few weeks at Biarritz or Marienbad were enough to let his strong constitution recover.

The occasional walks they took like this, with the King's restless mind leaping from topic to topic among his thousand interests, with comments and anecdotes, were to Ponsonby the most enjoyable part of his service. They were waiting for urgent, secret despatches from Arthur Nicolson in St Petersburg, but neither of them mentioned it. They talked of Marienbad itself, which had become the most fashionable resort in Europe through the King's visits, where Ponsonby was now manager of the golf club and where Lady Campbell-Bannerman had died suddenly on their previous trip. They had attended the mourning service, before C.B. took her body back to Scotland. To most people's surprise, Campbell-Bannerman had proved to be an outstanding Prime Minister, making the best use of the

304

immense but untried talents in his party, balancing and controlling his Cabinet with a master's hand, a difficult job with such different elements at the intellectual Asquith and the ambitious Welshman, Lloyd George, impatient for power. Bertie was afraid that, if anything happened to C.B., the radical tail would begin to shake the horse. C.B. was radical enough, himself, having pushed through the immediate grant of self-government to South Africa and now this Trade Disputes Act, giving wide powers to the Unions. One clause in particular troubled Bertie, the one allowing 'peaceful picketing'. 'An absurd description,' he said. 'As if it could possibly be claimed that any form of picketing could be free from occasional acts of violence, or, at any rate, of constant intimidation. It will lend itself to great abuse.'

But the subject they kept returning to was Germany. The Kaiser's Admirals were stunned by the reports on the trials of the *Dreadnought*, which Bertie had attended. With her speed, firepower and armour, she made every other battleship afloat obsolete. Now that England was laying down another three, Von Tirpitz conceded that she must be left unchallenged as mistress of the oceans. Even if they were to build their own Dreadnoughts, the Kiel canal was not deep enough nor wide enough to give them access to the sea. For the whole year, Kaiser Wilhelm had been remarkably restrained and had begged his uncle to meet him at Wilhelmshöhe on his journey to Marienbad. Bertie had brought Hardinge to talk with the Chancellor, von Bülow, and had refused to discuss politics himself. Wilhelm had been charming and unaccustomedly modest, taking great pains to be friendly to Ponsonby. 'My old friend, Fritz,' he smiled, shaking hands. 'I tried to read in the newspapers some account of the yacht-racing at Cowes, but all I could see was that your wife looked remarkably well and wore a new hat.' He had not been able to resist some military display and had brought a whole army corps to honour his uncle. Wilhelm also brought his plumply placid wife, Augusta, who lived most of her life apart from him, comforted by religion, and his daughters to increase the family atmosphere. For over a year, he had known that he was on probation. Even this meeting was only for a day. At the end of it, when his uncle confirmed a tentative invitation to him and Augusta to visit Windsor in three months' time, he was as excited as a little boy.

It was dark when the King and Ponsonby arrived back at the Hotel Weimar. All the lights were on and a Viennese orchestra played in the ballroom. Hotel guests, a selection of the international élite, were spaced out at tables along the elegant terrace. As always, a frisson of anticipation went through them at the sight of the King, but they had learnt to be very careful not to acknowledge him unless he seemed to wish it. Through the open main doors, Bertie saw his friend the Abbot of Tepl, whose rich monastery owned the whole of Marienbad and most of the surrounding countryside. Like his monks he wore the unusual combination of a white cassock and a black tophat to symbolise involvement both in affairs of the spirit and the world. Some visitors were coming out of the doors, among them a dark-haired, dark-eyed young woman, wearing an emerald-green dress in the new tighter style with a slight flare at the ankles and a high lacy collar nearly reaching her ears. Bertie had spotted her earlier in the day, when she had smiled to him. She was decidedly attractive. He nodded affably to the people coming out as they bowed and curtsied. The young woman curtsied a little deeper than the others and paused, her smile teasingly provocative. Bertie was tempted but noticed Sir Henry Campbell-Bannerman sitting alone at one of the tables. He raised his hat to her and moved to join Sir Henry. As Ponsonby made to follow him, the young woman stepped in front of him, stopping him. He raised his hat, surprised and intrigued.

Campbell-Bannerman was pleased that the King had joined him. They enjoyed each other's company, although they did not always agree on things. C.B. accepted that, perhaps, he was rushing some social reforms through too quickly but there was a great deal he wanted to do and he was afraid he did not have much time. His own health had deteriorated more quickly after his wife's death, but the energy he still brought to his work shamed his critics.

Bertie respected his shrewdness and found his odd, little habits endearing. When they strolled round town, he would bow and say good morning to his favourite trees. And when he picked up one of his collection of walking-sticks, he was reported to apologise under his breath to the others for leaving them behind. Bertie waved away a waiter who came towards them, bowing. 'D'you think the cure is doing you any good, Sir Henry?'

'Every year I tell myself so, Your Majesty—but every

year it seems to have less effect,' C.B. said, patting his stomach.

Bertie chuckled. 'I know the problem!' He leant towards him confidentially. 'Just think what we'd be like if we *didn't* spend a month here every year.' Just then, there was a flash from beyond the balustrade of the terrace. His head whipped up. 'Blast! There's another of those photographers! I thought they'd promised to leave us alone? . . . Fritz—where the devil's Ponsonby?' He realised that Campbell-Bannerman was laughing quietly. 'What?' he scowled.

'I was thinking of that photograph the other day, sir,' C.B. said, smiling. An enterprising photographer had taken a snapshot of them, sitting with their heads close together in serious discussion. It had appeared on front pages throughout the world and caused quite a stir with its caption. "Is it Peace or War?" 'The Cabinet was somewhat concerned. Grey wrote to ask if we'd reached a decision on the Balkans.'

'And?'

'I wrote back to tell him we'd been discussing whether halibut was better baked or boiled.'

Bertie chuckled. 'A very suitable discussion for two old gentlemen.' He had, in fact, just agreed to recognise Serbia where the regicide officers had at last been dismissed, and advised caution to Ferdinand of Bulgaria who had asked his help in declaring his country's independence from Austria. He leant back, his good humour restored. 'By the way, I have to congratulate you on refusing to support this idiocy of a Channel Tunnel.'

'Don't you think it's feasible, either, sir?'

'Probably it is, technically. But we don't want England attached to Europe by a kind of metal umbilical cord.' C.B. smiled. 'It's personal ties we need—not artificial ones.' Bertie paused, then went on 'Did you know Isvolsky, the Russian Foreign Minister, is coming to Marienbad?'

'No, I didn't, sir.'

'I invited him,' Bertie said casually. He saw C.B. become suddenly cagey. 'Well, the Anglo-Russian talks have been going on for four years now, and got nowhere. It'll do no harm if I flatter Isvolsky a little. Present company excepted, of course—most politicians are slightly vain.'

Campbell-Bannerman smiled. They eased apart as Ponsonby came to join them. Bertie nodded. 'So there you are, Fritz. What have you been up to?' He motioned to a chair.

'I was detained by a young . . . lady, sir.' Ponsonby said, as he sat. 'Whom I believe you noticed.'

'Oh, yes, very attractive,' Bertie murmured. 'Who was she? What did she want?' He saw that Ponsonby was amused but reluctant to speak. 'Come on—out with it.'

'Well, sir,' Ponsonby told him gravely, 'it appears she has come all the way from Vienna. She feels that her professional status would be greatly improved if she had the inestimable honour of sleeping with Your Majesty.'

Bertie blinked. The young woman had not looked like a courtesan. 'What did you tell her?'

'That it was out of the question, sir.'

There was a pause and Bertie nodded, conscious of C.B. staring at him. 'Ah. Of course.'

'Whereupon,' Ponsonby said, 'so as not to waste the price of the ticket, she asked if she could have the more dubious honour of sleeping with me.'

Campbell-Bannerman was forced to smile. Bertie glanced towards the hotel doors and back at Ponsonby whose eyes were twinkling. He chuckled and startled the decorous terrace as he leant back, roaring with laughter.

It was so silent in the Prime Minister's study that they could hear Big Ben strike the full hour. C.B. sat behind his desk with Edward Grey, the Foreign Secretary, standing beside him. Opposite them sat clean-shaven, solemn Herbert Henry Asquith, Chancellor of the Exchequer. David Lloyd George, with black hair and moustache and intense blue eyes, stood by the fire with his blunt-faced, redheaded friend, Winston Churchill. Lord Esher was with them. He had given up his arrangement with Cassel completely and returned to politics. As the King's adviser, he had quickly achieved the same acceptance by this Government as by the previous.

Churchill pursed his lips, looking from him to Campbell-Bannerman. 'So he's brought it off, Prime Minister,' he said in his gruff, slightly sibilant voice.

'It appears so,' C.B. admitted. 'The Anglo-Russian Agreement was signed yesterday in St Petersburg. We are now linked in a triple alliance with Russia and France.'

'Germany won't like that,' Lloyd George said dubiously. 'There's a lot in our Party who'll say we're condoning the Czar's oppression.'

'Then it's up to us to point out how beneficial it is for

both our countries,' Grey answered. He had little patience with foreign policy being criticised in terms of factory-floor politics. 'Apart from completing the balance against Germany and Austria, by this convention Russia has accepted our possession of India, Tibet and Afghanistan. And we have divided Persia into two spheres of influence. Matters which have been the possible cause of war for a hundred years have now been settled peaceably. The negotiations have been very delicate.'

'It is what the King has been working for ever since his visit to Paris,' Esher explained.

'Yes. But what I don't know,' Churchill said, 'what I'm not entirely certain of, is what part did King Edward really play in all this?'

'It could all have been handled without him,' Asquith said.

'Perhaps,' Campbell-Bannerman agreed. 'Yet he found ways to approach them we had not thought of—and never gave up when we had. It's him Isvolsky trusts. And on his trips this year he has visited the Kings of Italy and Spain, and the Kaiser. And had informal talks with the new French Premier, Clemenceau, and the Emperor Franz Joseph.'

'What is he?' Lloyd George snorted. 'The Monarch or the Foreign Secretary?'

'I, for one, am not too biased to take his advice,' Grey said stiffly.

'No disrespect, Sir Edward,' Asquith soothed 'Yet the belief abroad that the King dictates our foreign policy is extremely unfortunate. The Kaiser, in particular, sees every move he makes as a deliberate insult. It lowers European politics to the level of a family squabble.'

'What do you imagine we can do about it, Mr. Asquith,' C.B. asked.

'We must get King Edward to convince his nephew that we have no warlike intentions towards Germany,' Lloyd George insisted. 'Otherwise, he will see this new alliance as a direct threat.'

'So you deny that the King has any real effect or influence.' Esher murmured, 'and at the same time, have to appeal for his help as a peacemaker.'

C.B. and Sir Edward Grey smiled. Lloyd George had to have the last word. 'At any rate,' he said grudgingly, 'he's to be congratulated on his moral stand in walking out of that apparently disgusting, theatrical performance. It was warmly appreciated in my constituency.'

'As to that,' C.B. remarked drily, 'His Majesty assures me that he has no wish to pose as a protector of morals—especially abroad. He left because he was bored.'

When Churchill laughed, Lloyd George glanced at him, annoyed.

The State Visit to which the Kaiser had looked forward so eagerly was threatened on three separate accounts. Firstly, he was depressed and enraged by the treaty, especially after Nicholas's Ministers had rejected his own offer. Then, the Foreign Office offended him by hinting that there would not be space for a large escort of German battleships at Portsmouth. But most importantly, his Court and Government were suddenly convulsed by a sensational scandal when his closest friend, Philip Eulenberg, was accused and put on trial with other high-ranking officials for homosexual offences. The reaction inside Germany was so fierce that Wilhelm was forced, against his will, to condemn and disown them to save his own reputation. He was afraid of a disapproving reaction in England and wrote to explain that he was unable to come, due to 'Bronchitis and the acute cough effect of a virulent attack of influenza.'

Von Bülow was threatened with involvement in the Eulenberg scandal and terrified that, if the Kaiser did not behave as if nothing was wrong, they would all come crashing down. When Bertie wrote that if this visit was cancelled at the last minute there might not be another invitation Wilhelm recovered quickly from his diplomatic illness. He and the dumpy, rather plain Empress Augusta, known in the family as Dona, were met at Portsmouth by their cousin, Prince George, who escorted them in the royal train to Windsor where Bertie and Alix and an enormous houseparty waited to welcome them. Deliberately, Bertie had arranged no military parades, keeping everything friendly and sociable. Responding to it, Wilhelm relaxed and his charm astonished those who did not know him. At the reception, he teased Ponsonby's pretty wife about her newsworthy hats, swapped Latin tags with the Chancellor, Henry Asquith, who was a classical scholar, and flirted with Daisy of Pless, whom he accused of turning his sons' heads. His admiration of Alexandra was almost embarrassing, but genuine, while she was surprised to see how much older he looked after just a few years, his hair and waxed moustache streaked with grey. He was still handsome, but his face was lined and his erect figure heavier. 'You are so young,' he kept saying. 'Times spares no one but you.'

As used as they were to opulence, the great banquet in the Waterloo Chamber was the most sumptuous Wilhelm and Dona had ever seen, wih a hundred and eighty exquisitely dressed guests at the long tables which glittered with gold plate, gold and diamond centrepieces and candelabra, a liveried footman behind every chair and the walls, under the portraits of Wellington's generals and allies, lined with scarlet-coated Yeomen of the Guard. Among the guests were Alfonso and Ena of Spain, Bertie's daughter, Queen Maud of Norway, and the plump Amélie, wife of his cousin, fat and humorous Dom Carlos of Portugal. Wilhelm was flushed with pride to be guest of honour and his uncle's speech, proposing his health and Dona's, moved him deeply. He felt the arms of the family reaching out to enfold him. He had not realised it before, but his uncle had quietly achieved the dream of his father, the Prince Consort, Wilhelm's grandfather, with the Czar and Czarina his nephew and niece, the Queen of Norway his daughter, the Kings of Portugal and Belgium and the Prince of Bulgaria his cousins, the Queens of Spain, Rumania and Sweden his nieces. His brothers-in-law were the Kings of Greece and Denmark. And Wilhelm, himself, a major link in this incredible chain that bound all Europe together. As he looked at his Uncle Bertie, he felt an unusual sense of humility. Why had he tried to fight him? Why had he listened to those who said that England was an enemy? They did not understand the pride of belonging to this family, of sharing its strength and reinforcing its promise of peace. His speech in reply was thoughtful and sincere and drew warm applause.

The days of the visit were filled with parties, dinners, private concerts and theatrical performances. Bertie kept strictly to his decision not to talk politics with Wilhelm. Instead, he and his brother Arthur, Duke of Connaught, took their nephew shooting in Windsor Forest while Alix and her daughters showed Amélie and the shy Dona the beauties of the castle. Afterwards, they all met in the family sitting-room where they were joined by George and May.

Wilhelm had relaxed even more. Enjoying the informality, he even stopped wearing uniform and changed into ordinary suits like his host. Alexandra was sitting on the sofa beside his wife, Dona. 'Aunt Alix,' he said, 'have I told you how lovely you are?'

'Once or twice, Willy,' she answered, smiling. She was still not at ease with him and knew she never would be, but did not let it be seen.

'That is because I can't get over it! You are always so elegant-wunderschön,' he laughed. Beside Alix, Dona shifted uncomfortably, aware that he would give her a lecture later on her own dowdiness. He strode to the fireplace and spread his hands, warming himself. 'It's so comfortable here, so pleasant, My palaces are all so cold. Sometimes, I ask my Chamberlain if he thinks I want to skate.'

They laughed and George suggested. 'Tell him to light a fire.'

Wilhelm shook his head. 'It would be misunderstood.' He had to maintain his reputation for hardness and endurance. 'But this is a real home. We must all meet more often.'

Bertie had been lighting a cigar. 'I'd have asked you before, Willy,' he observed mildly. 'But of course, you were indisposed.'

The others held their breath. Dona stiffened with embarrassment and Wilhelm turned slowly. 'I should have known that a few days in England would cure me,' he said.

Bertie puffed on his cigar, watching through the smoke. 'It is an illness which I hope will not recur.'

'It can't possibly—now,' Wilhelm assured him. They smiled and the others relaxed. 'Strange,' Wilhelm murmured. 'Whenever I am here, I never want to leave.'

Arthur chuckled. 'Your people would think we were keeping you prisoner.'

'In a way you are,' Wilhelm told him. 'I suppose it's my English blood, the things my mother taught me as a child. I have longed to live here—to be one of you.'

'You are, Willy,' Bertie said softly.

'Only inside myself. And never completely.' For a moment Wilhelm sounded wistful, slightly lost. 'I have had to fight against it, for the sake of my country. For what I have sometimes had to do.' He shrugged. 'But—blood is thicker than water.'

It was a theme to which he returned the next day, when he was invited to London to open the new Admiralty Arch and to an official lunch with the Lord Mayor and Alderman at the Guildhall. Londoners were impressed by his friendliness and modest charm, when they had been used to thinking of him as a potential enemy, and gave his procession through the City a warm welcome. In reply to the Lord Mayor's address, which was presented to him in a gold casket, Wilhelm electrified his distinguished audience by a passionate and sincere plea for friendship between England and Germany. 'They are of the same blood and of the same creed and they belong to the great Teutonic race which Heaven has entrusted with the culture of the world. Our race has been chosen by God to work his will in and upon the world, brothers in everything but name. Surely—surely that is grounds enough to ensure peace between us and to foster mutual recognition and understanding in all that draws us together and to sink everything that could part us?' His speech, ending with the solemn words, 'Blood is thicker than water!', was received with deafening applause and, when he left the Guildhall, the crowds in the streets cheered him with wild enthusiasm.

Bertie was delighted with the unexpected success of the visit, but disconcerted when Wilhelm decided that, while Dona was returning to Germany, he would stay on for another month. He had been inspired by the reaction to his speech and wanted discussions with the British Government and to meet more of the people. He also wanted to fulfil a lifelong ambition to live for a time as an English country gentleman. Bertie arranged for him to rent Highcliffe Castle near Bournemouth from Col. the Hon. Edward Stuart Wortley, who remained in his own home as a guest of the Kaiser.

Francis, now 1st Viscount Knollys, was much more than a Private Secretary. He handled all the King's engagements, provided the bulk of his information and it was mostly through him that Bertie corresponded with his Government departments, Ambassadors and colonial officials from the Governor-General of Canada to the Viceroy of India. Knollys still resented being left behind in favour of Ponsonby on the King's trips abroad, but to be his principal adviser along with Lord Esher more than made up for it. He was with Bertie and Esher in the study at Buckingham Palace.

Bertie was very concerned by Kaiser Wilhelm remaining in England, and knew that the German Government was just as worried. If anything upset Wilhelm, he was liable to react violently and undo all the good of his visit. Edward Stuart Wortley had been in the Paris Embassy and had helped secretly to organise the King's tour of 1903. Now he wrote from Highcliffe to Knollys, keeping him informed of the Kaiser's attitude. So far, if his conversation was extraordinary, it showed a continuing desire for friendship. He had even been pleased by the Liberals' announcement that they would cut one dreadnought and several battleships from Fisher's naval estimates.

'He sounds really sincere, this time,' Bertie said. 'If only it lasts.'

'The Kaiser's very popular, sir,' Esher commented. 'People can't think why they distrusted him before. A pity he wasted his talks with the Foreign Office. He spent the whole of the first raving against the Jews. And the second, describing a railway he intends to build from Berlin to Bagdad.'

'What on earth for?' Bertie asked.

'He either couldn't, or wouldn't, say, sir,' Esher answered.

'There can only be one reason,' Knollys pointed out. 'To carry military supplies.'

Bertie stared at him. 'Don't even think it, Francis. He just hasn't been approached in the right way.' He reached for a pen and a sheet of notepaper. 'I'll write to Grey.'

As he began the note to suggest that another meeting should be arranged, there was a knock at the door and Fortescue came in. He seemed flustered. 'Excuse me, sir. His Imperial Majesty has arrived and wishes to see you urgently.'

'From Bournemouth?' Bertie was surprised and looked from Esher to Knollys. 'Thank you, Seymour. Show him to the private sitting-room and I'll——' He broke off as Wilhelm marched into the study past Fortescue. He was obviously agitated.

'Why am I being kept from you?" Wilhelm demanded. 'Why am I not allowed to see you?!' He glared at Fortescue. Bertie nodded and Fortescue withdrew, closing the door.

Esher and Knollys had risen and were bowing. They could see that the Kaiser was excited. The hand of his withered left arm was thrust into his pocket and he plucked at the lapel of his black coat with the other. 'I am free for you any time,' Bertie said soothingly.

'We have had no real chance to talk!' Wilhelm complained.

'I try to reason with your Government, but they do not understand me. I am always misunderstood.'

'Gentlemen——' Bertie hinted. Esher and Knollys bowed again, preparing to leave.

'No! Let them stay,' Wilhelm insisted. 'Anything I say may be heard by anyone.'

'I have promised my Ministers not to talk politics with you,' Bertie explained.

'This is not politics—it is life or death!' Wilhelm declared. 'This is a unique opportunity. I offer friendship, and they tell me they are cutting out one dreadnought and a few battleships. Why build any?'

Bertie had restrained himself as long as he could. 'All right, Willy. Cards on the table. We build, because you build. It's as simple as that.'

'But I have not the slightest wish to go to war with England!' Wilhelm protested.

'You don't need a fleet to fight France or Russia. They are on your doorstep,' Bertie said. 'So we must assume it is meant for us.'

Wilhelm was thrown for a second. 'It—it is only to defend our commerce.'

'You will not need to defend it,' Bertie stressed, 'neither of our countries would have to waste money on warships, if we had once been able to come to terms. If you and your Ministers sincerely wanted to join us in ensuring a lasting peace.'

The muscle in Wilhelm's jaw was jerking. 'You can't expect me to disband my army!' he exploded. They watched him as he began to pace. 'We are a new nation. We must be allowed to expand—to defend ourselves. All this talk of war is only because my people are nervous. But I can control them! Don't you realise I am the greatest friend Britain has?'

'How so?' Bertie asked quietly.

Wilhelm swung round to face him. 'You deny it now—you laugh. But it is only I who prevent the states of Europe from joining against you! It is only I who stop my armies from marching—from taking what should be ours!' His voice was thick, his eyes flickering. 'Only I keep my people in check. Everything—I have sacrificed everything for the affection I have for you, for our family! And see how I am treated! Cruelly—cruelly misunderstood—on all sides!'

'Willy . . .' Bertie said gently, and rose.

'I—I——' Wilhelm faltered. 'You will excuse me.' He bowed. 'Excuse me.' He bowed again, abruptly, and left the room.

In the silence after he went out, Esher and Knollys looked at each other, stunned. Unlike the King, they had never seen the Kaiser like this. Bertie sat again heavily at his desk. He picked up the letter he had begun to write to the Foreign Office and tore it slowly in half.

The day after Kaiser Wilhelm left England, reaffirming his sincere desire for peace, a revised Navy Bill was announced in the Reichstag, providing the Imperial German Fleet with twelve more battleships and ordering the construction of four dreadnoughts

The year 1908 began with the gaiety Bertie's people had come to expect. He had seen an operetta in Vienna, 'Die Lustige Witwe' by Lehar, and persuaded the impresario George Edwardes to put it on in London. All that winter, people were humming and whistling the Merry Widow Waltz. But Bertie himself was suffering another severe bout of bronchitis and there was a break in the routine of years. Owing to the illness of the Duke of Devonshire, the customary week at Chatsworth had to be cancelled.

His breathing laboured and painful, Bertie opened Parliament in State with Alexandra. He was determined to fight his illness, but felt permanently exhausted. He was also worried by the worsening health of Campbell-Bannerman. Then terrible news came from Lisbon. His friend, King Carlos of Portugal, had been assassinated with his heir. Riding in an open carriage towards his palace with Queen Amélie and their two sons, he had been fired at by a group of men with rifles. One had broken through the crowd and leapt on the back of the carriage, shooting him at point-blank range, while another pumped bullets into his elder son. Amélie had saved the life of their youngest son, Manoel, by covering him with her own body and had been wounded. Bertie and Alix attended a Requiem Mass at the church of St James's, Spanish Place, the first time a King and Queen of England had attended a Roman Catholic service since the Reformation. The following day, to silence protests, they went in State to a memorial service at St Paul's.

Bertie was plunged into the deepest depression by Carlos's

murder and went alone with only Alice Keppel to his son-in-law, the Duke of Fife's, house on the seafront at Brighton to mourn. Other friends tried to comfort him and his doctors begged him to leave for Biarritz before the coughing brought on a haemorrhage.

A message from Asquith that Campbell-Bannerman had collapsed made him return to London. The old Prime Minister had refused to admit that his heart condition was incurable and worked on until he dropped. Even now he would not resign and any suggestion of it seemed to distress him. Bertie went to see him and found him confined to his bedroom at 10, Downing Street. He was drawn and shrunken and Bertie scolded him gently for doing too much. He was following the example, C.B. said, of his Sovereign. Bertie introduced the subject of his resignation, for his own sake and the country's, and was touched when Campbell-Bannerman told him he had no intention of subjecting him to the strain of a change of Government while he, himself, was ill. He would not give up his office until he was certain the King had recovered. The next day Bertie left for Biarritz where Alice Keppel was waiting for him.

Ponsonby was glad she was there, for no sooner had the King's health started to improve than another hammerblow struck him with the news that Harty Tarty, the Duke of Devonshire, had died. For many years he had been a steady, guiding hand in British politics and, with his death, Bertie lost one of his oldest and dearest friends. When a despatch came from Asquith two days later, saying that Campbell-Bannerman had at last given up his own struggle, Bertie should have returned to London for the swearing in of the new Prime Minister, but even a short walk to the local church exhausted him. With newspapers in England demanding his immediate return, Bertie telegraphed to Asquith, the obvious choice as Premier, to ask if he had any objections to coming to Biarritz. Asquith left for the South of France at once.

Herbert Henry Asquith was a Yorkshireman. Brought up in modest circumstances, he showed his ability at school and, at seventeen, won a classical scholarship to Balliol College, Oxford, where he distinguished himself and was elected to a fellowship. He became a successful barrister, using his practice to support himself as a Member of Parliament, as M.P.s received no salary. He had been a

317

notable Chancellor of the Exchequer for the last two years. Like most of his colleagues, he had considered that the Crown, under King Edward, had reached a prominence that threatened the prestige of Parliament. He had resented it, yet working with the King, especially during those recent months, he had learnt to value his constructive advice. He had no wish to risk the King's health unnecessarily and, as he explained to Ponsonby, it was even an advantage to be away from London while engaged on the delicate business of forming a new Cabinet. Normally cool and self-possessed, he was surprisingly nervous at the thought of the approaching ceremony, but Ponsonby told him to leave it all to the King.

Bertie received him in his hotel drawing-room. Asquith was concerned to see him so pale and strained, but Bertie put him at ease at once, concealing his tiredness. As they talked through the changes in the Cabinet, Asquith realised that to discuss them with someone as impartial and knowledgeable as the King was of great use. Lloyd George was promoted, with slight reservations from Bertie, to take over as Chancellor. He was more pleased to agree to Winston Churchill replacing Lloyd George as President of the Board of Trade. At the end of the meeting, Asquith knelt and kissed the King's hands as Prime Minister. He was relieved and grateful.

But Bertie was given no peace. The newspapers and many Members of Parliament continued to criticise his staying in France. He had always done his duty and, against the advice of his doctors, left for London less than a week after Asquith returned, to hold an immediate Privy Council and swear in new ministers. They were shocked by his appearance and the critics were silenced, but he had been hurt by the accusation that he had put his own convenience before his concern for his country. By an incredible effort of will, he threw off his exhaustion and took Alix on a non-stop, three-country State Visit to Denmark, Sweden and Norway.

Margot Asquith had been to Sandringham before her marriage, but was pleased to return as the wife of the Prime Minister. A highly intelligent young woman from a prominent family, her outspoken directness had always amused Bertie. He was surprised when she had married the staid Henry Asquith and often smiled at Alix saying, 'Well, Mr

Asquith may run the country, but Margot will run Mr Asquith.'

Henry had gone to his room with Francis Knollys to decode an urgent telegram and Margot wandered through the hall, where the Queen and some of the guests were dancing, into the salon where the King and his friends were playing bridge. He seemed to have recovered completely but, in an odd way, he had suddenly become an old man. His partner was Alice Keppel and they played against Sir Ernest Cassel and Agnes Keyser. No beauty herself, with her thin figure, long face and drooping, hooked nose, Margot had always envied Alice secretly and wished that she could agree with the jealous ones who whispered that now she had put on so much weight she had lost her looks. But Alice's opulent figure only made Margot feel more envious.

Bertie was coughing on his cigar. He glanced across at Alice. 'I can't concentrate with all this noise. Sorry, partner.' As Alice smiled to him, he coughed again.

'If I may say so, sir, you are smoking too much,' Agnes Keyser murmured.

Cassel chuckled. 'If Sister Agnes had her way, we'd lose all our tobacco shares.'

'I'm not a candidate for your nursing home yet, Agnes,' Bertie said. 'And I am cutting down.'

'Not enough to worry Sir Ernest,' Alice remarked casually.

'That's not fair!' Bertie protested. 'I'm rationing myself to only two cigarettes before breakfast.'

'And three cigars,' Alice added.

'Small ones!' Bertie growled. 'At any rate, I'm trying, Alice. So don't nag.' Cassel and Agnes Keyser had been smiling, but were concerned as he began to cough again, his face congested. 'It's no use,' he muttered. He looked up and saw Margot. 'Take over for me, will you, Margot?' He rose and the others began to rise, too. 'No, it's all right. Carry on, carry on.'

Margot Asquith took his place and he moved to the fireplace, throwing his cigar on the fire. The coughing attack did not develop, but left him breathless. As he looked round, he saw the Prime Minister and Francis Knollys coming towards him. They bowed and Asquith said quietly, 'May I interrupt you, sir? It's a rather serious matter, a communiqué from our Embassy in Berlin.'

Bertie tensed.

'It appears that Kaiser Wilhelm has been trying to break our alliance with Russia,' Knollys reported. 'He forced Czar Nicholas to meet him on his territory, at Swinemunde.'

'What was said?'

'We cannot find out, sir,' Asquith told him. 'But our observers say the Czar left the meeting frightened and humiliated.'

'Fools . . .' Bertie muttered. 'They'll destroy each other.'

'The situation is very dangerous,' Asquith went on. 'Our agreement with Russia is too new to be put to the test.'

'If it's broken now, it could never be re-established,' Bertie said.

'Exactly, sir,' Asquith agreed. 'The Russians must be reassured and the Czar convinced where his best interests lie.'

Knollys stared at him as he understood what he meant. 'It's too dangerous for His Majesty to go to Russia!' he protested. 'There are assassinations, disturbances there every week. Do you realise what you're asking?'

Bertie was considering Asquith. 'There are many in your own party who won't like it. For various reasons.'

'I can handle them, sir,' the Prime Minister promised. 'I shall tell them that you are not going to arrange a new treaty, but to preserve what we have.' It was a tacit admission of how much the country and Government had come to rely on the King.

They broke off as Alexandra came towards them, smiling. 'Mr Asquith,' she chided, 'you were to dance with me.'

He bowed. 'I—I apologise, Ma'am.'

'Well, it's too late now,' she laughed. 'We're playing Hunt the Slipper. Come and join us. You, too, Bertie.'

As she turned away, Bertie stopped her. 'Alix,' he said, 'it appears we may be going on a little trip.'

Bertie and Alix sailed to Russia in the *Victoria and Albert*. In addition to Ponsonby and Fortescue, Bertie brought with him Arthur Nicolson, Jacky Fisher and General Sir John French. The Government had wanted him to take a Cabinet Minister but he insisted on being accompanied by Charles Hardinge as usual. Alix brought Charlotte Knollys and Louisa Countess of Antrim. They were escorted by cruisers and torpedo-destroyers.

The crossing of the North Sea and the Baltic was extremely rough and, apart from the King and Queen who were both exceptional sailors, everyone suffered. To their

320

amusement, the worst sufferer was Admiral Fisher. But the weather cleared to blue skies and calm sea as they neared the large Baltic port of Reval, where the two Russian Imperial yachts, the *Standart* and the *Pole Star,* were waiting for them with the Czar's Ministers and most of the imperial family. They were guarded by two battleships, all that remained of the Russian Fleet.

The situation inside Russia was so bad that the police could not guarantee the safety of the King and Queen and so the visit was carried out on the yachts. It was paradoxical, Ponsonby thought, that on the first visit of a reigning English King to Russia, he could not land. Yet from the start, everything went well. The moment the King, dressed in cavalry uniform, boarded the *Pole Star* and greeted the guard of honour with the Russian formula, 'Good morning, my children,' and the sailors roared in answer, 'God Save the King!' the atmosphere thawed. Bertie had been carefully briefed by Nicolson and Hardinge and astonished Isvolsky and the Prime Minister, Stolypin, with his grasp of events and personalities inside Russia. They also knew that before he left London he had entertained Fallières, the President of France, and that everything he said now was with his assent. Any threat there had been to the Triple Agreement disappeared.

Bertie's greatest success was with Nicholas, himself, in their private meetings on each other's yachts. With Alix, he cut through the first stiffness and formality. They were both pleased to meet their four grand-nieces again, now growing into pretty girls, and especially, to see little Alexis, the Czarevitch, a delicate, fairhaired boy who stayed close to the hulking sailor who was his permanent guard and nurse. From Minny, who was also on the *Pole Star,* they had heard that he was suspected to have haemophilia, the bleeding disease which had attacked so many of Queen Victoria's descendants and from which Bertie's own brother, Leopold, had died.

On the first afternoon, Bertie held Alexis as they posed for Charlotte Knollys who was taking a group photograph on the deck. The girls sat awkwardly on either side of him and he made fun of them until they laughed and relaxed. 'That's better,' he said. 'Move in closer, Nicky.'

Nicholas was at the side and edged in. 'You, too, Mama,' he called. As Minny joined her son and he put his arm round her, Bertie saw the Czarina Alexandra glance sharply at them. Alicky was still distant and reserved, estranged from her mother-in-law.

Charlotte finished and Alix ran out of the group to take a snap of Bertie as he rose, holding Alexis.

'Careful, Uncle Bertie——!' Alicky warned.

'Don't worry,' he smiled. 'I've never dropped one yet.' He posed, then handed Alexis over to his sailor nurse who was hovering, anxiously. Bertie turned. 'So many grand-nieces, and all so pretty. Still, if you'll excuse us, your papa and I have to finish our chat.'

'Of course,' Nicholas said, and the girls rose, bobbing curtsies.

Bertie bowed to them and to the Czarina, then took Nicholas's arm and they walked together into the state-room.

After they had gone, the girls were downcast. 'What shall we do now?' Alix wondered and they looked at her hope-fully. 'I know—you can show Charlotte over the ship,' she decided. 'Only you mustn't lose her over the side.'

In the state-room, Bertie and Nicholas could hear the girls squealing with laughter. Nicholas was grateful to his aunt and uncle. He had not seen his children so relaxed and happy for a long time and it pleased him to have his mother with them, instead of her being excluded as she was so often. He was reading a copy of the speech Bertie was to make that night at the banquet on his yacht. Its theme of universal peace appealed strongly to Nicholas. Peace was the one thing he longed for. They were with Hardinge, Fisher, Isvolsky and Stolypin, a tall, grave man with a long, grey beard. At their meeting that morning, Bertie had raised the subject of the harsh treatment of Jews in Russia, as the Rothschilds had begged him to. Stoly-pin now assured him that laws would be prepared to protect them.

Nicholas finished the draft speech. 'These are my feel-ings, too, Uncle Bertie,' he said. He hesitated. 'I may have said unfortunate things in the past—but only because I was confused and misled.'

Bertie smiled. 'We have both been misled, and from the same source.'

Slowly, Czar Nicholas's smile answered his. He was so much more at ease with him than with his cousin, Wilhelm. Just talking to his uncle, he felt more self-confident, while Wilhelm always increased his feeling of uncertainty and in-

322

security. He wished he had modelled himself on his uncle Bertie, as he had once wanted to, and when Bertie chuckled to him, he laughed back, suddenly unrestrained.

On the deck, Alix sat with Minny on a swing seat under a striped awning. They were watching Alicky who sat apart from them, cold and withdrawn, with Alexis on her knee. 'You see how she behaves?' Minny said.

'She is a good mother,' Alix insisted.

Minny shook her head. 'She has no affection, no warmth. We are only a family again because you are here.'

Alix was sad for her. 'Why don't you come and live with us, Minny?' she asked gently.

'I can't leave Russia,' Minny said. 'There is an evil man who has gained influence over both Nicky and Alexandra. They think he is a holy man with the power to cure Alexei, but he is a charlatan! He will cause great harm. Many people are turning against us because of him.' Alix had heard of this peasant mystic, Rasputin, who posed as a monk. Alicky dismissed from court anyone who spoke against him. Minny's voice was bleak. 'I am afraid that the trouble we have seen is nothing to what will come. If Nicky needs me, I must be here.'

In the state-room, Bertie had mentioned the choral society which had sung for him the evening before. Orders had been given that both men and women were to be stripped and searched first by the police, although they were not even on the Imperial Yacht but on a steamer moored alongside. Ponsonby had managed to have the orders cancelled, in view of the possible reaction if it was reported in England. 'We must take every precaution,' Stolypin shrugged. 'It is only two years since my daughter was blown up by Nihilists. Now they are sworn to kill me. And we have heard of many plots to attack both His Imperial Majesty and yourself, sir, while you are here.'

'Surely you find this situation intolerable?' Fisher said.

'Wouldn't it be better to give them some of the freedom they call for?' Hardinge asked.

Isvolsky sighed. 'It's so simple, looking from outside. Our people are not used to freedom. Unless they are educated first, they will misuse it.'

'Do not leave it too long,' Bertie suggested quietly.

Nicholas had been listening. 'I, too, would like to trust my people—and have them trust me, as yours do. I have let the Duma assemble again. But all they do is insist on impossible reforms.'

'Any reform in one direction brings immediate demands for reform in others,' Stolypin explained. 'Where do we begin?'

They were seated round a table, drinking kirsch, and rose as the Czarina Alexandra came in, with the sailor who carried Alexis. 'Excuse me,' she said to Nicholas. 'He wants to say goodnight to Uncle Bertie.'

Bertie smiled. 'So early?'

'He must rest,' Alicky told him. 'I don't want him to become excited.'

'Well—good night then, Alexis,' Bertie chuckled and kissed the little boy's hand. Alexis smiled shyly as the sailor carried him out and Alicky curtsied before following them. Bertie was near Nicholas and saw his affection and concern. 'Take good care of him. I lost my first boy. No one can know the pain.' Nicholas nodded, responding to his sympathy. 'After all,' Bertie went on, 'that's what we work for—the world we leave our sons.'

Nicholas had had a hideous vision for a second of his own children lying dead, like Stolypin's daughter. 'If we have the courage,' he breathed.

'I am sure you have the courage, Nicky,' Bertie said. 'I only hope you have the time.'

Chapter
18

Bertie was grateful to Alix in Berlin. She was laughing and gay, interested in everything, charming to everyone. None of the people they met could have guessed that for years she had refused to visit Germany officially. She had never forgiven the unprovoked attack on Denmark in her youth and, although she had liked Vicky and her husband, Fritz, she had never trusted their son, Wilhelm. How right she had been, Bertie thought. Yet when he explained how imperative this State Visit was, she consented at once.

The six months since Reval had been difficult. The meeting with the Czar had caused a storm in Germany, with the Kaiser making wild speeches claiming that England planned to encircle Germany and provoke him into starting a war, so that he would be blamed and not his uncle. Bertie had managed to calm him at a meeting on his journey to Marienbad. On his annual stay with Franz Joseph of Austria a few days later, the aged Emperor had agreed on the need to urge restraint on Wilhelm. He had returned Bertie's visit at Marienbad, where the King induced the Emperor to ride in a motorcar for the first time. During the drive, Franz Joseph complimented Bertie on the perfect balance Britain had achieved in Europe, which nothing must be allowed to upset. Scarcely had Bertie arrived home, when Austria annexed without warning two Serbian provinces which looked for protection to Russia. Cunning and autocratic behind his kindly mask, the Emperor Franz Joseph was making a bid to restore the prestige of his crumbling empire, taking advantage of Bertie's determination to preserve peace and his ability to hold back Russia. He had not even told his ally, Wilhelm, who flew into a panic, first terrifying his people with warnings that Fisher was coming with the British Fleet, then complaining that his uncle had visited every capital city except his, proof that he hated him. Bertie was sickened by Franz Joseph's duplicity, but neither he nor his Government would go to war over two minor Balkan provinces. Yet the situation was increasingly tense, with the European nations incensed by Austria's apparent readiness to risk a general war and the Kaiser behaving as though it might begin at any moment.

Such a war, Bertie warned, would be like nothing ever seen before, a holocaust of which only the American Civil War could give an idea, and that merely a faint impression. He decided that, as soon as possible in the New Year, he must pay his long-delayed State Visit to Berlin, to try once again to pacify Wilhelm, and, more important, to prove to the German people that his offer of friendship was genuine.

Alix was glad she had come with him to share some of the strain, and that he had brought one of the royal doctors, Sir James Reid, whose skill and devotion had prolonged Queen Victoria's life. They had come in February, the worst month for Bertie. He was grey-faced, racked by coughing fits which left him breathless and shaking, but he drove himself on. His relaxed geniality broke through the distrust and hostility of the people he met and the crowds began to respond warmly.

The visit had a farcical beginning when he went to Alix's salon on the train to make sure she was ready. The traindriver drew up carefully in the Lehreter Bahnhof, so that the red carpet was directly outside the door to the King's salon. The Kaiser, Dona and their family and officials were all waiting by the red carpet and, when they saw Bertie and Alix getting out a hundred yards further down, had to run along the platform to take up new positions. Then, on the procession through the city, the horses pulling Alix and Dona's carriage stopped and refused to go on. They had to change into the carriage behind, which meant that everyone had to change carriages all the way down the line in an undignified scramble. When Bertie and Wilhelm's carriage reached the courtyard of the Imperial Palace, splendidly decorated, with a guard of honour in uniforms of the age of Frederick the Great, they looked back and found that they were quite alone. No one had told them what had happened.

Throughout the crowded programme of the visit, Bertie worked hard to create and keep a friendly atmosphere wherever he appeared, but the pace was exhausting, parades, receptions, State Banquets, a Court Ball and constant speechmaking. At a performance in the Royal Opera House of 'Sardanapalus', an opera designed by Wilhelm himself, Bertie could not stop himself falling asleep. He woke up to see real flames licking round the funeral pyre on stage and he struggled to his feet thinking the theatre was on fire. The signs of fatigue worried his doctor and Alix and grew harder to conceal. On the next morning, he had his greatest success of the visit in a speech at the City Hall where his sincerity and faultless German convinced the City Fathers that he was one of themselves and he was received with loud applause.

From there he went to an enormous luncheon at the British Embassy. Before the reception which followed lunch, Wilhelm, Dona, Alix and he toured the Embassy. Ponsonby and Hardinge were with them and a few special guests, including Princess Daisy of Pless, who was as much a notable in Berlin as in London. Bertie flirted with her as a relaxation from his formal duties and a relief from Wilhelm who veered from exuberance to tension, nervous in case anything else should go wrong. He was the one person Bertie had failed to relax.

As they came back down the wide staircase, Bertie felt out of breath and could not face the guests in the main rooms without resting. He led the way into an anteroom on the excuse of finishing the large cigar he had lit. 'I remember this room from my first visit here, as a boy,' he chuckled. 'There was a little Polish Countess. I managed to hold her hand for five minutes.' Wilhelm smiled stiffly, the others more openly. 'It's always been a good place to talk,' Bertie added, and they laughed.

'Are you enjoying your stay with us?' Dona asked Alix.

'Very much,' she smiled. 'But we haven't stopped since we arrived. I hardly had the strength to dance at the ball last night.'

'Yes, I didn't notice you on the floor much, either, Fritz,' Bertie said to Ponsonby.

The ball in the Weisser Saal had opened with the Royal Quadrille for the Princes and Princesses, led by the King with Dona and the Kaiser partnering Queen Alexandra. To Ponsonby's amazement, all the other dances had been from the time of Beethoven and Mozart. Wilhelm would allow nothing more modern. 'I'm afraid I don't know the minuet, sir,' Ponsonby explained.

Bertie coughed on his cigar, chuckling. 'Before your time, eh? Before yours too, I suppose, Daisy?'

Daisy was very fetching, her blondness set off by a royal blue silk dress whose close fit had made the Empress Augusta frown. 'Are you offering to teach me, Your Majesty?' she coquetted.

'I might take you up on that,' Bertie murmured. 'But I expect you prefer the Two Step.'

'It is not permitted,' Wilhelm said pompously. 'As Daisy well knows. People do not come to Court Balls to enjoy themselves, but to learn deportment.'

For a second, Bertie thought Alix was going to giggle. 'Yes, yes, Willy, of course,' he said, and nodded to the others. He took Wilhelm's arm and drew him across the anteroom to an ornamental sofa against the far wall. Tiredness was like a dull weight pressing him down and the uniform of the 1st Prussian Dragoon Guards, which he wore out of courtesy, was so tight around him it restricted his breathing even more. He sat heavily and Wilhelm sat beside him, with some reluctance. He had determined, on this visit, to fight the pull of his uncle's charm. He wanted to impress him, not be impressed. He had resented the King falling asleep during *his* opera. He had deliberately not attended the function at the City Hall in the morning to show his disapproval of the socialist leanings of the municipality and was disturbed at reports of the ovation his uncle had been given. It unsettled him and made him wary. The others talked quietly, a little self-consciously, trying not to overhear. The Chancellor, von Bülow, was edging nearer, but Hardinge stepped in front of him.

'Have you thought over what I said?' Bertie asked. 'I've been completely open with you.' Wilhelm was silent. 'This time I speak for my Government,' Bertie stressed.

'Which has isolated Germany from the rest of Europe,' Wilhelm muttered. It was his unending complaint.

'Don't you see, Willy?' Bertie urged. 'We hold a balance between us. If we can steady our allies and you can control yours, as long as we can talk like this, neither of us has anything to fear.'

Wilhelm nodded. What his uncle said was true. There was no need of a treaty between them; it was not realistic.

Alix had been watching without appearing to and judged the moment correctly. She moved to them. 'We should go back to the reception.'

Wilhelm rose and bowed. 'Of course, Aunt Alix.'

Bertie had been depressed by his nephew's reluctance to

come to an agreement. His breathing had grown shallower and he could not make the effort to rise. 'You go back,' he said. I'd like to stay here for a minute.' The others had turned towards him and he saw their surprise. He knew Alix would understand he needed to rest, and help him.

'A good idea, Bertie,' she nodded. 'But don't take too long finishing your cigar.'

'No, no,' he promised. 'Daisy'll sit with me. Won't you?' Daisy of Pless dimpled. 'I'd be delighted, sir.'

'Good,' Bertie smiled. 'So would I.' He indicated the place beside him and Daisy came to sit on the sofa. Now the others were smiling and von Bülow smirked to Wilhelm as they crossed towards the door to the hall.

Daisy had not realised that the King was in difficulty and that he had not wanted to alarm the others. The tight, high collar of his tunic bit into his throat and he was finding it hard to breathe. He smiled to her and tried to puff on his cigar, but choked on it. 'Do I remind you of your Polish Countess, sir?' Daisy asked, flirting. In the last few years she had learnt how to please him.

'She was small and dark, spoke no English,' Bertie coughed. 'Otherwise you're very similar.' Daisy laughed. Bertie was aware of her waiting for him to go on. 'You've no regrets marrying a German? You like it here?'

'In many ways,' she said. 'But life is very formal.' He nodded, coughing. She glanced away. It was an important opportunity for her to help relations between their two countries. She smiled. 'Yet they're very like us, very friendly. If only——' She stopped, alarmed. The King's coughing had turned into a gasping wheeze. As she turned to him, he stared at her for a second, his face contorted and darkly flushed, then his eyes glazed and his wheezing breath cut off. He fell back into the corner of the sofa.

Alix and Wilhelm had paused at the door to have a word with Ponsonby. He was facing into the room. 'Ma'am—' he said urgently and Alix turned.

Daisy was rising from beside the King. She was terrified. If he died here, it could have the most awful consequences. The cigar had fallen on to his lap and she snatched it up. She saw his chest heave and she fumbled with the buttons of his tunic, but could not undo them. She looked round wildly as Alix and Wilhelm hurried to them. 'He just— He just——' she stammered.

'Yes,' Alix said. Wilhelm had halted, gazing at his uncle,

329

shaken. All at once, he could not move. Alix was the only one with the presence of mind to do what was necessary. She bent Bertie's head back and tugged at the clips of his collar until they snapped open. Beside her, Daisy cried out when they heard his breathing again, as he gasped for air. Wilhelm hurried in and raised him to a sitting position, cradling him in his arms. 'Uncle Bertie——!' he pleaded.

Bertie's eyes flickered open and he gulped in air which slurred in his throat.

'Are you all right?' Alix asked anxiously.

'Couldn't—couldn't breathe——' he muttered. 'But I'm fine. Fine now.' He eased out of Wilhelm's arms.

'Gruss Gott!' Wilhelm whispered. 'I couldn't bear it. I thought. . . .' He was trembling with emotion, all the quarrels that had ever divided them swept out of his mind.

Bertie managed to smile. 'Don't worry, Willy. I'm still here.'

'I'd rather die myself than have anything happen to you,' Wilhelm swore. 'I—do you believe me?'

'I believe you, Willy,' Bertie said gently.

Ponsonby hurried back into the room with Sir James Reid, who had been at the luncheon. Seeing the King trying to stand up, Reid said, 'Please, don't get up, sir. You must rest.'

'I'll send everyone away,' Wilhelm offered.

'No. No, I'm all right now,' Bertie insisted. He drew himself slowly erect and clipped his collar shut. 'We must show ourselves together. That's what we're here for.'

He took Wilhelm's arm and they walked towards the door. Alix supported him on the other side until they reached the hall.

At the reception, everyone remarked on the new closeness between the two rulers and the surprising gentleness in the Kaiser's voice when he spoke to his uncle.

On the first night home, Bertie and Alix dined alone at Buckingham Palace.

Bertie was sombre. He had achieved one of the objects of his visit, reaching a rapport with Wilhelm he had never thought possible. But it was too late. Hardinge had confirmed what he suspected. Wilhelm no longer held the reins of power inside his own country. His erratic behaviour and hysterical outbursts had alienated the Reichstag. In any crisis, his Government would take complete control, defer-

330

ring to him but making the ultimate decisions themselves. But they, too, were puppets, jerking on strings held by a small group of powerful generals and admirals, products of the military machine, whose mailed fist policy would shape Germany's future. And Bertie had largely failed in his second object. He had made some impression on the German people, had convinced some of his sincerity and, through him, of his country's. Yet he had not had long enough, nor been seen enough to end the bitter hostility that had been built up over the years. It would need more trips and harder work.

Meanwhile it had been made more difficult by Lloyd George, who had toured Germany to study their system of National Insurance. While there, he had made statements on foreign policy, of which he knew very little, embarrassing his own Government by declaring that most people in Great Britain wanted an alliance with Germany and not with Russia. He returned home as a hero of the extreme Left, who had denounced the King for agreeing to meet the Czar, 'a common murderer—a bloodstained creature.' In spite of the fact that the elected Duma had written to say they welcomed the meeting and King Edward's liberalising influence on Czar Nicholas. Bertie knew that the Left did not want conciliation and reform to succeed in Russia. Only by confrontation and revolution could the leaders of the proletariat seize power.

And now Lloyd George, aided by Churchill, had asked for the higher taxation voted for defence to be used, instead, for Social Services. Fisher and the Admiralty had asked for six dreadnoughts to be built in the current year. Lloyd George and Churchill claimed that four were all that were needed. When it was discovered that Germany was also building another four, the Opposition protested that the old two to one ratio had been shelved and the cry, 'We want eight, and we won't wait!' swept the country. Reluctantly, Bertie agreed. Britain's power depended on the supremacy of her Navy. The race to build dreadnoughts was on.

Alix was hurt. She had conquered her own feelings to go with him to Berlin, and he admitted she had been an invaluable help. Now, however, he intended to go again to Biarritz, when she had asked him to come with her to Hvidore. He tried to explain, but she would not accept that the cold and fog of Denmark would be bad for his lungs.

All she saw was that, once again, he was setting aside her wishes.

As soon as he had opened Parliament, he left for Paris where he reassured Fallières and Clemenceau that Esher's reforms of the Army were proving effective. Few members of the Cabinet except Asquith and Grey knew that he had authorised secret plans for British intervention if France was attacked. The German High Command described the size of the British Army as 'contemptible'. It is small but highly trained, Bertie told Clemenceau, and will more than hold its own. At the same time, he warned them that the main threat to peace lay in Austria, as dangerous in its death throes as a wounded snake. If Franz Joseph, in his struggle for self-preservation, moved against Serbia or Rumania, the German High Command would take the first opportunity to join in. That was what they must seek to prevent.

In Biarritz, Bertie took longer to recuperate than usual, being forced to rest with only Alice Keppel and Caesar for company. His exhaustion had gone deeper than ever before. The weather had been blustery but, as soon as it cleared, his health started to improve and Soveral arrived to help Alice restore his spirits. Soveral was grateful to Bertie for the help he had given to the boy king, Manoel of Portugal. He had invited him to England, fêted him and given him confidence. With the promise of King Edward's support behind him he had returned to Lisbon and the menace of civil war had receded.

With Alice and Soveral, he began to go for walks and drives again, and they knew he had recovered when he took them to stay overnight at Pau. He was bubbling with all his old enthusiasm and the reason became clear when the American inventor, Wilbur Wright, appeared. He and his brother Orville were in France to receive a gold medal from the French Academy. The aeroplane which Wilbur brought to demonstrate to Bertie was an improved model of the heavier-than-air machine in which the first flight had been made five years before. On the second of the two demonstrations, it stayed in the air for over forty minutes. Bertie was fascinated and regretted that his age and weight made flying an impossibility for him. It was an expensive toy but could have a practical use, he told Wilbur, in carrying urgent letters and despatches.

* * *

The crowds watching the Derby of 1909 were in a ferment of excitement during the last furlongs. Herbert Jones in the royal colours of gold, scarlet and purple had nursed the King's colt, *Minoru* throughout the race and made his bid coming round the last bend. When *Minoru* thundered down the straight to win by half a head, a shout went up from the spectators like none that had been heard before at Epsom.

The sight of the King beaming with pleasure in the royal box, with the Queen clapping her hands beside him, had the whole vast concourse in delirium. He had won the Derby twice as Prince of Wales and this win gave him the hat-trick as Sovereign. The hubbub was unending, with thousands of people laughing, cheering, singing 'God Save the King.' When he came down to lead in his winner, the police had no hope of holding back the crowds. The air was filled with hats thrown up and waved, tophats, bowlers, strawhats and cloth caps, while everyone cheered and shouted, 'Teddy boy! Good old Teddy!' Even the police had given up and were waving their helmets and the crowd parted of its own accord to make an avenue for him and *Minoru*. In a brief lowering of the noise, one voice in the crowd was heard yelling, 'Now, King, you've won the Derby. Go home and dissolve this bloody Parliament!' As an answering roar of laughter went up, Bertie laughed too and tipped his hat.

That evening, he gave his usual dinner at Buckingham Palace to members of the Jockey Club, then went to Lady Farquhar's ball in Grosvenor Square. In a room set aside for him to play bridge and entertain, he found a group of his closest friends grouped round Soveral who sat reversed on a chair, using the back as reins. He was re-enacting the race, while the others cheered him on. 'Into the last two hundred yards—we're falling behind!' 'Come on, boy!' Carrington implored. 'We're catching up! We're level!' 'Minoru! Come on, Minoru!' Fisher shouted. 'We're across the post in front—and the crowd goes mad!' Soveral cheered and jumped up, waving his arms as the others applauded, laughing.

Bertie stepped forward and took Soveral by the lapel of his evening dress. 'Come along, Luis,' he chuckled. 'I'll lead you into the paddock.' They laughed and he trotted Soveral round to a nearby bay window where Alice stood with Cassel and Esher.

'I'll never forget it,' Alice said, smiling. She was delighted at the change in Bertie, the firmness that had come back to his step and the sparkle in his eye.

He was still chuckling. 'I don't remember anything like it—shouting, hats in the air. And what did that fellow say?'

'Now you've won the Derby—go home and dissolve this bloody Parliament,' Cassel reminded him.

'And right he was,' Bertie nodded. They laughed, and Carrington brought him a glass of champagne. 'Thanks, Charlie.'

'Dissolve this Parliament,' Alice repeated. 'He meant, Destroy the People's Budget.'

Bertie paused and glanced at her, warning. 'Now then, Alice, I don't want to talk politics, not tonight.'

Alice smiled. 'All I want is your promise not to oppose Mr Churchill and Lloyd George without at least speaking to them.'

'They'll have enough opposition, anyway,' Bertie grunted, 'because of the higher taxes and death duties they're demanding.'

'Precisely, sir,' Carrington said. 'And if they're not defeated, they will bring in essential social services and benefits.'

Bertie glowered from him to Alice. 'Oh, very well. I can't refuse anything tonight. I'll consider their proposals fairly.'

They looked round at a burst of laughter. Soveral had rejoined Knollys and Jacky Fisher. 'It's a fact,' Soveral protested. 'At four to one on Minoru, if I'd put on ten million, I'd be as rich as Sir Ernest.'

Bertie had seen Lloyd George and Churchill. He told them that, while they had some justification in the viciousness of their opponents, they could only damage belief in their cause by the violence of their own speeches. He had no quarrel with their fight against illness and unemployment, the terrors of the poor. All parties agreed on the need for Labour Exchanges and some form of National Insurance but he warned them that the House of Lords would see an attempt to redistribute wealth as an outright attack on their class.

'The struggle is not so much between classes, sir,' Lloyd George said, 'as between luxury and squalor.'

334

Later, Bertie had a meeting with the Prime Minister in his study at Buckingham Palace. He knew that Asquith was concerned about Lloyd George who habitually overstepped his authority as Chancellor. He was too popular to be replaced, but too self-opinionated to take instructions from anyone. Bertie had seen that, behind the provisions of his first Budget, there was a deeper plan, to destroy the restraining control of the House of Lords. He hoped that, as a cooler head, Asquith would prevent it.

'I believe he is justified, sir,' Asquith said seriously. 'The debate is not merely between parties, but between Lords and Commons. The House of Lords has the power to veto. Up to now, they have passed the ruling Government's Finance Bills automatically—but if they throw this one out, for their own reasons, they will create a constitutional crisis. And I must tell you, sir, that my Government will accept the challenge.'

Alix had gone to Hvidore with Toria and Charlotte to regain her strength after a bad bout of influenza. It had been an exceptionally tiring Season, with threats of political disturbances. Bertie had worn out his secretaries with work and his friends with a restless need for distraction and relaxation. Even Cowes Week had been turned into a State Visit, when Nicky and Alicky arrived on the *Standart* with the children. Bertie had made a fuss of his little godson, Alexis, and taken the Czar on a review of the Fleet at Spithead. Alix was happy to see Alicky so much happier and more trusting. She had even joined in when they played uproarious games with the girls. Still, Alix was glad to escape to Sandringham afterwards, to take care of John for a while, George and May's youngest son. Poor boy, he would never grow up, except physically He was very loving and, to Alix, it was a pleasure and not a duty to look after him for May.

She had changed out of her travelling clothes and crossed to the dressing-room to look into Bertie's bedroom. She was annoyed to find him not there and turned to George, who was waiting. 'Georgie—where's your father? He met me at the station, then rushed off. Doesn't he want to hear about my holiday?'

'He probably has work to do, Motherdear,' George said. He hesitated. 'I wish you could get him to stop for a while.'

'If he thinks his paperwork is more important than——' she began, and stopped, seeing his anxiety. 'Is something wrong?'

'He's wearing himself out,' George explained. 'His doctors have begged him to rest, but he has meeting after meeting with the Government, the Opposition, representatives of the Lords——'

'Why?' Alix asked, surprised.

'Haven't you heard? The House of Lords rejected Lloyd George's Budget. Father has had to dissolve Parliament and call for an immediate general election.'

The election campaign was fought with great virulence. Asquith and Lloyd George were determined to end the traditional control of the House of Lords over the Commons. Throughout, Bertie worked unceasingly to find a solution, a compromise that would satisfy both sides. He had begged his friends in the Lords not to rise to the bait, the clauses in the Budget which were designed to make them throw it out. He suggested slight alterations which would allow them to accept it and he devised a scheme for voting in the Lords which would make it fairer to the party in power. Neither side would give way.

The Liberals were sure of success, but the election result was not what they expected. In effect, the voters agreed with the King that a compromise should have been reached. The overall Liberal majority was cut from 220 to 2. In any legislation they brought in, they would need the support of the Labour members and the Irish Nationalists. Asquith saw the dangers of being at the mercy of much smaller but more radical allies, yet determined to carry on the fight against the Lords. One major problem was that he would have to bring in a Bill, cutting down their numbers, their power and their right to veto, but they would obviously not pass it themselves by voting for their own destruction. Irresistible pressure had to be put on them and Asquith decided on the drastic measure of asking the King to create hundreds of Liberal peers, enough to defeat any opposition in the House of Lords.

It roused a sense of outrage in most of the country, as such an act would also weaken the position and authority of the Monarchy. Bertie was already a sick man, worn out with worry and overwork. He had seen the storm coming and done everything possible to avert it but, once again, the politicians would not listen to his advice. And once again, the strain had come at the time of year he was least able to bear it. Acute anxiety over the state of the country sapped what little energy he had left. In his illness and depression, he went again with Alice to Brighton to stay on the front with his friends, Mr and Mrs Arthur Sassoon, at 8 King's Gardens.

He was in their drawing-room with Alice, Arthur Sassoon and Francis Knollys. They were deeply worried about his condition. He was permanently out of breath and unable to sleep. Even in the cold of February, crowds assembled on the promenade, hoping for a glimpse of him and making it difficult for him to go out. He sat, hunched in his armchair with Caesar on his lap. He was smoking one of his cigars. 'They are using me—like a tool, a lever!'

'Is it possible to create so many Life Peers?' Sassoon asked.

'It's possible,' Bertie muttered. 'Like turning out sausages. And that's all a peerage would be worth, afterwards. They want me to ruin the very way of Life I've sworn to uphold. My only escape would be to abdicate.' The others tensed and he went on. 'Oh, I've thought of it. More and more lately. To enjoy what's left of my life quetly, let others pull the strings.'

'You wouldn't really consider it, sir?' Knollys asked carefully.

Bertie sighed. 'I suppose not. It would be running away. Besides—I've also sworn to uphold the Government, and in this matter they are right. Reform of the Lords is practical and necessary.'

Alice was upset for him. 'If only it could have been brought in without this.'

'It's the last battle of the old world,' Bertie coughed. 'We are now in the age of the common man.'

His coughing continued, low and heavy. Knollys looked anxiously at Alice and she decided to try again. 'Have you decided when you are going to Biarritz?'

He shrugged. 'I can't get away just now.'

'The winter fog is bad for you,' she protested.

'So they say.' He puffed shallowly on his cigar, panting. 'But I can't leave—not when I may be of use.'

There was a knock at the door and Ponsonby came in. He bowed. 'Mr Asquith is waiting, sir,' he said.

Henry Asquith was in Sassoon's study. Over the past months he had lost some of his urbanity. Margot had not hidden her opinion of the attempt to use the King as a political weapon and he had heard from Sir Francis Laking and Sir James Reid, the royal physicians. If the King was not allowed to rest and recuperate, they would not be answerable for the consequences. Overwork and anxiety, together with the constant struggle to breathe, had weakened his lungs and put an undue strain on his heart.

Asquith had acted only in what he believed to be the best interests of the country, but he had been so committed that he had paid little attention to the effect on the King. However, he had begun to have a high regard for him and was shocked by his fragile appearance. Although Bertie greeted him with perfect courtesy, the Prime Minister could see that he was on edge, expecting the demand for the peerages to be made now. Asquith blamed himself; he had asked for no prior guarantees from the King and had decided not to demand the peerages until there was no other alternative. He would do so, then, without hesitation, but he could have saved King Edward much unnecessary distress.

Bertie was grateful for his consideration. 'Do I take it the crisis has lessened for the moment?' he asked.

'Our resolutions on the future relations of the House of Lords and the House of Commons will be presented next month, sir,' Asquith told him. 'No action can be taken till then.'

Bertie schooled himself not to let his relief show too clearly. 'So I have a month. Good. Good.' He smiled. 'My doctors are trying to wangle themselves a holiday in Biarritz.'

With Sir James Reid in close attendance, Bertie travelled as soon as possible to France. He survived the journey to Paris well and insisted on receiving his friends at the Hotel Bristol and carrying out his normal routine to quell rumours about the state of his health which had disquieted the French Government. The day after he arrived, he went to the Théâtre de la Porte St Martin to see a disappointing play by Edmond Rostand. Because of the intense cold, the theatre proprietor heated the auditorium specially for him, but overdid it. It was like an oven and, after the perform-

338

ance, when Bertie had to wait for his car, he caught a chill. When he reached Biarritz, he collapsed and was confined to his rooms with only Alice Keppel and Luis de Soveral allowed to see him.

The Press agreed not to publish anything unless they were informed it was really serious. Even Alexandra did not know that it was anything more than a cold, until Ponsonby went out to Biarritz and found the King suffering from another severe bronchial attack with threatened pneumonia. Alix was distressed and wanted to go to him, but, in his condition, it might alarm him. And as Alice Keppel was with him, her arrival could cause embarrassment. Alix had never envied Alice Keppel until now. 'She is with him, I know,' she said. 'But how—how I wish it was me . . .'

Biarritz, for once, was unkind to Bertie. For weeks, the weather was raw and, when he started slowly to recover, the only exercise Reid would permit was walks in the hotel corridors with Alice and Caesar. At last, spring sunshine came and he could walk in the garden, then he was able to invite a few friends for the evening and to take a stroll on the promenade with Alice and Soveral. He was muffled in a greatcoat with a fur collar and wore a felt hat. He walked very slowly, using a cane. He had recovered, but looked like a man ten years older. Alice was concerned for him, when he made them extend the walk. His breathing was laboured again.

'Well, I really think I've gone far enough,' she smiled. 'I'm quite worn out.' Bertie hesitated, but was glad of the excuse to stop.

There was a public bench near them, facing the sea. 'If you sit here for a moment, Alice,' Soveral suggested, 'I'll fetch the car.' Bertie handed her to the bench and sat beside her while he recovered his breath. 'You're not serious about returning to London, sir?' Soveral asked. 'Dr Reid says you shouldn't travel yet.'

'Reid's an idiot!' Bertie growled. 'In a few days, Asquith is presenting a Bill to limit the House of Lords. If it isn't passed, the Government will have to resign, and the King must be there.'

Alice was about to protest, but Soveral signalled to her, seeing that Bertie was becoming agitated. 'There will be no need to return for that, sir,' he said. When Bertie glanced at him, puzzled, he smiled. 'It's bound to be passed. The

Irish Nationalists have promised to vote with the Government if they eliminate the duty on Whisky.'

Bertie laughed quietly and Soveral bowed, leaving him with Alice. She took his arm and they sat together, in companionable silence, looking out to sea.

Alix was upset by the news from Biarritz. George found her with Toria in the sitting-room at Buckingham Palace. He had expected her to be happy at the news that the King was getting steadily better. But she had cabled him, now that he was well enough to be moved, asking him to join her on a cruise where she could nurse him, herself. She would not listen when George explained that, on the yacht, he would be too far away, while, if there were another crisis, he could return from Biarritz in twenty-four hours.

'He's coming home now,' Toria said.

'Well, I won't be here,' Alix decided. 'I shall take the yacht myself—go to Greece to visit my brother.'

George was not used to seeing his mother like this, taut and hurt. 'He'll expect you to be here when he gets back,' he said.

'There's no point—since I'm clearly not needed,' Alix told him. She headed for the door to her apartments. 'Toria, you will come with me.'

Alexandra had sailed for Corfu by the time Bertie reached London. He was disturbed by her sudden departure, but carried out his unfailing routine, again to quash rumours about his health. He dressed and went to Covent Garden for a performance of *Rigoletto*. He sat alone in the omnibus box at the rear of the stalls and the few who saw him were struck by how drawn and saddened he seemed. He left after the first act, standing for a long time gazing into the auditorium, as if saying goodbye.

He had only partly recovered, but he plunged into a gruelling round of work, catching up on letters and despatches, giving audiences to Asquith and Winston Churchill, who was now Home Secretary, receiving Kitchener on his return from India and promoting him to Field-Marshal. They discussed Charles Hardinge's coming appointment as Viceroy.

He had an emotional meeting with Jacky Fisher. During the previous year, Charles Beresford had at last been forced to leave the Navy because of his gross insubordination. He had used his resignation to attack Fisher openly, calling for a committee of enquiry into his conduct and fitness as First Sea Lord. After many months, the committee upheld Fisher, and Charlie B.'s career was over. In recognition of Fisher's services to the nation, Bertie raised him to the peerage as Lord Fisher of Kilverstone, but his position had been weakened by the enquiry and, on his sixty-ninth birthday, he retired. 'I've been scrapped like an obsolete battleship,' he said. 'I've made too many enemies.'

'But you reformed the Navy in spite of them,' Bertie told him. 'They can't undo what you've done.'

Fisher's eyes were wet. 'It was only possible because of you, sir. You fought for me. I'll never forget it.' His voice was gruff. 'Thanks to you, the Navy's ready if it's needed.'

Bertie could not relax. Alice and Mrs Willy James came to play bridge with him and Ponsonby in the Chinese Room. He was too tired to make conversation and they went home early. The fought-over People's Budget had been passed by the House of Lords and now the Government was preparing its Veto Bill for after the Spring Recess. Bertie took Francis Knollys and Fritz Ponsonby down to Sandringham with him for the weekend.

It was bitterly cold in Norfolk but the rooms in the great house were unheated as the Queen was abroad. There was still no word from her. After dinner, when he sat alone smoking his cigar, he thought of Alexandra and how much he needed her. There was so much of his past he wanted to remember now and she was woven through it, inextricably. Yet he, also, could not live without Alice. Next morning, he drove to the little church in the estate where Eddy's body had first lain and, after lunch, inspected the farm, but the biting wind drove him indoors. Ponsonby went with him into the salon. He could see that the King was troubled and stayed silent.

Bertie was looking slowly round the room at the pictures and mementoes. 'I always liked this house,' he murmured. 'There's a lot of me here.' He had spoken to himself. He sat on one of the sofas for a few moments, then shook his head. 'I can't settle. We're going back to London, Fritz.' He pushed himself up. 'Call Miss Keyser at

Grosvenor Crescent. Ask if it would be convenient for me to dine with her.'

Agnes Keyser poured a measure of the brandy she kept for the King and gave it to him, where he sat at the side of the fire. 'Thank you, Agnes,' he muttered. 'I hope I haven't put you out?'

'Of course, not, sir.' She smiled and sat opposite him. He was pale and coughed intermittently. 'You sound so tired,' she said.

'The slightest exertion wears me out,' he panted. 'I don't sleep. I lie, turning things over and over in my mind.'

'What things?'

Bertie paused. 'What's to come. I wanted to leave the country steady and peaceful for George, when it was his turn.'

She was disturbed by his cough and pallor. 'You will, sir,' she assured him. 'These present troubles cannot last. And you will be spared for many years.'

The shake of his head was scarcely perceptible. 'After all I've tried to do in my life, what have I achieved? Precious little.'

'How can you say that?' Agnes asked. Her tone was indignant and he looked at her, jerked out of his dejection. 'It's not so much what you've done as what you stand for,' Agnes went on. 'The confidence and belief in themselves you've given to others. Your people know there's a real human being on the throne, who understands and cares for them. They are proud of our way of life, because it is yours, because so much of it comes from you.'

Bertie watched her for a moment, her warmth and certainty buoying him up. 'I'd like to believe that,' he breathed. 'But it's so fragile, a way of life.' He turned his face to the fire. 'I keep having the strangest feeling that I'm seeing everything for the last time. I had it at Sandringham. That's why I wanted to see you.' His cough racked him. 'Just—just another chill.'

George's telegram saying that his father's bronchitis had returned reached Alix in Corfu. She set off home at once, overland. When George met her at Victoria Station with his sons, Prince Edward and Prince Albert in their naval cadets uniforms, instead of Bertie, Alix was surprised. Never once had she come home from abroad without Bertie meeting her. Toria immediately realised that her

342

father was more seriously ill than they had supposed, but Alix did not suspect until George made her enter Buckingham Palace by the garden door, when all the palace officials were assembled at the front. 'I thought you'd want to go straight to him,' George explained.

'Your telegram just said he had bronchitis.'

'A series of attacks,' George said. 'His breathing almost stops at times and his heart is affected.'

Now that he was revealing his own anxiety, Alix was worried. 'His heart?'

George forced himself to tell her. 'No one can say how long he has. Perhaps a few days.'

She gazed at him, stricken, then hurried down the corridor.

She found Bertie in an armchair in their private sitting-room. He was dressed in a black frockcoat and sat, hunched and grey, a tartan rug wrapped round his legs. He was smoking a thick, black cigar, although every now and again it made him dizzy. Caesar sat by his feet.

When Alix came in, Bertie glanced up and smiled. He tried to rise but the effort was too much. 'My dear——' he husked. 'Forgive me, I wanted to meet you but these fool doctors . . .' He chuckled.

Alix had prepared for seeing him before she entered the room, and seemed very controlled. She smiled. 'How are you, my dearest?'

'Oh—a poor old thing,' Bertie shrugged. 'But I'll fight it.'

'It's all this worry,' Alix protested. 'All those demands they've made on you.'

Bertie coughed. 'No, no. No one's to blame. It's only my chest.' He saw the distress in her eyes. 'Now I don't want you to get upset, Alix.'

His voice was so low and hoarse she could hardly make out what he said. 'I—I can't hear you,' she faltered.

Bertie beckoned to her to come closer. 'I've reserved the box for you tonight at Covent Garden. I'm sorry, I can't go with you—but you must show yourself.'

'No! I'm not going to leave you.' He tried to speak but she would not let him. She could not forgive herself for staying away. 'My dearest,' she said softly. 'I came home to be with you. Now I'm here I won't ever leave you, ever again.' He was smiling to her. She managed not to cry, but to smile back.

343

'I didn't want you to feel you had to,' he coughed. 'But I'm glad. I've been waiting for you.'

She bit her lip. 'If only they'd let me know sooner. Shouldn't you be lying down?'

'I've just seen Ernest,' he told her. 'And I must get on with my work. I'm not going to give in.'

Alix had begun to recover. 'Why are you smoking?' she exclaimed. 'It must be bad for you. You need some air.'

She moved to open one of the windows in the recess. 'What difference can it make now?' Bertie chuckled. 'Don't fuss, Alix.' He pushed himself to his feet. 'See? I'm not finished yet. Now, you run along and change.'

Alix nodded. 'Yes. I'll change and come back and sit with you.'

'That would be nice,' Bertie murmured. She had not heard, but kissed his cheek. He spoke louder. 'I'm really glad you're here, Alix. I've missed you.'

She smiled to him, almost girlishly, and moved to the door. He smiled to her as she looked back before going out. He stooped and patted Caesar, whose tail jumped. 'We've got her back, eh?'

Still chuckling, Bertie moved slowly, panting, to the birdcage on its stand near the open window. In it were two canaries. He chirrupped to them and tapped on the bars. When one whistled in reply, he smiled and took another puff on his cigar. He stopped suddenly, his hand clutching his chest. His knees buckled and he slumped back against the seats under the window, then slid to the floor. It was a massive heart attack.

Alice Keppel had not moved from the telephone in her room. The news had burst on the world, all the more shattering for being unexpected. Vast crowds had gathered outside the Palace, silently watching and waiting for each bulletin as it was posted up on the board on the railings, with the information that the King had had a series of heart attacks and that his condition was now critical. They were afraid to look at the Royal Standard in case it began to lower on its mast.

Many of Bertie's friends had been to the Palace to find out the news. Some of them had met there, Soveral, Cassel, Carrington, Fisher and Esher. They took it in turns to telephone Alice. She was empty inside, except for the agony of waiting. She now knew that there was no hope and that Bertie had been given morphia to dull the pain, that the Archbishop of Canterbury had been sent for and the royal family was gathering. She could not believe the end was so near. Always before, he had managed to recover, to push back the shadows with his indomitable will to live.

The telephone rang again, startling her, and she had to nerve herself to pick it up. It was Francis Knollys, to say that a carriage had been sent to bring her to the Palace.

Alexandra was standing alone in the dressing-room, motionless. She turned as the door to the corridor opened and Ponsonby showed in Alice Keppel. He bowed and withdrew.

Alice curtsied. When she rose, she and Alexandra gazed at each other in silence for a long moment. 'He is just conscious, Mrs. Keppel,' Alexandra said gently. 'But refuses to be put to bed. He does not have long. I believe he would wish to see you.' Alice was nearly overcome by her generosity of heart. She could not speak. Alexandra moved to the door of the King's bedroom and opened it.

Through the door, Alice could see Bertie sitting in a chair near the bed, wearing his old silk dressing gown. He was barely conscious, but smiled to see her come in and raised his right hand slightly in greeting. Alexandra closed the door, leaving them together and Alice knelt by Bertie, gazing up into his eyes which told her what he had not the strength to say.

Later in the day, Bertie collapsed again and had to be lifted into bed, where he lay, propped up on pillows to help his shallow breathing. He was still just conscious and aware of May and his daughters, Louise and Toria, who stood at the foot of his bed. Alix sat beside him, holding his hand. He was glad she had kept the Bishops and the rest of the family from crowding into his small room. He had seen them all briefly, in turn, and remembered how distressful his mother's death had been for the younger ones. He had tried to think of something memorable to say but his gift had deserted him.

Alix was holding herself in check, very tightly, knowing he would not want her to weep. 'They all send their love,' she told him. 'Willy—and Nicky and Alicky—and Minny. Lord Carrington. Franz Joseph.' She saw his lips twitch in a fleeting smile and she stopped, not trusting herself to go on.

His lips were moving and she leant towards him. 'I am glad . . . I have done my duty,' he whispered.

Alix was almost in despair. 'I can't—I can't hear you, my darling . . .' He smiled again faintly and seemed to shake his head. Alix looked round as George came in from the dressing-room and stood beside her. He was also forcing himself to be natural.

Bertie recognised him with pleasure. 'George . . .'

'There's some news, Father, you might like to hear,' George said. Bertie nodded once. 'The Two-Year-Old Plate at Kempton Park Races. It's just been won by your horse, Witch of the Air. By half a length.'

There was a hush for a moment, then Bertie chuckled, quite loudly. '. . . I am very glad . . .' he said, and his eyes closed.

Toria began to cry quietly and George put his hand, comforting, on his mother's shoulder as the Archbishop's voice could be heard from the dressing-room, reciting the prayer for the dying.

In the pillared Cabinet Room in 10 Downing Street, members of the Cabinet sat waiting in silence. Lloyd George glanced across at Winston Churchill who was drawn and serious. 'It's the end of an era,' Churchill said quietly.

They rose as Asquith came in and moved slowly to his centre seat at the side of the long table. He glanced round the people who were there, as if not seeing them clearly, then sat in his chair, looking at his hands which he had placed on the table top. 'I have just returned from the Palace,' he said thickly. 'I was booed in the street . . . They said I—I killed the King.' He paused to collect himself and his head rose. 'The people are stunned. They cannot believe he has been taken from us.' He paused again. 'No man in our time has been more justly beloved. And no ruler in any time has been more sincerely true, more unswervingly loyal, more uniformly kind to his advisers and servants . . . He earned well the title by which he will always be remembered—the peacemaker of the world.'

Ponsonby stood waiting in the corridor outside the door to the dressing-room. Caesar sat on a chair near him, watching the door, and his ears pricked up when it opened. Ponsonby tensed as George and May came out. George closed the door and turned. 'He was my best friend,' he said desolately, and stopped, unable to go on.

Ponsonby moved forward slowly. As he knelt, George gazed at him, then almost reluctantly, held out his hand.

'Your Majesty,' Ponsonby said. And kissed King George's hand.

Alix would not let them move Bertie's body. For days, she sat by him quietly, not weeping, just watching over him as he lay still, his hands folded.

At last, Minny arrived from St Petersburg to be with her and told her he must be taken to lie in State. They were standing together by the bedside.

'Not yet,' Alix said.

'You must let them take him, Alix,' Minny repeated. 'It is right.'

Alix sighed and nodded. It had to end. She moved forward and looked down at him, seeing the golden-haired, blue-eyed boy who had first smiled to her shyly all those years ago in the Cathedral at Speyer. She had still not wept, for her memories of him were too real. 'This is the longest I have had him to myself for many years,' she said quietly. She was carrying a bouquet of roses and she laid them gently by the side of his folded arms. She smiled to Minny. 'But I'm not complaining. I always knew he loved me best.'